FIVE Magic Spindles

ROOGLEWOOD PRESS

Raleigh, NC

Published by Rooglewood Press
www.RooglewoodPress.com

Printed in the United States of America

ISBN-13: 978-1-942379-13-3

Book design by A.E. de Silva
Cover illustration by Julia Popova

Table of Contents

FOREWORD

W HEN THE time came to select the theme for Rooglewood Press's third creative writing contest based on a fairy tale retelling, I worried about choosing "Sleeping Beauty." Following up "Cinderella" and "Beauty and the Beast" is a challenge, since those tales feature active heroines who make choices and take chances that dramatically advance the romantic storylines. With such heroines, writers enjoy a full range of options to create fascinating adventures for their retellings.

But "Sleeping Beauty"? The famous legend of the heroine who . . . sleeps away half the story? Not exactly the stuff of dynamic characters and high adventure.

Nevertheless, with the support of my creative team here at Rooglewood, I decided to take the leap. Because, despite its tricky storyline, suggestive themes, and passive heroine, "Sleeping Beauty" is a timeless fairy tale on the same level as its more exciting counterparts. It simply makes no sense to publish a series of fairy tale retellings without "Sleeping Beauty" in the mix! So I made the call, we announced the contest, and I crossed my fingers, hoping the competitors would find ways to infuse energy into this story about a dormant princess.

Sometimes when painters wish to increase their own creativity, they will choose a limited color palette. In the hands of a talented artist, the result of such a limited palette can be the most stunning, the most creative and beautiful of paintings. The same principle often holds true in the realm of fiction writing. Though it may seem unreasonable, even inadvisable, to limit a plot to the confines of the "Sleeping Beauty" legend, the participants in this year's contest used those limitations as an opportunity to show us how amazingly creative they could be!

Choosing only five winners proved more difficult than ever this year. But in the end, the five writers we selected produced the most vivid, exciting, and unusual versions of this fairy tale I have ever seen.

The collection opens with possibly the most surprising setting of all. Rachel Kovaciny's "The Man on the Buckskin Horse" is a classic Western in all of its leather-and-gunpowder glory. I went into reading this story with a skeptical eye, wondering how any writer, no matter how talented, could pull off a "Sleeping Beauty" retelling with a cast of homespun characters and no magic. Within a single page I was hooked. Although the innocent young beauty is indeed out of the action for much of the story, Rachel gives the reader a dynamic heroine in her viewpoint character, Emma the midwife, who steps into the role of Good Fairy. And how can anyone resist an enigmatic prince wearing a cowboy hat, boots, and spurs? This author reminds us that classic Westerns are ultimately tales of chivalry like the King Arthur legends of old, including the same romance and drama, re-envisioned for a new audience. Thus the setting that seemed incongruous proved itself a natural fit for a fairy tale, and I became a believer.

Turning the page to the next story, readers will find themselves transported to a land quite unlike the American Old West. Kathryn McConaughy sets her tale in the ancient Near East, infusing her world with a magic so vivid that one cannot help being swept into the unfolding drama.

But it wasn't Kathryn's setting alone that made "Guardian of Our Beauty" stand out in the crowd—really, it was her exquisite writing that caught my eye and the eyes of the other contest judges. With a confident combination of poetic lyricism and humor, this gifted author weaves a tapestry of words into an unforgettable work of art. Rarely do I encounter a writing style that captivates me so completely.

Each year, the first story I read for these contests ordinarily suffers by soon being buried in my memory under countless other retellings of the same tale. This year, however, the first story I read was Grace Mullins's "The Ghost of Briardale" . . . and there was no chance in the world of its getting buried. This zany comedy—set in a haunted insane asylum of all things!— simply refuses to be forgotten. Grace's plot is madness itself with its many twists and turns, and her characters are numerous for such a short adventure. Yet she manages to make each character a distinct and loveable— and sometimes loathe-able—individual. How any young novelist could invent such a wild take on "Sleeping Beauty" while managing to maintain the most important aspects of the original is beyond me, but I knew I had to include her story in this set of five.

Michelle Pennington's "Spindle Cursed" arrived on my desk with a letter of effusive praise from the judge who read it before me. However, after reading so many unusual and even bizarre retellings, I paused when I saw that this story was a traditional fantasy. It seemed almost too tame a choice. Would the author be able to bring something new to her version of "Sleeping Beauty"? I shouldn't have doubted. Michelle's traditional setting serves only to highlight the breathtaking landscapes, the dynamic characters, and the palpable peril of the plot she unfolds. "Spindle Cursed" is a romance at its heart—the skillfully told romance of two genuine people learning to appreciate and understand one another. It's also a thrilling adventure featuring a menacing dragon, fascinating rules of magic, and numerous daring escapes and desperate schemes. Everything about Michelle's style reveals her highly developed sense of pacing and drama, resulting in a tale that is impossible to put down, one that leaves the reader craving more of her world and writing.

If I had to use only one word to characterize Ashley Stangl's "Out of the Tomb," that word would be *risk*. This story is risky in every possible way. A science fiction fairy tale retelling set on a distant planet and featuring non-human protagonists? How could this possibly work? Yet although Ashley's hero and heroine may not be human, they are such endearing people, so vividly realized and with such compelling motivations, that I found myself bonding deeply to both of them. The author takes her risky retelling one step further by being the only author in this collection to attempt a gender-role reversal, with a sleeping prince as opposed to a sleeping princess. The result of all this risk-taking is nothing short of stunning. A perfectly paced, heart-wrenching adventure, "Out of the Tomb" reinvents the old legend as something new, something . . . futuristic.

Every one of these five authors proved herself a force to be reckoned with, tackling this difficult theme head-on and infusing her story with unexpected life and ingenuity. Since launching these contests, I have never seen a more varied assortment of stories. But the diversity of these adventures simply underscores the lasting beauty and timelessness of the original. I could not be more thrilled with the collection you now hold in your hand.

So dive in, dear reader, and discover for yourself the wonders in store!

Anne Elisabeth Stengl

THE MAN
ON THE
BUCKSKIN
HORSE

RACHEL KOVACINY

For Dad and Mom, who taught me to love westerns and words.

And for Deborah, my trusty scout.

With loving thanks to Larry and our kids.

Soli Deo gloria.

1

I WASN'T back in town for more than three minutes before I learned that Mrs. Mortimer had gone and hired herself a gunman.

Folks like to say our town doesn't need a newspaper because it already has Emma Thornberry. Precious little happens here in Mortimer Junction that somebody doesn't tell me about. And I knew of only one reason why Adelaide Mortimer would hire such a man: She meant to have it out with Victor Owens once and for all.

To my everlasting disappointment, I did not witness the gunman riding through town myself. I had been out attending a different arrival: the fifth Cummings boy in a row, and the loudest yet. But I had barely climbed down from my buggy before the man at the livery told me all about Mrs.

Mortimer's new hireling, his big buckskin horse, and the fancy pistol he wore in a black holster. I got right back in my buggy, believe you me. Let no one call me a shirker! I drove straight out to the Owens place to warn Victor, for it seemed no one else had thought to do so. The closer I get to fifty, the rarer sensible folks become.

We've seen a lot of lone men passing through Mortimer Junction ever since the War Between the States ended. Some with a smile and a whistle to hide behind, and some you don't feel you ought to disturb. All still fighting battles, within themselves or against others. They drift in, maybe find work for a while, then drift on. Everything I heard about this stranger said he was a different sort altogether, though I doubted he meant to stay in town for long either.

It was late afternoon when I topped the small bluff that overlooks the Owens homestead. I could see there were no other horses tied outside the little picket fence that keeps the sheep away from the cabin. I'd beaten Mrs. Mortimer and her hired gun. Victor Owens would have some advance warning, thanks to me.

I was right glad to see sheep scattered all around the house and barn. I don't care much for sheep, but I must allow they look real nice from a distance, dotting the prairie like so many friendly boulders. Victor fences in more of his land for pasture every year, but the Owenses still have only a few hundred head. Just what he and his daughter can care for on their own. At times they graze to one side of the homestead or the other. The rest of the time they take the flock farther out on their land and camp near them. I was glad to see those sheep near the house because I knew that meant I'd not have to go traipsing about the countryside to find Victor.

I have long considered the Owenses' little place the prettiest this side of the Platte River. The cabin rests at the bottom of a small depression in the land, right along a reliable stream bordered by cottonwoods and such. I remember how poor Juliet brought roses with her from back East, bundle after bundle of dead-looking sticks so far as I could see. But somehow she coaxed them to grow around her new little home. I'm grateful she lived long enough to see the way they flourished, how they climbed up the walls clear to the roof and on over it. When those roses are in bloom, you couldn't paint a nicer picture, and their scent more than masks what you'll smell if the sheep are pastured nearby. I suspect that might be one reason Juliet planted so many of them.

But I wasted no time admiring the view that day. I drove straight on down and tied my mare to the picket fence. The Mortimer ranch was still a fair piece up the road, but I didn't know precisely when the gunman had arrived. He might have had plenty of time to ride out, learn what Mrs. Mortimer wanted from him, and head on back.

The cabin door stood open like usual. I knew from the constant, rhythmic clacking and whirring that Victor's daughter was hard at work with her spinning wheel. And this was no puny wheel you could sit by! I've often wondered how Juliet convinced Victor to haul that huge wheel west. It stood taller than my shoulder.

I stepped inside and saw Rosalind, barefoot, wearing a plain dress the color of a winter's sky. She spun the wheel with her right hand while in her left she held a length of wool that twisted into thread, winding onto a long, sharp spindle sticking straight out to one side. I had always given that spindle a wide berth when I visited the Owenses, for I suspected it could deliver a nasty jab if a person encountered it unawares. Juliet had kept a cork stuck over it whenever she wasn't spinning, which I thought right sensible. I noticed the spindle was nearly empty—Rosalind must have just begun.

I felt this was no time for pleasantries. "Rosalind, is your father home?" I asked, forgoing my usual cordial greeting.

"Afternoon, Miss Emma," she welcomed me, walking backward to spin the wheel again then slowly moving forward as the wool she held twisted up around the spindle.

Her calmness ruffled me, I will admit, and I spoke more sharply than I otherwise would. "Where is your father? I got something of real importance to tell him."

Rosalind had been too calm for several years. When her poor mother left us, the girl had retreated behind a stockade of tranquility. Once a spirited, joyful child, she no longer laughed, wept, or even grew angry. I'd wanted to tear down that emotionless prison of hers for years but had yet to find the necessary tools to do so.

Still, she was a lovely young lady, for all her unnatural staidness. I'd long admired Rosalind's looks. My hair you couldn't compare to anything but dead grass even when I was young and hopeful. But Rosalind's hair, thick and dark and glossy, reminded me of a bear rug by firelight. On that particular day she had it braided and wound around her head like a crown. I would have loved to have hair like hers. And her eyes! Dark eyes hold an enchantment, I do believe. Her mother, Juliet, had the same coloring. Part Spanish or Italian or something likewise exotic.

Now, though, I feared Rosalind's loveliness would be wasted, never to be passed along to a generation of beautiful babies. When she was young, we had all predicted she would make a splendid match one day. Certainly she should not lack for suitors. But after Juliet's death, Rosalind's aloofness kept most men away. Her detachment cooled any interest some man or other would show from time to time. At twenty, she seemed destined to join me in spinsterhood.

Rosalind raised her eyebrows but did not comment on my lack of manners in questioning her so abruptly. "We have a ewe about to birth her first lamb. Pa's brought her to the barn. I'm sure he'll be along directly.

Won't you stay and eat with us?"

"No," I told her. "I'll go find your father now."

"Why?"

"Because Mrs. Mortimer has hired a gunman, and we must warn him."

Rosalind blinked twice, taking in this information. "You don't think . . ." She let the wheel begin to slow.

"Mrs. Mortimer is a determined woman, as well we know. What she wants, she takes. And if someone refuses her . . ." I shook my head. "Your father must be warned."

From the doorway behind me Victor Owens asked, "Warned of what?" He signaled his dog to remain outside as he entered. I've often wondered how long it takes to train a dog as thoroughly as Victor has trained his. It may look like a nondescript black mongrel, but one word or gesture from Victor or Rosalind and that animal knows precisely what to do. I may not have much use for sheep, but a good dog I can respect.

"Miss Emma, won't you stay to supper?" Victor offered. He was not a tall man, but he carried himself well. Though his fair hair had begun to grey and thin, his mustache flourished, fierce as ever. I've always thought him comely in his own humble way. Certainly his face held character, which is more than I can say for many.

"This is no time for pleasantries, Victor Owens," I told him. "Mrs. Mortimer has hired a gunman. He rode through town this morning and asked for directions to her ranch. I have no doubt that by now he is on his way back here."

"To do what?" The corner of Victor's mouth twitched. "Force me to marry her at gunpoint?" Though he had mourned dear Juliet, he had not retreated inside himself as Rosalind had done. Smiles and laughter remained his companions still.

"You know perfectly well she gets what she wants, and since for some reason she wants you . . ." I put my hands on my hips, prepared to launch into a good scolding, for I saw he was trying not to smile. "Victor Owens, I wish you would take this seriously."

"What I take seriously is a young ewe close to her first lambing. I don't have time to worry about gunmen or Mrs. Mortimer."

"You and your sheep! I swear sometimes you think they're human."

"Sometimes I like them better than humans." Victor could hold back his smile no longer. "Did you speak to the man?"

"Not myself, no."

"Could be he was just looking for work." He started to close the door then paused. "What kind of horse did he have?"

"The man at the livery stable told me it was a big buckskin."

Behind me, Rosalind asked, "You mean you didn't see him yourself?"

"No."

Victor nodded toward the open door. "You're about to get the chance."

Rosalind and I moved closer to him so we could see out too. Down the bluff drove Mrs. Mortimer in her fancy buggy, and beside her came the stranger on his pale, dark-maned horse.

VICTOR," I said, "now would be a good time to get your rifle."

"You really think I'll have need of it?"

I drew myself up to my full height of five feet and one inch. "Victor Owens! You don't mean to say you're going to face that man unarmed!"

"If you shoot an unarmed man, it's murder," he said calmly.

Beside him, Rosalind touched his arm. "She wouldn't dare. Would she?"

"Think of Rosalind! And me! What if that man holds one of us hostage?" I glared at the approaching gunman, but then it occurred to me that if he was of a mind to take a hostage, I might not feel especially averse to his picking me. He had reached the picket fence, where I could get a nice look at him. Strong jaw, straight nose, and a cleft chin. Hair even blacker than the black shirt and trousers he wore, the same color and shine as his gloves. He wore a splendid blue vest too, glossy like satin. A man who did well for himself, clearly, which meant he knew his business.

Which meant he was good at shooting people.

Victor told his daughter, "Go on in my room and shut the door."

Rosalind shook her head. "No, Pa. I won't leave you to that woman." I was pleased that beneath her docility Rosalind had a mind of her own yet.

"I'll be fine. You do as I say." He snapped his fingers at his dog. "You there, Blue!" Obediently, the dog trotted inside. I've always wondered why they named that dog Blue. For his eyes, maybe.

"Stay in my room until I say it's safe," Victor ordered. When Rosalind started to protest, Victor told his dog, "Take her in," and pointed to his room.

Blue took Rosalind's skirt in his mouth and tugged. Rosalind said, "Pa, I think it's awful foolish of you not to get your rifle as Miss Emma said." All the while she was speaking, that dog was firmly tugging her into her father's room. Once she was inside, she shut the door as Victor had told her to.

The Owens cabin had only the two rooms. The main one held the spinning wheel, with a good-sized window behind it so you could see the trees down by the stream and the small kitchen garden behind the house. There was also a fireplace with Juliet's rocker by it, a small table and chairs, and a few crates stacked up to hold dishes and other kitchen sundries. Rosalind's cot was there against the front wall under a smaller window, not far from the hearth. The other was Victor's bedroom, where I'd spent two days tending Juliet while she slipped away. Since we have no doctor for hundreds of miles around, I have learned all I can about treating wounds and illnesses so that I can care for more people than expectant mothers only. Too often, though, I can do no more than hold their hand while we wait for the end.

Once Rosalind and the dog were safe inside, Victor stepped out to face this oncoming trouble. Before Mrs. Mortimer could descend from her buggy, he demanded, "What is it now?" I followed him, hoping the presence of a witness would discourage mischief.

While Victor spoke, the gunman dismounted and proceeded to tie his horse and Mrs. Mortimer's to the fence not far from where I'd hitched my own mare. Such nerve! As if he were an invited guest.

Mrs. Mortimer smiled, baring her teeth. I don't know that I have ever seen that woman smile with actual joy. "I think you know."

Adelaide Mortimer had passed her prime, but you had to get close up to realize as much. After her husband died, a scant two years back, she'd worn black just long enough to satisfy the demands of propriety. Now she wore a dove-grey riding habit that fit her like a snake's new skin. We all knew that she had set her cap for Victor Owens, which surprised many in these parts. Not that Victor wouldn't be an attractive prospect for a husband; he had more sense than God gave most men, and a kind heart. But I did not suspect Mrs. Mortimer of valuing such qualities. I figured she thought he would look decorative at the dining table, and his land would make a fine addition to her holdings, adjoining her ranch the way it did.

Victor said, "My answer is still no."

She smiled again. "Won't you ask me in?"

"Inside or out, I won't change my mind."

Mrs. Mortimer looked at her companion long enough that we were forced to acknowledge his presence. "This is Mr. Palmer. Surely you wouldn't leave a stranger out in the hot sun?"

The gunman, Palmer, didn't smile any fake smiles, which I felt was a point in his favor. He helped Mrs. Mortimer step down from her buggy like an attentive chaperone. I wondered why she didn't give up on Victor and try to interest this Palmer in matrimony instead. I may have long ago dispensed with all expectations of marriage myself, but I can still admire a fine-looking man when one passes. I'm sure polite society would never countenance a gunman for a husband, but out here in the wilds of Nebraska we tend to overlook a person's past if they're willing to behave themselves in the present. Besides, Palmer would look far more ornamental on Mrs. Mortimer's arm than Victor.

"Ride on, Adelaide." Victor crossed his arms.

"But I have a business proposition for you."

"I'm not interested."

"Be reasonable."

Victor glanced back at the cabin, doubtless thinking of Rosalind waiting inside, listening through the log walls. "What is it now?"

"Your ranch abuts mine. I need more land if I'm to expand the stockyards near town and still have enough grazing for my own herds. I want to buy your ranch. With what I'll pay, you can find twice as much land somewhere else."

"No."

"No?" Mrs. Mortimer pouted as prettily as a schoolgirl. "Why don't we go inside while you think it over." She opened the gate and walked inside its enclosure.

Victor moved to block her, so she pretended to notice me for the first time. "Good afternoon, Emma. I trust I'm not interrupting anything important?"

"It so happens, you are," I retorted.

"Oh, I do apologize. This really shouldn't take but a minute. Wouldn't you like to go on in the house, away from the stink of all these sheep?"

I pinched my lips together disapprovingly. While I found the smell of those sheep unpleasant myself, I had the manners not to make such a bold-faced comment about it.

Palmer took his place beside her. His right hand rested lightly on his pistol, making his wordless threat obvious. I suddenly realized that my presence could be less help than I'd thought. Victor might not mind a bit of peril himself, but it appeared he was reluctant to have me shot on his account, for he allowed Mrs. Mortimer and her gunman to push past him and enter his house.

I glared at them both as I trailed them all inside. Victor headed for the fireplace where he kept his hunting rifle, but Palmer stepped into his way.

"Now," said Mrs. Mortimer, taking a folded paper from her pocket, "I've had this bill of sale drawn up."

"I'm still not interested."

"After you sign this, we'll go to the bank before it closes to transfer the money. I'll give you a full week to pack up and move on." She gestured at her gunman. "If you don't want to, I'm sure Mr. Palmer can . . . persuade you."

I didn't see Palmer pull his pistol from its holster—it simply appeared in his hand. He pointed it nowhere in particular. Yet.

I put in, "Aren't you forgetting there's a witness here?"

"Ah yes," Mrs. Mortimer said, "I'm so glad you're here, Emma. It's always comforting to have someone near who is skilled at binding up wounds."

I'd never been sure that Mrs. Mortimer didn't hold me responsible for the loss of her three babies, though each clearly had perished some time before it entered the world. I bridled at her tone but made no reply. There are times, I have learned, when swallowing one's words before they're spoken is far less bitter than having to eat them after.

Victor said, "Shoot me then. I still won't sign it. I won't marry you, I won't sell my land, and I won't move on. You can't have everything, Adelaide Mortimer."

"Is that so?" She began to say something else but was interrupted by Rosalind's flinging open the bedroom door. The girl rushed out to stand in front of her father, arms spread wide.

"Please don't shoot my pa!" Rosalind looked that gunman in the eye, and for a moment everyone fell silent. She lifted her chin, and her eyes, so hollow for so long, seemed to fill with life while I watched.

If the situation had not been so dire, I would have applauded.

"Please, you don't even know us." She kept her gaze on Palmer's face, her eyes continuing to plead with him long after she stopped speaking. Mrs. Mortimer, she ignored, the way we'd all like to most of the time.

Victor's faithful dog stayed close beside her, teeth bared. I had long respected that dog for its good sense. Like most of its kind, it seemed to know the difference between a good person and a bad one. The way it watched Mrs. Mortimer only confirmed my opinion of its worth.

Palmer's black eyebrows drew together in a rather pleasing way, and he looked from Rosalind to Mrs. Mortimer. "You said he'd be alone." He had a deep, smooth voice that suited his comely features. If I were a young maiden so inclined, I might have swooned.

"Oh?" Mrs. Mortimer shrugged. "How was I to know he wouldn't be?"

While Mrs. Mortimer bickered with Palmer, Victor put a hand on Rosalind's shoulder to move her out of harm's way. Although Palmer had kept his gun pointed more or less at the floor, when he saw Victor's hand come up, he tensed and raised it. I thought for a moment that we were all finished—he would shoot Victor purely from reflex and then have to kill Rosalind and me because we'd seen him do it. I could see us, all three, tossed into some shallow grave or left out on the prairie to feed the coyotes.

But Palmer fired no hasty shots. I felt my knees tremble from relief. Instead, he said, "Mr. Owens, step back against that wall, please." He gestured with his head to the wall that separated Victor's room from the main one. "A little farther. Keep your hands away from your sides."

Victor moved slowly across the room until his back was against the wall. Beside Rosalind, the dog growled. Victor said, "Down." Blue whined and sank to the floor between Rosalind and me. I wished Victor would have trained his dog to attack gunmen on command. How convenient that would have been!

Rosalind begged, "We don't have much land. You don't need it!" She stood between Victor and me, her back to the spinning wheel, her hands half raised in supplication.

"Don't I?" Mrs. Mortimer shook her head. "Little Miss Rosalind, how would you know what I do and don't need?"

"I know you don't need our land. You have so much. What difference would our bit of range make? Is it my pa? Are you still after him?"

That must have struck a little too close to the bullseye for Mrs. Mortimer. Her reply cracked like a whip in the hands of a good cowhand. "This isn't about him."

"You only wanted him because everyone knows he's the best man anywhere around, and you think you always have to have the best." Rosalind turned to the gunman. "I'll bet she hired you because she heard you were the best. Same as she ordered that fancy buggy from St. Louis." She looked at Mrs. Mortimer with disdain. With her braid wound around her head like a crown, for a moment she looked positively regal. "You think having better things than the rest of us makes *you* better than us. But everyone knows that's not so."

I glanced at Victor and saw that he was watching his daughter with something like hope in his eyes. So he too had noticed the change in her.

"Enough!" Mrs. Mortimer gestured to her hired gunman. "Mr. Palmer, shoot her instead."

He had the decency to look startled. Another point in his favor. "Excuse me?" he said.

"Shoot the girl! In the leg or the arm, for now. Maybe that will shut her up." She looked at Victor. "Or are you ready to sign?"

Though Victor opened his mouth, Rosalind didn't give him a chance to speak. "No!" Her expression became fierce. "He will never sign your filthy paper!"

I wondered if I could distract Palmer somehow, perhaps fake a fainting fit. If I'd been close enough to ensure he'd catch me, I might have tried it.

Mrs. Mortimer swore a most unladylike oath. She threw the bill of sale down on the floor. "Must I do everything myself?" Grabbing the pistol from Palmer, she aimed it at Rosalind. "Will this convince you to sign? Or do you need even more encouragement?"

"You don't need to do this," Victor pleaded. He took a step toward her. I knew he meant to rush her and take his chances with the pistol rather than let her harm his daughter.

I sprang forward, hoping to put myself between Rosalind and that gun and to keep Victor from doing the same. But I had forgotten about the dog lying obediently on the floor between me and Rosalind. I am forced to admit that I tripped over him. Instead of shielding Rosalind, I fell against her.

At the same moment, Mrs. Mortimer fired, the noise from that pistol sounding like a cannon's roar in the small room.

3

HOUGH THE acrid scent of gunsmoke filled my nose and made me cough, I'd seen chips of wood fly out from the wall beyond and knew the bullet had not hit anyone.

For the moment I thought Rosalind was safe.

Rosalind stumbled backward, turning toward the spinning wheel, falling, hands groping for something to hold onto. I looked up from where I'd landed on the floor just in time to see her left hand, flailing as she fell, slam against the sharp wooden spindle. Rosalind cried out, a childlike noise of shock and fear, as the spindle pierced her palm so deeply its tip protruded from the back of her hand. She fell to her knees, her skewered hand above her.

Victor leaped at Mrs. Mortimer. He wrestled the gun away, shoved her back against the wooden wall, and pointed that pistol squarely at her face. His dog barked savagely beside him, obviously waiting for a signal or command to help in any way.

I may be nearing fifty, but I remain spry. I hoisted myself up off the floor and hurried to Rosalind's side. I told her, "Don't you pull on that, young lady. Hold your hand still." I feared she could damage the muscles and tendons in her hand if she moved it.

Rosalind looked at her bloody hand then at me, her eyes too wide. "Miss Emma," she said, her voice wavering. "Oh, Miss Emma."

"Don't you worry," I told her. "You're going to be fine. Don't look at it, look at me."

"Mr. Palmer!" Mrs. Mortimer howled. "Defend me!"

I prayed that God would strike that gunman dead with a lightning bolt before he could so much as twitch in her defense. Who knew how many more firearms he had concealed about his person?

The good Lord tends to answer my prayers in the most peculiar ways. Palmer had not moved from where he'd stood when Mrs. Mortimer snatched his weapon. I'd wondered at that—did he not know what to do without a gun in his hand? Why did he just stand there, not even trying to get his pistol back?

Now he said, "I've seen how much protecting you need." Instead of reaching for a weapon, he crossed his arms, hands remaining where we could see them.

Victor trembled with rage. I knew that at any moment he would do something foolish. Much as I would have enjoyed seeing Mrs. Mortimer punished for such vile behavior, I'd come to that house to save my friend, not watch him commit a hanging offense. "Victor," I said, hoping to divert his attention, "do you keep any sort of bandages in this house?"

"What?"

"Bandages. For Rosalind."

"There's some in the barn."

"That's too far. I've got plenty in my bag, but I can't fetch them myself. I don't want to leave Rosalind." I did not want her trying to pull her hand from that spindle before I was ready to stanch the bleeding.

Victor didn't move. Possibly he was afraid of what Mrs. Mortimer might do if he released her. I know I was.

She glared at him past the pistol he still held pointed at her face. She had more nerve than a Confederate whistling "Dixie" on the courthouse lawn, I will give her that. "All you have to do is sign the papers, Victor. Sign them, and you'll never see me again. You can help your daughter then. I won't interfere."

"Shut your mouth." Victor put more vehemence into those three words than most folks pour into an entire tirade.

Rosalind whimpered, her face squeezed up like a crumpled rag. The pistol in Victor's hand shook ever so slightly.

I steeled myself for another gunshot. "Don't," I pleaded. "Victor, no."

Palmer earned another point when he spoke up. "Where is your bag?" he asked me, his own voice steady.

"In my buggy, under the seat."

He went out and returned with my black leather satchel. "Are you a nurse?" he asked.

"No." I didn't bother explaining what I was since there's no real quick way to say "I'm a midwife who knows a goodly number of remedies and has more experience binding up wounds than she ever expected to get."

Instead, I took a roll of white bandages I'd rolled myself and a pair of scissors from my bag, and I cut off two sizeable lengths. I folded those two pieces into thick pads. All the while, I talked soothingly to Rosalind. "Don't worry, you're going to be fine. Hand wounds don't bleed all that much.

Now, if you'd whacked your head on this thing instead, why, we'd be swimming by now. You've got nothing to worry about."

When I had the dressings ready, I said, "Victor, I need you to help me."

"I can't."

"Victor Owens, you come here right now!" I demanded. "I need you to hold Rosalind still while I pull her hand free. If I don't do this just so, that spindle could rip right through her muscles. She'd never have good use of it again." I paused before adding, "Or do you want Mr. Palmer to hold her?"

The idea of a stranger's arms around his daughter did the trick. Victor dragged Mrs. Mortimer to the front door and shoved her through it. "Get out," he snarled. "Get off my land and never set foot on it again! If you ever do, I will shoot you for trespassing." His dog bolted for the door, but Victor caught him.

She laughed. "This gunman may have failed me, but I can hire another and another. I can lay siege to your house and starve you out. I—"

Victor slammed the door shut in her face and barred it. He tucked the pistol into his belt, crossed the room, and took hold of Rosalind's arm. I made my way around to the other side of them. "Hold it tight," I instructed.

"Wait," Palmer said. I'd nearly forgotten he was still there. "This will help." He picked up a wooden spoon and held it out to Rosalind. "Put this between your teeth," he said quietly. "Bite down hard when you need to."

I thought that a right good idea, though I didn't say so. It seemed this gunman had dealt with pain a time or two himself.

Beside me, Victor winced as Rosalind clamped the spoon's handle between her teeth. He knew how painful this was about to be for her.

She looked up at me and nodded. I grasped her hand in both of mine and tugged it free of the spindle. Rosalind made small, helpless noises, but she did not try to pull away from me. More blood snaked down her arm, soaking into her blue-grey dress. I kept her hand up above her heart to slow the bleeding.

"Victor, can you hold her arm up like this?" I asked. When he did so, I quickly pressed one of the folded wads of cloth against the back of her hand. With my other hand I picked off wool fibers from the yarn she'd spun. They had stuck to her palm while it was jammed against them over the spindle.

Palmer hovered nearby, watching me. He cleared his throat and suggested, "Might not washing the wound help ensure you've removed everything that might infect it?"

I pointed out, "The blood will wash it clean." As if I wouldn't know that any foreign matter in a wound could cause it to fester!

"It will help," he agreed. "But it's not bleeding that much. If you will permit me . . ." While I finished removing pesky bits of wool, he used the scissors from my bag to cut off a section of bandage, then soaked that in the wash basin. "It can't hurt and it might help," he said, holding out the wet wad of cloth.

I looked at Victor to see what he thought. He gave a small nod, his lips pressed too tightly together to speak.

"Very well," I conceded. I swabbed the wound in her palm with the sodden cloth then pressed the other dressing against it. "I suppose now you'll tell me I should wash the back, too."

"I would advise it."

I frowned at him. "Next you'll be wanting to bandage her up yourself."

Around the spoon handle still clenched in her teeth, Rosalind said what sounded like, "Clean it and be done. Please."

So I peeled off my original dressing and cleaned the back of her hand as well. Palmer gave me a fresh dressing when I'd finished. All the while, Victor had held onto her arm, keeping it still for me. I held the pads of white cloth in place while Palmer wrapped more bandages around them three times, then I pulled my fingers out so I could finish the job myself. No blood soaked through, and I offered up a silent prayer of thanks.

Victor helped Rosalind to her little bed beside the fireplace. She curled up on her side like a weary kitten, her hands tucked close to her. Although she'd stayed remarkably composed throughout her ordeal, once she lay down she began shaking. Victor spread her yellow wool blanket over her, smearing her blood from his fingers all over it. The dog sat alertly on the floor beside her bed, clearly intending to guard his injured mistress against any further attacks.

When he'd finished tucking Rosalind in, Victor turned to Palmer, who stood waiting near the door. "I intend to wire the sheriff down in Lincoln about this." He sounded more weary than angry, and I realized I was nearly spent myself. A crisis sure saps a body's strength.

Palmer nodded. "I would if I were you." He waited for Victor to unbar the door then walked out without another word, not even to ask for his pistol back. He even closed the door behind himself. One last point for Palmer, I thought.

From the window over Rosalind's bed, I watched the gunman ride off without waiting for Mrs. Mortimer. She sat there in her buggy for some minutes, staring at the cabin, though she avoided looking at me. Finally she drove away, sheep scattering to both sides of her buggy as she clattered off. Even a person as treacherous as Adelaide Mortimer can do only so much damage in one day, I expect.

I brewed a soothing tea and gave it to Rosalind to help her stop shaking. Before long she fell asleep, and I reckoned there was little more I could do for her. I left Victor with instructions to give her water and food whenever he could. I told him to keep her hand outside her blankets where it would get fresh air to it, and to change the bandages every few hours. I promised to come back first thing in the morning, but I assured him that Rosalind was young and strong and healthy, and she should be well in no time at all.

When I returned to the Owens place the next morning, I learned how wrong I had been.

I'D EXPECTED Rosalind would still be recovering that next day, but I thought to find her winding yarn or reading by the window over her cot, maybe occupied with some small household task.

Instead, she sat in her mother's rocking chair by the fire, huddled beneath her yellow blanket.

I saw that she kept her injured hand obediently out in the open, not tucked under her woolen wrapping, and I nodded with satisfaction. Victor had heeded my instructions. It's not every man who'll take advice from a woman, much less orders. But as I've said before, Victor Owens was a rarity.

However, he was also nowhere to be seen. I figured he was likely out tending his sheep and horses. Blue sat beside Rosalind; the dog was watchful but permitted me to enter.

"Good morning, Rosalind," I said softly. "How are you feeling this morning?" The previous day, while busy binding her wound and so on, I had not had time to feel guilty about my part in her injury. But that night I had slept poorly, filled with remorse. Now I dreaded what I would find when I examined her wounds. Rosalind was not one to laze about without some dire reason.

She looked up at me, her face pale and her eyes unnaturally bright. "Miss Emma?" she said softly. "What are you doing here?"

"I've come to see how you're getting on, that's all. Is your father about?" I noted the remains of biscuits and salt pork on the table, no doubt their breakfast. I would clean the mess up later.

"I don't know." She sounded guarded again, as if refusing to let life touch her. I had hoped that the glimmer of spirit I'd seen aroused in her the day before would continue to blaze bright and steady; instead, her injury seemed to have quenched it.

"How do you feel?" I checked her forehead for a fever and found it. I made sure to keep my voice cheerful, a skill I've had all too much practice developing over the years.

"This hurts. Like I burned it." She held up her hand weakly.

"Has your father given you anything to help with the pain? Whiskey or such?"

"Last night, I think."

"I'll fix you something in a minute that will help." I chatted about the weather and suchlike while I inspected her hand. Victor had changed the bandages, I was pleased to see. But the fingers were red and swollen. Red streaks straggled up her arm above the white cloths, heading for the elbow, as though some beast had clawed her. I knew only too well what that meant, and my insides churned with dismay. Infection.

I set to work changing the dressings, keeping up my steady stream of inconsequential prattle to distract her. As soon as I unwrapped her hand, I saw that the wound in her palm was covered with a yellowish crust and oozing pus. The wound on the back had a similar scab, though much smaller.

At that sight, the guilt I'd dammed up someplace deep inside broke through my bulwark of determined cheer. I don't generally waste much time fretting over what goes right or wrong with my patients. I just take the cards I'm dealt and do the best I can with them. But I was partly to blame for Rosalind's plight, though I had been attempting to save her from being shot.

Before I could stop myself, I said, "Rosalind, I am real sorry I hurt you. I never for a minute thought you'd fall onto that spinning wheel." I glared at the dog. "If that fool creature hadn't been in the way, I would have been able to pull you to the floor instead of pushing you like that. But that's my own fault for leaping when I ought to have been looking first, I expect."

Rosalind touched my arm with her good hand. "Miss Emma, I don't blame you. You did what you thought was best, same as always."

I smiled. "Thank you, my dear."

"It's Mrs. Mortimer who's to blame. If only—"

I took her good hand and patted it. "None of that," I told her. "Don't you go getting all worked up over her. For one thing, she's not worth one worried thought from you. And for another, you can't concentrate on healing if you're spending all your energy hating her."

My words soothed her perhaps as much as hers did me, but I still felt guilt sloshing all around inside me. I figured I ought to be done letting it leak out. I had more important things to think about, like how to save this poor girl's hand and maybe her life too. I mixed a good slug of the medicinal brandy I carry with brown sugar I found in their kitchen stores, knowing it would ease her pain some. Rosalind swallowed it with no complaints, though she twisted up her face like a small child taking medicine. I told myself to remember to use more sugar the next time. Then I took some dried willow bark from my black leather bag and steeped it in water. I used that to poultice her wounds, which I bound with fresh bandages.

That done, I stirred up the fire and set water to boil. Many's the time I've seen willow bark tea work wonders on a fever. I don't own to this around some folks, but much of what I've learned about healing came from a Pawnee elder who used to trade me his knowledge for coffee beans. I don't have fancy medicines like laudanum or carbolic acid the way a real doctor might, but the way I see it, poultices and teas are better than nothing.

I prayed that they would be enough, that the Lord would spare her, for I knew suddenly that if she died from a wound of my own infliction, I would leave Mortimer Junction. There was no way I would be able to face Victor ever again if I cost his daughter her life.

All the while, I kept talking to Rosalind. That's one of the benefits of knowing all the news there is to know—you don't run out of things to gab about. By the time I'd put the water on to boil, cleared away the breakfast remains from their table, and drawn up a chair to set myself down beside her, she knew all about the new Cummings baby, about a drifter who'd taken on work at the livery, and how something—or someone—had made off with three chickens from the back of the Petersons' henhouse.

The thud of hooves outside interrupted us. I looked out the small window over Rosalind's cot, expecting to see Victor ride back in from some chore out in the pastures.

To my shock, the rider was Palmer, the gunman. His big buckskin horse startled the sheep, which skittered off to one side or the other. He would be at the door in only a minute or two.

Where, oh where, was that Victor Owens when I needed him?

I LOOKED for Victor's rifle above the fireplace, but it was gone. He may not have taken my warning about Mrs. Mortimer's vengeful spirit seriously before, but clearly he did now.

"Rosalind," I asked again, forgetting to sound cheery, "where is your father?"

"I don't know," she said.

"Where's the pistol he took from that man?"

"I don't know." She tried to stand up and look out the window but dropped weakly back into her chair. "Who's coming?"

"Never you mind." I looked all around the room but could see few places where a gun might be hidden. I poked around the bedclothes on Rosalind's bed, thinking perhaps Victor had left it for her, but found nothing. Then I invaded Victor's own room and rummaged through his dresser drawers. Nothing again. Neither was the gun inside the big basket of unspun wool beside the spinning wheel.

That left me with no real means of protecting Rosalind or myself. I'm not generally in a position to require protecting, what with the Indians moved far off now and me past the age where I might expect an assault on my virtue. I briefly considered setting the dog on Palmer, but it had not moved from its post beside Rosalind, and I didn't trust it to obey me if I ordered it to attack.

I found a good-sized knife among the kitchen things. It would have to do.

Taking my place in the doorway, I prepared to defend Rosalind against whatever new devilry might befall us. Palmer may have been helpful, even sympathetic, the previous day; but Mrs. Mortimer had money aplenty, and he had the look of a man who knew how to spend money. Who knew what sidewinding scheme Mrs. Mortimer might conjure up for getting at Victor?

Palmer rode that handsome buckskin up to the fence, bold as a hydrophobic raccoon. He reined in next to my buggy and touched his hat brim. "Good morning."

I waved my knife in what I hoped was a threatening gesture. "I'll not be taken in by good manners!" I told him. "Mr. Owens ran you off once. I expect he won't hesitate to shoot you this time."

"Is he here?"

"Yes." It wasn't a lie, since surely Victor would not have strayed far with Rosalind in such a state.

"May I speak with him?"

It struck me that Palmer used words like an educated man. Who had seen to his schooling but neglected to teach him right from wrong? No honest man would trade on his ability to kill, I was certain.

"He is otherwise occupied," I said.

"And what of Miss Owens?" He kept his hands on his saddle horn, relaxed and nowhere near the gleaming pistol that had replaced its twin in his holster. He made no move to dismount.

"She is none of your concern!"

"That was a nasty wound."

"I said she is none of your concern!" I brandished my knife at him again. "If you have a message from Mrs. Mortimer, you can give it to me, and I will deliver it to Mr. Owens."

"I have no message." He grimaced, a bitter but not unfriendly expression. "I am no longer in her employ."

"I see." I felt my apprehension begin to fade, prey no doubt to his fine appearance and manners. Behind me, I heard a hissing noise that meant the water I'd set to boil was doing just that, now I was not there to watch it. Boiling over, in fact, and wasting the hot water I needed for willow bark tea. "Be off with you," I ordered, waving my knife again to remind him that I was not defenseless. "I must tend to something."

I hurried inside and took the heavy pot from the fire. I set it on the table and dumped in handfuls of willow bark. The knife I kept close by on the table, just in case.

Rosalind said, "It was that man again, wasn't it." She sat up straighter.

"What man?" I tried to sound casual. I failed and I knew it, but I stirred the tea with vigor and pretended I had not a care in sight.

"Mr. Palmer, the gunman. I . . . I recognized his voice."

I saw she looked a mite flushed, which I marked up to the fever's account. "I sent him packing, as I gather you heard."

"Oh."

While I worked, I heard a noise at the open doorway. There stood

Palmer, eyeing me curiously, hat in his hand.

I realized he might find my actions comical, a plump woman stirring a black pot like some storybook enchantress. "I am no witch," I felt compelled to explain. "I am a midwife and the closest thing to a doctor folks around here can find. I'm making tea, that's all." I will admit his good looks flustered me, aimed in my direction as they were.

"Tea?" he inquired.

"From willow bark. A remedy for fevers."

He glanced at Rosalind, a pitiful little bundle under her perversely cheerful yellow blanket. "For Miss Owens?"

His concerned tone and the worried way the inner edges of his eyebrows curved upward somehow convinced me he had not come to kill us. I told him, "Yes. Her wound has become infected. I'm trying to keep her from joining her poor mother."

He frowned but said nothing. Instead, he fidgeted, shifting his weight from one foot to the other and turning his hat around in his hands. Though I kept right on stirring my tea, I watched him closely. I gathered he was trying to make a decision of some sort. Finally, he said the last thing I could have imagined: "Can I help?"

"No." I busied myself with testing the tea. "Thank you," I added, feeling he deserved another point just for offering.

"May I come in?" he asked.

"That is not up to me," I said. "This is not my home." Though I would not have minded calling a cozy cabin like it my home rather than my cramped room at the boarding house.

"It is mine," Rosalind said. She twisted around in her chair to face him, not without a deal of effort. "Mr. Palmer, will you give me your word you mean us no harm?"

"I will. I do." His fingers crumpled the brim of his hat.

"You are nothing but a hired killer," I pointed out. "Why should we trust you?"

"I suppose I wouldn't, if I were you," he said quietly. "But I wish you could find a way to do so, just the same. I . . . I wasn't always a hired killer. I think I can help Miss Owens."

Rosalind sank back in her chair, causing it to rock back and forth. "Miss Emma, let him in."

The next thing I knew, he had taken my seat beside Rosalind. To my surprise, Victor's faithful dog did not protest. It didn't exactly wag its tail and lick Palmer's face, but neither did it growl or try to bite this intruder. That dog's reaction melted my fears about our visitor far more than any assurances from the gunman could have done. If Palmer had meant to harm Rosalind, I trusted that Blue would have sensed it.

"May I?" Palmer reached out, and Rosalind placed her bandaged hand on his. He examined the streaks on her arm closely. "Would you mind if I unwrapped this?" he asked me.

"I certainly would!" I marched over to him. "What do you want to do that for?"

"I'd like to see if rinsing the wounds would help," he said.

"Oh, you would, would you?" I wondered if perhaps that dog, Rosalind, and I all had faulty instincts when it came to trusting strangers. "Of all the nerve! First you came here pointing a gun at good honest folk, and now you wish to tamper with my patient? Rinse the wounds, indeed!"

"Sometimes it does a festering wound good to cleanse it and allow light and fresh air to the site."

"And how would a common killer know that?" I am not by nature a rude person, but I assure you that guilt and worry had worn my patience powerful thin by that point, and I felt no remorse right then over what I called him.

Palmer frowned. "As I said, I haven't always lived by my gun, Miss . . ."

"Thornberry," I supplied.

". . . Miss Thornberry. I know this will sound improbable, but I assure you it's true. I spent three long years as a surgeon during the war. I have seen more infections than you can imagine possible, and I will know by examining Miss Owens how serious her condition is."

"As if I would believe that." I shook my head so sharply, I could feel my hair start to loosen from the knot I wore on the back of my head. "How could a man go from saving lives to taking them?"

Palmer met my eyes. "Far too easily."

I held his gaze, searching for insincerity. A surgeon, here and now when Rosalind needed one, would be nothing short of a miracle. Too good to be true, my common sense insisted.

Still, something about the way he spoke seemed truthful. And his behavior of the day before, telling me to wash Rosalind's wounds, helping bandage them neatly and efficiently—all that testified to his veracity. As I've said, the good Lord sometimes answers my prayers in the most unpredictable ways. Perhaps this was one such answer.

But I still needed to know one thing. "Why are you no longer in Mrs. Mortimer's employ?"

"Because she lied to me. She said she had a troublesome neighbor who had threatened her, harassed her, and finally demanded that she buy his property. Had that been the case, I would have been only too happy to assist her. However, from what I could see here yesterday, I suspect the reverse is true."

A gunman with a conscience. And here I'd thought those were a myth.

Rosalind asked, "Do you always give notice when an employer lies to you?"

He almost smiled at her. "She also tried to shoot an innocent young woman with my gun. I returned the money she'd paid me and rode straight to town yesterday. But I couldn't leave without checking on your condition. I feared . . ." He looked down at her bandaged hand.

I said, "Then you were wiser than me. I told her father she would be fine."

"And perhaps she will be."

I sighed heavily and theatrically to make the point that I was still reluctant. "All right. I'll choose to believe you. For now. Examine her hand for yourself, if she will permit you. Though when her father sees you, I have no doubt he'll raise Cain over my allowing you in here."

"Thank you." He returned his attention to Rosalind. "May I?"

Rosalind nodded. Her gaze never left his face—not that I blamed her, for it was a face well worth perusing, as I have already noted.

I moved to look over his shoulder, curious as to his assessment of my treatment. He unwound the bandages as gently as he could. I noted approvingly the sure way his fingers worked, not jostling her hand in the slightest.

"Willow bark, you said?" he asked as he sniffed my poultice.

"Yes."

"Have you had much success with it before?"

"Indeed I have! I've—"

He interrupted me. "Have you tried carbolic acid?"

I frowned at him, irked more by the interruption than the implication that I lacked the necessary medicines and knowledge. "I told you, I am a midwife, not a nurse or a doctor. I have heard of that but never seen it. I've no notion where to get it or how."

"No morphine either, then?"

"None."

"Laudanum?"

"No."

"What do you do to ease a patient's pain?"

"Give them a little medicinal brandy."

He sighed. "Bring me the brandy, please."

"I've already given her brandy."

"I don't intend to have her drink it. I want to wash the wound with it. Or any other alcohol, if your brandy is too dear. And bring that wooden spoon again."

"Why should I?" I demanded. "I have nothing besides your word that you were once a surgeon. Or that you have broken with Mrs. Mortimer! For all I know, this may be some cunning scheme of hers to harm these good people yet again. Pretend to help us, get us to trust you, and then murder us all in our sleep, mayhap!"

Rosalind's eyes searched his. "You wouldn't shoot me yesterday. Not even when she ordered you to. I trust you."

"I think we should wait for Victor," I said.

"Then by all means, go find him," Palmer said. "But we have no time to waste here. The brandy is but a temporary measure. She'll need the other things, real medicines. But we must start somewhere."

I wasn't about to leave Rosalind alone with him to go off searching for her father. My qualms about his cleaning her wounds with alcohol were minimal, as I knew it to be as good as boiling water for sanitary purposes and wished I had thought of it myself. So I brought him the brandy and the wooden spoon.

"I'm so sorry," he told Rosalind, "but this will hurt." He offered her the wooden spoon. Once again she clamped it between her teeth. Then she squeezed her eyes shut. Palmer balanced the washbasin on his knees and held her hand over it, cupping his hand under hers and holding her fingers open with his thumb. Then he poured a little of the alcohol into her palm so that it puddled all around the wound.

Rosalind's eyes flew open, and she let out a wild yell around the spoon clenched in her teeth. But she didn't try to pull away. I grabbed hold of her other hand. "Squeeze as hard as you need to," I told her. I quickly regretted the offer, for Rosalind is a strong girl, used to manhandling sheep. But if she could stand the pain to her wounds, I told myself, I could stand having my fingers crushed by hers.

Palmer tilted her hand to let the brandy drain out into the washbasin. Then he turned her hand all the way over and repeated the process. The alcohol wouldn't stay puddled around the wound on the back, of course, so he simply poured a little over it at a time.

Rosalind's hand survived this, and mine did too. When he'd finished, he began binding her wound with a fresh dressing.

Rosalind took the spoon from between her teeth. "Thank you," she said weakly. "You see?" she added, glancing at me. "I knew."

"Knew what?" I asked her.

"Knew I could trust him. That hurt, Miss Emma, but it wasn't a . . . a bad hurting, if you catch my meaning."

Without so much warning as a footstep to alert us to his presence, who should appear at the window above Rosalind's bed but Victor, his rifle aimed squarely at Palmer. "Well, I sure enough don't trust him," he said.

We all jumped like pups caught licking out the stewpot.

"You get away from my daughter," he said.

P ALMER SET Rosalind's hand down carefully and raised both his own. "Just trying to help," he told Victor.

"I said get away from her." I'd never before heard Victor sound that angry. It was almost like listening to a stranger. He glared down that rifle, its butt snug up against his shoulder, looking ornerier than a wild steer.

I said, "How about we all talk this over like the sensible folks I know we are?"

"Not now, Miss Emma," Victor growled.

I admit those harsh words rankled me a good deal, coming as they did from a man I counted my friend. I put my hands on my hips. "I'm giving you the chance to be sensible, Victor Owens. You can come in here with your rifle and let this man speak his piece at gunpoint if you've a mind to. After all, it's your house. But any conclusions you've jumped to, you can just un-jump."

Victor narrowed his eyes, but when he spoke, his voice had lost much of its severity. "Rosalind, what has this jackleg shootist been up to here?" He did not lower his rifle.

Rosalind replied quickly, her words almost running together. "He washed my hand, Pa, that's all. Miss Emma's real concerned over it. He was a surgeon during the war." Her cheeks were flushed still.

"That so? Ain't that convenient."

Palmer said, "I came to check on Miss Owens's hand. And to ask if you'd wired the sheriff."

"What's it to you?"

"You could say I'm ashamed. For not doing more yesterday. I was caught off guard by Mrs. Mortimer's cruelty. I came to apologize. If you bring her to court for assaulting your daughter, if you need a witness to testify, you can call on me. Luke Palmer. A wire to the station master in Abilene, Kansas, will find me."

"I don't know."

Victor was a stubborn man and a proud one. I worried he might let his pride keep him from accepting Palmer's apology or his offer to help. So I put in, "Mr. Palmer no longer works for Mrs. Mortimer, which I'm sure you will see is a sign of his good sense."

"How do we know this isn't her plan? That she hasn't sent him here to get a man inside, and then finish us off?"

Though I had earlier thought that same thing myself, I now protested, "Victor Owens, be reasonable. Adelaide Mortimer has to keep on living in these parts. She knows full well that with me here to see what happened yesterday, half the town would have heard about it by sundown and the other half doubtless knows by now. If you or Rosalind turned up dead, there's not a person with sense in these parts who wouldn't know who's to blame."

"That's so," Victor conceded.

"Besides," I added, "if your dog has no objection to this man's presence, why should we?"

Victor eyed his dog through the window. He raised his eyebrows as if considering asking what the furry black sentinel could tell him about our intruder. For a moment I almost expected Blue to volunteer his opinion.

Palmer said, "I meant it when I said I've quit. I'm no saint, but there are some things I won't do. A man has to draw the line somewhere."

Victor studied Palmer. At last he lowered his rifle. "All right. If you let me have your gun, you can stay."

Palmer stood up, keeping his hands away from his sides where Victor could see them clearly. "Thank you. But truth be told, I need to leave. I must have medicines Miss Thornberry doesn't possess. I'm sure there's a doctor in Lincoln who has what I require."

I objected, "Lincoln is a day's ride from here." I also objected to his assuming it would be he who saved Rosalind's life, but I kept that to myself lest I sound like a spoiled child deprived of a treat.

"Which is why I must leave at once." He touched Rosalind's shoulder. "I'll be back soon." His gaze caught and held hers briefly. Then he hurried to the door. "Miss Thornberry, a word?" he said as he went outside.

I joined him and Victor beside the gate. Palmer said, "Your tea may help her fever, so by all means have her drink it. And any food or water she will take. Keep her wound clean—every few hours repeat what I did with the brandy. Don't wrap it again—let both sides get air to them. If we can't stop that infection . . ."

"We will lose her," I finished for him.

"She will lose her hand, at the very least."

Beside me, Victor gave a sort of sighing groan, as if he'd been trying to avoid that fact only to have it run headlong into him.

Palmer continued, "I will do everything in my power to prevent that, but . . ." He paused, and it seemed to me he looked almost frightened for a minute, though I couldn't think why. He continued, "But it may come down to a choice between her hand and her life."

I asked, "You think these medicines will help? If you can find them?"

He went to his horse. "I have seen them stave off infection and sometimes lessen it. I only hope I can find them and ride back here in time." He untied his bedroll from behind his saddle, unbuckled his saddle bags, and tossed them both inside the picket fence.

I had a sudden thought. "Shouldn't you stay here with her, then? We can get someone from town to fetch the medicines."

Palmer turned away to check his saddle's girth, making sure it was cinched securely. With his face still averted he said, "I'll need to get more than medicine. If that infection can't be stopped . . ." He took a deep breath. "During the war we amputated as often as we could—it was the only real hope we had of preventing a wound from festering like this." He looked over at us. "I wish I had stayed here yesterday. I lacked the courage, that's all. I hope I can make up for that."

Victor said gruffly, "Maybe I've misjudged you."

"No, you judged me about right. But a man doesn't have to stay on the same trail he's been riding, does he?" With that, Palmer untied his reins from the fence, swung into the saddle, and started off.

While watching Palmer and his horse lope up the rise, I asked Victor, "Before we go inside, answer me one thing: Where were you? How could you leave your child alone like that? She is seriously ill, do you not realize that?"

"No," he said, sounding as irritated as I felt. "I didn't realize that. She was a bit tired, but she said she would be all right. I knew that young ewe would birth her lambs any time, and I had to check on her, feed the horses . . . I can't just abandon my stock."

I glared at him, my frustration and guilt rising up in me again. "You can't abandon your stock, but you can leave your daughter to die?"

"I didn't know she might die. You told me she'd be fine." He spun around and headed back to the house.

I shivered. He was right; I'd as much as promised him that. And he'd believed me. Trusted me. Remorseful, I hurried to catch up with him before he ducked inside. "I'm sorry." I touched his arm to stop him. "I am so very sorry, Victor. I had no call to accuse you that way." I closed my eyes for a moment, searching for a way to divert our words, stop us from tearing at each other from worry and dread. "How was your ewe?"

"Fine. They're all fine, her and the two lambs she bore this morning."

"I'm glad."

He looked at me strangely. "Are you?" He went inside without another word.

I entered just in time to see him stalk straight over to the spinning wheel, grasp the spindle, snap it clean off, and toss it into the fire. "That's an end to that," he said.

7

E SPENT that day in a haze of chores and nursing. Victor kept himself busy outdoors during daylight, checking in at the cabin every hour or two to see if I needed help. I tended Rosalind, pouring as much willow bark tea and water into her as I could. I also started a batch of stew with whatever I could find in Rosalind's small garden behind the house.

Victor, being a thoughtful man, gave up his room and bed for me that night. He laid out a blanket for himself on the floor beside Rosalind's cot and promised to wake me if her condition changed in any way. I slept so soundly that when I awoke the next morning I was stiff, never having shifted position while asleep. If not for that I would have felt remarkably well rested.

In the other room Victor dozed on the floor by Rosalind. She was awake, moaning softly, her eyes open but wandering. My small bottle of medicinal brandy had not lasted through the previous day, but Victor had a dusty bottle of what he termed simply 'liquor.' After mixing a dose of that with some of their rapidly dwindling supply of brown sugar, I moved to stand beside them. I didn't like to rouse Victor, for his face looked just as weary as it had the day before. But I knew Rosalind was suffering, and he blocked me from reaching her.

I bent down and touched his shoulder. "Victor," I murmured. "Wake up, Victor. I'm here now." .

He stirred, mumbled something I did not understand, then opened his eyes and looked up into mine. I'd never realized how blue his eyes were, like small flowers that you find by accident, hidden away in the vast prairie.

"What is it?" He sat straight up and looked at Rosalind as if he feared to find her gone.

"Go to bed," I told him firmly. "By the looks of you, you cannot have had more than three decent winks of sleep this whole night, nor the one before. I will tend Rosalind; I will see to your horses and mine. When you wake, I will fix you something to eat. Now go."

He did not so much as mutter a protest but stumbled off to his room.

I was glad for the good night of rest I'd gotten my own self, for I could see it would be a long day. And we could not expect Palmer back before nightfall. I took Victor's seat beside Rosalind. "Good morning," I said to her with a smile, expecting no answer and getting none. She drank my draught with a scowl then turned her head toward the wall.

Pressing food on her just yet felt unwise, so I left a cup of cold willow bark tea on the chair by her bed and went out to the barn. I grew up on a farm, and though that was too long ago for me to admit to in mixed company, I still knew how to pitch hay and haul water. I'd barely finished seeing to the stock when a rancher from up north arrived with his half-grown boy whose leg was sliced open clear to the bone. They wouldn't say much about how it had happened, just asked me to stitch him up. I always leave word at the boarding house as to where I'm going, so folks in need can find me when I'm out tending someone else.

I treated the boy outside, right in the bed of his father's wagon. Mindful of Palmer's advice, I first swabbed out the gash as best I could, then gave the boy that well-gnawed spoon to bite while I poured liquor over the wound and the needle I stitched it up with. He downed a generous slug of the alcohol with considerably less face-pulling than Rosalind.

Their arrival had awakened Victor, who appeared briefly at the door with his rifle. When I'd finished bandaging up the boy, I instructed his father as to the care of the wound. He gave me two silver dollars warm from his pocket and promised me a dozen eggs if I would ride out their way in a few days to check on the boy.

When I went inside to wash up, I found Victor pacing restlessly, fiddling about with things, and being more bother than blessing. I sent him out to check on the new little mother and her lambs in the barn. Rosalind had not touched her tea. At first I thought her asleep, but she tossed her head back and forth at times, mumbling. Her face was flushed, and her skin was hot and dry to the touch. I wondered if I should try to sweat the fever out of her but decided she had too little liquid in her to make that advisable. Whenever I tried to get her to drink either willow bark tea or water, she pushed the cup away with surprising force. I gave up on that eventually and set about baking a pan of cornbread to go with what remained of the stew I'd made the day before.

Then the dog barked, startling me so that I dropped a spoon onto the table with a clatter. I spun around and saw Rosalind out of bed, hanging onto the chair, swaying. "Where is he?" she asked, her rasping voice painful to hear.

"He's in the barn," I assured her as I hurried to her side.

"I need to find him."

"He's in the barn, checking on the sheep," I soothed. I tried to guide her back to bed, but she pulled away.

"No, not Pa. The other man. Luke, he said his name was." She tried to move toward the door.

"Rosalind, you're not well," I said firmly. "How about some warm cornbread? I've just baked some."

"I've got to find him." She shoved me away.

Now, I am neither a light woman nor a weak one. Or so I thought. But Rosalind pushed me hard enough that I had to let go of her arm to keep myself from toppling onto her bed. Regaining my balance, I caught up with her as she reached the threshold.

"You come back in here," I ordered as I took hold of her good arm again.

She twisted and pulled against me. "Why won't you leave me alone?"

Hoping her father might be able to handle her better than I could, I called out the doorway for him. She tried to push past me, but I blocked her way. "Blue," I said, hoping that dog was as intelligent as I believed, "go fetch Victor. Bring help. Please."

Blue cocked his head to one side, gave a short yip, and ran out. Rosalind tried to duck under my arm and follow, but I got her around the waist and hauled her back inside, then quickly slammed the door shut. "You are staying here," I told her.

"I have to find him," she moaned. "Why'd he leave?" She began to pace the room, from door to spinning wheel to table to bed to door, around and around and around.

It couldn't have been more than two or three minutes before Victor arrived, but it seemed much longer as I stood guarding the door, watching her walk in circles like a sick calf. But then he was there at the window, calling, "What's wrong?"

"She's out of her head from the fever. Help me get her back into bed."

Victor and his faithful dog slipped inside, and I barred the door behind them. Then together we tried to convince Rosalind to lie down, or at least to sit by the fire. Finally she consented to sit in her mother's rocking chair, where she rocked back and forth, still agitated. She began to mumble half under her breath.

I sat down at the table, worn out by the struggle. Victor pulled the other chair up and looked at me with such anxious sorrow that I took one of his hands in both of mine and squeezed it reassuringly.

"Fevers are a strange thing," I said softly. "Distressing to watch and unpredictable as a jackrabbit. All we can do is keep her safe until Mr. Palmer returns."

"You really believe he can help her? That story about being a surgeon, the war . . ."

"If you're thinking it's too good to be true, I've felt the same. Yet, watching him—he certainly seems capable." I shrugged. "Sometimes the good Lord sends us what we need right when we need it. Even if it's not what we wanted."

Victor looked down at our hands. "I hope so." He placed his other hand on top of mine. "If you hadn't been here, Emma . . . I don't know. I just don't know."

"But I am. And I'll not leave until we've seen her through this." Not though ten babies all decided to be born that night. Their mothers would have to travel to me, for once.

Victor said, his voice faltering, "I can never hope to repay you." His eyes met mine, and he seemed about to say something else, but didn't.

"This is what friends do," I told him. "They help."

I DID not look for Palmer to be back before nightfall. Lincoln was a good twelve-hour ride away, and what with finding a doctor or druggist, resting his horse and himself, then riding back—even if he pushed, it would be late before he arrived. Or so I expected.

But it was only midafternoon when we heard a horse outside. Victor snatched up his rifle and hurried to the window, flattening himself beside it so he could peer out without being seen much himself. "It's him," he said.

"Him? Now?" I pushed away from the table. "Can his horse fly?" I went to the window to see for myself. Our visitor was indeed Palmer, but riding a different animal, a rangy dun far inferior to his own fine mount. I flung open the door. "Mr. Palmer, where is your horse?" I demanded.

"In Lincoln. I'll see him again in a day or two." He dismounted wearily.

"How is she?"

"Feverish." I watched him untie a canvas sack from his saddle horn. "Did you get . . . everything you needed?"

"Yes." He paused then added, "And I hope I won't be needing everything I got." With a rough stubble shadowing his cheeks and dark half-moons under his eyes, he made me worry I'd have another patient on my hands if he didn't rest soon.

Victor met him at the door, his face full of questions he didn't know how to ask. Or wasn't willing to, maybe.

Palmer stopped before he entered the house and handed me the heavy canvas sack. Unbuckling the fine gun belt from around his waist, he held it out to Victor, pistol firmly in its holster. "As you asked," he said.

Victor took it from him and went inside without a word.

I set the sack beside Rosalind's bed. It clinked softly, something metal against glass. I shivered at the sound. Palmer went right to where she still sat restlessly in the rocking chair. He spoke softly as he checked her pulse, felt her forehead, and stilled her rocking so he could look into first one eye, then the other. "How long has she been like this?" he asked.

"A couple hours," I said. "Since before noon."

"She's wearing herself out." He turned to Victor, who watched nearby, arms folded. "I'm going to give her laudanum to make her sleep. Once she's quiet, I'll treat her hand." He asked me, "When was the last time you gave her a dose of liquor?"

"Early this morning, when I first woke. She won't drink anything for me now though, or for her father either."

Rosalind put up a fuss about the laudanum Palmer coaxed her to swallow. Then suddenly her eyes lost their unfocused glaze and she recognized him. "Oh!" she said, smiling up at him. "I've been looking for you."

"And you've found me," he answered. "Now I need you to drink this. Please, Miss Owens."

She obediently swallowed what he gave her, and smiled again when he thanked her for cooperating. But before long she was back to muttering about needing to find him, rocking and rocking as if her life depended on it instead of on any medicine we could give her.

While we waited for the laudanum to take effect, Palmer drew Victor and me to the far side of the room. There he said softly, "While I was in Lincoln, I learned that Mrs. Mortimer has more than replaced me. She's hired three more gunmen. I have no doubt she intends to do just what she threatened: lay siege to this house."

"Three!" My voice squeaked on the word.

Victor said, "Well, how did you think this would end, Miss Emma? Some nice way? Like you said, she must know you've told the whole town what happened here. She needs to end this now, and the only way she'll want it to end is with us gone, one way or another."

"I agree," said Palmer. "I hope I didn't overstep myself, Mr. Owens, but I stopped at the sheriff's office while I was in Lincoln. I told him all that's happened here. He said he'd send a man to investigate when he could spare one. He'll bring my horse along when he does."

"I thank you for that," Victor said. "Whatever happens here, at least there's a chance for justice that way."

Palmer asked, "Can you fire a gun, Miss Thornberry?"

"Not with any degree of accuracy." I imagined myself wearing a holster and staring down a hired killer. If reality had not been so alarming, I would have laughed at the conjured image. I elaborated, "What I mean to say is, I doubt I could hit a moving target with anything you'd call dependability. But shoot a gun? Yes, I can do that."

"That's all we'll need," Palmer said. "Mr. Owens, when I've finished tending your daughter, I'd like to talk over some ideas I've had for how we could defend this place, see what you think."

"And then you will sleep," I told him. "What possesses you men to think you don't need sleep? Turns you into willful children quicker than anything."

"Yes, ma'am," he said.

I returned to watching Rosalind. It wasn't long before her head dropped back against the chair and her eyes closed. Victor carried her to her bed. At Palmer's request he put her in it with her head closer to the door, the reverse of how she usually slept. This placed her right arm to the wall and her left hand free to be doctored without our reaching over her all the time.

Palmer checked Rosalind's pulse again before examining her hand and arm. The red streaks reached up to her elbow now, twice as long as they'd been when he left. Scowling, he set to work.

While Palmer treated Rosalind using various bottles he'd brought back with him, Victor cleaned and oiled his rifle. Then he did the same for Palmer's pistols, both the one he'd taken from Mrs. Mortimer and the one Palmer had surrendered that day. He set out boxes of ammunition, a neat stack beside each weapon on the table. I hauled as much water from the stream as I could find containers to fill, so that if we did indeed find ourselves besieged, we would not lack water for Rosalind. I toted bucket after bucket until I thought my arms would pop from their sockets. When Victor finally finished with the weapons, he took my place. He said he would fill the horse trough and make sure the sheep and her lambs had water in the barn as well. Palmer's spare pistol was tucked into the front waistband of Victor's trousers, and he looked so fearsome that I was happy we were on the same side of this predicament.

I returned to the house, there to sink down into the rocking chair, worn out for the time being. Palmer had finished tending Rosalind's wounds. When I arrived, he was just washing off his own hands. He splashed water on his face while he was at it. By the looks of Rosalind's hand, he had peeled off the crusted scabs and drained the yellowish pus, then spread a paste of some sort all over and around the puncture wounds.

"Mr. Palmer," I said, "you need to sleep. You'll be no good to us if you're dozing on your feet when those three new gunmen show up. I doubt they've ridden all day and night as you seem to have done."

Taking his seat beside our patient once more, he replied, "I once stayed awake more than forty hours, operating on soldiers after a battle. I can sleep when this is over." He didn't look at me but focused down on Rosalind's arm. He traced his forefinger up the longest streak of infection to where it ended inside the crook of her elbow. "I ought to operate now." His voice became flat, as if he were reading from a book, not speaking his own thoughts. "I should take off her arm here. Minimize the muscle damage." He circled her arm with his fingers midway between elbow and shoulder.

"Then why don't you?" I asked. Though it would be an awful thing for Rosalind to lose her arm, I'd resigned myself to the fact it would very likely be necessary. She would be better off living life with one arm than not living it at all, I reasoned.

He looked over at me then, his expression as sorrowful as if poor Rosalind had already died. "I can't," he said.

"Why ever not?" I snapped. "You say you're a surgeon. You've amputated arms before, surely. If that's what must be done, let's begin."

Softly he said, "You asked me how a surgeon could turn killer." His voice was so low, I had to scoot the rocking chair closer to hear him.

Palmer avoided my gaze. "I said it was easy, and in a way it was. Easier than believing myself to be a coward, anyway. But that's what I am. I've spent these last few years proving time and again how well I can shoot, that I'm willing to risk my life in exchange for money. My life? Why, it isn't worth the price of a bullet."

I have learned from my dealings with all sorts of sick folks that there are some diseases you can't see: thoughts that eat you up from inside your own head, and you can't admit they're there until they're about to kill you. Some festering sores in your memory need a lot of time to mend. Some only start to heal once you've told someone else they exist. And some can't be cured, no how. I nodded and rocked and said nothing, hoping Palmer was one who would find voicing his troubles to be a healing process. Besides, I was curious as to what he would say next.

He went on, "I finished medical school the second year of the war and went right to work for the army. At first I treated more sick than wounded. Excepting when there was a big battle, we mostly had to deal with dysentery and . . . and other camp diseases. But when there was a battle, we'd be pressed hard for days." He lifted his head and stared out the window, his gaze focused somewhere in the past. "We'd find a barn or a big house, sometimes a church, to use for the amputations. We'd learned that a man had a better chance of surviving an amputation than a wound filled with dirt and gunpowder and a bullet and the devil knows what else. So we'd take off any limb we suspected would become infected.

"They'd lay a man on the table in front of me. If we were lucky, we had chloroform. Sometimes we didn't. We'd use laudanum if we had that instead, but sometimes . . . sometimes we just had a couple of strong orderlies to hold the man down and a leather strap for him to bite on.

"There were days when my arm would ache from using that bone saw. Ache like I'd been taking down trees with it. But that wasn't the worst of it. Nor the smell, nor the sight of all those mangled bodies."

He turned away from the window, his haunted eyes seeking mine. "It was the screams. I still hear them, Miss Thornberry. Men begging me not to cut them up. Others waiting their turn, crying for help, for water, for their mothers or their wives. And I could only treat one at a time. No matter how fast I worked, how long I stayed there, I could never help them all."

He rubbed his hands together, one inside the other, as if washing them. "One day, I . . . I couldn't stay. I was through. I'd cut off one limb too many, and yet I'd saved far too few men. I got sick. When I was better, they made me a clerk. I filled bottles and inventoried supplies and stayed as far away from wounded soldiers as I could without leaving altogether. I thought maybe eventually I'd be able to treat them again.

"But then the war ended. And I knew the truth. I knew I was a coward. I've been lying to myself ever since that I wasn't. I let myself get shot at; I shoot other men. But it's never really fooled me. Well, now I'm through fooling anyone else too."

I leaned forward. "Mr. Palmer, you've come to a fork in your trail. You said yourself that a man doesn't have to stay on the path he's been following. Here's your chance to find a new one." I gestured to Rosalind. "A few hours won't make that much difference, will it? You'd still be able to save her if you waited three or four hours to operate?"

"I think so. That's morphine I put on her wounds—we used it in the war to stave off infections and sometimes treat minor ones. I hoped it might help a little."

"Then get some sleep," I said. "You'll have a clearer head and a steadier hand if you do. And if you can't operate, then maybe you can . . . can tell me how to do it." The idea filled me with dread, but if it was the only way to save Rosalind's life, I would do what I had to.

Palmer rubbed his eyes with his fists the way a little child would. "Maybe you're right." He stood. "I'll sleep in the barn's hayloft. Good vantage point if someone . . . visits." He stopped halfway to the door, right hand flat against his leg where his pistol ought to be.

"While you're at it, might as well take Victor his rifle," I suggested.

"Good idea." He gathered up several boxes of ammunition and the rifle, and left.

I knew then that Palmer was not so different from the other men who drifted through Mortimer Junction after all. The war wasn't finished for him yet either.

PALMER NEVER got a chance to sleep. Only a thimbleful of minutes after he left for the barn, I heard several horses approaching. The dog rushed to look out the door, growling. I joined him and saw six men riding down toward the cabin. And I would have recognized the fancy buggy up at the top of the bluff as belonging to Mrs. Mortimer even if we hadn't been expecting her to return.

I bolted the door then hurried to the table where Palmer's belt and pistol still lay. The gun was heavier than I'd expected. I held it out in front of me, aiming at the spinning wheel, to see if I would need both hands to fire it. I decided I would. Once I got used to the feel of the weapon, I moved to the window above Rosalind's bed the way I had seen Victor do, sidling up to it so I could see out without showing myself.

The newcomers fanned out as they rode down the slope, not sticking to the track. Three of them I recognized as cowhands who worked on Mrs. Mortimer's ranch, which meant the other three must be the hired guns. They got about halfway down the hill before I heard Victor shout, "Stop where you are. You're trespassing."

One of the hired gunmen motioned for the others to stop but moved a little ahead of them before he reined in his horse. "As far as we're concerned, this land belongs to Mrs. Mortimer," he called back.

I would have disliked that man even if he hadn't been here to do Adelaide Mortimer's dirty work. His long face had too much jaw and nose and not enough anything else.

"Not yet, it doesn't," Victor yelled.

"Seems to me it's her word against yours. Why don't you come out and talk it over with her, peaceful-like."

"I'm warning you, get off my land or I'll shoot."

The man with the long face laughed. "You and the midwife against six of us?"

Palmer's voice floated down from somewhere, cool and confident. "Hello there, Job Dixon. Last I knew, you were over in Colorado doing work for the railroad. I heard someplace you had some strong reasons for avoiding this part of the country."

The man looked up, and I knew Palmer must be in the barn's hayloft, speaking from the opening cut there to swing hay bales in through. "Luke Palmer, that you?"

"It is."

"You working for this sheep farmer?"

"No. I'm through selling my gun."

The man called Dixon grinned. I'd been wrong—he didn't just have too much chin and nose, he also had too much mouth. "Then we've got nothing to worry about."

"I didn't say I was through using it."

Dixon scowled. "You can't get all six of us at once. Be sensible. Come on down before this starts, and I give you my word you can ride out of here before any shooting starts."

"I don't have to get all six of you myself. I've got friends too. Why don't *you* be sensible and ride off this place before you get shot for trespassing?"

One of the other gunmen growled, "We didn't count on going up against Luke Palmer. She said it'd just be an old man and his daughter."

I glared at him for calling Victor Owens "old," though of course he couldn't see me. Why, Victor wasn't any older than me, and I wasn't nearly ready to be considered "old."

Palmer laughed. "Mrs. Mortimer has a real bad habit of neglecting to tell her employees all the facts."

Dixon said, "This is your last chance, Palmer. I don't fancy being the one to end you, but you can be sure one of us will unless you come on out here right now."

"I like it where I am," Palmer replied.

"Your call." Dixon clucked to his horse and began riding back up the hill. For a minute I thought he'd decided to leave after all. The other five men did the same, but they didn't ride all the way back up the bluff. Instead, they turned around again a little before they reached the top, and I realized they'd just been moving out of range of Victor's and Palmer's guns.

Dixon cupped his hands around his mouth and hollered, "Me and my pals aim to stay here until you get sensible. Might take a few days, but eventually you'll have to leave the barn. And when you do, here we'll be."

I knew then that Mrs. Mortimer had won. If Palmer couldn't come back to the house, he couldn't operate on Rosalind. She would die a slow, horrible death from infection. Or Palmer would try to sneak over here in the night; but even if he made it safely, that awful man Dixon was right: We couldn't stay bottled up here forever. And what if someone took sick and needed me?

I decided I would call out to remind Victor of all that, but before I could, there came a piercing whistle from the direction of the barn, one low note, one high note, and then another low note.

Victor's dog scrambled up on Rosalind's bed and jumped out the window before I could quite comprehend what he was about.

"You there, Blue! Bring them down!" Victor yelled.

I wondered if the poor man had taken leave of his senses. The men outside must have thought so too, for I could hear their laughter. As I watched, the dog ran off up the bluff and over it. He yipped a few times, and then sheep began bleating unhappily. They sounded for all the world like old women protesting the necessity of taking their rheumatism medicine. The bleating grew louder, rowdier, and soon a sheep or two drifted into sight over the rise. Then more and more of them. Blue yipped and growled somewhere behind them. And then a veritable flood of sheep poured over the bluff from where they'd been grazing up near the road. They pounded down the slope, surrounding Mrs. Mortimer in her buggy, engulfing the six men on their horses.

The horses shied at the sudden onslaught of wool-covered intruders bent on escaping the little dog driving them. The men tried to hold their horses steady, but their mounts were swept up in the rush, and they had no choice but to move on down toward the buildings.

Mrs. Mortimer fared even worse. Her horse bolted down the slope at an angle, the buggy lurching along behind it. As I watched, one front wheel hit an old tree stump and the buggy flew up into the air. When it landed on its side, Mrs. Mortimer tumbled out of it. I couldn't see her anymore for all the woolly bodies in the way.

A rifle shot rang out, but either it went wild or Palmer meant it as a final warning, for none of the men outside fell from their saddles the way I'd expected them to. Dixon and the other two gunmen began firing at the barn, but their horses lurched and shied, so that I was hopeful they could take no real aim. However, that made them difficult to hit as well. Though Victor and Palmer fired back, all their shots missed, as far as I could tell.

Victor called more instructions to his dog, but I couldn't hear them clearly over the sound of all those sheep. I'd thought they were headed for the barn, but as they reached it, the dog steered them on down toward the stream. That creature seemed to have multiplied into two or three dogs, for one minute I would see him in one place, and the next he would be on a different side of the herd. Always snapping at disobedient sheep, his sharp barks reminding them to go where he aimed them and not get any silly ideas about trying to get inside the corral or barn.

As the riders drew closer, Mrs. Mortimer's regular cowhands began shooting too. It got so I couldn't tell which shots came from where. The Owens cabin and barn are both set broadside to the river, the barn back just a bit instead of right in line with the house. That meant I couldn't see the barn unless I stuck my head out of the window and looked around the house, and I was loath to do so lest someone notice me and aim a few shots my way.

First one rider and then another passed beyond where I could safely see. I began to wonder if Palmer and Victor were ever going to hit one of the attackers, or if they were missing on purpose. Or if real gunfights went this way, with more noise and movement than killing. This being the first in my experience, I had no way of knowing.

Then I heard a cry of pain and chanced looking out the window far enough to see Dixon slide sideways off his horse. When he hit the ground, his horse bolted, leaving him lying there, sheep running on both sides of his body. I couldn't tell if he was dead or just wounded and did not think it wise to keep my head out the window long enough to find out. It was just as the last of the sheep streamed past that I heard a noise at the back of the house. It sounded like fabric ripping, a noise so out of place that I knew I needed to investigate at once.

I rushed to look out the window in the cabin's opposite wall, just to the right of the spinning wheel. There at the side of the house, holding a pistol of her own, stood Mrs. Mortimer. A strip of her skirt fluttered from the picket fence where she'd climbed over it. Whether she planned to fire in through that window at Rosalind and me or if she intended to sneak on past to the barn, I did not know. But I lifted Palmer's pistol and pointed it at her. "Stop where you are, Adelaide Mortimer," I said good and loud.

She jumped, but she did not drop her gun. "Emma, this is not your fight," she said.

I laughed. "It most certainly is my fight. You made it mine when you attacked my friends. When you hired strangers to come here and kill them."

"But you wouldn't shoot me. I know you wouldn't." She tried to sound confident, but I have been around enough people trying to be brave to know when they are pretending.

"I'd rather shoot you than look at you. And unlike Mr. Palmer, I have no qualms about shooting a woman." I realized suddenly that the gunshots had stopped. "The fight is over, and you have lost," I told her. Unlike most people, I have had enough practice feigning certainty to convince most anyone that what I say is so. Far too often I've had no knowledge of how to treat an ailment, but simply telling a patient they would be fine soothed them enough to buy me time to think of something helpful. I prayed that my trust in Victor's and Palmer's abilities to dispatch their adversaries was not misplaced.

Mrs. Mortimer hesitated. To help her decide, I put my thumb on the pistol's hammer and pulled it back to cock it. But it had a stronger spring to it than I'd anticipated, and the hammer slid out from under my thumb before I could pull it all the way back. The gun fired with a great thudding noise, shoving me backward from the recoil. I dropped it in my surprise, as startled as if someone else had fired it at me. But I wasted no time returning to the window to see if I had killed Mrs. Mortimer half by accident.

She had her hands over her face; her pistol lay in the dirt at her feet. I could see no blood anywhere, and with unexpected relief I concluded that the bullet had gone wild. I snatched up Palmer's gun from the floor and aimed it at her again. "You stay there," I told her. "You know now I mean business, so you stay right there."

From in front of the house, Victor yelled, "Miss Emma! Are you all right?"

The sound of his voice relieved me mightily, and I called back, "I am, but I'd be most appreciative if you'd come guard Mrs. Mortimer for me." I did not take my eyes off her, lest she try to retrieve her gun and trade me a bullet for the one I'd sent her way.

Victor appeared around the corner of the house, picked up Mrs. Mortimer's pistol, then led her back the direction he'd come.

I lowered my weapon with some relief and hurried to look out the door.

The gunman called Dixon lay where he'd fallen. One of his fellow gunmen leaned against the barn wall, clutching his left arm. Blood soaked out from under his fingers, but not so much that I worried he would die from its loss anytime soon. The third gunman and one of Mrs. Mortimer's hired cowhands stood in the yard with their hands up, Palmer's rifle trained on them from his vantage point in the hayloft. Mrs. Mortimer's other two regular men were nowhere to be seen.

"Where are the others?" I called to Palmer.

"They skedaddled when they realized they were in range of this rifle. Did Mrs. Mortimer shoot you?"

"No," I said proudly. "I fired at her. She tried to sneak up on us around the back of the cabin, but I stopped her with no difficulty whatsoever."

I couldn't be sure, but I thought Palmer chuckled.

10

VICTOR TIED up Adelaide Mortimer, her remaining gunman, and her cowhand. I tended the other gunman's wounded arm in the shade of the barn, trying to ignore the body lying not far away. Palmer had put his own blanket over the dead man, and I could tell he regretted the man's death, even though Dixon had come here with the intent to kill us. I wanted to ask how it had all happened, but I knew the story would keep.

I'd just finished tying off the bandage when I heard hoofbeats at the top of the bluff. Not again, I thought.

Palmer grabbed Mrs. Mortimer and yanked her toward the house. "If that's more of your men, you tell them to leave or they'll have to try collecting their wages from a dead woman."

Before Mrs. Mortimer could reply, three horses showed along the top of the bluff. Only two of them bore riders, and the third was a familiar buckskin. Victor said, "Friends of yours, Palmer?"

"They are now." Palmer loosened his hold on Mrs. Mortimer's arm. "Looks to me like the sheriff from down in Lincoln, bringing my horse and looking into this like he said he would."

As it turned out, we needed nearly an hour to give the sheriff a clear explanation of the situation. When it came time for me to relate how I had captured Mrs. Mortimer, I omitted the detail of firing the gun, accidental or otherwise, not wanting to seem either a braggart or foolhardy. He did not press me for more details than those I freely gave.

While the sheriff took charge of our prisoners, his deputy heaved Dixon's body over the back of the dun horse Palmer had borrowed. I offered the loan of my buggy to transport Mrs. Mortimer back to town, where they intended to hold the prisoners until they could travel to Lincoln aboard the next day's train. But that woman said she would rather ride a strange horse than sit in my buggy, so they put her on the dead man's horse and took her that way.

Once they had gone, I hurried inside to check on Rosalind, having neglected her shamefully in the excitement. She still slept, but I thought her forehead felt cooler, though I could not be certain. The red streaks on her arm had retreated at least an inch. I wondered if Palmer's treatment had helped enough, or if we still faced a grisly operation.

When he and Palmer came back inside, Victor asked, "How is she?" His voice was husky with worry.

"I can't tell." I stood up and motioned for Palmer to take my seat. "See what you think."

Palmer examined her arm. He said nothing for some minutes but took her pulse, felt for fever, and sniffed the wounds. At last he said, "I didn't think there was any hope, but . . . I do not think we need to amputate. I . . ."

I confess I interrupted him by grabbing Victor by both arms and whirling around him in a circle. "We have won!" I crowed.

Victor surprised me then. He wrapped his arms around me and gave me the most sincere embrace I had ever received from a man. "Thank you," he choked out.

I patted his back in what I hoped was a comforting way. "You're quite welcome."

He stepped back and looked at Palmer. For a moment I thought he might grab the gunman and hug him as well, but instead he held out his hand. "My sincere thanks," he said.

Palmer shook Victor's hand without a word. Then he stood and gestured for Victor to take his place beside Rosalind. "If you don't mind, I think I'll try getting some sleep." He moved to the doorway but paused there and looked back just in time to see Victor lean over and kiss Rosalind's cool forehead.

At her father's touch, her eyelids fluttered open. "Pa?" she whispered.

Palmer smiled then, a look so joyous it momentarily chased away the regret I still read in his expression.

"I'm here." Victor's voice had crumbled with emotion. "I'm right here. Are you thirsty?" He reached for the ever-present cup of willow bark tea.

Rosalind opened her lips again but didn't say anything. Victor slid one arm under her shoulders so he could lift her enough that she could drink easily. She managed a few swallows before her eyes closed with weariness. Victor lowered her head to the pillow again.

I followed Palmer outside, wanting to let Victor and his daughter have some peace for a minute or two. Dusk had crept up on the cabin while we were tending Rosalind, and I spied the first two stars peeping over the bluff at us. "A strange day," I commented.

"It's ended far better than I ever dared hope."

"So it has." I searched for something else to say. "Are you hungry?"

"I will be."

"I'll fix something for all of us. Come get it once you've slept." I went back inside while he headed for the barn and the rest he'd earned three times over.

WE SAT near her far into the night, all three of us, drinking coffee and watching Rosalind sleep. Enjoying the relief. The red streaks on her arm retreated steadily, and her fever did not return. The dog kept his post beside her bed, but his head lay on his paws, and once or twice I thought I heard him snore. Even he knew that the angel of death had passed over the cabin.

As I sat there between Victor and Palmer, I couldn't help thinking that Victor had been right: Mrs. Mortimer couldn't have everything. She could never have this companionable silence with these two handsome men.

I glanced at them both in the firelight. Both so fierce and yet so kind. We'd gone down a hard trail together, a trail I had not foreseen when I rode out to this cabin only a few days earlier. I'd meant to keep the man who now sat on my right from hurting or killing the man on my left, never dreaming that it would be Rosalind who would need saving instead. Or that she would be saved by the man we'd thought our enemy. What an oddity life can be!

Finally Victor spoke. "What are your plans now, Mr. Palmer?"

Palmer shifted in his chair. "I don't rightly know."

"We could use a doctor in these parts. No offense to you, Miss Emma." Victor smiled at me, the corners of his mustache lifting in a rather becoming way. Of course, everyone looks particularly nice by firelight.

"None taken," I said. "It would pleasure me greatly to turn over the serious ailments to someone capable and confine myself to midwifery." It would mean a considerable loss of income, but I had few wants and had already been setting aside cash money in the toes of my winter boots for some time. I had thought perhaps I could buy a house one day, a home to call my own. But the boarding house was not the worst place one could live, and if having a genuine surgeon in town meant I must give up that small dream, it was a sacrifice I would not fuss about making. I had kept vigil beside too many dying folks who could have been helped if I'd only had the proper training or medicines or tools.

Palmer took a long drink from his cup. "Miss Owens will need tending for a few days at the least. To be sure she's out of danger. Beyond that, I don't know."

Victor said, "Thank you."

"Do you think people would accept me as a doctor? After all, I arrived here as nothing more than a hired gunman."

I said, "We're a forgiving set of people here, Mrs. Mortimer excepted. What you do now matters more to us than what you've done in the past. I think there would be few objections."

"Then I'll ponder it."

I hoped that saving Rosalind had somehow brought him healing as well. Surely telling me about his past had helped. I could see that his burdens had not been lifted completely, not so soon. But perhaps he would be able to stay here and not drift on again like so many others. Maybe he had made a start toward winning his own war. His next words gave me real hope that it was so.

Palmer took a deep breath. "Mr. Owens, I must also ask if you would consider granting me your permission to call on Miss Rosalind. When she's better, I mean. If I stay. She's a remarkable girl, and . . ." He stopped there.

Victor cleared his throat. Twice. Finally he said, "I'll wait to give you my permission until Rosalind is better and can tell me how she feels about the idea."

"That's as fair as I could ask."

I felt a little thrill of wonder at the love story that might begin unfolding right before me. I have never tried my luck at matchmaking, but I do enjoy a good story of true love conquering all obstacles, and to see such a thing in person was so exciting, I wriggled my toes with glee at the thought.

Victor drained his mug. "Would anyone like more coffee?"

I held out my cup, and when he took it from me, his fingers lingered on mine.

I quailed inwardly, startled by the way my hand welcomed his touch. "No, thank you, no more coffee," I stammered. "It's time I got some sleep." I stood up so abruptly I knocked my chair backward. Only Palmer's quick reflexes saved it from crashing to the floor and waking Rosalind. Flustered, I murmured "Good night" as I hurried off to the safety of solitude behind a closed door.

But once alone, I found my thoughts restless, and sleep eluded me for a long time.

In the morning, when I made my way out into the big room, everyone else was awake. Victor sat beside Rosalind, holding her good hand. By the table, Palmer stirred something in a bowl, his sleeves rolled up and Rosalind's apron on, of all things. "Good morning," I greeted all and sundry. "Is that bacon I smell?"

Palmer said, "It is." He glanced at Victor and looked to be suppressing a knowing smile. "I'll be right back." He headed outside without even removing the apron.

"What an odd man." I wondered then why both Victor and Rosalind were staring at me. Had I forgotten to pin up half my hair? I touched it nervously, but it felt the same as usual, pulled back in an obedient knot. The cabin was so quiet, I could hear the sheep bleating their morning greetings to each other.

Victor stood, an expression on his face I'd not seen before. "Emma," he said, "this may come as a surprise to you. It did to me at first. But I would like . . . I wondered if you would . . . might you consider marrying me?"

I blinked. I fear my mouth fell open from the shock. A good dozen years after I had given up all thought of marriage, all hope for a home of my own, here stood this man, this friend, asking me to be his wife!

"Victor Owens," I cried before I could stop the words, "have you taken leave of your senses?"

"I think I've come to them."

I frowned suspiciously. "Is this your way of spiting Mrs. Mortimer?"

Victor threw back his head and laughed heartily. "No," he finally answered, "though now that you mention it, perhaps it will convince her I will neither marry her nor sell her my land."

I pursed my lips. "This is the strangest proposal of marriage I have yet heard tell of." But I could not help smiling then. For I realized that I could live happily there in that rose-covered cabin, passing the rest of my days side by side with Victor Owens. "I'll not give up midwifery just to keep your house," I cautioned him.

"I didn't expect you would. No more than I'll give up my sheep." He took both my hands in his, still smiling.

I looked at Rosalind, who lay propped up in her bed. "What do you think?" I asked her.

"I think it would make us all happier than we have been in a long time." She smiled too, and Blue gave a couple of joyful yips. Seeing Rosalind's smile widen when Palmer walked back inside, I suspected that we had the real Rosalind back with us for good.

"Are congratulations or condolences in order?" he asked.

"Both, I expect," I said, linking my arm through Victor's. "But first, breakfast."

ABOUT THE AUTHOR

BORN ONLY a few miles from where Jesse James robbed his first train, Rachel Kovaciny has loved the Old West all her life. She now lives in Virginia with her husband and their three homeschooled children. In her free time, Rachel writes for the online magazine *Femnista*, reads, bakes, blogs, watches movies, and daydreams.

To learn more about Rachel, visit www.RachelKovaciny.com

Guardian
of our
Beauty

KATHRYN MCCONAUGHY

To the late H. McConaughy: father, professor, writer.

And to the four R's (RP, R, HR, and RH),
without whom I have never finished a story.

ND IT happened in the days of the great heroes, in the years of the warrior shepherds, that the king of Gubla had no son. He took young wives and old wives, rich wives and poor wives, wives from the country and wives from the city. He sent for wives from Piyampetcha to the north, and from Uzu to the south. (He even begged a wife from the King of the Four Quarters, the master of the Black-Headed People; but the Great King did not send him a wife. The Great King did not even receive the king of Gubla's messenger.) But no matter how many wives the king of Gubla wed, they bore only daughters. Daughters, and more daughters.

"How can I live? I'm drowning in daughters!" the king complained to his chief priest. He sat leaning on one arm of his throne, his back to the wide windows that opened toward the sea. The lesser lords of Gubla stood in ragged clumps on the far side of the white-walled hall and tried to pretend that they were not listening.

The chief priest, Kashap by name, shook his head slowly from side to side. His predatory glare terrified every junior priest in Gubla; now he turned it on the king. "O mighty king, great ox, warlike shepherd," he began.

"You aren't composing an epic, Kashap," the king grumbled. "I know my own titles. Give me a solution!" The king, who was a veteran of more battles than he could remember, was not afraid of Kashap, priest or no priest.

"This plague of daughters—it is a curse," Kashap replied.

"So you've said, but I've sacrificed enough sheep to lift a thousand curses. Are the gods not listening? I must have an heir!"

Kashap ran his fingers through his oil-streaked beard. "Obviously the gods are not disposed to lift the curse. My king, it is time to choose an heir who is not of your house."

The king rubbed the horns of the bull that made up his right armrest. "I had . . . thought of that, though the thought is bitter to me."

Kashap smiled. "You can either adopt your chosen man as heir directly or marry him to one of your lovely daughters."

"Heir by marriage," the king said at once, sitting straight. A stranger at the court might have thought the king's stocky build came from too much royal food; but he would have changed his mind if he had seen the king sparring with the captains of his guard each morning. "But which daughter should the fellow marry? I have so many . . . Kashap, how many daughters *do* I have?"

Kashap blinked and tried to call the princesses to mind. He knew them only as objects, interchangeable pieces of the royal furniture; he could hardly have named one of them, let alone all of them. "As many as the stars of the heavens, O great ox," he said smoothly. "The appropriate daughter must be selected by inquiring of the gods, of course."

The king growled. "If you're going to insist on asking the gods, we'll have a long wait! If they were going to help me and not just take every sheep in Gubla, they would have given me a son by now."

Kashap muttered a quick aversion ritual under his breath, making sure to speak just loudly enough that the king would know what he was doing. "Don't blaspheme," he said piously after he had finished. "Perhaps there is some man, favored of the gods, who has been chosen for the kingship."

The king leaned forward over the arm of the throne. "I remember when you said that *I* was the favored of the gods," he said in a low voice. "Were you wrong, Kashap? If you were wrong then, why should I believe you now?"

He leaned back. "Inquire if you must, but bring me an answer!" he boomed, his voice reverberating across the room so that that every man present could hear him.

Kashap bowed and made his way out, shaking with anger. As he passed through the gate and his retinue of lesser priests fell in behind him, he hauled his two chief assistants under the cover of his sunshade. "Start the inquiry as I told you before!" he snarled. "Follow every procedure! Study every omen! But see that the lot falls on the oldest unmarried girl!"

Thaiyu the divination priest shook the arrows one last time and let them fall into the circle. He looked at them gloomily and made a mark on his tablet. It was exactly the same mark he had made the last forty-eight times. He had re-cleansed the circle, changed his arrows, substituted goat's blood for ram's blood—but the result was always the same. In all his years as a divination priest he had never seen anything like this.

Some god was actually answering.

Generally speaking, Thaiyu divined answers by the tried-and-true "best out of eleven" method—or whatever number he had to reach to make sure that the answer matched what Kashap had ordered the answer should be. This time, though, there wasn't a single different answer that he could interpret as ambivalence on the part of the gods.

Leaving the last set of arrows lying on the table, Thaiyu picked up his tablet and left the room, feet dragging.

The priestly court of the Ladytemple was already filled with diviners. "Fourteen livers I cut open, but it was all the same answer," one complained. "Cow livers! Frog livers! Dolphin livers!"

"You don't understand!" one of the astrologers shouted at a colleague. "The star of the Cave shouldn't *be* visible at this time of year! It upsets everything . . ."

The chief reader of omens, his arms full of scrolls, swayed from foot to foot, his hair standing on end. "I went through the whole omen cycle! The flight of birds . . . numbers of pregnant women . . . the shapes of oil on water . . . the actions of the temple donkey . . . I checked everything."

Kashap strode out of the temple to stand in the inner gate. "Silence!" he cried, eyeing them as a snake eyes its prey. The priests' wild babbling ground to a halt. "What answer have you received?"

Thaiyu looked at the chief omen reader, who shrank back behind his husky assistant. No one seemed ready to speak.

"Well?" Kashap demanded.

The astrologer coughed, tugging nervously at his beard. "The . . . positions of the stars are quite clear. There can be no doubt."

"Yes, yes?"

The astrologer looked around miserably. Some of his fellow priests edged away from him. "The *next* daughter to be born to King Shokorru is the one who should wed the king's heir!"

"What?" Kashap roared, flying down the hill to breathe hotly in the astrologer's face. "A child not even born yet? Incompetent wretch! You don't know the sun from the moon! I'll have you banished from Gubla!"

The liver-examiner raised a hand. "Ah? O-mighty-high-priest-chosen-of-the-gods, this was also the result of my liver omens. Fourteen separate livers I cut up, all astonishingly similar! I've never seen anything like it!"

Kashap whirled to attack this man too, but now every one of the priests began to speak at once. "The daughter not yet born!" "The donkey lay down as if to give birth!" "The wind—"

"This is a conspiracy!" Kashap shouted.

"It is a god!" the astrologer insisted shrilly. "A star is there that should not be there! It must be a god!"

"Which god?" a stocky arrow-shaker growled. "What god answers?"

"A new star in the heavens!" the astrologer cried. "A new god! One we have not known before!" Then he was on the ground, his mouth open in surprise, a red stain spreading on his robe.

"There is no new god," Kashap hissed, holding a bloody sacrificial knife in his shaking hand. "We will report that the eldest unmarried daughter was selected by the omens! Do any of you want to argue?"

The priests looked at the astrologer's still body then looked from Kashap to the skies above. Which was more dangerous, Kashap or the gods? Yesterday, each of them would have named Kashap; but if the gods were starting to pay attention, then—

A burly figure in a brown hood pushed to the front of the crowd. "You won't report any such lie."

"How dare you!" Kashap sputtered, raising the knife.

The figure pushed back his hood. "I dare because I'm the king," Shokorru growled, his grin like the grin of a lion. "Whoever this new god is," the king went on, "I like him. See that he gets some sacrifices."

Kashap swallowed, letting his hand drop until the knife was hidden in his robe. "An unborn daughter to be married to your heir," he said in a strangled voice. "Eleven years until she can be given in marriage! Would you leave your kingdom without an heir for so long? What if something happened to you? Who would be the Guardian of Gubla's Beauty?"

"Would something be less likely to happen to me if the marriage took place this year?" the king asked sharply. "Or would I meet with an accident soon after the bride price was paid?"

"I don't know what you mean," the high priest gritted from between clenched teeth. "Eleven years until she can be married!"

"More than that," the king said. "My daughter will be a princess, not a worker at the olive press. Let her be well grown before her marriage."

"But you don't know what might happen!" Kashap cried in anguish, all his plans in disarray.

The king leaned close. Though shorter than his high priest, at this moment he loomed. "One thing I can tell you, Kashap," he said in a soft voice which nonetheless rang all through the temple's inner court. "When my daughter reaches her sixteenth birthday and is married to the man who will be king after me—that man will not be you."

Kashap howled. "Curses on you! May the moon be eclipsed toward you! May the sun be eclipsed toward you!" He drew the knife from his cloak and held it high. "I made you king! I will unmake you! I—Let go of me!" But the omen reader's large assistant had him by one arm, and Thaiyu had him by the other.

"Kashap," the king said. "You are banished from Gubla. My good servants, throw this wretched priest over the cliff. Let the sea gods deal with him."

The king watched steadily as they dragged Kashap away. "Now . . .

who's in line to be the next high priest?"

Several of Shokorru's wives were pregnant at the time of Kashap's downfall. In seclusion as they were, none of them heard about the priests' new prediction.

The first wife to give birth was the girl Perakha. Stolen from a people that lived far south of Gubla, she had been sold to the king by an Ullazan merchant. Enchanted by her huge black eyes, the king had married her.

Those eyes were brilliant with joy now as Perakha rocked her new daughter in her arms. The midwife went out to deliver the news. Out in the city of Gubla, as the sun rose over the horizon, the king announced a week-long feast.

Blissfully unaware, Perakha fed her daughter and sang her a lullaby from her own childhood.

For forty days, mother and child remained in seclusion; but on the forty-first day, heralded by horns and bull-hide drums, both were placed in a sedan chair and carried from the women's palace up the main street of the city, through the courtyards of each of the seven temples, and finally to the palace gate, as part of the grandest procession any of the people of Gubla had ever seen.

The nervous omen reader, now the new high priest, stood at the edge of the royal dais, frantically reviewing the newly composed princess-dedication ritual one last time. When the sedan chair arrived and the king, his nobles, and the important priests had all arranged themselves on and around the dais, the omen reader began the ritual, spraying the sedan chair with hyssop flicked from the end of a long rod. One of the king's nobles, rigid with the honor of participating in the ritual and the dread of doing something wrong, took the baby from her mother and moved to stand before the king.

After various invocations of the divine (complete with a hastily added hymn to the new god, the God Who Answers), the high priest painted the baby's hands and feet with white and black ochre and declared her to be the vessel of the kingship. The whole crowd cheered.

Now the king stepped forward. Laying his hand on the head of his baby daughter, who watched him with big, unworried eyes, he called out: "This is my daughter! Her name is Aplati-shamirat-yaftinu—My Heiress, Guardian of Our Beauty! He who marries her will be king in Gubla after me!"

All the people cheered, waving palm branches and long brown arms.

Now was the time for the blessings from the priests of Gubla's twelve principal gods: the Great Lady of Gubla; the Benevolent Bull; the Thunderer of the Seven Anchors; the Sea; the Sun, Determiner of Destinies; the Warrior Girl; the twins Dusk and Dawn; the sisters Oily, Dewy, and Earthy; and, substituted for the usual god of serpents and scorpions, the new god, the God Who Answers. Each of the twelve had an altar and a priest standing ready to make that god's favorite offering and to proclaim their own, shorter blessings for the princess.

No one had volunteered to make the sacrifice for the God Who Answers; no one knew what kind of sacrifice he might like. And so, standing by the twelfth altar with his too large robes pooled on the ground around him was the most junior priest in all of Gubla, rubbing wretchedly at his nearly invisible beard.

The first eleven sacrifices went on as steadily as the turning of the seasons. The priests sacrificed their rams, swans, grain, donkeys, lions; they shouted their blessings out toward the crowd. "The reign of her husband will bring peace with the south." "The reign of her husband will bring the expansion of our borders and the growth of our power." "The reign of her

husband will last year after year, and every nation will tremble at his name."
As each one finished, the king's servants went forward on their knees to
pour out bags of gold and silver at the bases of the altars. The king's nobles
followed, bringing other gifts: a necklace of topazes for the Lady Sun, a
golden footstool for the Bull.

When the parade of gifts was finally finished, the priests turned to
their youngest member, the newly appointed priest of the God Who
Answers. He tugged on the rope that went around the neck of the washed
and perfumed goat he was to sacrifice. The goat bawled irritably and refused
to move. The young priest, shaking like water in an earthquake, turned his
back on the king to wrestle with the goat.

At that moment there was a horrible shriek.

Everyone turned and looked up. There! On the roof of the Ladytemple,
the figure of a man, his head tilted back toward the sky as he blew on the
wailing horn! He blew until he ran out of breath then threw the horn down
at the king's head. Shokorru ducked. The man on the temple top glittered
with the full regalia of the high priest; his robe was stiff with golden thread,
and his turban gleamed with gemstones.

"Kashap!" Shokorru roared. "Guards! Take him!" He waved his
guardsmen toward the temple; several vanished inside at a run, looking for a
way to the roof, while the others drew tight around their king. None of them
had brought arrows to the princess's dedication.

Kashap gave a warbling yell then screamed, "The first man who
touches me: may he be cursed! The serpent will always drop down upon
him! The scorpion will ever curl below him! This will be for his destruction,
for the destruction of his body, for the destruction of his form!" He keened
again, and the people of Gubla shuddered. No one wanted to cross the high
priest at the best of times, given the many rumors of his magical powers.
And now—hadn't he been thrown from the cliff into the mists between sea

and land? How had he survived? He must be far more powerful than any of them had ever dreamed!

"Get down from there!" the king shouted. "Kashap! You are no longer the high priest of Gubla! You have no right to wear those robes!"

"Can a king change the will of the gods?" Kashap jeered. He waved his hands, and a black mist formed in the air, curling around him like a thundercloud. "You have insulted the God of Serpents by not asking for his blessing! So I will speak to you on his behalf. Hear me, King Shokorru! Hear me, all of you!

> *"Hear the curse of the spurned one,*
> *The evil word of the one whose mouth is opened!*
> *A child is born to the king of Gubla,*
> *A female child to the warrior of Gubla,*
> *His daughter, guardian of its Beauty,*
> *His heiress, sustainer of his family!*
> *On the day of her sixteenth birthday,*
> *On the day of the daughter's marriage,*
> *On the day that he chose so that he might reject me!*
> *On that day the child will perish,*
> *Will perish from a tiny wound;*
> *She is wounded by a spindle of juniper,*
> *She is slain by a yarn-spinner of wood!*
> *The Beauty of Gubla will fall into ruin,*
> *The fame of Gubla into desolation.*
> *In the midst of six distresses Gubla sinks,*
> *And in seven, evil will defile it!*
> *Then the vineyards and olive groves will turn to desert,*
> *The fields of the sown land fill with thorns and briars;*

Where the beasts of the field once grazed and drank,
Now serpents and scorpions will make their homes.

No one will pass through the land,
And no one will dwell in it.
This is the end of the Beauty of Gubla!"

Kashap threw up his arms, black smoke pouring from behind him and filling the courtyard. The space filled with panicked cries as the people tried to run away from the black cloud, but it grew more quickly than a man could run, until the darkness covered the whole city of Gubla. Then, as suddenly as it had appeared, the smoke vanished.

Shokorru, who had fallen to his knees from the force of his coughing, struggled to his feet. He grabbed a spear from one of his guardsmen and ran out to the edge of the dais, turning to aim at the roof of the palace. But Kashap was gone, vanished with his smoke.

"My daughter!" the king said hoarsely.

"She is well, my king," said a soft, accented voice. Sitting on the edge of the dais was his wife Perakha, the baby held tightly in her arms. The nobleman who had been holding the child during the ritual was flat on his face, scraping dust onto his head and muttering aversion rituals.

The omen reader came trembling toward the king. "What shall we do, O wild bull?" he asked in a voice that cracked. "Kashap has cursed the child and the city!"

Shokorru growled and pulled at his beard.

Perakha pressed her forehead to the top of her small daughter's head. "Ah, Lord," she whispered. If only she had been at home in her land far away. Then she would not have been afraid of Kashap's curses.

In her too tight hold, her baby squirmed and started to cry.

"Hush now," said a new voice. "Don't be frightened, little one." Perakha glanced up and found an old man looking down at her. His face was tired, and his hair was gray; he wore worn-out clothes on his back and worn-out sandals on his feet. He did not look like a man of Gubla.

"Who are you?" King Shokorru barked. "Don't speak to my wife!" With the guardsman's spear still in his hand, he strode forward until he stood within striking distance of the old man.

"Then I will speak to you," the gray-haired man said. "I've come a long way."

"What king do you come from? Can't you see that this is no time for a state message?" Shokorru asked him. "Speak to me some other time!"

"I will speak now," said the graybeard. "King Shokorru, I come to you on behalf of the God Who Answers."

Perakha looked up into his face. "Oh!" she said. "I know who you are."

"We've had enough of men speaking for the gods for one day," the king said, jabbing his spear at the old man's face. "No more!"

"Not nearly enough," the old stranger said, a fierce expression coming over his face. "Unless you like the cursed future that your priest has laid out for you?"

"Please, my king," Perakha asked, looking up with wide eyes.

Shokorru looked at her and sighed. "Very well. Speak. But if you say something I do not like, I will kill you where you stand."

"Mmm," said the stranger. "Hear this:

"The words of the God Who Answers,
The god of a people without a temple,
The god of a people without a king;
The god who made the earth and the skies,
The god who stops the rain, and sends the sun across the far horizon.

Hear the words of the God Who Answers.

An enemy will come from the north,
An adversary from the shores of the sea;
Enemies from the far off isles,
And adversaries from the distant coastlands,
For they have made a treaty of hatred,
And they have planned a plan of destruction.
They will bring desolation on the empire of Arinna,
They will destroy the cities of the Sea!"

"What? Do you stand before me and dare to curse my city more?" Shokorru roared.

The stranger frowned. "Listen," he said.

The priests and nobles on the dais waited for Shokorru to strike the old man dead, but he did nothing.

"On the day of her sixteenth birthday,
Your child will be wounded;
Yet to die is only to fall asleep.
She will sleep, but her breath is in her.
She will sleep, with all your kingdom—
Gubla will sleep, both men and beasts.
Thorns and briars will grow around it,
Scorpions and snakes will dwell on its border,
But all within will sleep in safety.
The enemy from the sea will see it,
The adversary will see and turn away.
'There is no plunder to be taken from Gubla,
There is no wealth to be gained from this thornfield!'

> *Thus shall Gubla escape the sea band;*
> *If the city sleeps, then she sleeps peacefully."*

"But how shall we wake, good seer?" asked Perakha in a small voice. He smiled at her.

> *"The city sleeps till a man is sent,*
> *A noble heart from a far off place.*
> *Caught by a dream, he journeys to Gubla;*
> *Seized by a vision, he follows the road.*
> *He will not be stopped by serpents and scorpions;*
> *He will not be stopped by an evil curse.*
> *Though seven evils shall defend it,*
> *Yet seven strokes shall surely smite it!*
> *A faithful heart, a brave traveler,*
> *A warlike shepherd for the city of Gubla.*
> *He will wake your daughter, who guards your beauty;*
> *He will know her among the thousands of Gubla,*
> *And the thousands of Gubla will wake with her.*
> *Then you will know that the God Who Answers*
> *Is the one who brought all these things to pass.*
> *This is the declaration of the God Who Answers."*

"That is a better prophecy," Shokorru said, lowering his spear.

"I said the words I was sent to say," the stranger said sternly. "I would not have changed them at your request." He looked down at Perakha. "Do you want to stay here, little one, or would you rather go home to your people?"

Perakha held her daughter close. "I will stay here, good seer."

"Peace, then," he said, and vanished.

Everyone stared for a long moment then rushed forward. But there was no sign of the old stranger.

S MALL PALLI believed herself to be the most ordinary princess in all the cities of the Sea. Like her older sisters, she lived in the Palace of the King's Women, where she learned the things of women: how to weave and dye and paint and make pots; how to sew and mend and braid hair. (Palli did not learn how to spin, though. Her-father-the-king had forbidden it.) She was not as pretty as her glorious oldest sister, Shapsh-yishma-tsalati; nor was she as pleasantly ugly as her favorite of the-king-her-father's wives, Shiunan-ashui. Even her nickname was very ordinary. After the curse on her naming day, no one wanted to call her "Aplati-shamirat-yaftinu." Speaking her name might anger the gods. So she, like dozens of other girls in Gubla, was called Palli, "My daughter."

Palli was different from her older sisters in only three things.

The first thing was the story of her naming day. Every first day of the week, Mother gathered Palli into her arms. "How are you, my lily of the valley?" she would whisper, her black eyes lighting with her smile. Then she would tell the story of that day. As Palli grew up, she came to believe that her mother was very brave. She was not afraid to repeat the curse that Kashap had laid on her. She was not afraid to say Palli's name: "My Heiress, the Guardian of Our Beauty."

Mother often smiled with her eyes, but she only smiled with her mouth when she spoke of the prophet from far away. "You will have a great trouble, my lily," Mother always said. "But you will be delivered, and by enduring you will save all Gubla."

Palli did not know how she could save anyone. But if all she had to do was sleep—well, she could do that! She slept every night. When her other small sisters wondered why Palli went so willingly to bed, Palli only blinked at them and said, "It is good practice."

So the story of her naming day was the first thing that was different about Palli.

The second thing was cut from the same cloth. Because Palli was her father's heiress and would one day marry the next king of Gubla, she was brought out every year on the day of the Beautification of Gubla and made to stand behind her father. So she watched as he and the priests offered the sacrifices that were meant to appease the gods for any blemishes on Gubla's Beauty. Every year she heard her father proclaim, "I am the Guardian of Gubla's Beauty, and I have guarded it! And here is my daughter who will guard it after me!"

This was almost the only time Palli saw her father when she was young, so she always looked forward to it. Her father was a very great king, she was sure; strong and wise. She hoped—oh, so much!—that she could save his city for him when the time came. Then perhaps he would smile at her as her mother did.

These first two things—the story of Palli's naming day and her part in the ritual of Beautification—were things everybody knew, but the third thing that made Palli different was something nobody else knew.

She saw things.

Not ordinary things, but odd things. Things out of the stories her beautiful sister Tsalat told.

"Hold my hand, Palli," said Tsalat. "It's a long way down."

They were walking along the edge of the sea cliffs, looking north toward the harbor. Tsalat, who was almost thirty years old and oversaw everything to do with the Palace of Women, was much taller than delicate Palli, even though Palli had been growing a lot.

Palli curled her fingers happily through Tsalat's and smiled up at her, using only her eyes. She was nine years old, and the seven years until her wedding day seemed like a lifetime.

"You are so quiet, Palli-palli. What are you thinking about?" asked her big sister.

Palli looked out at the sea, which ran roughly here over the rocky shallows. A mist of spray hid the shoreline. "I'm thinking about the road to the Deeps," Palli said at last. "In stories, if you pass through the mist between sea and land, you will find yourself on the road to the Deeps."

Tsalat looked down at Palli, worry in her brown eyes. "But why would you want to take that road, Palli? Haven't I told you enough stories about the dangers in the Deeps?"

"Kashap must have gone there," Palli answered, still staring out to sea. "That's why he didn't die. That's how he had the power to . . . to curse us."

"Hush, Palli. Don't say his name."

"I'm not afraid," Palli said. "The God Who Answers is stronger than any old serpent god."

"Palli," Tsalat said, "promise me you won't try to go to the Deeps. Many people try to go, but most find only the current and drown; or else they find the rocks. Promise me."

"I won't go to the Deeps, Tsalat," Palli promised obediently. This was no great sacrifice. There were, after all, other magical places. To the north, there was the Double Mountain towering over a realm that could only be reached through moonlight mirages. To the south, near Uzu, there was the Cedar Forest, which on foggy nights became a strange, strange land. And, of course, there was the road to Far Horizon, which began where the sea met the sky.

Sometimes Palli thought about going to one of those places. Surely just going to sleep wasn't enough to protect Gubla? Surely there was something else that she should do?

A shape in the ocean caught her eye, and she stopped, digging in her heels when Tsalat tried to tug her forward. "Wait!"

A great black shadow like a ziggurat glided just under the water. Then it rose, water pouring from its black scales. As it rolled onto its side, showing the paler gray of its belly, it fixed Palli with a great orange eye. She knew that it saw her, even across all that distance. "You are beautiful," she whispered.

"What are you looking at, Palli?"

"It's the Litan," Palli whispered.

"The sea monster? Where, Palli-palli?" Tsalat laughed.

"There," Palli said, pointing.

"That's just a raft of logs, little sister, waiting to be floated down to the Black Land."

Rafts don't have eyes, Palli thought, as the Litan completed its roll and sank back into the Deeps. *Rafts don't look back at you.*

Shiunan-ashui—who despite being one of the king's wives was even younger than Tsalat—did not tell stories. She was from the great kingdom of Arinna, far to the north. "Prophecies, prophecies," she scolded Perakha. "Stop filling that child's heads with prophecies! They never come out the way you expect. We know that in Arinna. You fish-bellied sea-coasters rely too much on your gods."

Perakha shook her head. They had had this conversation many times. "I rely only on the God Who Answers," she gave the well-worn reply. "His prophecy will come true."

"Palli girl," Shiunan-ashui said, putting her hands on her wide hips. "You need to concentrate on practical things. Like how to be pleasant to this man you are supposed to marry in, what, six years now? He'll be stuck with you, so you need to learn how to make him happy. I'll teach you how to make perfume. Come here, help me grind this."

Palli nodded and trotted over to cradle the big stone mortar in her lap. She wrestled contentedly with the pestle as Shiunan-ashui talked on. "We make the best perfumes in Arinna. It was my perfume that got me married to King Shokorru. His envoy said that I smelled better than any of the other ladies in the Silver City. Now, your father will choose your husband, but you should still try to please him."

Palli looked up at Shiunan-ashui with guileless eyes. "But won't I marry the one who wakes me from sleep, Aunt Ashui?"

Ashui threw up her hands. "There, Perakha! You see what comes of filling the child's head with prophecies! Keep grinding, little one."

Palli ground on, but with a frown on her face. How could Aunt Ashui, whom she loved so much, say something different from what Mother said? Why would Tsalat never talk about Palli's naming day or her wedding day at all?

She needed to go and talk to someone wise, Palli thought. She would go to the Ladytemple. Surely the priests would know what was true. So, once Aunt Ashui had gone to her nap and Mother was busy weaving, Palli carefully put away the mortar and pestle and crept out of the Palace of Women.

Her father's dogs found her at once. They were thin and brown and tall, bred for hunting lions. "Palli!" they barked. "Palli! Palli!"

"Shh," she told them, rubbing the tallest's furry head. "I'm going to the temple."

She let them walk with her to the temple precinct. "Now, stay here," she told them gravely. "You can't come in." Palli wasn't really supposed to go into the temple either; some of the gods were cross about that sort of thing.

The biggest dog gave a great snuff, raising his head high. *Snuff! Snuff!* "Lion!" he barked. "Lion! Lion!"

"Hawk! Hawk!" barked another dog, leaping onto the first dog's back then sliding off again.

"Shh! Stop that," Palli scolded. "What is it?" She looked up.

Crouched on top of the wall, gazing hungrily down into the temple's sheep pen, was a woman. Her skin was black as night, her slitted eyes as golden as the skin of a temple statue. Her cloak hugged her back like a pair of folded wings.

Palli did not know of any reason to be afraid of the golden-eyed woman. "Health to you," she said politely.

The woman's head jerked up, and she stared at the little girl. "Did you speak to me?" she rasped.

Palli could see that the woman looked very tired. Gray splotches like bruises mottled her skin. "Yes. I'm Palli," she said. "Are you all right?"

"The storm—it blew me so far," the woman muttered to herself. She narrowed her eyes and clicked her teeth together. "I am very hungry and thirsty too."

"Oh!" said the little princess. "Won't you come with me? My mother will give you something to eat and a place to stay for the night. You don't need to be frightened. My mother is not at all frightening."

"*I* don't need to be frightened?" said the woman, amused. "I suppose you aren't frightened of me."

"Oh, no," said Palli.

"I have flown all the way from the Double Mountain," the dark-faced woman said, looking carefully at Palli's face. "I am a child of the Storm-Makers."

"It's pleasant to meet you," Palli answered politely, although she didn't know what a Storm-Maker might be. "Will you come?"

"I will not come under any roof, little Palli."

"Oh." Palli thought about this. "Then I must bring you something here!" She ran into the temple and over to the washing well. Keeping an eye out for any disapproving priests, she hauled up a bucket of water and carried it quickly to the wall. She lifted it as high as she could. "Can you reach it?"

The woman blinked at her doubtfully then leaped down from the wall as lightly as any cat. She leaned over the bucket while Palli held it and lapped up the water with her tongue. Palli giggled.

When the woman was satisfied, Palli ran the bucket back to the well. Upon returning, she asked, "What do you want to eat? Would you like some bread?"

The golden-eyed woman made a disgusted face. "The Storm-Makers do not eat bread," she said in a grand voice.

"What do they eat?" Palli asked curiously.

The woman's mouth twitched. "We eat meat."

This was something of a problem. Palli was not sure where to get meat. She was sure that she should not take it off any of the temple altars. "Cooked?"

"If necessary I will eat it cooked," said her odd visitor, looking nauseated at the very idea.

"Oh! That's why you were looking at the sheep," Palli realized. "Why didn't you take one?"

"That would be stealing. Storm-Makers do not steal."

Palli had not thought of this. "My father is the king. If I give you a sheep, is it still stealing?" she asked.

"Do you give me a sheep?"

"Yes," Palli said, making up her mind. Feeding a person was a more important use for a sheep than feeding a bunch of gods that didn't answer. "Take one."

The woman sighed. "You have given me food and water. I owe you a favor, little Palli." She fixed Palli with one golden eye. "Call my name, and I will help you. Call Dirigga."

"Dirigga," Palli repeated.

The woman gave her cloak a shake. In the instant before it was still, it changed into a pair of wings. The woman blinked, and before her lashes opened, her face was the face of a black cat. She lunged into the air, and her body was the body of an eagle. "Don't forget!" she called to Palli, then swooped forward. The sheep in the pen burst into a chorus of indignant bleating, but there was nowhere for them to go. Dirigga swooped low, catching a sheep in her great claws, and powered up into the sky.

Palli stared after her wistfully. How wonderful, to be able to fly!

"What's all this racket?" cried Thaiyu, running out of the nearest temple entrance. "Child, what are you doing in here? This is not a place for children or women! Shoo!" Flapping his hands like birds' wings, he chased Palli out of the temple precinct.

"Lion! Hawk!" barked the dogs as she ran out.

"What wise dogs!" she praised them. Glancing over her shoulder, she saw Thaiyu hauling a woven barrier across the doorway. She didn't think he would want to answer questions about her prophecy now, so she trotted away to throw sticks for the dogs until Aunt Ashui came looking for her and dragged the dusty little princess back to the Palace of Women.

Before dawn on her thirteenth birthday, Palli woke. Picking up her slippers, she crept out of the room where she slept with her mother and slid out a broad window, avoiding the guard who sat snoring on his seat outside the door. She shook out her slippers carefully—one could never be too wary of scorpions—and paced slowly to the sea cliff. She did not see the several guards posted outside of her father's palace, who stood leaning against the warm stone walls; nor did they see her, a slim gray figure with a silent tread.

Palli tasted salt in her mouth and knelt, feeling a hint of spray on her bare arms. Below, the waves battered their heads against the cliffs.

"I'm not afraid," she whispered to the ocean. "I'm not afraid of you." She wondered if the high priest had been thrown from this very spot. She wondered if he was still down there in the mists. Watching them. Waiting for his curse to come true.

"Sleep? Is that really all I have to do?" she asked the sky. It brightened; the rim of the sun rose above the horizon. Palli held her breath and watched carefully.

A line of gold stretched across the water. It broadened, not like oil spreading but like a door opening. Then . . . the waves stopped. The wind fell. There was only the golden road across a glass-like, silent sea.

Palli held her breath. Just when her pulse began to pound in her ears, the wind rose again; the waves took up their pounding. And the golden road flickered and vanished into the haze of sunrise.

The Road to Far Horizon. Palli could hear Tsalat saying the words, her lips curving into a mysterious smile. If Palli needed to do something more than sleep—if she needed to know more—she would take that road. But she would not take that road against the wishes of the god who had sent the prophet on her name day.

She bent low, her arms wrapped around her, so low that her forehead pressed against cold stone. Screwing up her eyes so no light could get in, she whispered, "God Who Answers, if you want me to go, let Mother be the first person to speak to me this morning." Palli always asked for something, sometimes one thing, sometimes another; but whatever she suggested never happened.

She supposed she should stop asking. But what if the God Who Answers only answered some of the time? What if he didn't pay attention to little girls? Her mother said that the god was the great king over skies and earth; and kings, as Palli knew, were busy people, not interested in the doings of women and children. So she came out once or twice a week and prayed her prayer.

"O small princess, is that you?" asked the familiar voice of the watchtower guard. "You might get sick, lying there in the cold, Lady avert it!"

"I'm not cold, thank you," Palli said primly, standing up. The watchman shifted uneasily under her eyes, which were as large and serene as her mother's. "I will go now."

She went, but she did not go in. Instead, she trotted along the cliff, behind the palace and the Ladytemple and the clusters of small houses, until she came to the ramparts that protected the city. She climbed up over them and down again on the other side.

She meant to go and look at the ships in the harbor. They were so interesting—bringing all sorts of things from everywhere. The king of the Black Land had sent three ships and a good deal of gold to Shokorru; the ships had gotten to Gubla, but the gold had not. "Pirates," Aunt Ashui had told Palli, along with some bloodcurdling details that she wished she hadn't heard. "There are so many more pirates these days," Aunt Ashui complained. "Where are they all coming from, I ask you?" Then Tsalat said that the-king-her-father was considering whether to send logs to the Black Land in spite of the lack of gold.

Palli wondered if you could take a ship on the Road to Far Horizon.

"Mama!" came a high-pitched cry. "Ma-a-ma!"

It sounded like a young animal. Palli turned away from the shore and ran inland, past more clusters of houses and a group of young women gathered at a well. Soon she reached the barley field.

"Ma-a-ma!"

"Where are you?" Palli called breathlessly. The coarse stalks of the barley beat against her legs, but she ignored them.

"Mama!"

There it was, half hidden by the barley. It looked like a baby donkey, except its ears were smaller and its coat was soft and fine. It was a pale reddish brown all over, except for a great spot of white on its chin. "Oh, don't cry!" Palli told it. "I'll help you find your mama."

It gave a startled snort and tried to lurch away, small nostrils flaring.

"Are you a little horse?" Palli asked in a confiding tone. "Have you come from the chariot house east of the city?"

He blinked large brown eyes at her then reached forward to poke his nose into her skirts. "Poor colt!" Palli said, stroking his soft neck. "Where— Oh, you're trapped!" His hoof was stuck in a small round hole. The princess ran her hand carefully down his leg. "I'll get you out."

A flicker of dark movement in the barley made her look up. A shiny black snake eyed the little horse maliciously. Barely opening its mouth, it hissed, "Myy hhole!" and writhed, filling the air with a sweet, sinister smell.

"Ma-a-ma!" screamed the colt, trying to rear. Palli pulled him tight against her side, her face white.

"Go away for a little while," the princess said in a tight voice. "Go away for a little while, and we'll be gone when you come back."

The snake tilted its head to one side; light glinted off its fangs. "That'ss myy hhole!"

"We don't want to spoil your hole," Palli told it, trying to keep her voice from shaking. It was best not to let the snake know that she was frightened, that she knew what sort of snake it was. From its nasty expression, she suspected it could tell anyway. "Go away!"

"Ssss," it sneered, and glided forward toward the colt.

Palli stamped heavily on the ground. "If you bite him, I'll stomp you!" She slid around in front of the little horse. He whuffled miserably into her back.

"Yyou firsst," the snake promised, coiling to strike. It did so slowly—to give her time to be frightened, Palli knew.

The wind shifted. In an instant it changed from a breeze to a blast. There was a shrill, angry whistle, like a gale rushing through a sea cave, and the snake was whirled up and flung high into the air, flung so high and so far that Palli couldn't see where it came down.

"Mama," the colt whickered happily.

The wind turned, swirling around them; the barley danced. As the chaff rose, Palli could almost see the shape of a mare, her mane like a river of air flowing behind her.

"Thank you," whispered the wind-mare. "You saved my child."

Palli shook her head. "I couldn't stop the snake."

"You gave me time." The wind-mare snorted, making the dust dance. "Who are you? It has been long since any two-legged creature looked me in the eye."

"Palli," said Palli. "But who are you?" In her mind she searched through

Tsalat's stories for a horse made of air, and didn't find one.

"I am the Mother of All Horses." A soft puff like a breath touched Palli's cheek. "If ever you need my help or the help of my children, call for me, child of beauty."

"Oh! His foot," Palli realized, bending down. Carefully she twisted the little hoof free.

"Pa-alli," the colt nickered, ears pricked. Palli smiled sweetly at him.

Then he and the wind-mare galloped away to the east, the mare racing around and around her colt so that he hardly touched the ground. Palli waved farewell then turned to walk home.

I wonder if the snake will ever come back to its hole. She shivered. She did not want to see it again. If the mother mare had not come, it would have killed her. Then neither the curse nor the prophet's words could have come true.

Palli shivered again and wondered whether the angry God of Serpents or the wise God Who Answers had been the one in charge of what had just happened to her.

As she climbed lightly back over the barricades, ignoring the stares of the shieldmen, she thought, *It must have been the God Who Answers who sent the mare. The God of Serpents wouldn't want me to die till my sixteenth birthday. He wouldn't have let a snake attack me in the first place.*

It was odd, how much you appreciated being ignored by some gods, Palli thought. You sacrificed goat after goat, supposedly so that the gods would give you nice things, but most of the time you just wanted to keep them from doing something dreadful to you.

KING SHOKORRU sat on his throne with his royal spear in his hand. If he clutched it a little too tightly, no one was close enough to see; and if he listened more to the sounds floating in through the window than to the words of his counselors, no one could tell it from his face. If the warrior king was afraid, he hid it even from himself.

The time for Kashap's curse to be fulfilled was drawing near.

The man who had been speaking to him stepped back with a deep bow, and another stepped forward. "My king, mighty spearman, wild bull, one comes to you with a message from your brother, the king of Pirulat. Will you hear his message?"

When the wind was right, Shokorru could hear the sounds from the northern harbor. At the moment he heard nothing; either nothing was happening there or the wind was in the wrong quarter.

"My king?" The young man stepped forward, tugging insistently on the sleeve of the messenger, pulling him forward. "My king, my father, will you hear?"

Shokorru took a sudden breath, and his eyes focused on the young man's face. Etlu-kashid had been Shokorru's shield-bearer in his last campaign; he was a strong fighter, a good companion. And he was Shokorru's chosen heir-by-marriage. "Open your lips," said the king.

Etlu-kashid pushed the envoy forward. The man's face was gray under the brown of his skin. He bowed, clasping his hands tightly together. "King of battle, warlike shepherd," he faltered. "This is the message of your brother, the king of Pirulat, fair Pirulat."

This was a very short introduction, so short that it was almost rude. The men of Gubla frowned and muttered to each other as the messenger went on. "Thus says the king: In days of old, my father, the king of Pirulat, loved you, and you loved my father. Now I tell you that the monuments he built are being destroyed and the walls he built are being broken. Now I send this message to you and say, send troops. The navy of Gubla is famed through all the lands; the spear-carriers of Gubla are mightier than the spear-carriers of the east; the archers of Gubla are finer than the archers of the south. The harbor of Pirulat, my city, is blockaded by these cursed sons of the islands, who spring up in our waters like poisonous snakes. How can I send you tin and silver with these raiders before my gates? Send troops quickly, O my brother, and we will divide the spoil." He ground to a halt, swaying slightly.

"Is there no more?" Shokorru snapped after a moment. His finger joints ached from his grip on his spear.

"Mighty king, only the earnest good will of your younger brother—"

Shokorru lunged to his feet and slammed the butt of his spear against the floor. The envoy gasped and stumbled back, trembling before the rage in the king's face.

"Take him out! Take him out!" Shokorru roared. "Am I to be troubled with the actions of every pirate and islander who comes to these shores? Take him out!" As the messenger was hurried away, the king sat down again with a thud.

"Will you send no one, O king?" snapped Etlu-kashid, stepping forward toward the throne. Shokorru stopped him with a glare, and he stepped back. Still, he went on: "Have we not traded with our brothers in Pirulat for generations? Have we not fought beside the sons of Pirulat in many wars?"

The king growled, and one of the priests darted forward to tug at the young man's arm. Etlu-kashid shook him off with a snarl. "If you will not go, O king, let me go! I will take the young warriors, and we will bring back plunder!"

"If you go, you go alone," the king growled back, a storm gathering in his face. "You will not take any of my other warriors on this fool's errand!"

"You don't think your warriors can stop a fleet of pirates?" the shield-bearer challenged him, looking over his shoulder at the men behind him. The other warriors in the room drew closer.

"Be silent, you young fool!" Shokorru snapped, surging to his feet again. He spread his arms wide and spoke to his men in a battlefield roar. "Why does the king of Pirulat write to me? He is vassal to the king of Arinna! The great king, king of three dozen cities! Why does he not ask *him* for help?" He stared at Etlu-kashid. "I will tell you. He *has* asked him, and the king of Arinna has not sent help. He too is being attacked by these sons of the sea. If the king of Arinna cannot drive them off, how shall we? This is a fight for empires, not cities."

"They have not come here!"

"But they will come," Shokorru answered, his voice low. "They will come. They are sailing south. They began with Arinna; now they reach Pirulat. We are next, Etlu-kashid. This is not the time for any warrior to leave the city."

His shield-bearer clasped his hands behind his back, his face still tight. Then, in a voice so quiet that only Shokorru could hear, he said, "When I am king, I will send help to our brothers. I am not afraid."

Shokorru grunted. "If you do not stay here to marry my daughter in two months' time, you will never be king in Gubla."

Although none of the men who had heard the message of the envoy from Pirulat admitted to having repeated it, within a few hours everyone in Gubla was talking about it.

"I don't know why everyone is so upset," puffed Aunt Ashui, who was growing plump. "The Sun of Arinna will drive these raiders away from his shores, and then he will clean them out of Pirulat."

"Your cousin has not driven them away during these past seven years when they have been coming in greater and greater numbers," Tsalat said, her face as beautiful as ever but thin from care. "*We* certainly cannot expect help from Arinna."

"Shokorru ought to have made his bow to Arinna years ago instead of keeping up this absurd pretense of a tie with the Black Land," Ashui snorted. "Then he would know where to look for help!"

"You will not speak so of the-king-my-father," Tsalat ordered in a dangerous voice.

"Peace," Perakha said softly from where she sat half-reclining on her couch. "Let us not quarrel. We knew that the raiders would come, for the prophet told us on Palli's name day: 'Enemies from the far off isles will bring desolation on the empire of Arinna; they will destroy the cities of the Sea.'"

Shiunan-ashui gasped and crossed to Perakha in one quick stride, raising her hand as if to strike. Palli, who had been sitting cross-legged beside her mother, rose smoothly to block her way. "Do not curse my people!" Ashui snapped, thwarted.

"Ha," Tsalat muttered. "Is your heart still with your mother in Arinna? Where is your loyalty to your husband's city?"

"I do not curse anyone," Perakha said gently, reaching out to grasp Ashui's clenched fist. "But the word of the God Who Answers will come to pass."

Palli held her breath until her aunt turned away. *I'm so sorry, Auntie,* she thought, watching the older woman storm off. *I'm sorry that your friends and your family are in danger. I'm sorry that you might lose your old home.*

"That woman!" Tsalat snapped, drawing herself up elegantly. "She understands nothing. If we must lose all, let us do so with courage and dignity." The princess's eyes were bright and fierce.

"Gubla will be safe," Perakha reminded her.

"Will it?" Tsalat asked wearily.

"It was promised."

"No god cares for the promises he makes to mortals," Tsalat said, shaking her head. "The gods are not to be trusted."

"The God Who Answers—"

"Don't speak to me, Perakha. If we are saved, speak to me then. But until then, don't speak to me." Tsalat swept away after Ashui, her hands plucking feverishly at the upper flounces of her dress.

Palli looked bleakly after her. In two months, she would be sixteen years old and Gubla would either be saved—or not. The older she got, the more frightened she was; and yet the more determined she was that Gubla would not be lost through any act of hers.

She thought almost constantly about her wedding day. She was glad she would sleep—that *a faithful heart* would come from far away to wake her. She did not want to marry Etlu-kashid. He cared only about fighting in wars. *He would not be a good king for Gubla,* she thought, *even though my father chose him.*

Her wedding troubled her. If her father truly believed in the prophecy of the God Who Answers, why would he hold a wedding for her? Sometimes she thought that she and her mother were the only people who remembered what the prophet had said. *If it were really true, wouldn't more people remember it? Wouldn't more of them care?* she wondered.

But she would not stop believing now. Not so close to the end of her long wait. *God Who Answers, can you hear me? Please remember your promise. I couldn't bear it if you changed your mind like all the other gods. Please.*

The morning of Palli's wedding, she woke to a world covered in dew. The ground sparkled with crystal gems, and the sea was so clear and so blue that Palli could see the reefs below the cliff.

Her mother helped her into her flounced dress, its hems decorated with shell and tiny lapis lazuli beads. Tsalat brought out the royal jewelry, the jewelry that had belonged to King Shokorru's mother until she died: precious beads and a crown of golden flowers, a golden pendant and lapis lazuli earrings. Palli would have protested—there was so much, and it was so heavy—but Tsalat insisted. "Today you marry the king-to-be. As his chief wife and your father's heiress, you will be queen in Gubla. So wear the jewelry, Palli dear." Aunt Ashui, determined to be generous and good-natured after her long sulk, brought out her best perfume. She was so generous that Palli was nearly suffocated by the smell.

"I smell like an incense offering," she whispered to Tsalat when Ashui had gone out into the hall.

"Isn't that what you're supposed to be in this prophecy of yours? A sacrifice for the good of Gubla?" Tsalat said in a hard voice.

Palli dropped her eyes and said nothing. After a moment she heard a sigh, and her sister leaned forward to kiss her forehead. Palli smiled with her eyes, the hard words forgotten.

There was a procession, the people of Gubla lining the streets and throwing flowers at Etlu-kashid in his chariot and at Palli in her sedan chair. Palli smiled shyly at the children but didn't look anyone else in the face. Everyone looked so happy and excited; she didn't want them to see her nervousness. There were sacrifices to two dozen gods, major and minor; this took a long time, as each sacrifice had its particular blessing. Then she sat behind a screen while envoys from various places (almost all, she noticed, from south and east of Gubla) gave congratulatory speeches and laid out their gifts. She wished she had been allowed to sit in the upper rooms of the palace with her mother and Tsalat and Aunt Ashui and to watch it all out the window; then she might have enjoyed the sight.

"A fine bronze image of the Lady of Gubla, from your brother the king of Uzu," one of the envoys was announcing while Shokorru's scribe scratched away busily with his stylus, recording the gifts.

"A humble object set with sea glass, from a humble admirer of Gubla's Beauty," said a smooth voice, much nearer. Palli looked up with a start. An old man in a long cloak and an embroidered skullcap bowed before her, holding a tapering wooden . . . *something* across his palms. The wide, rounded base was indeed set with sea glass.

"Shouldn't you present it to the-king-my-father?" Palli asked softly. Perhaps the old man was a foreigner and did not know the way of things in Gubla.

The old man looked up. "This gift is for you, great queen," he said, a spark of malice in his eyes.

A spindle. He's giving me a spindle, Palli realized, suddenly recognizing the object. *I suppose this must be Kashap. He didn't trust the Serpent God to deliver his curse for him, so he came to do it himself.* Now that it came to it, she wasn't frightened at all.

"Thank you," she said, and put out her hand.

"Palli!" came a woman's scream from an upper window.

I'm sorry, Tsalat. Palli wrapped her hand around the spindle. *Ouch!* She pulled back her hand, and a single drop of blood fell from her finger.

"Aha! So much for your plans, King Shokorru!" Kashap shouted, his face contorted with sudden glee. "Where is the Beauty of Gubla now?" He lifted the spindle triumphantly above his head. Palli's blood trickled down the wood to splash unheeded on his leathery cheek.

But I don't feel anything, Palli thought, a little worried.

Gloom gathered around the sorcerer, seething around his feet then rising like the tide. The last thing Palli saw before the darkness took him completely was a glimpse of his malevolent face. Then the cloud of darkness rose into the air and blew away toward the sea, where it sank into the mists and vanished.

"Magic!" Shokorru roared. "KASHAP!"

Palli stepped out from behind the screen, and the crowd surged toward her. But even as the first of them reached her, they slowed, eyes closing. With a sound like a sigh, the people of Gubla fell asleep.

Palli saw her father falter and fall; she saw Etlu-kashid, eyes dim, crumple into a heap on top of one of his companions; she heard Tsalat's screams fade. Someone's pet monkey gurgled and curled up on a guardsman's chest.

She was on the ground without knowing how she had gotten there. A rug made of thin braids dug into her cheek. Her eyes, flickering shut, saw her crown of golden flowers lying fallen on the ground. *The curse has come true. God Who Answers, save . . . my . . . city . . . .*

Palli slept.

From his mist-veiled rock off the coast of Gubla, Kashap the magician stared at the city. He didn't know how the curse would look when it took effect—What was *that*?

Thorns, a wall of thorns shot up from the ground to snatch bitterly at the sky and tie themselves into an unbreachable wall around the city. "Trapped! You're trapped, Shokorru!" Kashap shouted. It was even better than he had expected! But the people of Gubla must not escape . . . .

He sat and waited, fingers plucking at the rock. *No one will get out of Gubla alive,* he promised. Not if he had to sit here for a hundred years!

The former high priest, his eyes lit with madness, began muttering an incantation.

ALLI WATCHED as clouds curled around her, turning gold as the sun set. *I wonder if there is another road to Far Horizon in the clouds,* she thought. How beautiful it was to be looking down on Gubla, on the sea sparkling against the rocks.

I'm dreaming, she realized, not surprised. She had, she thought, been dreaming for some time without realizing it. *My city* . . . Her heart turned to Gubla, and it grew nearer. A great tangled wall of briars covered the barricades and barred the gates, a thorn grove more than fifty feet thick. Brown and black shapes scuttled and slithered along its base. *Snakes and scorpions,* Palli thought, disgusted. She hoped they couldn't get into the city; the sleeping people could not defend themselves.

The instant she thought it, she began to sweep low along the inside of the wall. Stone rushed past; her father's guardsmen slept peacefully at their posts with no sign of Kashap's curse-creatures around them.

Is this real? Palli wondered for an instant. *Am I seeing what is truly happening?* Then the thought fled away.

The moon rose. Palli rose with it, soaring high above the clouds; she did not notice the thin tendrils of black mist that seeped through the barrier of thorns, creeping along the ground until they reached the faces of the sleeping people. The scraps of mist drifted over the closed eyes, over the prone bodies, then blew out to sea again, to where the sorcerer sat chanting.

High in the pure air, Palli flew for a long time. At last she came down again, attracted by wavering lights shining up from below.

Set in a swathe of once-green farmland not far from the sea was a city. It was burning. An army swarmed around and through it; a long column of prisoners was already forming.

No! Palli did not know the city or the place, but her heart ached. She spiraled low toward the broken entrance. The bronze-banded gates were now blackened with fire, their reliefs battered out of recognition.

Someone threw something over the wall, and a cheer rose up from the victorious army. "The king of Pirulat is dead! Let us divide the plunder!" The man at the top of the wall said more, but Palli did not know the language.

Palli cried out, and a few of the soldiers turned, scanning the skies. "Only a night bird," one said to his companion.

With a twist and a thought half-thought, Palli swirled into the burning palace. She did not know what she was looking for, only that she must find—find—

The royal nursery, yes! A child crouched, staring toward the door.

You can't stay here! Palli tried to shout, but the girl did not look up.

God Who Answers! Answer and let her hear me! I know this wasn't in your prophecy—that I would still act while I slept—but please don't make me watch without being able to help!

"What are you?" asked the child, eyes narrowing suddenly.

Follow me! Palli insisted, and swept out the door. *Cover your mouth and nose!*

Coughing, the child followed. Palli led the girl out of the palace to a group of the palace servants; but before she could think of a way to get them all out of the city and to safety, the city slipped away and she sank into the dark of dreamless sleep.

Palli dreamed, and dreamed again. She saw smoke rising over the Silver City of Arinna, its walls broken, its empire fallen. She saw ships burning on the water. She tried and tried to help—but she could touch nothing, and often none could hear her. Sometimes she was in the midst of helping when the world slid suddenly sideways and she found herself in Gubla, looking down at her own sleeping self.

Will these pirates destroy the whole world, and only Gubla be left? she wondered.

The sun shone in her eyes; she came up out of sleep and knew that she was dreaming again. Something had half woken her, something she had heard with her body's ears.

There it was again: a horn sounding a higher note than the horns of Piyampetcha. *Ships coming to the harbor—the pirates!* A fleet of two dozen ships swept down the coast, just far enough offshore to miss the reefs. They must have seen the palace and the Ladytemple atop the cliffs.

The thorn wall protected Gubla on the land side, but if the raiders could scale the cliffs, they could get into the sleeping city. Would they fall asleep then too? Palli didn't know, but she feared that they would not. The sleep had come from the prophecy, and the prophecy had said nothing about people from outside Gubla.

God Who Answers! I must stop them, Palli thought, feeling more alert than she had in a long time. But what could she do? She couldn't touch the ships, or the sailors with their feathered headdresses and copper earrings.

The water rippled below her, light shining down like a road into the Deeps. *The Deeps! The Deeps!* she thought. Was anything there that could help her? She pivoted and dove, her dream spirit moving through the water as easily as through the air.

Down and down. She thought she flew for hours, but it might only have been seconds; it was hard to tell in the dream. She hoped she would not get lost in the dark.

A great triangular shape loomed before her, drifting like a sunken ship. She caught the faint glitter of an orange eye. *Litan! Litan!* she called. *Please help!*

The sea monster rumbled and turned, eyes opening. "Who's there?"

It's me, Palli, she answered. There was no reason the creature should recognize her, but Palli thought, dreamlike, that her name would be enough.

"Oh, is it?" he hummed. "Why do you wake me from my sleep? I'm tired. These are sleepy waters nowadays."

I came from Gubla. The pirates are coming! They'll get into the city and kill everyone, Palli explained. *Is there something you can do?*

"Gubla. The city up above?"

Yes. Please!

"There used to be many fishermen in these waters," the Litan rumbled thoughtfully, turning belly-up in the water. Upside-down, he eyed Palli, swishing his thick tail slowly back and forth. "When I was hungry, I just took a net full of fish. Not a boat; boats are prickly and make my throat sore. Now I have to find my own fish."

If the pirates kill everyone, there may never be fishermen here again,

Palli told him. *You'll have to catch your own food or go and live somewhere else.*

"Hmmph," he puffed, turning slowly right-side up again. "But I like it here."

Palli waited.

"I suppose I'll have to do something," he sighed, orange eyes glittering. Slowly he rose upward through the water. Palli, stifling her impatience, rose with him.

The pirates had never seen anything like the Litan.

He surged out of the water, his black scales gleaming like broken rock, and rammed one of the larger boats, pushing it sideways against another. With a roar, he grabbed the anchor ropes of another ship in his mouth and plunged down into the Deeps. The boat stood nearly on end and began to sink; the sailors, yelling shrilly, managed to cut the anchor ropes. The ship crashed back onto its keel with a crack that suggested its seams had split. The Litan capsized a fourth boat, jaws gaping in a monstrous grin, and amused himself by making little rushes at the others until the refugees from the four damaged boats managed to load themselves onto the undamaged ones. Then he chased them out to sea.

When he returned, his eyes were gleaming with interest. "That was more fun than I've had in years," he told Palli. "If they come back again, I will eat them!"

Palli had expected the Litan to go back to sleeping in the Deeps, but instead he spent his time gliding dangerously up and down the coastline, menacing the fish and sunning himself in the harbor. The pirates tried to come back, and the Litan chased them off again.

Palli wasn't sure, but she thought she might be dreaming less frequently now. Perhaps she only forgot her dreams. She thought that she dreamed of the pirate fleet approaching a smaller fleet up a wide muddy river; but she also dreamed that they were sunk by a combined force of tan-kilted warriors and giant crocodiles. While this was possible—she had seen winged cats and horses made of wind, after all—she had never known creatures out of myths to cooperate so closely with groups of mortal men.

Gubla slept, the barrier of thorns growing thicker and higher with every year, like a great dome between the city and the sky. In time, the city was forgotten.

THE THIRD and youngest son of the King of the Four Quarters did not go to the feast at his father's new palace. He had not been invited.

At the moment he didn't mind this a bit. How glad he was that he had gone out for a walk instead of joining yet another lion hunt!

Prince Nerbalatan flung himself down on a rock, laughing. "Mercy, mercy! I need a moment to breathe!" His beard itched as if a mess of tiny scorpions had come to nest in it; the fringes of his robe, which had been soft and colorful this morning, were dusty and full of burrs.

"Eh—you're old, Neriya!" his new friend accused him, swinging his throwing stick. "I'm not tired!"

"I am old," Neriya agreed calmly. He certainly was in comparison to this boy (who couldn't have been more than ten), although his own older brothers still teased him about the sparseness of his square-cut beard.

"Ready yet?"

"Not yet," said the prince, dropping his own throwing stick. He didn't think the boy would attack an unarmed opponent.

The lad bounced up and down then jumped up onto a rock, brandishing his stick overhead like a mace. "I am Karduniash the Great!" he shouted with a flourish. He pointed the stick at the prince. "Who are you?"

"Prince Nerbalatan," said Neriya, taken by surprise.

The boy lowered the tip of his stick and frowned. "Who's he? I don't know any tales about a Prince Nerbalatan."

Neriya realized his own mistake, but explaining would mean telling the boy that he was truly a prince, which was not a fact that had ever done Neriya much good. So instead, he said, "There aren't any tales about him, because he was not a hero and could never be a king."

"But why couldn't he be a king, if he was a prince?" asked the boy, scowling ferociously.

"He had older brothers?" Neriya suggested.

"Well, he could kill them, couldn't he?"

"Hmm." The prince hid a smile. "That wouldn't be very brotherly."

"Lots of princes do it," the lad said breezily, swinging his stick and looking willing to cut down any number of older brothers.

"The real reason he could never be king is because he had a birthmark on the right side of his face, which showed that he was inauspicious."

"What?"

"Bad luck," Neriya tried. "Nobody wants a bad-luck king. He'll attract demons, and none of the gods will ever bless him."

"He had a mark like you?"

"Er, yes," Neriya said, unconsciously lifting his hand to his cheek. His beard covered only half of the mark, which was even darker than his skin.

"I've never heard of him. Be someone else," the boy commanded imperially.

Be someone else. It was a tempting thought. But a man's place in the world was not so easily changed. "I'll be your faithful herald," Neriya decided. "O people of the whole universe! Harken to the might and wisdom of Karduniash! Master of the Black-Headed People! Keeper of the Hundred Gates! Linchpin of the Heavens, the Four Quarters, and the Underworld!"

"You're good at this," the boy said, his face lighting up with approval.

"Thank you," said Prince Neriya.

Later that evening, Neriya wound his solitary way through his great-grandfather's palace. The old palace was practically deserted tonight; he caught sight of a few servants scurrying here and there, carrying off some of the nicer movables to the new palace, but that was all.

He walked slowly through the maze of halls and into the audience court. The stars above gave just enough light for him to walk across the room without running into any of the date palms in their pots.

The carved reliefs on the walls were barely visible, but Neriya's memory supplied the pictures where his eyes could not. As a child he had always loved to look at the pictures and make up stories about the people from far away.

Arinna . . . He ran his fingers gently over the name carved just under someone's foot. *A northern kingdom, wasn't it? But you've been gone a long time.* Perhaps a hundred years. *Is that long? To the stone of this palace, not long at all.*

If the Arinna man carved here were alive, I wonder what he would think about everything that's happened? Neriya wondered then shook his head. *I know what he would think. What could he think about the fall of his kingdom?* He put his hand on his heart sadly then walked on.

The stone watchers loomed out of the dark. Great winged bulls with human heads, they wore noble crowns and stared always straight ahead, their carved faces set in slight smiles.

"What do you think of all this?" the young prince asked companionably, patting one watcher's shoulder. "I'm afraid you will have a great deal less to watch, now that the King has finished his new palace. No more long audiences on hot days, with people coming from all over the empire. But I daresay the birds will still nest in the date palms. Maybe that will be enough. Perhaps you're tired of people." He rubbed the thick neck with its carefully carved garlands of hair. He always expected the watchers to turn and answer him, they looked so alive. He wished they would answer. He wished . . .

"I wish," he said to the stars and the date palms and the stone watchers-at-the-gates, "I wish there were someone I could help without bringing down curses on his head. I would like to be of some use in the world. A useless prince is a sorry thing."

Are you a prince? asked a voice like murmuring water. Neriya jumped, tripped over his own feet, and caught himself against the stone watcher's carven shoulder. He looked up. Sitting—or floating?—on the back of the huge winged beast was a shifting shape—something like a girl in a gauzy gray veil or a dove with fluttering gray wings.

"Yes," he said. "Who are you?"

I am the Guardian of Gubla's beauty. Do you know where Gubla is?

"No," he said, not missing the fact that she hadn't given him her name.

We have slept so long! The faint shape flickered in distress. *And I dream so rarely now . . . God Who Answers, you promised . . .*

"Can I help?" Neriya asked, stretching up on his toes for a closer look.

The shape was plainly not that of an ordinary person; surely his expected bad luck would not affect her?

Help? The shape was suddenly still, and its shifting edges settled, like a bird's feathers smoothing. *Will you help?*

"I will," he said. "I promise. What do you need me to do?"

Come to Gubla. Wake it from its curse.

"How?" He had never heard of the place. It might be in the third heaven, for all he knew.

The coast—we sleep on the shore of the sea to the west of here, south of what was once called Arinna.

"Near Uzu?" he asked, casting about for the name of a place on the coast.

North of there. Come! I will try to guide you. Suddenly the shape lifted from the watcher's back and vanished with a sound like a sigh.

Two days after his strange meeting in the old palace, Neriya found himself on a battered old barge being rowed slowly north against the current of the Great River. Wide, slow, and shallow, the River was still the fastest road north from his father's city.

Neriya hadn't told any of the bargemen who he was, but he thought some of them might know. They gave him a wide berth and never asked him to help them row.

"Can I help?" Neriya asked the captain.

The captain eyed him warily then offered a polite grimace. "Noble lord, it would not be fitting."

It was a long trip north, with nothing to do but watch the banks go by.

It was too long a trip.

The little gray dove—in his memory, his strange visitor looked most like a dove—had seemed frightened, her plea urgent. This was taking too long!

"Is there a road from here to the sea coast?" Neriya asked every time they stopped at a village.

The captain always gave him a strange look. "You'll have to wait until we're farther north, lord. There is no caravan road through here. Do you see those mountains?"

Finally, Neriya asked one of the village people, a young man who had come to help the bargemen unload their cargo.

"There is a road through the pass—there," said the young man, waving toward the foothills. "But you don't want to go that way, lord. There are masterless men in the mountains. Robbers."

"I don't have much to steal," the prince told him, staring toward the purple-hazed hills. "Do you know where I can buy a donkey? I need something to carry my gear."

"If you have a donkey, they will steal it, lord," the village lad told him, frowning. "If you don't have enough for them to steal, they may kill you. Or eat you."

Neriya's mouth quirked. "Eat me?" It sounded like a story to frighten children. He didn't believe there were cannibal bandits in these hills.

Two days later, Neriya thought about changing his opinion.

The robber band had come right up to his camp in the middle of the night. In hindsight, the fire had been a mistake. But he had never been anywhere dangerous before! He had thought the flames would be hidden well enough, camped as he was in a narrow part of the pass. Now the bandits were going through his saddlebags and laughing, while the donkey's haunch roasted slowly over the fire.

Somehow he had expected that the bandits would be small men, thin from starvation, glad to take his silver and run away. These were not small men. They were giants, or Raffa, such as Neriya had thought existed only in stories. Each one stood head and shoulders taller than Neriya and had coarse black hair tied back in a ratty tail . . . and each one had twelve fingers instead of ten.

"Ah, little patron," smiled one, baring his teeth. He whacked Neriya heavily on the shoulder. "You have made our moon a good one! Are we not rich men, my brothers?" The others laughed.

"Aren't you worried that the king will send soldiers against you?" Neriya asked. It was worth a try. Didn't his father send out soldiers to protect travelers? Perhaps this was a little far away, but in his father's palace, no one would have questioned the king's ability to send armies to the far end of the world. "Don't make trouble for yourselves. Let me go on my way peacefully."

"What king?" one asked through a mouthful of meat. "The King of the Wall? He will not come for you, little patron. No one important comes through this pass."

"Then why do you rob travelers here and not go somewhere else?" Neriya asked. The smell of roasted meat made him hungry, but he remembered the donkey's patient eyes and felt guilty for even thinking about it.

The giants growled. "Ah, do you think yourself wise?" mocked the leader, who wore a band of silver around his throat. "Why ask us such questions, dog?"

"What kind of fool comes through this pass?" one muttered to another. "Is this a trap of the Wall King? Or some move of the King of the Gate?"

"He must be a spy! We should warn the Prince of the Hinterland. If the kings have planned to move against him, he may pay to know it!"

Neriya did not know any of the kings and princes they spoke of, but he did know the kind of treatment a supposed spy could expect. He had to find a way to escape!

"We will take this dog along with us and see what knowledge we can wring from him," stated Silverband. "As soon as the sun rises, we will go." He leaned down to grab the prince's throat, hauling him to his feet. "Sleep by the fire, where we can see you." He threw Neriya down; one of the prince's hands went into the fire, and he stifled a yelp. This was not the time to complain about being hurt. Instead, he lay still and hoped they wouldn't think to tie him up.

Now the giants were sleeping, all except one sitting on a ledge some distance up the cliff. Neriya, lying with his face to the stars, sometimes saw a glint of light reflected from the giant's eyes. He was sure that the robber was watching him.

Ahead of him the pass continued to rise; it might be another day or week through to the other side, for all he knew. His best chance of escape was back the way he had come. At least he knew how far away help would be. But with the gray shadow's plea ringing in his mind, he hated to take a single step back.

Is that you? a voice asked softly. Neriya thought he dreamed it. But then he looked up and saw a faint gray glimmer in the air.

"Yes," he whispered. "Am I going the right direction?"

You are going so quickly in the right direction, it took me a long time to find you. And now you're in danger. I'm sorry.

"Don't worry," he breathed. "I'll get away somehow. Unless . . . can you do something, little dove?"

I can touch nothing. If these Raffa should wake, they would not even see or hear me.

"Doesn't everyone see you? Then how can I see you?"

You saw me because you were looking and because you did not think me impossible, she told him in her voice like a sigh. *Children see me, but no one else does.*

The wind rose, howling through the pass and sending a gust of burning ash from the fire. Neriya ducked his head under his cloak until the wind died. "If only the wind would go down a little," he murmured ruefully. The giants slept sensibly in the shelter of the cliffs; only he and one or two others—the lowest of the band—were unprotected here.

Wind, he heard. The gray shadow described a thoughtful loop in the air. *Don't be frightened. I'll go for help.*

"But if no one can see you—"

She was gone.

Neriya kept himself awake all night, staring up at the stars with weary eyes. He was not sure that her soft voice would be enough to wake him if he slept. But she did not come back.

Palli drifted far and far above the hills, chasing the wind. It was hard to dream so long. She felt the edges of things beginning to dull, and deeper sleep lurked around every hillock. *I can't . . . but I must go on!*

She had spoken to the prince. The first grown person to hear her in many a year! And now he was in danger of his life. Palli had never meant for *that* to happen. He was not a fierce man like Etlu-kashid or her father; she didn't think he would be able to rescue himself. He might be her father's height, but his shoulders were narrower, and his dark eyes were as bright and earnest as a child's, his squared beard still thin with youth. His hands were peaceful hands, not hands that had known hard work and harder fighting.

Her vision blurred, and she could no longer tell up from down. *Mother of All Horses!* she cried, as the dream faded. *Come as you promised and help Prince Neriya!*

Even if she could not catch the wind, perhaps the horse-of-wind could hear her.

In the morning, Neriya could hardly stand, he was so stiff. The little gray dove had not come back. *I'll have to rescue myself,* he decided. Besides, if he was to free her city from a curse, he would have to deal with more than a double-dozen of giant bandits.

In a heroic poem, he thought ruefully, he would bash a few giants' heads together, wrest their weapons out of their hands, and kill them all in a few short stanzas. The Hero of the Forest would have had no trouble with these robbers.

Neriya eyed the Raffa. He wasn't even sure he could *reach* some of their heads, let alone bash them together. He was going to have to try something different.

"Peace to you, may you receive good news," he said politely to the leader of the band. "May I say a word?"

Silverband, who was tying his packs over his broad shoulders, gnashed his square black teeth. "Speak quickly if you speak at all, little dog!"

"I am not a servant of any of the kings you spoke of last night," Neriya told him. "I have no interest in reporting anything to anyone, except that this pass is dangerous, which the local people know already. Take my goods, take my cloak, but please let me go. I am travelling toward the sea, because I have seen a vision of a—a flying being that asked for my help. I am only trying to help her, O commander."

"Not a servant of any of the kings?" another sneered. "Where does anyone see such fancy beards as among the servants of the King of the Wall?"

They're going to condemn me because of my beard? Neriya thought numbly.

"But the worm sounds more like a son of the Gate," another argued.

"He's trying to trick us! Kill him!"

"Shut your lips!" the leader snapped. "A flying being? What are you saying? Do you say that a goddess appeared to you? Was it the Bloody Maiden?"

"No, no," Neriya said hastily. He did not know who the Bloody Maiden was; there was a warrior goddess in his father's kingdom, but "maiden" was not the first word one would use to describe her. "Not a goddess, certainly not a goddess."

"Oho! Been speaking to demons, have you?" said Silverband. "As the Thunderer thunders, if I let you get away from me with such a story! If you are lying—well, then you are lying and deserve whatever I might do to you. And if you are telling the truth, you are a sorcerer!"

"She isn't a demon," Neriya protested as two giants grabbed his arms. "I am no sorcerer—"

"Look at the mark on his face! He is cursed by the gods!" shouted one of his captors.

Oh no! Neriya thought. Even in his father's kingdom a peasant man with such a mark could be killed lest he curse others. Here and now, his royal birth would not help him. He struggled desperately as the two giants lifted him off the ground. The leader unsheathed a short curved blade.

"Let us see what omens are in his guts!" the massive bandit shouted to his men. They let out a cheer.

A breath of wind brushed Neriya's cheek. Then, suddenly, there came the scream of a gale. A tremendous blast of wind threw the bandit leader across the narrow pass, slamming him against the rock wall. The wind gave another howl—and *turned* to whirl the other way! Robbers yelled and roared as the very air became suddenly powerful and hostile, flinging them this way and that.

One of the huge bandits, the one clinging to Neriya's right arm, let go and tried to run, only to be thrown after his fellows. The other hung on determinedly, his hands shaking. "Sorcerer!" he screamed. "Curse you, sorcerer!" With his free hand he pulled out his knife, ready to kill Neriya and thus end his supposed magic.

"Don't!"

The wind stole the breath from Neriya's lungs, and his feet left the ground. He and the last of the bandits tumbled, falling up into the sky. Cloud and land whirled before their eyes. With a gasp the bandit let go of the prince, only to drop like a stone. Neriya snatched at him reflexively but couldn't reach him before he himself was propelled still higher, before the ground was hidden by a haze of thin cloud.

"Little dove, little dove!" Neriya cried, too dizzy to be properly frightened.

"Not a dove, but the Mother of All Horses," came a warm, grass-scented voice. "Put your arms around my neck, and I will carry you toward Gubla—for the sake of the child who saved my child long ago."

Neriya could see nothing but air; but he closed his eyes, reached out his arms, and found that they wrapped around something. It was neither fur nor air nor sunlight but felt rather like all three under his fingers. He held tight. He almost felt as if he were astride a mare, with the long hairs of her mane whipping past him.

"Don't be afraid. I will not drop you." Air screamed past his ears as the mare of wind galloped over and around the jagged mountains.

After a while he opened his eyes, only to laugh in delight. So quick, so high! The speed might steal his breath, but the sight of the rocky hills with their patches of green, their twisted trees, and their flocks of goats, filled him with joy. It was a beautiful country, even if it was full of bandits.

The Mother of All Horses carried him a long way, until the mountains shrank and the foothills settled into miles and miles of deserted wilderness. Heat rose off the rocks; parched-looking plants made sparse shade, as still as death with no breeze to stir them. The wind-mare grew slower and slower, and sank lower and lower, until she set him gently on the ground. "The wind does not travel here at this season," she told him. "Now you must make your own way."

He stood on top of an anchor-shaped rock and watched her gallop away, tearing up the clouds in her wake. Then he turned back to the wilderness. *The sun is sinking now. She must have carried me for most of the day,* he decided. *It sets in the west, so if I walk toward the sunset, I will be walking toward the sea.*

Pleased with his reasoning, the prince set off through the desert.

When Palli woke into a dream again, it took her some time to find Prince Neriya. He was far from where she had left him. He looked ragged and dirty, and he talked quietly to himself as he stumbled over the ground.

Neriya, she whispered, worried. *Neriya, can you hear me?*

"Peace to you, little dove," he said cheerfully, although his eyes did not quite focus on her. "Am I still going in the right direction?"

Have you been wandering long?

"A few days, I think," he answered calmly. "I find that one gets used to being hungry. It wasn't something I ever had occasion to learn before. I don't feel hungry now."

Palli was sure that there were things to eat in the wilderness; people lived here, after all. But she, like Neriya, had never learned the ways of the wilderness folk. She hovered anxiously over him. *Have you found water?*

"Hmm?"

That much she could do, Palli decided. With a twist and a sigh, she sent herself gliding over the ground, around hills, and through broken rocks until she found a spring—a tiny trickle of water seeping from the side of a hill. Now, quickly, quickly, back to Neriya . . .

This way, she coaxed him, fluttering around his shoulders.

"Little dove," he murmured absently, and trudged obediently after her. It took much longer for her to guide him to the water than it had taken her to find it, but she got him there at last. He would not die of thirst, at least.

"Thank you," he said, looking rather more alert. "I didn't know how thirsty I was."

Now you should rest, Palli told him. *Unless you can carry water with you, you should always rest in the heat of the day.*

"But don't you need help? Is there time to rest?" he protested.

I would rather that you lived to reach Gubla instead of dying while trying to get there, Palli told him a little sharply. *But you must have something to eat.*

Neriya looked around him. "I fear I cannot eat rocks," he said, sounding genuinely apologetic.

I will see if I can find help, Palli said, and whisked away.

"I wish you wouldn't keep leaving me, little dove," the prince whispered. But Palli was already far away.

Dirigga! Dirigga! she called. One friend had come to save him from the bandits—perhaps another would help Palli get him to Gubla alive.

Neriya slept until late afternoon next to the little spring. He woke when a sudden gust of air washed across his shoulders. *Mare of wind . . . ?*

It was not the horse of air but a creature just as strange: a winged creature with the face of a cat. "Stormbird!" It was just like the ones painted on the walls of his great-grandfather's palace, although the artists had gotten the colors wrong. This one was as black and gleaming as diorite.

The creature looked at him dubiously. "This one is too heavy for me to carry," she told her gray, flitting companion.

But you can bring him food.

It sneered at him. "Men are troublesome. They shoot at us. Hunt us."

Please. You did promise.

"Very well—a favor for a favor, food for food," the Stormbird agreed grumpily.

"Thank you," Neriya said, bowing deeply to her. She ignored him, but he wasn't annoyed. He was too amazed to see a mythical creature roosting on his rock.

Dirigga continued to ignore him through the weeks that followed, although she brought him food almost every day. And every day he kept struggling westward over the hills, with his little gray bird hovering overhead and pointing out the way he should go next.

I must not sleep, I must not sleep, Palli told herself. Who knew how long it would be before she found him again? He might get lost. Dirigga might stop bringing him food if Palli were no longer there. So she struggled to stay in the dream. *Tell me about the place where you live. Tell me about your family. Tell me about your life.* His answers interested her and helped her to keep dreaming.

"But my life isn't very interesting," he would always say after a little while. "Tell me about what *you* have seen. Tell me about your life, about Gubla."

Talking about Gubla was easy. She told him about the Litan, whom he hoped he would see. She told him about the gleaming blue-green ocean, about the Road to Far Horizon. She told him about Tsalat and about Tsalat's stories. She told him about her parents. Last of all she told him about her naming day and the prophecy of the God Who Answers.

"I'm not much of a warlike shepherd," Neriya said thoughtfully. "I have hunted lions and hippopotami, yet I have never been to war. But if all I must do is wake you up, I don't suppose much war will be required."

The kings of Gubla have always been warriors.

"Well, this Etlu-kashid fellow you told me about—you'll wake up and finish your wedding, and Gubla will have a warrior king again."

Palli had never wanted to marry Etlu-kashid; but she could see that Neriya hadn't entirely understood her story, and telling him that she wasn't planning to marry Etlu-kashid would have required some awkward explanations.

The prophecy means that I will marry you, she said quietly to herself. It was a pleasant idea. Neriya was a most unusual man, she thought, to set out on a long and dangerous journey just because a half-seen person asked for help.

They journeyed on until the wilderness grew green at last and they reached the more fertile areas of the coast. Dirigga flapped off for the last time, looking glad to be rid of her responsibility. The next day, Neriya got food at a village.

There were many villages for a while; but as they got closer to Gubla, they began finding abandoned ones that were collapsing slowly back into the ground. "There was a city here in my great-grandmother's time," one of the villagers warned Neriya. "But it was cursed and lost! Don't go there—no one who goes there ever comes back."

"Is that true?" Neriya asked Palli later. "Is it really so dangerous?"

There is the wall of thorns, Palli said slowly. *And the snakes and the scorpions. Some of the scorpions are very large.* She had not paid attention to them for a long time; they could not touch her.

"Ah," Neriya said thoughtfully. At the last inhabited village before Gubla, he traded the remnants of his fine clothes for a kilt, a short spear, and a bronze ax. He did not care to fight snakes with his bare hands.

On the last day of their journey, Palli grew more and more excited, fluttering around Neriya like his own personal whirlwind. *Almost there, almost there!* Neriya, caught up in her excitement, broke into a run and ran until he could run no more. He stopped to breathe, leaning on his spear, then balanced it on his shoulder and ran again, laughing.

There it is, Palli told him at last. *My city!* She spun so closely by his face that the wind of her passing was like a touch on his cheek.

Neriya looked across the plain at the city hidden under a dome of briars with the sea flashing green and gold beyond. "Well, little dove," he panted cheerfully, "I think you will be awake again in time to go to sleep tonight!"

aS NERIYA approached the thorn-walled city, nothing moved on the plain of Gubla. *No snakes and scorpions? Maybe this won't be so hard,* thought Neriya.

But as he came nearer, he changed his mind. The briars, which were covered in purple and yellow flowers, had been weaving themselves together for generations—the old branches dying, the new thorns wrapping themselves around the old. So closely were they woven together that Neriya could not see the smallest bit of light through the briar hedge. Getting through that would be like chopping a forest down! Still, as long as there was no danger, it would be only a matter of time before Neriya broke through to the city.

He drove the spear into the ground beside him, where it would be easy to grab if something happened, and lifted his axe.

Be careful, Palli told him, fluttering to and fro. *These briars sprang from a curse. Don't let them scratch you.*

"Peace, don't worry." Neriya struck a thick spiky stem—once, twice.

Before he could strike a third time, there was a scuttling sound, and a flood of amber-colored scorpions rushed out from under the brambles. Neriya yelped and leaped into the air, coming down with a crunch on half a dozen brown-striped backs. As they died, they struck with their tails; some of them stung him, leaving burning spots on his skin. He kicked a few away, but hundreds more poured out from the shadow of the thorn wall.

Too many and too small to kill, he decided at once. As long as he didn't let too many of them sting him, their stings should only be painful, not deadly. He jumped up, setting his foot on one of the trunks of the briar bushes, and struck again with his axe. *Thrice.*

A snake dropped down onto his head.

Neriya let out a yell and threw himself backward, sending the snake flying but landing in the middle of the scorpion army. "Ah! Ouch!" He rolled to his feet, dancing from foot to foot and shaking palm-sized scorpions off his tunic. "Aah!"

He heard a chorus of hisses and looked up to see serpents slithering toward him through the thorns: gleaming black vipers and brown-striped adders, all intently focused on him. They dropped gracefully to the ground and glided toward him, ignored by the yellow scorpions.

They're poisonous! Look out, Neriya! Palli warned him. She darted at the snakes. They hissed and struck at her, but they could not touch her any more than she could touch them.

At least they're bigger, Neriya thought grimly and went to work, trying to ignore the burning in his legs as the scorpions swarmed him. Snakes dropped; Neriya pinned them with his spear and cut off their heads, bending uncomfortably low. *I should have gotten a bigger axe.* He kicked wildly between snakes, shaking off their smaller brethren.

He leaped and struck and danced, gasping, but a tiny part of him sat back and thought, *More of them came when I struck the thorns the third time.*

My goal is to get into the city, not to kill these creatures. They are a distraction.

A very effective one, he had to admit. How he was going to chop through all those thorns with ten thousand scorpions scuttling around underfoot he didn't know. *But I can strike again now.*

He made a standing leap and hit the briars a fourth time. Their flowers shuddered, dropping petals and tiny snakes in all directions.

Neriya!

The prince spun to find yet more scorpions curling their tails to attack. But these scorpions were a little different. For one thing, each stood as high as his waist, its tail curling at shoulder height.

"You didn't say they were *this* large, little dove!" Neriya gasped, stumbling back. But there was no time for fear. The nearest struck at him; he whacked its tail away with his axe and warned it off with a stab to the head. It fell a half step back then sidled toward him again. He watched it carefully. As it struck again, he leaped aside and parried its tail with the shaft of the spear even as he brought the axe down on its head. It stumbled. He hit it again, and it collapsed to the ground. *At least they're not as quick as lions,* he thought.

A second giant scorpion went the way of the first. Then two decided to rush him at once. He ran quickly to one side, so that only one could attack him at a time; he was faster than they, but they had far more reach. He caught up a snake on the end of his spear and threw it at them. The closer one struck at it reflexively, and he stomped on its tail as the barb hit the ground. But he only managed a glancing blow before it pulled its tail loose, sending him sprawling.

The city, he told himself. *Don't forget!* To think that he had complained about having to chop through fifty feet of briars . . . He rolled and scrambled away from the approaching scorpions.

His little dove was flitting around before their eyes, distracting them from attacking him. He ran around them to strike the thorns again. *Five, six.*

There was a horrible scream. It came from far away, yet it was deafening. Neriya started to put his hands over his ears and whacked himself in the head with his own spear. Even the scorpions stopped short, curling their tails aggressively.

A black cloud rose from the sea. Boiling angrily, it swirled toward Gubla and dropped down before Neriya. The darkness faded, leaving behind the skinniest, oldest man he had ever seen. The man was bent nearly double, his wispy beard full of lichen, his cloak rotting on his shoulders, his eyes full of hate. "No one enters my city! No one!"

Kashap, Palli whispered in the prince's ear.

"It has been six sixes of years since I had to kill a stranger here myself," Kashap rasped, reaching into his pouch with contorted fingers. "But no one can survive my incantations! *A man, a young man, a warrior of the Wall, who has travelled far—may his joints be weak, may his eyes be dim, may his hand grow slack, may his breath stop. Six times I will say it, seven times I have said it: let it be for his destruction!*" the sorcerer chanted, his voice gaining strength with every phrase. At the last word, he pulled a clay figure of a man out of his belt pouch, threw it to the ground, and stamped on it.

Palli gasped. Neriya felt a moment of intense pain, but it passed, leaving him weak but still standing. *Where is this kingdom of the Wall that everyone keeps talking about, and why do they all think I come from there?* he wondered. Then his mind caught up with his heart, and he realized that the sorcerer had misnamed him. That was why the incantation hadn't worked. He had to hurry before the old man realized his mistake.

"Stop your lips! You see that you haven't hurt me," Neriya said, raising his chin. "Haven't you done enough harm with your curse? Let it go now."

Kashap went white around the lips. "How? How are you alive?" he screamed. "My magic always works! How—what's that?" He jerked, his eyes fixed on Palli's hovering shape. "What *is* that? A demon? You have magic of your own!" He rounded on Neriya, pointing an accusing finger. "I see that mark on your face! You are gods-cursed! Get out! This is *my* city! Find your own place!"

"I've come to set this city free!"

"If an incantation won't kill you, I'll use another way!" Kashap howled, flecks of spit flying from his shrunken lips. He raised his arms, and darkness boiled up from the ground. Neriya felt it like a cold breath and stepped back, not wanting it to touch him.

When it vanished again, Kashap had changed.

This is worse than giant scorpions, Neriya thought in disbelief.

Hardly a spear length in front of him was a tannin dragon. Its head and body and tail were shaped like those of a lion, but covered in gleaming green and black scales. Its neck was long like that of a snake, ringed by thick folds of scaly skin. It blinked mad eyes, Kashap's eyes, at him, then threw back its head and roared.

The ground shook. With a symphony of frightened hisses and chitters, the snakes and scorpions fled from the dragon. Half a dozen scorpions sprang from Neriya's clothes and skittered away.

That's something, at least, Neriya thought. Although his legs were so swollen already that he hadn't been feeling the stings anymore. He felt the scorpions' venom only in the catch of his breath and the shaking of his hands.

"Little dove," he rasped, "I don't want you to see this." Whether he won or lost, there was nothing she could do to help.

The God Who Answers promised that you would wake the city, she told him, flickering just over his shoulder. He could almost imagine he felt fingers brush his face. *I won't leave you!*

The dragon lurched forward, clumsy in its unaccustomed shape, jaws gaping to reveal double rows of teeth. Neriya dove aside then rolled to his feet and chopped at its flanks. Its head whipped around, darting on that long neck, and it hit him with open jaws. It probably meant to bite, but instead it knocked him away. He rolled and leaped high, stabbing into the dragon's open mouth with his spear. But it shut its jaws with a snap, breaking the spear in half.

Well, that's unfortunate, Neriya thought distantly. He whacked the broken spear-haft across the dragon's nose then turned to run. If he could reach the thorn wall, surely there would be somewhere he could wriggle in, where the dragon couldn't reach him? *In with all the snakes and scorpions.* It wasn't a very good idea, but it was the only one he had.

No! Palli cried. Neriya whirled to see the Kashap-dragon right behind him, beginning to strike. The small gray shape darted at the dragon's eyes, wrapping herself around its head. Blinded, the dragon roared. Neriya ran forward.

Kashap shook his head wildly. The dreaming princess clung for a moment then lost her position and drifted away. Kashap stretched out his neck and belched a cloud of darkness toward her. It curled around her, and Palli screamed. The dragon's lip curled in satisfaction.

Neriya saw the darkness swallow her. "Little dove!" he shouted, and leaped. The dragon, distracted, didn't move in time. Neriya's axe bit deep into its neck.

With a hissing gurgle, the tannin fell to the ground. Black ichor trickled from around the axe head. With a furious hiss, Kashap lurched, trying to get up and attack again—but his writhing was his undoing. Neriya still clung to the handle of the axe. When the tannin's thrashing tail caught Neriya in the ribs and knocked him sprawling, the axe was pulled free, tearing the wound wider.

The tannin still tried to get up, but the ichor pouring from its neck dispersed into black mist. Scales rained down from its body, turning to smoke before they hit the ground. The dragon twisted and shrank, its great claws and long neck vanishing, until it became a man once more.

Kashap looked up at Neriya through the film of age that covered his burning eyes. "I have still won," he choked. "If you do not wake the city before night falls, everyone within it will die!" He gave a final gasp and lay still.

Neriya did not know whether the old man spoke truth or lies. But he had no further interest in the sorcerer. "Little dove!" he shouted. "Little dove!" But there was no fluttering gray shadow anywhere. *Could the sorcerer have hurt her with his magic?* Neriya thought with a thrill of fear. He turned and rushed toward the wall of thorns, striking with all his might—a seventh time.

With a crack, the thorn trunk parted. Other cracks followed as the briars beyond pulled back, leaving a narrow path toward Gubla's walls. Neriya ran in without a thought for snakes or scorpions. Brambles caught at his clothes and his beard, but he ignored them. He passed through the wall of thorns and scrambled up the eroding bulwarks, using the last of the briars as footholds to climb the city wall. His hands bleeding from the thorns, his legs numb with scorpion stings, he ran down into the city.

It was dark here already, the thorns overhead shutting out the light. He nearly stumbled over the first sleeper. "Wake up!" he cried, shaking the man. But the man did not stir.

How can I wake them? His little dove had not told him. *I must find her!* She would know what to do. *If only—if only the sorcerer's magic did not—*

The thought was too horrible; Neriya could not let himself think it!

Neriya ran through the city, stopping only to look into the faces of the few people that he found. Then, when he reached a wider street, he began finding more. Hundreds of people, all in their finest clothes, tumbled in heaps on the road. He looked into face after face, but there were too many of them. And how could he be sure if he found her? He had never seen her face, not really!

"She said she was the guardian, the guardian of their beauty," he muttered to himself. "She was getting married . . ." She should be apart from the others, not buried under one of these piles. He ran up toward the larger buildings. The palace and temples ought to be in the highest part of the city, surely?

Here was a dais, a collection of altars. There—didn't that man look like a king, with his graying hair worn in a royal club at the back of his head?

"Little dove!"

There she was. She lay sleeping like all the others, face down on the dais with one hand outstretched toward her father. He knew her at once.

Carefully he knelt beside her and turned her face toward the sky. The braided rug had left a pattern on her skin, a mark like the one on his own cheek. "Wake up, little dove!" He shook her gently. She didn't stir. "Little dove!" he shouted, but that didn't wake her either.

Wincing, he pinched the skin on the back of her hand then smoothed the mark out apologetically. "Little dove?" *I should have made her tell me her name! Maybe then she would wake for me.*

Was it getting even darker in here? He looked up toward where the hidden sun ought to be. Were Kashap's last words true? Would the people of Gubla die when the sun set? How terrible, to journey so far, only to be the instrument of the city's final destruction instead of its help! And yet he might have known it would be this way—was he not cursed from his birth? He reached up to scratch futilely at the mark on his cheek.

Her face—it was so still. The rise and fall of her chest was so slight that it hardly stirred the beads of her necklace. "No, little dove," he whispered. "Don't die!" He had to wake her somehow!

He leaned down and kissed her.

Palli sighed. Her last dream had been very unpleasant, she thought as she rose toward waking. She was surprised when, instead of floating in the sky, she found herself lying on the ground, her head pillowed on someone's leg. She opened her eyes. "N-Neriya?"

"Peace, peace. Everything's all right now," he said, his face slack with relief.

As the people of Gubla woke, light began to filter down from overhead. The thorns were withdrawing from above the city.

Palli rose to her feet, wobbling slightly, weak after a century of dreaming. *Waking at all is a miracle. You truly do answer, don't you?* she breathed toward a patch of sky.

"Did Kashap hurt you?" Neriya asked, tugging worriedly at his beard. "I didn't think anything could touch you!"

"I'm all right," Palli told him, patting him gently on the shoulder. She thought dimly that this was not how she would have acted toward a man once upon a time, but that time was long ago. She reached up and touched her own face. *Don't I look any older?* Yet she remembered a hundred years of dreams!

Her father groaned, and she threw off her bewilderment to run to him, half tripping over her own gilded sandals. It felt so strange to walk on feet instead of floating weightless through the air. "Father, are you well?"

Shokorru took her hand without looking at it, and she pulled him to his feet. "Yes, yes," he rumbled. Then he looked at her and dropped her hand with a frown. "Is the curse broken, Aplati-shamirat-yaftinu?"

Palli shivered. It was a long time since she had heard her name. She bowed her head a little and stepped back. "It is broken, O-king-my-father."

Shokorru's gaze went past her, and he fixed Neriya with a glare. "So you're the son-in-law I was promised? Tell me who you are and how you broke the curse."

Son-in-law? Did the city not fall asleep in the middle of the princess's wedding? Neriya thought, puzzled, but let it go. Perhaps the king was still confused from his long sleep.

The king of Gubla looked like a mighty warrior, but he was nowhere near as fearsome as the King of the Four Quarters, Neriya's own father. Neriya bowed and said, "Mighty king, your servant is Nerbalatan, the third son of Ilnadinshumi, King of the Four Quarters, Master of the Black-Headed People."

"Ilnadinshumi?" Shokorru said suspiciously. "I know the name of the King of the Four Quarters—that isn't it."

"I fear that you have slept long, O king," Neriya told him sympathetically. He was watching his dove out of the corner of his eye. She looked as if she were deciding whether to glide away or not. He did not want her to go, so he offered her his arm. She took it with a little smile. "Much has happened since Gubla began to sleep."

"Arinna and Pirulat are gone," Palli told her father quietly. "But the pirates are gone too, fled or resettled years ago."

"Aplati, stop your lips," her father said, not unkindly. "You, Nerbalatan, tell me the whole tale."

"Now?"

"Now."

So Neriya told it all—how he had seen his little dove hovering in the palace; how he had travelled; how he had faced the snakes, scorpions, and Kashap-dragon. As he spoke, the king's expression grew stranger and stranger. When Neriya finally stopped, Shokorru muttered to himself, "'A noble heart from a far off place; seized by a vision he follows the road; he will not be stopped by serpents and scorpions.' By the third heaven, it is just as that old man said!"

"I don't believe it!" came a loud voice. Etlu-kashid pushed through the crowd that had grown around them as Neriya told his tale. "Dragons! Giant scorpions! Birds! What kind of fools do you take us for? This man is no brave warrior! So he is dusty—so he fell into a scorpion nest! This proves nothing!"

"He is telling the truth," Palli said sternly, holding a little more tightly to Neriya's arm. "He did all the things that he has said, and more."

"King Shokorru, *I* am your heir," the angry shield-bearer insisted. "You chose me to marry your daughter! You never believed that old prophecy! This *foreigner* has heard the tale and come to fool us with fanciful words! Let me kill the lying dog!"

Neriya, who was beginning to feel provoked in spite of his exhaustion, rested his hand on his axe handle and stared at Etlu-kashid. "I did not come here to challenge you for the kingship. I came because this lady asked for help." *He hasn't even looked at her! Does he care only for the throne and not for her?* He didn't think his dove should marry this fellow after all.

The young shield-carrier snorted. "If anyone would believe such a claim, let the Lady of Gubla smite me!"

"You are fortunate that the Lady of Gubla never hears us," Shokorru growled. "Because I believe him. The God Who Answers has not only answered but has delivered what he promised. I am not such a fool as to go against the only god I have ever found who cares about my city."

Etlu-kashid fumed, but he backed away.

"This young man is right that I am not a mighty warrior," Neriya told the king. "Worse than that, I am cursed by the gods, as you see by this mark on my face. Let him be king, if you have chosen him." He stopped and swallowed hard. "But—such curses do not usually attack women—I would—if you do not fear the curse—" He stopped, blinking helplessly at Palli.

"He would like to marry me, O-king-my-father," Palli said quietly, her gray eyes steady on Neriya's face.

"Yes," the prince agreed, looking back at her. "Just so."

"Hmmph," grunted Shokorru, looking from one of them to the other. "First! I have said that the man who marries my daughter Palli will be king after me, and so he shall. Second! If any gods have cursed you, they can take it up with the God Who Answers, who has obviously blessed you. Third! If a god is going to trouble himself to find me a son-in-law, I'm not going to reject him. So marry my daughter, and I'll make you my heir, and we'll be done with it."

Neriya took a deep breath and let it out again before he could speak. At last, in a strong voice, he said, "If you are decided, mighty king, then let it be as you say."

And behold, it was as the king had said. Palli and Neriya were married, and Neriya was made heir. Almost the first thing he did with his new position was to put Etlu-kashid in charge of driving all of the snakes and scorpions out of Gubla. The shield-bearer drove them into the sea—to the great excitement of the people of Gubla, who watched from the cliffs as the Litan devoured the nasty creatures in great gulps.

And if, after Neriya became king, the king of Gubla fought in far fewer battles and had far fewer wives than his predecessor (declaring insistently that one wife was enough for him), nobody seemed to mind. The new King Neriya sent messengers to Perakha's people, asking for someone to come and tell Gubla more about the God Who Answered; and when the messengers returned, the whole city was seized with an unusual cheer. It was a strange and wonderful thing to have a god who kept his promises and cared about right and wrong rather than incantations and laments.

And sometimes, when the royal children had been borne off to bed by the doting triumvirate of Perakha, Tsalat, and Ashui, the king and queen of Gubla would go out to sit side by side on the cliff and watch the sun go down.

"There it is—the Road to Far Horizon, little dove," said Neriya. "Should you like to go adventuring there?"

Palli smiled and leaned her head on his shoulder. "Not yet, my shepherd; wait a little while. We shall all go there someday."

ABOUT THE AUTHOR

KATHRYN McCONAUGHY is a Christian and has studied at Geneva College (as well as sundry other institutions of higher learning).  She is reliably informed that she wrote her first story in the second grade; most recently, she has been writing a series of young adult fantasies set in the world of King Arthur. When she's not writing stories, she enjoys gardening, reading, sword-fighting, and writing papers on obscure aspects of Semitic grammar. Kathryn lives in Maryland with her list of dissertation ideas and her large personal library.

To learn more about Kathryn, visit
www.TheLanguageofWriting.blogspot.com

the Ghost of Briardale

Grace Mullins

To Mama and Daddy, my heroes.
Thank you both for all of your love, encouragement,
and support . . . Oh, and the chicken nuggets!
I love you both.

Chapter 1

O N THE *day of the princess's eighteenth birthday, mere moments before her kingly father was due to arrive at the hidden castle to celebrate that momentous occasion, the princess, in a fit of temper, stormed from her bedchamber and escaped the ministering hands of her three aunties. In her desire to find peace from their constant nagging, she fled to the highest tower of the keep and hid in the stairwell. Just as she shut the tower door, she heard them calling her name from somewhere far too close for her comfort.*

"No, my dear aunties. I shan't come out until sundown," she whispered, the words making her feel ever so much better. "You'll believe your stupid curse has fallen and be all in a tizzy when Father shows up. Ha! That will teach you three a lesson you won't soon forget."

So saying, she climbed the twisting stairway to the tower room, which she expected to find deserted. Instead, upon opening the creaky door, she discovered there an old woman—so old and so deaf, she must never have heard of the king's command to destroy all spinning wheels in the realm, for there she sat, spinning and spinning.

The princess, who had never seen a spinning wheel before in her life, was much more surprised by that strange instrument than by the sight of the old woman herself.

"Whatever are you doing, good old mother?" asked the princess, for she could be polite when the mood took her, and respect for the very old was one of the few manners she'd not abandoned.

"I am spinning, my pretty child."

The princess took several paces into the room. "How do you do it? Let me see if I can spin also."

So saying, she took the spindle in her hand and, in a moment of rare clumsiness (for the princess had always been graceful beyond measure, due to the blessings allotted her at her birth) she pricked her finger.

Immediately she fell to the floor, as still as the dead.

The old woman clucked and shook her head. "Dear me, the poor girl," she crooned, but a cruel smile twisted her lips.

Footsteps rang on the stair. As the princess's three aunties burst into the chamber, the old woman flung up her ragged cloak and disappeared before they had so much as glimpsed her gloating face.

"Members of the board, allow me to recount a summary of the proceedings which have engaged our attention for the past three days."

The judge's feeble voice quavered almost as hard as the hand holding the summation document before his withered face. He was so old that one could easily imagine he'd lived during the fabled time of tall elves and fluttering fairies, hundreds and hundreds of years ago! His age-clouded eyes squinted hard through the thickest glasses ever seen by man, and he rolled his lips several times over his wooden dentures as though gearing up for the effort of speaking again.

Nonetheless, the presiding judge of Yoleston court was the most awe-inspiring person Franz had ever seen. Perhaps not for any great personal merit, but simply because he held Franz's future—his very life—in the palm of his quivering old hand.

Franz sat in the dock, ringed on all sides by solid bars as though already in prison. Two nervous guards flanked him, unwilling to meet his eye whenever he turned to them. Were they . . . were they *frightened* of him? But he was innocent!

Well, practically innocent.

"Mr. Thrombold P. Teabody," croaked the judge, and peered over the edge of his documents, seeking out a face in the crowded courtroom, "has stated and produced evidence of this"—and now his old eyes moved to the dock, meeting Franz's stricken gaze—"this young man's violent behavior, culminating in the vicious flinging of a knife at Mr. Teabody's face."

Franz bit the inside of his cheek. It had been a penknife! A penknife used for sharpening quill pens, such as any clerk working for Mr. Teabody used on a daily basis. And he hadn't flung it at Mr. Teabody. He'd flung it at . . . at . . .

"And I've got the scars to prove it!" the thunderous voice of Mr. Teabody declared. With a scrape of chair legs, the spindly banker rose from his seat, pointing at a nearly invisible pink line along his left temple. Really, the penknife had barely grazed him!

Mr. Teabody wasn't the forgiving sort. And, by virtue of a large purse, he owned half the town, including every single member of the medical board and, most likely, the judge himself.

Franz sank into his seat, his shoulders slumped in defeat. He was doomed.

"The lad's a menace to society!" Mr. Teabody said. "He ought to be locked up in prison, away from all those innocents his violence will inevitably harm!"

The watching crowd murmured in approval. They might not actually agree with Mr. Teabody, but the drama of the whole thing enthralled them. And after all this drama, one couldn't help but desire an exciting ending! Prison would be acceptable.

Why then did Franz feel that fate would hit him with something far worse than mere imprisonment?

The old judge's head bobbed on the end of his skinny neck, giving the impression that it might at any moment break off like the head of a dried flower. "Yes, thank you for the reminder, Mr. Teabody," he said.

He then addressed himself to the medical board which sat in place of a jury, for this wasn't a criminal trial, but a medical inquest: "Esteemed members of the board, you know the details. Franz Happernickle, clerk, was seen on numerous occasions by coworkers and by Mr. Teabody himself to rave and gesticulate wildly at thin air, rendering all who saw him uneasy, for these fits of mania grew ever more violent. The violence culminated in the events of last week, during which young Master Happernickle did take up a knife . . ."

A penknife! Franz screamed inside his head.

" . . . and fling it with brutal force at the head of his employer."

No! At her! I threw it at the . . . the . . .

. . . at the ghost . . . .

Franz hung his head in shame. Even in the privacy of his own mind he sounded like a lunatic.

"You have examined the lad," pursued the judge, though each word wheezed from his lungs as though it might be his last, "both in the context of this court and in private consultations. It is now up to you to reach a verdict." He dropped the paper and folded his shaking hands. Was that a smile twisting the corner of his withered old mouth? "Esteemed doctors of Yoleston, how do you find the accused?"

The board head stood on cue, his bearded face solemn under the light of the electric bulbs shining starkly down from the ceiling above. "By unanimous agreement, my fellow board members and I do officially declare Franz Happernickle to be insane."

The crowd murmured again, delighted at the news. One or two dewy-eyed spinsters might have cast young Franz a sympathetic glance—for he was a nice-looking young man despite the extreme redness of his hair and the freckles abundant across his nose—but these were by far the minority. Franz had no family and, apparently, no friends in all of Yoleston to care as his doom was pronounced.

He buried his face in his shackled hands. It wasn't as though he'd expected any better, but still . . . perhaps a small piece of him had hoped that he'd wake up and discover the events of the last week to be nothing more than a nightmare!

A nightmare prominently featuring a hideous, green, glowing face . . .

The judge pounded his gavel three times, like a foreboding echo. Once the crowd had hushed, he turned his mummified visage upon Franz, who looked out from between his fingers as if through the bars of a prison window. "In light of this pronouncement made by our venerated team of medical experts," said the judge, "you, Franz Happernickle, will be sent immediately to Briardale Asylum for the Mentally Infirm until such time as you might prove yourself once more a fit member of society."

The gavel sounded one last time.

"Take him away."

Chapter 2

WHEN THE *three aunties stepped into the room, they cried out in dismay. For the past eighteen years they had worked so hard to keep the princess hidden, to protect her against the curse hanging like a precarious sword over her life! Curses might sometimes be avoided, after all, if one takes proper precautions.*

But the princess had never been a cautious sort.

"Oh my! Oh me! What can we do?" cried the youngest of the three, clasping her hands as she knelt beside the prone body of the princess.

"Wait a hundred years, I imagine," said the middle auntie. "Thanks to that counterspell of yours, she won't be wakened any sooner. And then only if we can find a True Hero in time."

"A True Hero," sighed the third auntie, who was the oldest of the three

and the most beautiful. She shook her head ruefully, rubbing her temple with one long finger. "Oh, Viola! What possessed you to concoct such a counterspell?"

The youngest fairy—for indeed, the three aunties weren't aunties at all, but fairies—wiped away a tear. "It seemed the right choice at the time. And how hard can it be? Heroes aren't so rare as all that."

"True Heroes are," said the second fairy irritably. "A True Hero has to have performed one of the Three Great Deeds: save a kingdom, slay a dragon, or move a mountain."

"Well," said the youngest fairy, trying to smile through her tears, "at least we have a hundred years to find one—"

She didn't have the chance to finish her thought, for before the words left her mouth, the sound of a heralding trumpet rang out in the courtyard below, signaling the arrival of the king and his retinue, come to celebrate the princess's birthday. "Batwings!" the oldest fairy snapped, moving to the window to gaze down at the horses and courtiers pouring through the gates. "And here I told him it looked as though we would avoid the curse rather neatly. He's going to be so disappointed."

"It could have been worse," said the middle fairy. "If not for Viola here, the princess would be dead. As it is—"

"As it is, she will die even so!"

All three fairies flinched at the sound of this fourth, unexpected voice in their midst. It was a voice of poison, a voice of evil.

A voice they knew all too well.

They whirled around and saw a shadow drop away like a cloak, revealing, not an old, deaf woman, but a tall, powerful Lady of Darkness.

"Mara!" the oldest fairy exclaimed.

No one ever returned from Briardale.

This thought whirled inside Franz's mind like an out of control spinning top. He thought it over and over again as they bound him into a straightjacket, propelled him out of the holding house into the street, and guided him toward the somber coach waiting under the streetlamp in the foggy gloom of early morning.

No one returned from Briardale. People went away, locked up far from polite society, and . . . vanished. Forever. And it didn't much matter if they were *really* lunatics or not. How many greedy guardians had taken care of inconvenient wards by having them declared insane and shipped away to Briardale? How many husbands or wives had managed to rid themselves of undesirable spouses by a word in the right ear and a one-way ticket to that foreboding edifice deep in the Black Swamp?

But . . . one never expected to find oneself straight-jacketed and climbing into that dreaded coach.

Franz couldn't look at the crowd gathered along the lamp-lit streets that morning to watch the unfortunate lunatic as he was sent away. He knew that if he dared meet any of those gazes, he would see the same thought reflected in each pair of eyes: *Poor boy. A death sentence would be better.*

The coach's windows were shuttered fast. The seats inside were cushioned but still managed to be hard as stone. Once the door closed behind Franz, he heard the *clink* of a lock. All was dark as night inside, without even a faint crack of light to alleviate the gloom.

When the coach jolted forward, Franz fell heavily on his side, unable to support himself because of the restricting straightjacket. He wanted to scream but clamped his jaw tight. He wouldn't give all those onlookers the satisfaction of hearing a lunatic's yells. The coach bumped over the cobbled street, and Franz almost tumbled from the seat onto the floor, only just managing to brace his feet against the opposite seat and keep himself in place.

Was this the end of everything for him? His existence hadn't been particularly pleasant up until now, but at least it wasn't utterly, beyond all reason *horrible*. Sure, life as a poor coalman's son wasn't all ease and smiles, but he'd learned how to read and write, and managed to clean himself up enough to acquire a clerk's position with Mr. Teabody. He'd earned a full three shillings a day, enough to keep a very small room at the boarding house, sleep on a clean-ish straw mattress, and eat two square-ish meals a day.

All of those luxuries seemed long ago now . . .

Time passed. The coach left behind the cobbled streets and turned onto the main road outside of town, then passed to a smaller, dirt road. The rattling and rumbling became unbearable, and Franz half wondered if he'd arrive at Briardale with his limbs broken to pieces.

What would life in a lunatic asylum be like? Would he be forced to share a cell with other madmen? Visions flashed through his mind, horror stories told of Briardale and its inhabitants. Somehow he knew, he just *knew*, they would eat him alive.

"Dear me, you're still angry, aren't you?"

Franz's heart stopped. He stared in horror as, on the seat opposite— just where he'd braced his feet to keep himself from falling—something green and misty materialized, swirling and shapeless at first, but resolving at last into the face and form of . . .

"You!" Franz snarled.

Sitting cross-legged before him, her chin on her hands and her eyes blinking with deceptive innocence, was the ghoulish green girl who was the source of all his woe.

She smiled at him, displaying a full set of glowing teeth. "At least you're acknowledging me again." She closed one eye as though to study him more intently through the other, then screwed up her face. "They surely haven't been kind to you through this whole business, have they? Calling you insane! The nerve! But then, that's what you get for throwing things at people."

Never before in his life had Franz wished this much to throttle anyone, but there were important reasons why he couldn't. First, she was a girl, and he would never hit a girl even if she were as annoying as this translucent green creature.

The second reason was that he was helplessly strapped, so, even if she's been some sort of brute, the only harmful thing he could do was glare.

So Franz slouched down in his seat, satisfying his fury by sending her a glare that bore the weight of a thousand hurling penknives. "During our last conversation, I believe I made it quite clear to you that I never wanted to see your ugly face again."

She "tut-tutted" at him, shaking her head. "Sorry, but I'm afraid I can't abandon you now that we're actually on our way. I knew it would all work out in the end! While this isn't perhaps the *best* way to get you there, we should arrive well before nightfall. And that leaves a whole night and a day for you to do what you need to do and save us all. I think that's plenty of time, don't you?"

Franz blinked at her, his glare melting into an expression of confusion. "Save you? What in the . . ." He squeezed his eyes shut, hoping he could squeeze the image of her out of his head for all time. But when he looked again she was still there, smiling at him. "Why are you haunting me?" he asked, his voice weak from exhaustion.

"I'm not haunting you!" she answered with a terrifying little laugh. "I've *chosen* you. You see, Franz Happernickle, you are our last hope—"

She didn't get to finish, for the coach lurched to a sudden stop. Franz tumbled from his seat onto the floor and lay stunned, his vision clouded.

Vaguely he saw the green form of the girl rise from her place on the seat and—though this could be a trick of the eye caused by the bump to his head—stick her head out through the coach roof. The rest of her body, from her shoulders down, remained visible, but she slowly turned in place, as though taking in everything to be seen outside.

Franz felt sick. The sight of her headless body gave him a better appreciation of her frightening face.

She pulled back in, and her smile was gone. "They're making the exchange," she said. "Now take care you don't let on that you can see me, because if you do, they'll know—"

She broke off with a little "Oh!" and vanished from sight just as the lock jangled and the coach door opened. Franz, still lying in an awkward heap on the floor, looked warily through the opening.

Instead of the pale, solemn-faced guards who had loaded him in at Yoleston he saw . . . a most remarkable face! Indeed, he was awe-stricken, for he had never before seen anyone so terrifyingly impressive! A tall man, youthful yet commanding, with flowing golden hair, a square jaw, and glinting grey eyes . . . the sort of man one reads about in legends but never meets in real life.

This mighty specimen reached in, caught Franz by the collar, dragged him from the coach as though he weighed no more than a small sack of beans, and set him on his feet. As Franz caught his balance, he looked up and saw . . . another one! Another amazingly powerful, broad-shouldered man speaking to the two Yoleston guards.

This second man gave Franz a quick once-over, his finely formed lip curling with distaste. "This is the lunatic?" he asked in a voice of sonorous power.

"Yes sir," said the guard captain. "Franz Happernickle."

"And what exactly is his ailment?" asked the first man, still holding

Franz's collar.

"He sees ghosts, sir," replied the guard. "They make him violent."

"Ghosts, eh?" said the second man, and turned to study Franz closely. "How many ghosts do you see, lad?"

"Don't you dare answer that!"

The voice in his ear startled Franz so that he let out a little yelp and would have jumped three paces had he not been held so firmly. He glanced sideways and saw the green girl floating at his shoulder. She shook her head and put a finger to her lips. "Don't answer them, not a word! They can't know about me or we're done for!"

"Ghost steal your tongue?" said his captor, giving Franz a shake. "Speak!"

Franz gaped up at him then shrugged. He didn't really care what the ghost girl told him, but neither did he want to admit his own lunacy in the face of this heroic figure. He felt small, foolish, and more hopeless than ever.

"It doesn't matter," said the second man, who might have been the twin of the first except that his hair was raven black instead of sun gold. He extended his hand to the guard, who gave him a stack of papers to sign. Franz watched as the exchange was made . . . and as the green ghost girl, entirely unseen by everyone else, floated up to look over the raven-haired man's shoulder.

Suddenly she put out a finger and poked him in the eye. He didn't so much as flicker an eyelash.

The papers signed, the Yoleston guard captain indicated Franz with a wave of his hand. "He's all yours!" he said with a nervous laugh.

The golden-haired man tightened his grip on Franz's collar and pushed him into motion. Only then did Franz notice the cart waiting some little ways up the dirt road. A pair of black horses stood in the harness, and somehow Franz suspected that their eyes were red and flaming behind their blinders. They just had that look about them.

Beyond the cart, the road wound away from all civilization—away from the villages and farm fields through which Franz had already traveled, albeit in darkness—into a deep, shadow-filled forest.

The road to the Black Swamp. The road to Briardale.

"Get in there, boy," said the heroic man, and shoved Franz into the back of the cart, which was basically a large cage that might be used to haul a wild animal. The second heroic man tossed a canvas over the cage, again blocking the world outside from view. Franz didn't mind—it wasn't as if he wanted a better look at the Black Swamp. Not to mention, there were probably hordes of mosquitoes in it that wanted to feast on him.

As the two men climbed into the driver's box, one said to the other, "Do you think he is the one?"

"Can't be. Doesn't look the part."

"But he sees ghosts," said the first. "And they're running out of time. Isn't tomorrow the last day? She's got to bring someone, or they might as well give up now."

"But . . . him?" said the second. "He can't possibly be a hero. Not a True Hero. Can't picture him saving kingdoms!"

With that, they urged the horses into motion. Franz, having nothing to brace himself against, fell over on his side and rolled around on the cage floor until finally managing to push himself into one corner and, using all the strength in his legs, press himself hard against the cage bars. This would be a long journey.

"They're a couple of traitors."

Franz didn't even gasp when the ghost girl appeared in the corner opposite him, sitting cross-legged in the air just above the cage floor. She folded her arms, and her ghoulish face scowled. "A couple of stinky, no-account traitors!" she repeated. "I thought they were Heroes, you understand, True Heroes. Both had slain dragons, and everyone knows that's one of the Three Great Deeds. But they failed me. Failed all of us."

"What—what are you talking about?" Franz whispered, afraid the two men might hear him through the canvas.

"Those two!" said the girl, waving her hand over Franz's head in the general direction of the heroic figures. "I chose them first, you see. I have to choose a new hero once every hundred years. To break the curse. But first one then the other succumbed to Lady Mara's temptations, and—"

Before she could finish this baffling speech, her voice was cut off by the most blood-curdling roar ever to shatter the eardrums of a living man. Surely dragons could not make such a din, nor even demons. Franz screamed—making the two men in the driver's box laugh—and flopped down on his side, trying to hide his face in the floor. The roar sounded again, and a third time. Each roar seemed to go on for an age.

At last all was quiet. Franz, his heart ramming in his throat, turned his face to look in wide-eyed dread at the ghost girl. "What was that?" he gasped, his voice nearly silenced by his own terror.

The ghost girl gave a little shrug. "Oh, that's just the Slavering Swamp Beast. Nothing for you to worry about."

Chapter 3

HOW DID *you find this place?"* the oldest fairy demanded, taking a step forward as though to protect her two younger sisters. "I placed the wards myself. You should never have so much as glimpsed Briardale from afar! Not unless invited in by a member of the household."

The Lady of Darkness only smiled. "I have eyes and ears in more places than you can possibly imagine. Though you never realized it, you practically did *invite me in."*

She took three steps into the room, her long cloak billowing behind her like tattered storm clouds. Her sweeping eye landed on the princess's still form. The spindle lay as though just fallen from her fingers, and a trickle of blood fell from the tiny wound its point had inflicted.

"I've had eighteen years," said the Lady, breathing the words like poisonous fumes, "to think what I might do to circumvent that counterspell you"—with an evil glance at the trembling youngest fairy—"dared cast to destroy my original curse. Did you think I would sit idly by all that time? My enchantments have only grown more potent and dreadful!"

She flung out her hand. Before the three fairies could even twitch their wands, dark streams of enchantment shot from the tips of the Lady's fingers, wrapping around the princess like the coils of a huge serpent.

And the princess's rose-petal complexion paled . . . then darkened to hard gray.

"What is she doing?" cried the youngest fairy, nearly dropping her wand in terror.

"She's turning her to stone!" the middle fairy replied. And she was right—for as the enchantment dissipated and drifted away, they saw their princess's image in perfect stone lying upon that floor, stone curls still covering part of her face.

But, the oldest fairy noted with some grim satisfaction, her mouth, though hard and uninviting, still lay exposed, the lips gently puckered as though waiting for a kiss.

She did not dwell upon this thought, however, for she saw then that the dark tendrils of sorcery had not dissipated. Instead, they flowed along the floor of that tower chamber, crawled up the wall, and poured out the window. With a cry of dismay, the oldest fairy leapt to the window and looked down into the courtyard below . . .

The courtyard where the king and his retinue were now dismounting and looking around for some sign of greeting from the castle inhabitants. The king himself—tall, noble, beautiful beyond the ken of mortal minds—seemed to sniff the air, his fair brow constricting. He looked up just as the first snakelike enchantment reached him, winding about his head and body before *he had time to draw breath.*

One by one, every member of that noble company—and even their noble steeds—fell under the Dark Lady's spell.

The courtyard, which only moments before had brimmed with life, was now full of statues.

The roar of the Slavering Swamp Beast still ringing in his ears, Franz pushed himself upright and faced the ghostly girl. "I-I don't believe in-in Swamp Beasts," he said at last.

He'd heard stories, of course, but stories were just . . . stories. Make believe. Harmless horrors used to frighten unruly children into obedience at bedtime or when the boiled greens looked particularly unsavory. They weren't real.

"For that matter, I don't believe in ghosts," he added.

She laughed. "How about elves? Do you believe in them?"

"No."

"Fairies?"

"No . . ."

"Heroes? Please tell me you believe in heroes."

Franz didn't answer. Maybe he was a lunatic after all. Maybe Briardale was the perfect home for him. Otherwise, how could he explain his current situation?

Her cheerful laugh reminded him of a songbird in spring, and her green, shimmery form momentarily brightened. Then it dimmed again, and her face became serious. "I don't need you to believe in me. *I* wouldn't believe in me if I could help it. Being a ghost isn't pleasant; though it has its uses where locked doors and suchlike are concerned. But I can't actually touch anything in the mortal world, which can be right frustrating at times!

And flying about disembodied loses its charm after a few centuries." She sighed heavily then shook her head. "No matter! I don't need you to believe in me, but I *do* need you to believe in heroes. More importantly, I need you to be a hero. A True Hero."

Franz considered the two mighty figures currently driving the cart, then pictured the face and form he knew from the mirror—the freckles, skinny shoulders, and sad eyes. He tended to stoop from the hours he spent each day hunched over his desk, and his fingers were permanently ink-stained.

A hero? Unlikely!

But this ride through the Black Swamp might continue for hours, and he needed something to distract his mind from the horrors no doubt waiting for him at journey's end. So he asked, "Why do you need a hero?"

"That's more like it!" said the ghost girl, rocking eagerly back and forth. "That's the curious spirit I knew you possessed!" She folded her hands like a school girl about to give a recitation. "Once upon a time," she began.

Franz interrupted her. "I don't need a story, thank you. Please, just tell me what you want with me."

"It involves a story, I'm afraid," she replied a little sharply. "So settle back and listen. Once upon a time—more than five hundred years ago, if you must know—King Pintamore of the Elves ruled this land and the three kingdoms surrounding. He was a wise and just king, beautiful, noble, beloved . . ." The girl trailed off, giving Franz a sharp look. "But you don't believe in him either, do you."

Franz shook his head. The straightjacket made him much too warm for comfort underneath that canvas, and the air of the Black Swamp was muggy. Sweat dripped down his face, tickling as it went, and he could do nothing about it. So he pressed against the cage bars in sheer misery and listened to this unbelievable tale related by this unbelievable girl.

"No matter," said she with a shrug. "Whether you believe it or not, King Pintamore was the most perfect of all perfect kings, the greatest ruler ever seen across all the magical realms. But he was a born a twin. A younger twin at that. And this proved the source of all his troubles.

"His sister, Mara—older than him by mere minutes—could not inherit the throne, due to a law set in place by the Elders many centuries ago." The ghost gazed off into some hazy distance, as if she could see the ancient king and his sister even now, right through the canvas covering. "Mara grew up with bitterness in her heart that her right to rule had been stripped away by some narrow-minded decree made by those who had never met her or her brother. Though she may have begun this life as beautiful and noble as her brother, that bitterness festered, blackening her very soul.

"No one realized what was happening, however, for Mara always wore a smiling face in public, always played the part of the deferential sister, loyal to her brother in all things. Who could have guessed at the tragedy brewing?

"You see, the royal family of the elves is gifted in magic more potent and powerful even than the magic of fairies. But in Mara, that magic took a dark turn. As her powers blossomed, they just as quickly rotted until, by the time she reached full maturity, she was already the first true and terrible sorceress seen in the living world in a millennium. Still, she kept it a close secret. Rumors abounded, but no one knew if those rumors were true . . . and no one traced them back to the king's own sister."

Despite himself, Franz was caught up in the tale. The ghost girl's straightforward but eager delivery made a fellow almost believe the impossible things she said.

"Disaster might still have been averted," the ghost girl continued. "Lady Mara might have kept her evil magic to herself, might even have eventually gotten it under control and turned back to goodness. But then the king's firstborn child was born . . . a daughter. And King Pintamore made a decision that tipped Lady Mara right over the edge.

"You see, King Pintamore had always thought it unfair that his sister should have her kingdom taken from her. He'd suspected the bitterness in her heart, however, so he made no move to protest the law or to renounce his crown, accepting it as his duty when the time came for him to rule the Elf Kingdoms. But when the baby princess was born, he thought again how wrong it would be for her to never claim her inheritance as queen, particularly if a younger brother should ever come along. Determined that she would not be likewise ill-used, he set to work rewriting the ancient law.

"It took time and effort, but on the morning of the princess's Naming Day, the good king was able to celebrate not only the reveal of his daughter's name, but also her assumption of the role of heir to the throne. When the time came, she would become Ruling Queen of the Elves."

Franz watched how the green glow around the ghost girl brightened and her eyes shone with admiration for the ancient, and probably fictitious, king. He couldn't help being moved by the story.

The ghost girl met his gaze, and her shining eyes dimmed with foreboding. "Just when the celebration was at its highest pitch—just when King Pintamore lifted his infant daughter above his head for all his court to see—that's when—"

Bang!

The cart came to an abrupt halt, and Franz fell again, this time hitting his head rather badly. Sparks danced before his eyes, and his vision darkened so that he almost couldn't see when the ghost girl got up and put her head through the canvas and cage bars. She pulled back inside again, her eyes huge. "We're here already!" she gasped. "Oh dear, I don't have any time . . . If she guesses who you are, she'll lock you up in the dungeon, and I don't know what I'll do then! I need you to make your daring escape now, if you don't mind, then follow me quickly."

Franz, still lying on his side, the jacket holding his arms in a tight self-embrace, gaped at her. "You want me to *what?*"

"Make your daring escape. Your sudden burst free," said the ghost girl, flitting this way and that, her hands clasped anxiously. "You know, like heroes do. They always burst free at the last moment."

"But . . . but . . ."

The two mighty figures outside spoke together in low murmurs. Then Franz heard the crunch as though of boots landing in gravel outside.

"Then we'll have to hide somewhere, you know," the ghost girl continued. "I'd take you directly to the tower if I could, but with the barrier in place . . . we'll need to find the missing wands before we can get through . . . Oh, *do* hurry, please."

"You're crazy!" Franz hissed, rolling onto his shoulder and struggling to get himself upright. "You're crazier than I am! I'm *not* a hero! I can't suddenly burst free of anything, and I can't—"

The canvas whipped off the cage, letting in a whole world of blinding gray swamp light. With a little "Oh!" the ghost girl vanished, leaving Franz blinking and wincing in that glare even as the two heroic figures unlatched the cage door.

"Still in there, I see," said the raven-haired one. "Not much of a hero, are you?"

"I tell you, he *is* her Chosen One," the golden-haired one replied, his deep voice full of warning. "We'd best keep a close eye on him, just in case."

The cage door creaked open. Franz, still mostly blind from the sudden light, saw huge hands reaching toward him, then found himself dragged across the cage floor and falling, falling . . .

Thwack!

His back hit the ground, and pain shot through his already battered head. He blinked once, twice . . . his gaze blackened, the world spun, and for one blessed moment he thought he might slip into unconsciousness and be able to forget the tangled web his life had become.

But it was not to be.

The darkness receded, and he found himself at a wicked wall of briars and thorns. Just beyond the wall a tall tower loomed above the swamp trees. It was an intimidating structure, especially since it was . . . upside down? Panic almost seized Franz at this sight, but then he realized that it was *he* who was wrong-side up. He had little time to revel in this newest confirmation of his sanity, though.

"Get up, little hero," said a mocking yet epic voice. Another huge hand grabbed him by his shoulder, set him on his feet, and held him upright when his knees tried to buckle. "Welcome to Briardale."

Franz gazed first upon a gothic gate of scrolled black iron then on through the gate into a courtyard full of gaping-mouthed, hollow-eyed statues. Beyond those statues rose a fortification of moss-encrusted, briar-choked stone . . . a proper home for minds gone mad.

Minds like his.

Chapter 4

THE ELDEST *fairy turned from the window, her beautiful face stricken with horror. The Dark Lady's power had grown indeed, festering into such a force of evil that she might ensorcell the king himself, so long as he was taken unawares. Such power was far too great for any one fairy to combat on her own, not even a fairy as strong as she.*

But she was not alone.

"Sisters!" she cried, lifting her wand and springing across the room to stand between the other two. "Counterspell, at once!"

The magic in their spirits brimmed, finding focus in their wands, which glowed in three different hues of glorious color. But the youngest fairy whispered, "What counterspell do you mean, exactly?"

The eldest fairy blinked, for her mind was still galloping to catch up with their circumstances. And in that moment of hesitation, the Lady threw back her head and laughed.

"Did you think," she declared, her voice made more terrible by that laugh, "that I've not had time these last eighteen years to consider what to do with you three fools as well?"

With that, she lifted her hand—for elf magic requires no wands for focus—and spoke a single harsh word: "Il've!"

The word was like a slap across the eldest fairy's face. She staggered and felt her sisters, one on each side, grab hold of her arms. Time seemed to slow, as though dragging through bog muck. The fairies could not move, could do nothing but stare in horror as an onyx ball formed in the Lady's fingers.

With a flick of her hand, the Lady sent that ball rolling through the air toward the trio. As it came, it broke into three parts—three snarling wolves made up of shadows and dark enchantment. Each wolf lunged for one of the fairies, mouths gaping wide, wider than should be possible, ready to swallow them whole.

Botheration! *the eldest fairy thought.*

Then the darkness of that wolf throat enveloped her. Tiny stings covered her face, her hands, her wings. Amidst the growing pain, the eldest fairy felt herself tilting, plummeting . . .

A thin wisp of ghostly greenness floated over the heads of the two heroic figures and the one wretched figure wrapped in a white straightjacket. She hesitated a moment, hating to abandon her Chosen One. But if she spoke to him, tried to offer him advice or comfort, he might respond . . .

And the two former heroes would know exactly what that meant. They were already too suspicious.

So the ghost—whose name was Roselee—darted away, a thin stream of ghost-smoke passing through the iron bars of the gate into the courtyard beyond. The statues standing at intervals about the yard seemed to watch her with their sad stone eyes.

Roselee shivered and looked away quickly. All those glorious, noble folk depending on her for their salvation! She had not asked for that task, and as the centuries passed, she'd begun to fear it wasn't a task she could fulfill.

Nevertheless, she paused before one particular figure. Tall, kingly, his head upraised as though even now he looked upon the dark spell that descended upon him centuries ago.

His gaze was the one Roselee most dreaded facing. But she offered her best attempt at a curtsy, which was rendered still more awkward by virtue of her insubstantiality. "This one," she whispered, "he'll be a True Hero for all of us. I promise."

Was it a promise she could keep? By sunset tomorrow they'd know for sure . . .

One of the former heroes—the raven-haired one, her first Chosen One—pounded on the iron gate, his deep voice echoing across the courtyard. "We're here, my Lady! We've brought the new one!"

A chill shuddered through Roselee's phantom being. Though she knew no one but Franz could see her, she could not help ducking behind the imposing marble figure of King Pintamore.

A door opened in the castle keep. Though it was only mid-afternoon, darkness poured into the courtyard, rendering all as gloomy as dusk.

Lady Mara appeared.

She stepped from her fortress dwelling and crossed the courtyard, her pace slow and sedate, as though the heavy robes of black shadow she wore weighed her down. Roselee had never seen her face, not once in the five hundred years since she'd awakened to find herself insubstantial, realized she was a ghost, and began haunting the grounds like a proper ghost should. Many times she had crossed paths with the sinister Mistress of Briardale, but always the Lady wore a veil. Roselee couldn't guess why. Did she hide some hideous disfigurement? Or was she a monster more terrible than a ghost or ghoul?

It hardly mattered. The veils themselves were almost more horrible than anything they might hide.

When she stood within touching distance of King Pintamore's statue—Roselee might have reached out and passed a ghostly hand through her shoulder if she dared—Lady Mara raised one arm and spoke a word of command. The iron gates creaked open.

The two former heroes dragged Franz into the yard. He tripped over his feet and certainly didn't look prepared to make a sudden burst free. That was the trouble, Roselee reflected, with picking a Chosen One based on *potential* heroism rather than actual mighty deeds. He lacked the practice necessary to get on with things.

Poor Franz! He'd been through so much in the last week since she first began appearing to him in Mr. Teabody's office. But she knew, she just *knew* that he possessed every quality of an honest-to-goodness True Hero!

If only he could realize that potential . . .

The poor lad could hardly lift his head as the two former heroes pushed him to his knees before the Lady. When he did manage to look up, he averted his eyes almost immediately, trembling with dread at the sight of those awful veils.

The Lady loomed over him, silent as death. At last she said, "What is the nature of your malady, poor boy?"

The sweetness of her words merely underscored the poison in her voice. Roselee ducked her face into stone King Pintamore's shoulder and shuddered. The Lady could neither see nor sense her, but not even five hundred years had helped Roselee overcome her dread of the sorceress.

But would Franz be taken in by that honeyed tone? Others had been . . . two heroes and many, many more besides!

Though she hated to look, Roselee forced herself to peer over the king's shoulder again to see what took place. So much rested on these next few moments. If the Lady believed that this new human inmate was merely a lunatic sent to Briardale for health and healing, she would simply put him in with the other inmates. There were no chains or complex locks to those rooms, and even an unpracticed hero like Franz should be able to figure out a way to break free, with a few helpful hints from a ghostly friend.

But if the Lady realized who he was, if she realized who had orchestrated his coming to Briardale . . .

Franz tried again to look up at his strange hostess. This time he maintained his gaze. "I . . . I . . ." he stammered, trying to figure out how to answer the question put to him.

And Roselee could only whisper into the stone fabric of Pintamore's tunic, "Don't tell her. Don't tell her, Franz!"

Though she knew the Lady could not hear her, she dared not call out; for if the Lady saw Franz suddenly perk up as if listening to a voice no one else heard, she would know at once! Roselee urged him in whispers, her whole spirit begging him to heed her. "Don't tell her that you can see me!"

Perhaps he understood her even across the distance, because not another word crossed his lips. He simply knelt there gaping like a codfish on market day. Roselee could have kissed him in relief.

Her relief was short-lived, however. For the golden-haired former hero cleared his throat and said, "I believe, my Lady, that he's been seeing . . . her."

Batwings and bug shells! Roselee pounded an insubstantial fist against

Pintamore's shoulder. How had she ever been stupid enough to choose *that* one as her True Hero?

The Lady's silence was weirdly expressive even without a glimpse of her face. At last she said, "*This* one? A *hero?*"

"Well," said the former hero with a nervous shrug, "the news from Yoleston is that he sees ghosts. And they've got to be pretty desperate by now, with the Magic Cycle almost complete."

"Desperate, yes," the Lady whispered. "But I didn't think they'd be . . . *idiotic.*"

Simmering with wrath, Roselee narrowed her eyes at the sorceress. Franz wasn't as terribly unheroic as all that! Maybe no one else saw in him what *she* saw, but that didn't mean . . . didn't mean . . .

Drat. The former hero was correct. She was desperate. At her wits' end, in fact.

The Lady tilted her head as if to look down upon Franz. She folded her arms, the sleeves of her midnight cloak wafting like a rook's wings. "Tell me, boy, and tell me truthfully," she said. "Are you a hero?"

Franz gulped, his Adam's apple bobbing impressively. Then he shook his head and pushed a few frightened words from his throat. "There aren't any heroes anymore . . . are there?"

"Let us hope not," the Lady replied. Her interest in Franz used up, she addressed her two henchmen. "My army is big enough. One more lunatic won't make a difference, and we're so close to the end that it's best to take no chances. Send him to the dungeon and lock him away with the other two. Come sunset tomorrow we'll deal with all of them . . . once and for all."

Roselee's hopes plummeted. She watched as the two former heroes dragged Franz to his feet and half carried him across the courtyard. Away from the statues. Away from the tower. Away down a winding stair into labyrinthine passages and cells where the sun never shone.

Still Franz didn't make a sudden burst free. He simply hung there, suspended between those mighty arms. He cast a desperate glance about, his eyes searching for something . . . Wait, did he look for her?

Roselee couldn't even bring herself to come out from behind Pintamore. She watched her Chosen One until he vanished through the door and down the stairs into the bowels of Briardale.

Then she twisted and looked at the tower high overhead, where three fairies and a stone princess even now awaited her return, eager for word that this time, *finally,* she had managed to do something right.

Heaving a sigh, she drifted up on the breeze, reluctant yet determined to admit her failure.

The atmosphere hung heavy with clouds, and streaks of lightning licked at the sky. Ignoring this threatening display, Roselee rose up and up until she reached the tower's balcony. She peered through the window.

The same gloomy grey light that shrouded the whole of Briardale that dismal day revealed a humble chamber used only for storage back in the day. If Roselee remembered the story correctly, it had been empty when the princess crept up the tower stairs five hundred years ago . . . except for a spinning wheel, which should not have been there, standing in the center of the chamber.

The spinning wheel stood there still. Otherwise the room held only a few old crates and boxes . . . and the beautiful girl upon the floor, sleeping away the centuries. Once the stone curse struck, the princess had been far too heavy for anyone to lift. So there she remained, her hand outstretched as though she had only just dropped the spindle, waiting for her True Hero to come along and kiss her.

Roselee didn't remember the princess from the time before she woke up and discovered herself to be a ghost. In fact, her memories were so few that she'd had to trust the three Guardians to explain events to her as best they could. She couldn't help thinking that all of this was quite a lot of bother for one rather spoiled girl . . . however beautiful she might be!

"Roselee, what are you doing out there?" a sharp voice hissed.

Roselee looked from the sleeping statue to the spinning wheel. It stood just where it had first been discovered five hundred years earlier, its wheel now spinning in a steady, unaltered rhythm. On the floor beside it sat a tiny, fluffy-tailed squirrel . . . a squirrel wearing a dress, a mobcap, and a sour expression on her whiskered grey face as her front paws pressed and pressed at the treadle, keeping the wheel moving.

Shame filled Roselee to brimming at the sight of that cranky little face. How desperately she had hoped to return to the tower with better news . . . and with the True Hero right behind her. Instead, she floated outside the window empty-handed, as it were.

She opened her mouth . . . and closed it again.

The squirrel *harrumphed* and returned her attention to the wheel. "So I assume you brought a new one. Where is he then? Please do not tell me that look on your face means he's he already fallen prey to Lady Mara's persuasions and betrayed us?"

"Oh no, not at all!" Roselee answered at once. She tried to rush forward, forgetting herself. As a result her nose hit, not the window glass— which she could pass through as easily as smoke—but an invisible barrier. A barrier as solid as stone; more solid, in fact, for it could keep out mortal and immortal, the living and the dead. No one passed through that boundary.

"Ouch," Roselee groaned, and floated back again, rubbing her nose.

The squirrel continued to push the treadle, eyeing Roselee from beneath the spinning wheel. "So, our last Chosen One," she said, the faintest trace of anxiety tingeing her dry voice. "Our final hope. A True Hero."

The color of Roselee's cheeks deepened to a rich emerald. "Yes, absolutely," she said with less conviction than she should.

The squirrel narrowed her eyes. "Has he saved a kingdom?"

"No . . ."

"Slain a dragon?"

"Um . . ."

Guardian Alicia chittered, her huge front teeth rattling together. "Tell me, dear Roselee, tell me that he has, at the very least, moved a mountain!"

Once again Roselee opened her mouth . . . and closed it.

The squirrel let out a squeak that brought dust raining down from the rafters. Two lumps among the abandoned crates stirred, snorted, clucked, and two sleepy heads reared from the shadows, blinking round at the gloomy chamber.

Then, with a ruffle of feathers, a chicken jumped to her feet. She bobbed her head this way and that, the pointed peak of the elegant cap she wore fluttering with veils. She pranced out of the shadows into the gloomy light in the center of the room, leaving her companion to follow in her wake. This companion gave an enormous yawn, a long sticky tongue flicking momentarily from her open mouth and licking her eyeball. Then, with a little shake of her sinewy body, a lithe spotted lizard wearing a furry purple coat darted out after the chicken.

"What's wrong, Alicia?" the chicken clucked, approaching the spinning wheel. She noted the direction of the squirrel's gaze and followed it to the window. "Oh, hullo, Roselee dear!"

"Hullo, Guardian Lolly," Roselee answered glumly.

"Roselee! Oh, Roselee!" exclaimed the lizard, sitting upright, using her tail for balance, and clasping her front claws together eagerly. "You're back, dear Roselee! Where is the hero? Have you brought the hero? Have you found our wands?"

"Hush your babble, Viola," snapped Alicia, pushing so viciously at the treadle that the wheel whirred in a blur. She trained a bright black eye on the glum-faced ghost. "All right, girl. Out with it. If he's not saved a kingdom, slain a dragon, or moved a mountain"—the chicken and the lizard gasped in dismay at this—"what exactly *has* your hero done to make him a True Hero?"

Roselee's ghostly form faded until she almost disappeared into thin air. How could she explain in the face of Alicia's justifiable wrath? How could she defend her choice when she hardly understood it herself? The first two heroes she'd chosen because they'd slain dragons. But they had both betrayed the cause, joining forces with Lady Mara. Her third hero had also slain a dragon—albeit a very small one—and the fourth had moved a mountain, an actual *mountain*.

But while those two had remained true-hearted to the last, neither had succeeded in penetrating the tower barrier before the time was up. And with not only Lady Mara's enchantments but also the two former heroes to contend with—not to mention the Slavering Swamp Beast, more terrible by far than any dragon Roselee had ever seen—well, it was a lot to ask of a fellow, True Hero or otherwise.

The point was, brawn and courage had failed. And with the end of the Magic Cycle looming and the fate of all Briardale's inhabitants left in her insubstantial hands, Roselee had gone in search of her final Chosen One full of despair.

Until she'd seen a red-haired lad walking down the streets of Yoleston. Not an especially impressive specimen, threadbare and hunch-shouldered, hands in his pockets. Nothing for her to particularly note.

But just as she'd made ready to float on by, continuing her desperate search, she'd seen him turn off the street and enter a dank alley where a creature in rags huddled on a doorstep. A figure so smelly that everyone else who even caught sight of it hastened to the other side of the road!

Not this fellow. As Roselee watched, amazed, she'd seen the young man kneel and lay his hand on the creature's shoulder. A wrinkled old face lifted from the rags, hideous to behold with boils and the ravages of poverty.

"Here, good mother," Franz Happernickle had said, plunging his hand back into his pocket and pulling out every coin he owned, which were few indeed. He pressed them into the crone's withered hand. "Have a meal and a night's rest somewhere, for me?" And he'd smiled sweetly.

"Bless you, Franz!" the old woman had croaked, just as though she knew him. As though this was a regular part of her sad, miserable life, the one part that brought a grin to her toothless face.

"Don't mention it," he'd replied, and planted a kiss on that fetid, lice-ridden head.

He'd gone without supper that night.

"Maybe . . ." Roselee whispered even as the three Guardians—squirrel, chicken, and lizard—stared at her with earnest dismay, ". . . maybe there's more to being a hero than saving kingdoms and things. Maybe a True Hero needs a true heart . . ."

Her words trailed off into the sky.

Viola blinked enormous eyes. Then she burst into tears, wailing, "We're all *doomed!*"

"Come now, Viola," Lolly clucked, putting a wing around the lizard's back. "Stiff upper lip, what, what? We've faced so much already, we don't want to lose our heads now, do we?"

Alicia ignored her two sisters. Her work at the treadle had slowed to a more sedate pace, but the wheel kept spinning even as it had for centuries now. Oddly enough, Roselee saw a considering look on her furry face.

"Tell me one thing, girl," the squirrel said. "Is our last Chosen One . . ." She paused as though hating to ask the question, then spoke all in a rush. "Please tell me that he isn't *human*."

Roselee didn't answer. Which was all the answer Alicia needed.

"Batwings and buzzards!" The squirrel's voice was more mournful than angry by now. "Bad though your memory is, you do *know* how susceptible humans are! Look what happened the other times you picked a human hero. At least the last two didn't turn on us!"

"Franz won't turn," Roselee declared staunchly. She may not be able to promise much, but this she knew. "He'll be true to the cause . . . just as soon as he knows what the cause *is* exactly."

"What good does that do us?" Lolly demanded, the feathers round her neck ruffling. "If he's not a True Hero, it doesn't matter if he finds the wands, doesn't matter if he gets through the barrier, doesn't matter if he kisses the princess until his lips turn black and blue! Viola's counterspell was specific: Only the kiss of a True Hero will break the curse. All of the curses!"

Viola sobbed even harder, hiccupping so violently that her tongue shot out. Alicia merely closed her eyes and muttered something like a prayer for patience before asking Roselee one last question. "So . . . where is he, exactly?"

Roselee wished she could melt away into thin air. It took all her will-power to remain visible. "Lady Mara sent him down to the dungeons."

"*Doomed!*" cried Viola.

Even Lolly shook her head, clucking sadly. "Viola's probably right. Don't see much hope for any of us now. We'll all be turned to dust. Without King Pintamore to stop her, Lady Mara will set upon the kingdoms with her horde of lunatics . . ."

But Alicia went right on pressing the treadle. She flicked her bushy tail, a strangely commanding gesture coming from her. "All right, Roselee," she said. "Maybe your choice isn't one any of us would make. But you're our only hope now."

Roselee dared a hasty glance the squirrel's way, meeting those stern black eyes.

"Go fetch him at once!" said the fairy, lifting one paw in a sweeping motion.

Galvanized to action, Roselee offered a sharp salute and slipped away down the side of the tower. She would fetch him! Somehow! She would get him out of that dungeon, and she would help him find his way up and through the barrier! Somehow!

Franz might not be anyone else's idea of a hero . . . but maybe, just maybe, he didn't *need* to be.

Chapter 5

THE DARK *Lady gazed down upon the fallen forms of the three fairies. She laughed to see them, still recognizably themselves, yet wearing new faces, new bodies. Ah, but it was the perfect spell to deal with those meddlers!*

She turned from them to survey the stone princess. The enchantment had almost completely taken her over now, her and her royal father! Their outer shapes were already hard as rock, and the spell crept now into their veins, down to their hearts.

And when their hearts were stone, they would die. No one could stand in her way to the throne then! No one would dare!

"Any moment," Lady Mara purred, her smile ghastly to behold. She knelt, reaching out a hand to touch the top of the princess's stone head. "Any

moment now, your soul will slip away. And then—"

ZING!

The Lady clenched her hand, feeling a sting as if a needle had been plunged into it. Whirling around, she snarled as she saw . . . the impossible!

The three fairies—one a lizard, one a chicken, and one a bristling, furious squirrel—stood awkwardly on their strange new limbs. The squirrel clutched a silver wand in her dexterous little paws.

"You may change our bodies," she squeaked ferociously, "but you cannot change what we are!"

Even as she spoke, the lizard wrapped her whole body and tail around her wand, and the chicken picked hers up in her beak. Lady Mara stared, aghast. But surely, with such altered forms, they would not be able to tame their wild fairy magic even with the wands to assist them!

She raised a hand to cast another spell, something to send all three little creatures flying across the room and out the window. But to her dismay, she realized that her powers were momentarily drained! Casting that enormous petrification curse—one that could even overwhelm her own brother—had depleted her strength.

"No!" she cried even as the squirrel waved her wand.

"I set free the spirits of those turned to stone," declared the squirrel. "Liberated from their stone bodies, they shall live on in this world, always near. And once the curse on the princess is broken, all shall be restored!"

So saying, she held the wand as straight upright as her little arms could manage. Instantly the wand began to burn bright until, with another ZING, hundreds of tiny lights shot up from it, flying out the window and every which way, including a group of lights that fell upon the princess like snowflakes.

Lady Mara felt a chill clutch her heart even as she watched the glittering fall of enchantment. But she snarled through her fears, "Fool! I know how your fairy magic works! The Magic Cycle lasts only five hundred years, then *all your efforts will come undone. I have only to wait until then, have only to prevent a True Hero from reaching the princess's side in that time. Then the stone curse will come to completion, and I shall win anyway!" She smiled again, her confidence growing even as she spoke. "How many heroes will you lure here for me to kill until the Magic Cycle ends?"*

"BWAAAWK! Bwok-bwok-bwok!" a valiant voice clucked defiantly. Lady Mara turned, her lips curled in a snarl, and saw the chicken, a wand gripped in her beak, fling a stream of glittering magic directly at her. Even as she did so, the lizard, standing at her sister's side, cried, "And we curse you, Lady Mara, to die the moment you cause the death of another soul throughout this Magic Cycle!" In a whisper she added, "That's what you meant to say, right, Lolly?"

The chicken ruffled her feathers in a shrug. But Lady Mara did not hear her answer, for the ribbons of shimmering light struck her full in the face, knocking her from her feet.

Just when Franz thought he couldn't feel any worse, he realized how foolish such a thought was. If all that had happened to him wasn't bad enough, now he could not even comprehend his surroundings. He was vaguely aware of being dragged down a spiraling stair, of red torchlight punctuating deep gloom. His skin shivered with cold and damp. But all of this seemed to pass over him in such waves of dread that afterwards he could recall none of it.

Awareness returned when he found himself in a gloomy corridor so cavernous that the very echoes of his breath seemed to resound around him forever. They must be deep beneath the foundations of Briardale now. If not for a bobbing sphere of lantern light approaching from the middle distance, Franz could well believe they'd done away with him, and an angel was making his way to take him to a happier place. But the thought of being dead was even less pleasant than being in an asylum.

Come now, the reasonable side of his mind protested in the midst of this madness. *Aren't lunatics sent here supposedly to rest and recover? An actual* dungeon *is just a bit much . . .*

"Ho there!" boomed one of the heroic figures—the golden-haired one, Franz thought, though it was difficult to tell them apart in the dark. "Dungeon keeper! We have a new one for you."

The swinging lantern, now much nearer, revealed the person carrying it. Such an ungainly creature he was! A tall man, but hunched over as though the weight of gloom itself had bowed him almost to breaking point. His ears were large and pointed, and his eyes, ringed by dark hollows, bugged out from a pale face. Deep lines scored the sides of his thin-lipped mouth, though otherwise his skin was smooth, if clammy. He wasn't old . . . but his eyes were ancient.

He bowed to the two heroes, saying nothing. He did not even look at Franz.

"Another hero for your collection," spoke one of the henchmen—the raven-haired one this time, Franz guessed. "See that he's properly restrained and all."

"Don't worry, little hero," the golden-haired man said, slapping Franz on the shoulder. "You won't be staying here long. The Magic Cycle is almost up, and then . . ." He ended in a chuckle that wasn't at all nice.

The dungeon keeper blinked. He reached out his free hand, the one not holding the lantern, and took hold of Franz by a straight-jacketed arm. With a silent nod, he indicated that Franz should walk with him.

Though he hadn't exactly the fondest of feelings for the two traitorous heroes, Franz found himself reluctant to leave their mighty company in exchange for this miserable new companion. But it wasn't as though he had much choice.

So he fell into step beside the dungeon keeper, who shuffled along the dark passage. The lantern offered feeble illumination, but the dungeon keeper seemed to know exactly where he was going.

He stopped suddenly before a low door with a barred window. With an old key he forced the lock open, and the door creaked on its hinges as though it hadn't been opened in a hundred years.

Perhaps it hadn't.

Total darkness waited on the far side of the door. Franz stood as though on the doorstep of Hades. Was this to be his fate? Shut away in this blind hole, lost forever, forgotten? And all for . . . for nothing?

A hand patted him on the shoulder. Franz looked around and, to his surprise, saw real sympathy in the dungeon keeper's gaze. With a little shake of his head, the bug-eyed fellow reached behind Franz and undid a few straps. For the first time in many hours, Franz was able to draw a full, deep breath. The straightjacket slipped off him into the dungeon keeper's hands.

"Th-thank you!" Franz gasped.

The dungeon keeper shrugged. Then, with a firm push, he propelled Franz into the dungeon cell.

The door creaked shut, slamming in its frame with a final clang. Franz felt as though he'd been shut into his tomb. Maybe he *was* dead. Maybe that's what had caused all this trouble. Maybe seeing ghosts—or one particular obnoxious ghost—was a result of his fatal disease, and everything horrible that had happened to him since was only a terrible afterlife? Maybe—

"So what's your name?"

"*AHHHHHHHHHHHHHHHH!*" Franz dropped to his knees, hands over his head. His heart pounded in his ears, and his blood raced so fast, he thought he might burn up with the pressure.

"You're a skittish one. Come now, there's no need for such dramatics."

The voice that had spoken didn't sound particularly threatening. Indeed, it was quite friendly, a distant part of Franz's fear-strained mind realized.

Then a light was struck. Its flare was so bright that Franz had to shut his eyes, and even then the glow penetrated painfully through his eyelids. But the pain soon lessened, and he found himself able to squint at the world from his crouched position on the cell floor.

An enormously powerful person stood over him, grinning a friendly grin. He wasn't actually any taller than Franz, but his muscles bulged beneath dark brown skin, and his shoulders, wider even than the shoulders of the two traitorous heroes, looked as though they could lift whole mountains. His arms were log-crushingly huge.

Strangely, however, the foremost thing Franz noticed about this stranger was the gleaming pin he wore on his shirtfront, a gold pin topped in a blue gem the size of a thumbnail. Light from the newly lit lantern gleamed off this gem, making it wink like a bright little eye.

"Blast it, Crete!" a second voice snarled, startling Franz and sending him peering into the shadows beyond the massive young man. "Shut that light off! I swear, I almost *had* it this time, but you threw off my concentration!"

"I want to see the new chap," the enormous fellow replied, still grinning down at Franz. He knelt, bringing his brown face down on a level with Franz's freckled one. "So you're a hero, right?"

Franz blinked like an owl. Then he shook his head vehemently. "Of course I'm not!" he said, raising his hands as though to defend himself against these accusations, which were somehow worse than the accusations of lunacy he'd faced in Yoleston. "Why does everyone keep bringing up heroes around here? I'm a banker's clerk, that's all! I check lists and write on ledgers and incredibly boring things like that!"

A stamp of feet, and the second figure stepped into the sphere of lamplight. Franz stared so hard that his eyeballs nearly popped from their sockets. For this person was a dwarf! Not even half as tall as Franz, broad and strong, with angry blue eyes and a bristling beard. An actual *dwarf!*

Franz couldn't help the little exclamation of surprise that burst from his lips.

The dwarf uttered a vicious curse. "Don't tell me you can *see* me."

Franz swallowed back further exclamations, gulping hard. "Um," he managed. "Um . . . yes?"

"You mean," said the dwarf, his face darkening with an angry red flush, "I'm still *visible?*"

He looked so enraged that Franz didn't know how to answer. But, as the little man continued to steam, Franz started to piece everything together: *Wait. I'm in a lunatic asylum. That's why they're all talking about heroes and things. They're all mad!*

And this dwarf wasn't a dwarf at all, surely! He was simply a very short man suffering from a delusion of invisibility.

While this realization did little to calm Franz's frantically beating heart, it at least gave him something reasonable to grasp onto. "Oh, wait," he said, speaking slowly as though to a child. "No, you're right. I *can't* see you at all. Is . . . is someone there?"

The dwarf's face brightened. "Really?"

"No," growled the muscular fellow, and smacked Franz up the back of the head. Though the blow was gentle enough, it knocked Franz forward, and he barely kept his nose from striking the floor. "Don't give him false hope," the big fellow said. "That's not nice."

"Liars," snarled the dwarf, flinging up his hands and stumping out of the circle of lamplight. Muttering to himself, he struck another light, and the glow of two lanterns now filled the cell. Franz, still on his hands and knees, now had a much better view of his prison.

It wasn't all that bad. Dark, cramped, windowless, yes; but three beds stood along each wall, the covers basically clean. Chains hung from iron rings in the ceiling, but they were rusty with disuse. On one of the beds, a thick, leather-bound book lay open to an illustrated page. On the floor near both walls sat several little bowls of milk.

This last sight gave Franz pause. Bowls of milk? On the floor? Were they expected to eat like . . . like animals?

The big fellow, noting the direction of Franz's gaze, said, "For the rats, you know. Prisoners need a hobby. Like taming rats." Franz gave him an uncomprehending look, and the big fellow shrugged his vast shoulders. "We've got to pass the time somehow, right? Mutey tries to help us as best he can."

"Who . . . who's Mutey?" Franz croaked, sitting upright and tucking his hands under his armpits. He didn't quite feel up to standing yet.

"Mutey. The dungeon keeper. Don't know his real name, so we call him Mutey on account of he can't speak," the big fellow replied. "He's a good sort. Ugly as sin, sure, but a good sort. He gives us lamps and oil. Sneaks in extra food and milk for the rats. That kind of thing. He even gave us a book once. It's got nice pictures."

Franz glanced at the open book on the bed again. But he wasn't interested in literature of any kind at that moment. "And . . . and who are you two?" he asked.

"I'm Crete," said the big fellow, tapping a hand to his chest. "I'm from the Kingdom of Homunculi."

"Hom—Homunculi?" Franz repeated. "Where's that?"

Much to his astonishment, Crete took the pin off the front of his shirt and held it out to Franz. The bright jewel gleamed like a slice of summer sky.

Crete pointed at it. "There," he said. "Right down there. If you look really, *really* close, you can just make out the tallest peak, Mount Homunglous. On a clear day you can see the whole Homunglic range! My hometown is in the foothills, the king's own city."

Franz blinked. His gaze flicked from the jewel to Crete's face and back again. So this man was a lunatic too! But of course he was. They were all lunatics here in Briardale. It stood to reason.

"It's . . . great," he offered weakly.

Across the room, the dwarf snorted. "He doesn't believe you."

Crete put the pin back on his shirt, patting it affectionately even as he tossed the dwarf a sour glare. "He doesn't believe you can turn invisible either. No one does, actually!"

"What, you can see me *now?*" the dwarf demanded, sitting upright on his bed, his eyebrows bristling with ire.

"Yes, Eidor. We can see you." Crete indicated the dwarf with a jerk of his thumb, saying to Franz, "This is Eidor. He's a dwarf, if you couldn't guess. Son of the King Under the Low Ceiling."

"Yeah. I'm a blooming prince," Eidor snarled, crossing his arms and slumping back against the wall.

"More to the point, he's a True Hero," Crete said, nodding sagely. "Moved an entire mountain overnight once, he did! That's the stuff of True Heroes."

Franz gaped at the two of them, his mouth hanging open like a broken trapdoor. How had he, a simple clerk, ended up in this windowless dungeon cell, flanked by genuine lunatics? This was madness! Out-and-out madness.

"As for me," Crete continued, crossing the room to take a seat on one of the other beds and leaning back against the headboard, "I killed a dragon once. The Slitherer of Homunculi, as the bards named it!"

"About the size of a speck, wasn't it?" Eidor asked nastily.

Crete gave him a withering stare. "It's all a matter of perspective. It was big to me, I tell you! And I killed it and claimed my place as True Hero of Homunculi. It was soon after that when . . . when *she* showed up."

A little shiver raced up Franz's spine. He pulled himself to his feet and, moving shakily, made his way to the nearest available bed, the one on which the open book lay. Pushing this to one side, he took a seat, drawing his feet up under him cross-legged. "She?" he asked. "Do you mean . . . do you mean the green ghost?"

"Ah!" said Crete with a triumphant gleam in his eye. "See, Eidor? I told you he was a True Hero too."

"He doesn't look like one," Eidor grumped.

"Neither do you or I to most folks in this world," Crete answered, waving this protest aside easily. "True Heroism is about the Great Deeds, not appearances." He turned back to Franz. "So she found you like she did us, huh? Looking for a True Hero to wake the princess."

"To . . . to wake the what?" Franz repeated.

Crete went on as though he hasn't spoken. "I saw her too . . . must be a hundred years ago now! She was pretty desperate by then and came all the way to Homunculi, looking for someone who could break the curse. I thought it would be an appropriate follow-up deed to dragon-slaying, so I agreed to try." His cheerful face creased suddenly with sadness. "I made a good go of it. Fought through the traitorous former-heroes. Dodged Lady Mara's evil enchantments. I even eluded the Slavering Swamp Beast! But . . . well, I couldn't make it through the barrier. Just couldn't do it! Roselee— that's the ghost girl, you know—said we had to find the missing fairy wands before the barrier could be broken. I couldn't find them in time, though. The sun set on the last day of the four hundredth year of the Magic Cycle, and my chance was gone."

Franz realized he'd been staring so hard that his eyes were drying out.

He rubbed them with the back of one hand. He wanted to ask questions but couldn't think what to ask. Crete sounded so . . . so *sincere*. As sincere as he'd sounded when pointing out his kingdom on the head of a pin.

Eidor chuckled, twitching his mustache. "The look on your face! What? Did you think you'd do any better than the rest of us? Didn't the ghost girl warn you what happened to her other Chosen Ones?"

"You . . . you were a Chosen One too?" Franz asked weakly.

Eidor nodded. "My try was two hundred years ago now, I'm guessing. It's hard to say. Time passes weirdly here in Briardale; doesn't feel like more than a few months. But yeah. I had the same trouble as Crete here: Couldn't find the wands. Couldn't get through the barrier. Then my time was up, and Lady Mara threw me in here to wait."

Though he was quite certain he didn't want to know the answer, Franz couldn't help asking, "To wait for what?"

Crete and Eidor exchanged glances. Then Crete answered in a most reluctant voice: "Truth is, once the Magic Cycle ends tomorrow night, Lady Mara will have us all killed. You too, of course."

Chapter 6

"WELL DONE, Lolly. Well done, Viola," said the squirrel, scampering over to the fallen form of Lady Mara. The sorceress twitched, her eyes blinking rapidly, but for the moment she lay numb, the stunning force of the fairy spell flowing through her. "That's taken care of her for the time being. Now, if we all work together, I'm sure we can think of a more complete binding to restrain her through the Magic Cycle, which should give us plenty of time to find a True Hero—"

She broke off suddenly, and all three animals turned at the sound of footsteps on the stair. They had thought themselves completely alone in the tower. Who else could possibly be lurking nearby?

A tall, commanding figure appeared in the doorway. He was slim and elegant yet powerful as well, and his face was beautiful beyond the beauty of *mere mortals, his eyes shining with the elf-light of distant stars.*

He twisted his hat in his hands.

"Why, dear boy!" the chicken clucked, recovering herself more quickly than the other two. "What are you doing here? As you see, we're in a pickle, and you might want to come back later. The curse has fallen, and . . ." Her voice faded to nothing as realization caught up with her.

The squirrel sprang forward, her front teeth chattering with fury, for she had guessed the truth a little sooner than the other two. "You!" she squeaked up at the beautiful young man. "You were our princess's friend! She trusted you! You . . . you're practically a member of the household!"

"What's going on? What's happening?" the poor lizard begged, swiveling her huge eyes from chicken to squirrel and back again. "I don't understand!"

"He let Lady Mara into Briardale," Lolly answered, her voice strangely dark and dangerous coming from a chicken beak. "He's the one who betrayed us all."

"Oh, surely not!" the lizard exclaimed, sitting upright on her tail and clasping her little clawed hands. "He's our princess's best friend! He could never do such a thing, could never let the curse catch up with her! Could you?" she added with a forlorn glance up at the beautiful young man's face.

He could not meet her gaze. "I'm sorry, Auntie Viola. I'm sorry, Auntie Alicia, Auntie Lolly." He gulped and lifted a hand.

Before any of the three fairies quite realized what was happening, he uttered a few words in a dark tongue—the dark elf language of sorcery. Power shot from his fingertips, three jagged lines of rippling shadow that struck each fairy in the heart. They stood not as stone, but frozen. Only their eyes moved, turning this way and that as though trying to see some way out of this new dilemma.

An evil laugh filled the tower chamber. Lady Mara, recovered from the stunning blow dealt her, rose up, her dark robes billowing about her feet. "Did you think," she said, sneering down at the three fairies, "that I would not prepare myself in case of weakened magic? Lady fairies, meet my loyal apprentice!"

Three pairs of furious eyes glared up at the young man. "You thought him nothing more than the princess's sweet little friend," the Lady said, her voice mocking and horrible. "You thought him harmless and innocent as a lamb. But he has been my servant all along!"

Even as the sorceress's laughter rang out like the tolling of funeral bells, the apprentice hung his head in shame, unable to so much as look at the fallen form of the stone princess.

The Dark Mistress of Briardale passed like a shadow through the passages of her abode. The old castle was not her favorite choice of headquarters, but following the events of five hundred years ago, she had thought it best to remain at the center of things until the Magic Cycle ended. It was a cramped, moldy sort of place in the most ill-begotten corner of the kingdom.

Little wonder her foolish brother had elected to hide his precious daughter here all those centuries ago.

Lady Mara held her head high as she strode along the corridor like a queen moving through the streets of her kingdom. Voices sounded through the heavily barred doors on either side—wild, ranting voices of the lunatics she had collected over the last several centuries.

The mortals in these parts had needed a convenient place to send their madmen and madwomen. Why not to Briardale Castle, where the Mistress welcomed all with open arms?

The Lady smiled behind her veils, listening to the animal-like howling on either side of her. Those who had not been mad when they arrived, she'd quickly turned mad using her evil arts. What a fine, ravening army they would be when the Magic Cycle ended! Not even the remaining elf hosts—who had all gone into hiding when the curse took their king—would stand against her.

She would wear the crown at last. The time was so near, she could taste it! Tomorrow at sunset her wait would end. Only twenty-four hours to go . . .

A dark, scuttling form caught her eye as it tried to dart out of her way into the shadows. She whipped out an arm, caught the figure by one big ear, and hauled him before her. The bug-eyed dungeon keeper cowered before her, falling to his knees and wringing his long-fingered hands.

"It is sunset," the Lady snarled down at him. "Time to bring in the Slavering Swamp Beast. Don't imagine you can slack off in your duties now, just because the Cycle is almost at an end!"

The dungeon keeper nodded, his lips moving soundlessly, his whole body cringing away from her.

Lady Mara chuckled. Even after all this time the sight of his ugly face still amused her! And when the Cycle ended and all the fairies' magic vanished? Oh, then she would have her proper revenge upon him! Everyone would see how she dealt with those of her servants who dared defy her will.

She slapped him hard across his pasty face. "Go on!" she snarled. "Fetch in the Beast."

Her slave crawled away to follow her orders. Lady Mara, still smiling, continued on her way down the corridor.

She passed out of the castle proper into the courtyard, making her way across the paving stones and between the assorted statues of those who had once been her friends and fellow courtiers. All those noble elf lords and ladies who had not raised a finger when her crown was snatched practically from her head and placed on the head of her brother. They deserved everything that was coming to them . . . tomorrow night . . .

And him. Pintamore himself, standing there with that shocked expression on his face. How little had he expected his sister to summon a power potent enough to rival his own! Lady Mara paused before his statue, studying the marble visage she knew and loathed so well.

"How aware are you, deep down in that stone?" she whispered. "Since that foolish Alicia set your spirit free, have you been watching all that I do? Have you seen the heroes try and fail again and again? Have you seen this last, most pathetic hero who even now languishes in my dungeon?" She reached up and patted her brother's hard cheek. "I hope you do see all and see it well, dear Pintamore," she snarled. "And I hope you are counting the minutes until sunset tomorrow as eagerly as I am!"

With that, she moved on to the tower doorway only a few yards away. She opened it and climbed the long spiral staircase. The barrier she had set in place was so strong that not even she could pass it. But the door to the uppermost chamber stood open, and Lady Mara might pause just outside the barrier and look into that dismal little room.

She saw the sleeping princess, waiting there even as she had first fallen. Beside the princess, curled up in little balls of fur and feathers, lay two of her guardians, sleeping. And in the center of the room stood the spinning wheel with a lizard in a purple fur coat pushing, pushing at its treadle to keep it going.

"Are you still at that useless task, little fairy?" Lady Mara asked with a cruel chuckle.

Startled, Viola almost lost her rhythm; but then she stiffened her tiny spine and redoubled her efforts, refusing to look Lady Mara's way.

At the sound of the sorceress's voice, Alicia's head appeared from behind her fluffy tail, and she sat upright, straightening her mobcap with one paw. "What are you doing here, Mara?" she demanded, her squeaky voice waking the chicken, who pulled her head out from under her wing.

Lady Mara smiled hugely at the sight of those three absurd creatures (though no one could see her smile behind her veils). Even now, almost five hundred years later, she felt a thrill of satisfaction over a curse well executed. "I came to see if you still persisted in spinning that wheel," she said with a careless shrug. "After all, your doom is certain now. Come sunset tomorrow you will all turn to dust, no matter what! Why prolong the inevitable? You might as well give up."

At Lady Mara's words, the chicken ruffled up her feathers and marched to the treadle, where she began to assist the lizard, spinning the wheel faster than ever. Alicia nodded proudly at this gesture and folded her tiny squirrel arms over her chest.

"Go away, Mara," she said. "You may gloat and preen all you like. But good will triumph in the end!"

A sliver of anxiety passed through Mara's heart at these bold words, but she shook it off. "Do you still believe that somehow the curse will be broken? Your little ghost girl has failed again! She brought the most feeble of all heroes—hardly what anyone would call a True Hero. He even now languishes in my dungeons along with the others. Your situation is hopeless! Give it up, Fairy Alicia. Give it up and rest in eternal peace."

Alicia said nothing. Instead, she marched over to the treadle and joined her sisters. They continued to push and push, spinning the wheel. As though it would make any difference now!

Lady Mara turned and descended the stairs. She had half feared that perhaps the fairies were even now concocting some final, desperate venture that might undo all her plans. But they were as hopeless as ever. The Magic Cycle would end. Her reign as queen of the elves—and, indeed, of all the kingdoms surrounding—would begin tomorrow night!

"Oh, Alicia," whimpered Viola when the sorceress had gone. "Maybe she's right! I am so tired of spinning this wheel. And is there any use to it anymore? Even if Roselee can break the hero free, how can he possibly find our wands? The others couldn't."

With those words, the little lizard succumbed to tears and could not even manage to keep pushing the treadle. Lolly and Alicia exchanged glances, then the chicken led the lizard away, one wing gently wrapped about her shoulders.

But Alicia kept on spinning. To be sure, they hadn't much hope left.

But sometimes a final, desperate hope is all that's really needed . . .

Chapter 7

THE SQUIRREL *tried to twitch her tail. She felt a burning sensation there at its tip, and she knew the paralysis enchantment wouldn't last much longer. But for now she was trapped, as were her sisters.*

The Dark Lady, still laughing, stepped lightly around to each of the three frozen fairies in turn and snatched the wands from tiny hands and tiny beak. They brimmed still with fairy magic, though that would quickly fade— for the wands had no magic of their own, only that which they channeled from the center of the fairies' magical beings.

But without their wands the fairies would have no channel for their power. Their magic would be unfocused and potentially disastrous. Without their wands they dared not try to work any big spells.

Lady Mara smiled at the squirrel's furious glare even as she drew the wand from her little grasping claws. Suddenly the squirrel's smallest clawed finger twitched. The paralysis was wearing off!

Jumping back beside her apprentice, Lady Mara hissed, "Quickly! My powers are still depleted. Do something before they are free!"

The apprentice, his beautiful face drawn with wordless woe, stepped into the room and past the three frozen fairies, then knelt beside the stone body of the sleeping princess. For half an instant his gaze lingered on her lovely face, half covered though it was by her stone curls.

Then he reached out and plucked up the spindle, blood still glistening on its sharp point. He stepped to the spinning wheel, affixed the spindle in place, and spoke a few words of dark elf enchantment, finishing with:

"I curse the spindle once more. The wheel must spin for as long as it takes for the princess to awaken. If it stops once during the next five hundred years, before the princess receives her waking kiss, then any object of stone within and around this castle will crumble to dust."

Lady Mara cackled with mirth even as her apprentice took the wheel in his hand and spun it. It whirred with motion, then slowed . . . slowed . . .

Energy flowed through the squirrel. With a squeak and a flash of her bushy tail, she flew across the room. But she did not fling herself in rage at either Mara or the apprentice, no matter how she might wish to. Instead, she rushed to the treadle and began to push it for all she was worth. She had to keep the wheel spinning!

The apprentice backed away then joined his mistress in the doorway. Even as he did so, the lizard and the chicken also broke free of his curse and rushed to the aid of their sister at the treadle.

"Five hundred years, sweet fairies!" Lady Mara declared. "I can't say I'm delighted at this delay in my ultimate plans, but then again, what are five hundred years to the elves? Keep on spinning, little sparkly ladies . . . keep on spinning until the sun sets on your Magic Cycle. Perhaps I'll let you live long

enough to see me crowned!"

With those parting words, she drew her apprentice out the chamber door and into the stairwell. She clutched the three wands against her breast and realized suddenly that although each was individually much depleted in power, the three of them together still boasted some magical potency.

Inspiration struck. Mara urged her apprentice several steps down before her, then turned back to the open doorway of the chamber. She waved the three wands, using their fairy magic to channel her own slowly returning elf magic, and declared in a voice of enchantment: "With these wands, I curse this tower! No one will be able to enter this room until the Magic Cycle passes."

She laughed again, her voice ringing down the winding stair and out into the courtyard where the king and his court stood frozen. "Best wishes finding a True Hero now!"

She did not see her apprentice bow his head and bury his face in his hands.

A horrible, screeching roar—like the creak of the world's most enormous gate being shut by the hand of a howling banshee—shot through the corridors and halls of Briardale, bouncing off every wall and crashing down into the deepest levels of the castle asylum.

Franz, seated on his bed in the dungeon cell, snatched up the nearest thing to hand—which was the illustrated book—and clutched it to his chest as a sort of shield, cowering behind it as the hideous noise assaulted his ears.

Eidor, who lay across from him on his own bed, saw him jump and chuckled. "What's the matter, hero? A little noisy slavering never hurt anyone."

"Leave him alone," said Crete, perched cross-legged on his own bed, slowly spinning his jeweled pin in two fingers. He glared reproachfully at the dwarf. "The Slavering Swamp Beast is an intimidating monster to even the most experienced hero. Why, I found it quite the dreadful sight the first time I saw it, and I'm an actual dragon slayer!"

"Yeah, but compared to that dust mite of a dragon you fought, most anything would look ferocious . . ."

The two of them launched into back-and-forth bickering which, oddly enough, served to soothe Franz's rattled nerves. At length they subsided—along with the din of the Slavering Swamp Beast, which really did sound much too close for comfort—and Eidor went back to lying still on his bed, periodically holding his breath and straining every muscle in his body. Franz guessed he was trying to turn himself invisible but found watching him struggle to do the impossible rather unsettling. Crete, by contrast, sat calmly on his bed, spinning the pin slowly as though in planetary rotation, his gaze focused as if he were trying to see his homeland on it somewhere.

Needing to distract himself from his mad companions, Franz slowly lowered the book from his chest down onto his lap and took his first good look at it. The illustration on the open page depicted . . . well, if he was honest, a princess more gloriously beautiful than anything he had ever dared imagine! She lay as though she had just fallen to the floor, her golden curls tossed about her perfect face and shoulders, her lavender skirts spread like the petals of a dainty flower around her feet, one slim white ankle just showing beneath the lace hem. A spindle, its tip stained with blood, seemed to have just rolled from her fingertips.

The opposite illustration showed the same princess again—only this time all the colors were muted to grey and her skin and hair were hard. She was solid stone.

Franz stared at the two images. Was it possible . . . could this be the same princess the ghost girl had started to tell him about in the carriage?

The one Eidor and Crete claimed to have been brought here to rescue?

The illustrations were so distracting that Franz almost missed the text written in a small, spidery script beneath. He drew the book up close to his face now and read:

And the princess's rose-petal complexion paled . . . then darkened to hard gray.

"What is she doing?" cried the youngest fairy, nearly dropping her wand in terror.

"She's turning her to stone!" the middle fairy replied. And she was right—for as the enchantment dissipated and drifted away, they saw their princess's image in perfect stone . . .

Curious, and feeling that he must be missing something, Franz turned back a few pages to an illustration of a tower chamber with a spinning wheel standing in its center and an old woman seated on the stool. He saw the stairway leading up to that chamber, the same beautiful princess in her lavender dress climbing the stairs, a petulant expression on her lovely face. He read:

On the day of the princess's eighteenth birthday, mere moments before her kingly father was due to arrive at the hidden castle to celebrate that momentous occasion, the princess, in a fit of temper, stormed from her bedchamber and escaped the ministering hands of her three aunties. In her desire for solitude, she fled to the highest tower of the keep and hid in the stairwell when her aunties passed by . . .

Before he knew it, Franz was caught up in the unfolding story of the princess and the spindle enchantment. He turned a page and saw the three beautiful fairies as they discovered their princess fallen deeply asleep. He turned another page and there saw a terrible dark sorceress depicted almost entirely in jagged strokes of black ink. Could it be . . . ?

He peered at the scratchy text and saw the name—*Lady Mara.*

A shiver rattled him to the bones. Though he had not seen her face, somehow he did not doubt that this was the same Lady Mara he had met when first dragged through the gates of Briardale. Was this illustration a true depiction of her hidden face? If so, it was a beautiful face in its way, though marred by deep lines of bitterness about the mouth and eyes.

Franz gave his head a little shake. Why was he taking such interest? This was just a picture book, a fairy story for children! He'd have to be as mad as Crete or Eidor to believe it.

But then . . . he couldn't deny the conversations he'd had with the ghost girl . . .

"What are you doing?"

Franz looked up to find Eidor's icy blue gaze fixed upon him. "I'm reading," he said, almost defensively.

"What? As in *actually reading?*" Crete exclaimed, his head jerking up from contemplation of his pin. He tucked the pin into the front of his shirt, then sprang off his bed and rushed over to sit beside Franz and peer over his shoulder. "You can actually *read* this stuff?"

"Yes . . ."

"Told you he wasn't a *real* hero," Eidor said, but he too sat up on his bed, his face full of interest.

"You may be right," Crete admitted but cast Franz an admiring gaze. "We heroes, we're trained in sword fighting, bow-and-arrow slinging, jumping on and off of running horses, scaling tall buildings . . . you know, hero things. But we never learn to actually *read.*"

"We just look at the pictures," Eidor added. He slid off his bed and stomped across the room. "They're good pictures, and we can put together most of the story what with everything the ghost girl told us too. But there are bits she never mentioned that I can't make heads or tails of. Like this!"

He swiped the book right out of Franz's hands and flipped the pages back to passages before the story of the princess falling under the curse. He found the illustration he was looking for and turned it around for Franz to see.

It was another image of the princess, looking more beautiful than ever, for she was depicted in the middle of the Black Swamp, and the ugly surroundings served only to enhance her natural loveliness. She stood with her arms crossed, her expression cross, and one foot planted in the deep, dark muck of a bog pool.

Across from her, on the opposite page, another figure emerged from the trees—the best-looking man Franz had ever seen, so idealized in his perfections that he hardly seemed real. Not even the two heroes who had dragged him around Briardale earlier could compare with this fellow, though his shoulders were less broad and his face more angular.

"Who's this bloke, then?" Eidor said, stabbing a stubby finger at the image. "We can figure that the girl is the princess we've been brought here to rescue, and Lady Mara is recognizable enough. The ghost girl mentioned the three fairies and all that. But I haven't got the first idea how this chap figures into anything!"

"What's it say, Franz?" Crete asked eagerly.

Franz read out loud:

The princess was lonely in her solitary life, hidden away at Briardale. With only her three fairies—disguised as her aunties—and a housemaid for company, she longed for a friend with whom she might share adventures. But her aunties were so fearful of Lady Mara, they did not allow the princess out beyond Briardale's protective walls.

One day, however, the princess slipped out from under the fairies' watchful eyes and took a walk into the Black Swamp. She figured she would rather have an adventure on her own than no adventure at all! But she had gone scarcely a mile out of sight of the castle when she came to a bog. Stepping unwarily, she planted her foot in sucking mud and became perilously trapped.

"Botheration," she said, folding her arms. "And these were my favorite shoes!"

She had no notion of the danger in which she stood. Her three aunties, solicitous of her care and keeping, had protected her from any possible harm, not even allowing her to take a tumble or two when, as an infant, she first learned how to walk. So the princess knew nothing of danger or of fear. She stood there, the bog muck sucking her down, and simply cried out:

"All right then, will someone please come along and rescue me now? I don't have time to stand here all day!"

Things might have gone very ill for the princess had not someone happened to be passing nearby. She heard movement and turned in time to see a strange young man of just about her own age step through the thickest patch of trees across the bog. He was a glorious sight to behold, the most beautiful of all his kind.

He stepped over the marsh as nimbly as though he had lived in this place all his life . . . though the princess knew this to be impossible. Only the lowly Swamp Elves lived in the Black Swamp, and they were an ugly race, nothing like this handsome youth—

Eidor made gagging sounds. "All right, skip over his perfections, please. Get to the good parts!"

Franz obligingly turned a page or two, passing over images of the princess and the handsome stranger apparently bonding in friendship over various adventures in the Black Swamp. Then he came to a much more interesting illustration depicting the princess, still beautiful but in a state of extreme wrath, with her hands upraised as though she would like to claw someone's eyes out. And who should kneel before her on the ground, his hands clasped and tears in his eyes? None other than the handsome stranger.

"See, this is the picture that's always made me wonder," said Crete, pointing at the man in the image. "I mean, what could possibly have happened to make him all crumpled up and pitiful like this? I mean, at first I thought he was a hero like me or Eidor or even like those two lugs upstairs. But this doesn't look too heroic to me!"

Franz scanned the image for the scrawling handwriting in the margins. "*And so it seemed that the two would be fast friends for life,*" he read, "*and that one day perhaps something truer and more profound might blossom in their youthful hearts. But fickle fate did play an evil hand when—*"

A rattling at the door interrupted him. He and the two lunatic heroes looked up and saw a face peering at them through the bars of the door window: an ugly face with bug-eyes set in dark hollows.

"Hullo, Mutey," said Crete with a friendly wave. "Guess what! Franz here can read that book you gave us all those years ago. Isn't that great?"

Mutey's solemn gaze fixed upon Franz and on the book. He would be an unnerving fellow to look at under the best conditions, and in the context of a lunatic asylum's dungeon, he was positively ghastly. But when he looked at Franz with that dumb appeal—as though he were trying, desperately trying, to communicate something of vast importance with his bulbous eyes—Franz almost felt that he'd rather come face-to-face with the Slavering Swamp Beast.

He looked away quickly, shuddering.

A creak of bars, and the little cell window opened. Eidor stepped across the room and retrieved the tray of food Mutey passed through. "Thanks, mate," he said.

The dungeon keeper shrugged and shut the window. They heard his footsteps retreat along the dark passage.

Franz, the memory of that ugly gaze still burned his mind, focused his attention on the illustration even as Eidor brought the tray of foul-smelling prison porridge over to share. Something about the picture caught Franz's attention, something that made his brow pucker and his mouth frown. Something in the face of that handsome man struck him as somehow . . . familiar? What was it about those shining, tear-filled eyes—

"*There* you are, Franz dear!"

Franz screamed and flung up his hands, accidentally knocking the tray of porridge right out of Eidor's grasp, which made Eidor scream too, and then Crete. Globs of gray porridge flew straight through the glowing green form that had materialized suddenly in the middle of the room, smiling right at Franz.

Chapter 8

N O LIGHT shone in Briardale's high tower that night. But anyone standing down below, straining his ears, might have heard a distant whir-whir-whirring as of a wheel spinning, accented by the clunk-clunk-clunk of the treadle moved by tiny feet.

The fairies were hard at work, determined not to let down their princess even if it took five hundred years to save her.

A lonely figure in a deep hood passed between the statues in the courtyard, afraid to meet their solemn stone gazes. Instead, this figure darted at great speed to the tower door, one hand reaching out to the latch, the other clutching something secret within the folds of his cloak.

Lady Mara's apprentice wondered—would he count as a True Hero? He had not moved a mountain, saved a kingdom, or slain a dragon. But he had slain a Slavering Swamp Beast deep in the Black Swamp and stolen its cub (which was even now being brought up by Lady Mara for use as the most vicious watchdog ever seen). Slavering Swamp Beasts were known to eat dragons for luncheon, so surely a man who dared face one could be considered a true enough hero to satisfy a curse!

He had to hope.

In his hidden hand he clutched three slender wands. He need only throw them through the barrier, for Lady Mara's curse had stipulated that "no one" would be able to cross the barrier, not "nothing." And if the fairies regained their wands, they could bring down the barrier and let him through to try his kiss . . .

"I thought as much."

The apprentice stilled, his hand just touching the latch on the tower door. An ominous figure materialized out of the shadows. Lady Mara loomed tall.

"Liar," she hissed, her mouth twisting in an ugly smile. "You told me that your friendship with the princess was all a ruse, just as we planned. You told me you were still my loyal servant . . . and I believed you! When you invited me into Briardale, allowing me to complete the spindle curse even as planned, I thought you were indeed true to me!"

The apprentice drew back his hand slowly. Then, spinning quickly, he darted out his fingers, his mouth opening to form a paralysis enchantment such as he'd used on the three fairies earlier that day.

But Lady Mara intercepted him with a word of her own and a powerful blast of enchantment. He froze mid-gesture, his cloak settling about him, his hood tossed back from his pale face.

"You see that my powers are recovered," Lady Mara said. "And I don't need them at full capacity to deal with my own apprentice!" She approached, extending one finger to press its nail into his cheek so hard that a dot of blood appeared. "I never believed you would be such a fool as to fall in love with the girl," she sneered. "What would she say, do you think, if she knew what you really *are?*"

She spoke another word, and a shimmer of magic surrounded the apprentice like a veil. It wavered with silvery light then darkened to black, rotting away slowly. When it vanished, the beautiful man was gone . . .

And in his place, frozen in the same position, stood a Swamp Elf—a creature of pasty skin and bulbous eyes, with teeth as pointed as a goblin's.

"No fit companion for the king's daughter, are you?" said Lady Mara cruelly. "A pretty girl like her would laugh in your face if you dared speak to her." She bent her head, her eyes level with his. "I gave you the beauty spell so that you could get close to her, win her trust, and ultimately gain me access to Briardale. I would have let you keep the beauty forever had you only remained true to me! But now I take it back . . . and more!"

With that, she snapped her fingers, uttering yet another dark phrase. Black tendrils curled out from her nails and plunged into the Swamp Elf's open mouth, down his throat. He gasped, gagged, but could not otherwise move. The tendrils retreated, drawing back into Lady Mara's hand.

"I have taken your voice," she said. "Until someone calls you by your real name, you will remain dumb, powerless, unable to work enchantments. You are no longer my apprentice, no longer my servant . . . you are my slave! And when the Magic Cycle is complete, you will join your lovely princess in death."

She snapped her fingers, releasing him from the paralysis. He collapsed to his knees, tears streaming, his mouth open in a silent howl of dismay. Lady Mara reached under his cloak and snatched the three wands from his grasp.

"I'll take these," she said, "and hide them where no one will ever find them!"

Few things in the world could be more pathetic than a ghost who was afraid—just a *tiny* bit afraid—of the dark.

Roselee considered this truth with a grimace as she hovered outside the doorway leading down into Briardale's dungeons. Oh, how she hated venturing down there! The passages were twisty, and it was all just so . . . *dark!*

But Franz was down there. Franz and . . . other things.

No. No, she could not let herself think about that! Besides, it wasn't as if anything could actually *hurt* her, immaterial specter that she was. Alicia would be disappointed with her nonsense if she suspected, and Roselee had disappointed Alicia enough to last a lifetime. A dozen lifetimes, really!

So, making herself flare as brightly green as she possibly could, Roselee held her breath and darted through the shut door into the absolute blackness of the descending stairwell beyond.

That first plunge was the worst. The shudders of terror sweeping through her ghostly being, the whispers of panic, the awful *creepiness* of it all. But after that initial horror it wasn't so bad, much like plunging into a pond on a cold morning. Sure, that first dagger of icy water through the skin is bad, but then the blood starts pumping and everything starts to feel fine.

Roselee didn't have blood to pump anymore. But her ectoplasm flared with renewed courage, and she spiraled her way down the stair to a place where it branched into three distinct corridors. Which corridor housed the heroes? She didn't visit them often, for what was the point when they could no longer see or hear her?

The rules of the various interlacing enchantments were complex, but Viola's original counterspell stated that the princess could be kissed awake after a hundred years. Thus, at the tail end of every century a new hero could be Chosen. But if he failed to kiss the princess before the century was up, his window of opportunity passed. His kisses would never work, and he couldn't even perceive the guiding ghost spirit anymore. It was terribly frustrating.

Roselee wavered before the mouths of those three corridors. She didn't want to waste time wandering . . . and she *really* didn't want to accidentally end up at the den of the Slavering Swamp Beast! It would have been brought in for the night by this time, and would even now sit brooding and slavering in its den somewhere down here, its wicked red eyes keen for any glimpse of intruders, ghostly or otherwise.

Roselee shivered and wrapped her translucent arms around her immaterial body. Then she tilted her head, listening. Was that Franz's voice she heard?

"I'm coming, Franz!" she trilled cheerily and darted down the corridor, all thoughts of the Slavering Swamp Beast forgotten. She scarcely even noticed the dungeon keeper when she passed him.

Franz's voice trailed off, no longer speaking in that steady rhythm. Where was he? Her eye caught a gleam of orange light through a window in one of the dungeon cell doors. He must be in there!

With a sigh of relief, she darted through the heavy door into the lamp-lit room. She saw Franz seated beside one of her former Chosens with a heavy book open in his lap.

"*There* you are, Franz dear!" she cried and popped into full visibility.

His reaction was not quite what she had hoped. Rather than a happy exclamation of recognition, he let out a yell and flung up his hands and the book. The other two heroes yelled as well, and one of them dashed right through Roselee—an unpleasant sensation that gave her the shivers—as he dove for cover under the bed. Glops of something gray flew through the air, and all was singularly unwelcoming.

Roselee folded her arms. "Really, I might have expected better of you," she said, scowling at Franz, who crouched on the bed with his knees drawn up as though preparing to leap for freedom. "Aren't you happy to see me?"

"*You!*" Franz exclaimed. "It's . . . it's really you?"

"Really who?" the grouchy growl of Eidor demanded from his place huddled on the floor with the meal tray over his head for protection. Across from him, Crete's feet poked out from under the bed.

"They can't see me," Roselee said, indicating the two heroes. "Only you can."

Franz blinked. "I . . . I was hoping maybe I'd just imagined you after all," he whispered.

She deflated, sinking down until her feet went partway into the ground. "Oh, Franz," she said, "that's cruel. Why would you *hope* that? And here I go trusting you, picking you out of all others, believing in you . . ."

"Is it the ghost girl?" Eidor asked, peering out from under the tray. "Is she back?"

"Roselee?" came Crete's voice from under the bed. He shuffled, lifting the bed partway off the ground as he turned about and scrambled free. "Is it really her?"

"See?" Roselee with a sniff. "*They* believe in me."

Franz nodded slowly, glancing at his two companions. "Yes. It's her. She's . . . she's floating in the middle of the room. Right in front of me."

Eidor shuddered. "Never did like ghosts," he muttered. "Especially when I can't see them!" He touched his forehead respectfully then, offering a little bow. "No offense meant, miss."

He couldn't see her, but Roselee gave him a gracious smile anyway. "*Some* folks still know the meaning of the word *courtesy*." Then she shook away her disappointment and faced Franz, her pale, stoop-shouldered, frightened Chosen One. The Chosen One with the true heart.

He would have to do.

"Have you figured out how to burst free yet? Like a proper Hero?"

"I've told you," Franz said, relaxing a little as he readjusted to her otherworldly presence, "I'm *not* a proper Hero. I can't burst free of anything."

"She wants you to burst free?" Crete asked, standing and dusting off the front of his trousers. "Tell her we've tried that. Both of us. We're experts at it, you know. But this room, it suppresses all of our usual abilities. Some sort of enchantment on it, which is why Mara keeps us here."

"That's why Crete can't shrink," Eidor added. "And I can't seem to remember how to turn invisible."

Franz stared at them open-mouthed, his eyes roving slowly from Crete to Eidor to Roselee and back around again. "So . . ." he said slowly, addressing himself to Roselee. "So this one . . . he really does come from a microscopic kingdom on the head of a pin?"

"Him?" Roselee glanced at Crete. "He's a homunculus, isn't he? They all come from Homunculi, the Smallest Kingdom. Didn't you know that?"

"And him?" said Franz with a nod at Eidor. "He really can . . . turn invisible?"

"Of course I can, you dolt!" Eidor snarled.

"He's a dwarf," Roselee said. "All dwarves can turn invisible. Why else do you think you've never seen one before? They never let themselves be seen by humans."

"And you brought them both here to . . . to try to kiss the princess?"

"I tried two humans first," she reminded him, flushing emerald with embarrassment. "Lady Mara couldn't rid herself of the True Hero curse-breaking, but she *did* make it more difficult for us by casting a spell preventing elf heroes from waking the princess. There were more than enough of those left in King Pintamore's kingdom who would have been glad to save the princess! But once that particular counter-curse was set, I had to look for heroes among other races. I tried humans first and . . . well . . . you've seen how *they* turned out. So I tried Eidor and then Crete. But . . ." She shrugged sadly. "They did their best! We simply couldn't find the wands."

"What's she saying?" Eidor demanded.

"Hush," said Crete. "They are probably plotting our daring escape even now."

Franz ignored them both. "So you picked me as your last chance." He pointed at the book. "Because the Magic Cycle is about to end."

Roselee sucked in a surprised breath. "How did you know about the Magic Cycle? I never told you that!"

Franz shuffled uncomfortably under her intense scrutiny. "Crete and Eidor told me some. And I read the rest here—"

"You can *read?*"

In her burst of excitement, Roselee shot to Franz's side, hovering above his shoulder and pointing eagerly at the book. "Quick! Quick! Turn the pages! No one else has been able to read it! Oh, I just *knew* I'd picked you for a reason!"

"What . . . what do you want me to look for exactly?" Franz asked with a shiver. Her ghostly presence so close was terribly disconcerting. He obediently opened the volume, however, and paged past the images of the three fairies and their spell-battle with Lady Mara, past the images of the apprentice's arrival.

"I want to know if there's anything in there to indicate where Lady Mara hid the wands," Roselee said. "Crete and I looked over all the pictures a hundred years ago, but they didn't tell us anything, and neither of us nor Eidor could read the words. But you see? You see?"

She pointed eagerly as the book opened to an illustration of Lady Mara and her apprentice. The Dark Lady was pulling the fairy wands out of his hands, and simultaneously seeming to cast a spell over his handsome face. It was difficult to see through the inky clouds surrounding him, but it looked as though he was being transformed into . . . into . . .

"Hold on a minute," Franz whispered, staring hard at the image, obscure though it was. "Is that . . . ?"

He read the text on the page. He drew a sharp breath. "Crete? Eidor?"

"Yes, mate?" said Crete.

Franz looked up at the two heroes. "Do either of you know what Mutey's real name is?"

The dwarf and the homunculus exchanged glances. "No," Eidor admitted. "He can't talk, so he never told us. We just call him Mutey 'cause it seemed better than nothing . . ."

A strange excitement caught hold of Franz. Roselee could feel the energy streaming out from his very spirit, and it thrilled her as well. Was he finally beginning to tap into that heroic instinct she *knew* he had deep inside?

He shut the book with a slam then opened the front cover. There on the first page a couple of words were scrawled in the same spidery script as the rest of the book. Franz's mouth moved as he read: "*This book was written by . . .*"

Leaving the book on the bed, he crossed the cell in a few strides, put his face to the cell window, and grasped the bars with both hands. "Excuse me? Mutey?" he called into the darkness. "Mutey, are you there?"

He let out a little shout when the dungeon keeper appeared suddenly before his vision. Stumbling back several steps, Franz recovered himself. "Oh! Yes, hullo. Um . . ."

The dungeon keeper's frog-like eyes brimmed with mute appeal.

"I say," said Franz with a little shake of his head, "is your name by any chance . . . *Paisley?*"

A blinding burst of light! Roselee screamed and sank down into the floor, trembling there in insubstantiality. Then, her ectoplasm still pulsing, she slowly floated up to peek out of the floor. She saw Crete's feet sticking out from under his bed. She saw Eidor standing on the same bed, his back plastered to the wall. She saw Franz crouched down on his knees, his hands over his head.

And in the doorway stood . . . the ugly dungeon keeper with the goggly eyes. Apparently that magical blast had done nothing to improve his appearance.

But on second glance Roselee noticed a striking difference in him: He was smiling. Not once in five hundred years had she seen this ghastly man smile!

"You have liberated me from Lady Mara's curse, hero!" he declared. His voice was pleasantly mellow despite coming from between those pointed teeth. "You have freed my voice and thus freed my magical abilities. Now I, in return, can free the three of you!"

"Hoorah!" Roselee cheered, though only Franz could hear her.

Franz pulled himself up off the floor, though he practically left his sagging jaw behind. "You *are* the apprentice then!" he breathed. "But you aren't on Lady Mara's side?"

"Certainly not!" the Swamp Elf replied. Then he lowered his eyes. "That is . . . I was her devoted servant for many years. She took me in and fostered my magical abilities. Swamp Elves aren't supposed to be magical, you know, and the other High Elves scorned me. But not Lady Mara. She saw my potential and decided to train me. I was devoted to her for giving me that chance! And when she sent me to spy on the princess . . . to gain her trust, and to infiltrate the barriers of Briardale . . . I was more than happy to oblige."

Tears brimmed in his eyes, rendering his pasty face less appealing than ever. "How could I have guessed that I would fall madly in love with dear, beautiful, brave Maralyn?"

"Maralyn?" said Eidor from up on his bed. Then he gave a loud *harrumph* as the bed shifted and Crete appeared from beneath it.

"Is that the princess's name?" asked Crete. "I never heard it before."

"Yes. Princess Maralyn, named for her aunt mere moments before her aunt betrayed her," sighed the Swamp Elf, placing a hand over his heart. "A rose too fair for a worm such as I to dare even look upon!"

He did speak prettily, Roselee admitted, pursing her lips in appreciation. One could *almost* overlook his ugliness, so deftly did he turn a phrase in that rich, deep voice.

"We became friends," he continued, "the dearest of friends! I knew that I could never betray her, could never let Mara into Briardale and allow the curse to fall. But . . . but . . ."

"Yes?" Franz urged gently.

The elf let out a despairing sigh. "On the morning of her eighteenth birthday, we had a fight. A foolish fight. I said something . . . something unpardonable to her, and she vowed she would never, *ever* speak to me again." He choked on his own voice, and Roselee feared he would succumb to tears then and there. He rallied himself, however, squaring his hunched shoulders. "I then made a foolish decision: I determined to let Lady Mara have her way, to let the curse fall upon the princess. But I intended to sneak back into the tower that very night, kiss her awake, and save them all. Then, I thought, she would *have* to forgive me."

"That was a pretty barmy plan, now wasn't it?" said Eidor.

Paisley the Swamp Elf couldn't bear to answer for several moments. At last he said, "After Mara stole my voice and made me her slave, I did what I could to help any future heroes. I assembled that book, detailing the whole story in hopes that someone would realize what had happened to me and break this spell. Then I left it here for you. How could I have guessed that True Heroes never learn to read?"

Franz stepped to the dungeon keeper's side and patted his shoulder awkwardly. "No matter," he said. "You're free now. And maybe . . . could you use your magical powers to get us through the tower barrier? We've got several True Heroes here—surely one of them could kiss the princess."

"No, Franz," said Roselee, rising completely out of the floor and shimmering before his eyes. "It has to be you. Their chances are up. You must kiss the princess to save all of us."

Franz looked at her—making the others, who couldn't see her, most uncomfortable—and shook his head. "But I'm not a hero, Roselee! Certainly not according to the . . . erh, the *exacting* standards of True Heroism. It can't be me."

"It *has* to be."

"But I can't—"

"I say," said Crete, taking a step forward and inadvertently walking into the middle of Roselee's ghostly aura. She shuddered and jerked back, pulling a face. "I say, let's not waste time arguing. Let's just try to get through the barrier and see what's what. I mean, it's our only shot at survival anyway, isn't it? Lady Mara will kill us all tomorrow at sunset, just as soon as the Cycle finishes. We might as well try as not."

"Right," said Eidor, brandishing his fists. "I'd rather die fighting than while sitting in here twiddling my thumbs! I'd particularly like a shot at one of those two handsome idiots upstairs, I don't mind saying . . ."

Franz gave his head a sad little shake but did not protest. Instead, he turned to Paisley. "Can you get us through the barrier?"

"Not in my own strength," the Swamp Elf replied. "But I can tell you where Lady Mara keeps the three fairy wands. If you can retrieve those and return them to the fairies in the tower, they'll be able to break the barrier for you."

"Excellent!" cried Roselee, clasping her hands. "Now we're getting somewhere! Ask him, Franz. Ask him where the wands are, and we'll go fetch them at once!"

But Franz hesitated. Something in Paisley's frog-eyes told him he wouldn't like the answer to the question he was about to ask. "So . . . uh . . . where are the wands, exactly?"

"In a place where only True Heroes may dare to tread," said Paisley. He lowered his melodic voice to speak in a tone of dire portent:

"The den of the Slavering Swamp Beast."

Chapter 9

LADY MARA never slept at night. When she slept at all, she chose the brightest hours of midday, hiding away in her darkest chamber, slinking into shadows as far from sunlight as she could get.

At night she walked the halls of Briardale, inspecting the cells of the mad inmates, studying the stone faces of the elves she had caught in her curse. Five hundred years, and still she did not tire of this nightly trek. Indeed, it would be strange after tomorrow night—after the statues had crumbled to dust and the lunatics had been set loose upon the countryside to ravage, pillage, and destroy—to find her centuries-old habit suddenly interrupted.

She passed along the corridor where the mad murderers were housed. She had amassed quite a nice collection over the centuries, all kept in perpetual youth by the magic hanging over Briardale. But unlike the lovely princess, they did not sleep through the centuries but festered in their lunacy, growing more vicious and more violent by the year. Even True Heroes must tremble to face them now!

Mara smiled at this thought—then suddenly the smile broke into a thousand pieces, scattering away at the onset of a frown. What was that? What was that rippling sensation flooding through the air, wafting over her in shudders of . . . of shattering? One of her spells? Broken? Impossible!

She reached out with her spirit, testing the numerous curses and counterspells that clutched Briardale in a magically oppressive net. Which curse? Which curse had broken? Which curse had—

"Paisley!" The name spewed from her lips for the first time in half a millennium.

Then her shout rang through the halls of Briardale: "Heroes! Heroes, where are you?"

Her two handsome henchmen appeared at the end of the hall, hands on their sword hilts, their stern faces alert and ready for action. Mara swept toward them, her veil wafting behind her like trailing smoke.

"My slave, the dungeon keeper, has betrayed me!" she declared. "And he's let the other three idiots loose! Hunt them down at once and make certain they cause no further damage. Chop off limbs if you must—*but don't kill them!*" she added hastily, for even ordering someone else to commit murder would bring that wretched chicken's curse down upon her head faster than lightning.

The two former-heroes saluted and sprang into action, their short cloaks flying. Mara followed them out of the murderer's hall, her eyes bright behind her veils, her magical senses straining. Paisley! His magic was no match for hers; but she had trained him herself, and she knew the potential of his restored powers. He would be determined to rescue the princess, fool that he was. As if he had hope this side of heaven of *ever* winning her vain little heart!

A flash of something caught her eye. Red hair?

"There!" she screeched, and her two henchmen, ahead of her by several yards, turned back to see where she pointed. They too glimpsed a shadowy figure darting down the passage—a very short figure running on two stumpy legs. "There they go! After them!"

The heroes charged into action, and Lady Mara pursued behind them, building up magical power in the tips of her fingers. She would turn them all into gnats, and the moment the Magic Cycle ended, she would squash them with her thumb, one by one! Then she would—

She stopped abruptly, as though hitting a wall. Her eyes narrowed to evil slits, and she turned. Something called to her magical senses, some slight plucking on the strings of her unconscious awareness . . .

She peered into a side passage of Briardale. There in the shadows . . . an extra shadow that should not be there . . .

"Did you think you could distract me with your little illusions?" Mara cried. "I *taught* you those tricks!" She flung out her hand as though throwing a dagger with terrible precision. *"Il've!"* she screeched.

Darkness rolled from her fingertips, forming the shape of a giant, leaping wolf.

"Do you think it will work?" Franz whispered.

He and the ghost girl crouched in the dungeons below Briardale. Franz stood with his back pressed to the wall; Roselee's back sank a little *into* the wall. They thought they heard rushing footsteps above.

"Paisley seems pretty good at illusions," Roselee replied with a little shivering shrug. "Those images of you and Crete and Eidor were good enough to fool me! They should definitely keep those two lugs busy for a while."

"Let's just hope it's long enough." Franz turned his gaze to the dungeon corridor down which Crete and Eidor had just disappeared. The corridor which, according to Paisley, led to the den of the Slavering Swamp Beast, which slept on a chain beneath the castle each night, foaming at the mouth and as alert as a watchdog.

"Should I go with you?" Franz had asked when the two heroes set out.

But Crete shook his head. "You . . . um . . . you need to save your strength for the kiss, right? Wouldn't want you to get worn out by all the rest of these heroics."

Franz hung his head at the memory. Though Crete's words had been kind, Eidor had rolled his eyes, expressing in one gesture that Slavering Swamp Beasts were the business of True Heroes, not bank clerks.

Roselee, sensing Franz's distress, reached out an insubstantial hand and patted through his shoulder a few times. "Don't worry," she said kindly. "After five hundred years, I think I've learned what to look for in a hero. I've searched all over the world through every race, magical and mortal. And I picked you."

Franz couldn't meet her eye. Wanting to change the subject, he asked a question which had been preying on his mind for some time. "Why are *you* the one to choose the heroes? I read most of Paisley's book and looked at all the pictures, but I didn't see you anywhere in there. Who exactly are you in all of this?"

It was Roselee's turn to hang her head. "To tell the truth," she said in a whisper, "I don't remember. My first memory is of waking up here at Briardale and realizing that I could fly and pass through walls, and that my complexion was extraordinarily green and see-through. I recall only little flashes of what it was like before . . . you know. Before I died? If I died. I'm not really sure about that."

She sniffed as though trying to hold back tears, though Franz wasn't sure if ghosts could actually cry. "Alicia, Lolly, and Viola—the three fairies from the story—told me my name and explained that they'd summoned me to help since they can't leave the tower. They were *trying* to summon the spirit of King Pintamore, but without their wands their magic is unfocused. So the summoning went wild, and they called me instead. At that point they simply had to make do. And I really have done my best!" She smiled weakly, not quite meeting Franz's studying gaze. "I've gotten to see parts of the world I'm sure I never would have seen otherwise. It's been quite the adventure when all's said and done."

Franz considered this, standing there in the darkness with only Roselee's ghostly aura to light the dungeon around him. Suddenly he realized who she must be.

Really, who else could *she be?* he asked himself. *It makes sense that she would be the one to choose the hero . . .*

Then he wondered, *But can I be hero enough for her when the time comes?*

This thought broke off abruptly as the roar of the Slavering Swamp Beast careened down the passage. Following hard upon the heels of that roar came the shouts of the two brave heroes facing a monster like none other.

The two heroes—one short and bearded, one broad and dark—paused in the narrow doorway and peered into the cavernous chamber beyond. This was the deepest point of Briardale, down in the bedrock under the castle's foundations. A natural cave etched out eons ago loomed before them, a trickle of river water flowing into a shallow pool in its center.

On the edge of that pool lay the dozing form of the Slavering Swamp

Beast. It gnawed on its own mighty forepaw like a child sucking its thumb, waiting for morning when it would be set loose to prowl the swamps.

"Whoa," Eidor breathed, supporting himself with one hand against the doorframe. "I'd forgotten how *big* he is!"

"Never mind him," Crete replied, though his voice trembled. "You see better in the dark than I do. Spot any wands lying about?"

Eidor tore his gaze away from the many coils of Swamp Beast to survey the cavern. This was a dwarf's element after all: dark and underground. His gaze quickly scanned every corner and crevice.

"Uh oh," he said.

"What?"

"I think I see where the wands are hidden."

"Where?"

"Do you see that iron chest?"

"No."

"Across the pool. On the far shore."

"Don't see it."

"The Slavering Swamp Beast is resting his chin on it like a pillow."

The two heroes were silent. But they weren't True Heroes for nothing, and Crete rallied himself almost at once.

"Right," he said, "here's the plan: You turn invisible—you can do that now that we're out of the dungeon cell, right?"

"I think so," said Eidor. The next instant he vanished completely, and Crete blinked at empty space. "Can you see me now?" came a voice from somewhere around waist-height.

Crete shook his head, impressed despite himself. "You're as invisible as a white rabbit in a snowstorm! Bet even the Slavering Swamp Beast can't see you."

Eidor flickered back into sight. "He can *smell* me though."

Crete shrugged. "That'll make your next act all the more heroic." He bent and whispered instructions in his friend's ear.

Not long afterward, the Slavering Swamp Beast stopped gnawing its paw and lifted its enormous head, dripping foam on the lid of the chest. Something smelled funny. It drew a deep breath, its slitted nostrils constricting then flaring as it let out an enormous, echoing snort.

Something smelled like . . . hero.

With a huff that sent more foam splattering into the pool, the Beast heaved itself up onto its stumpy forelegs, which, strong though they were, could only just lift its barrel chest clear of the rock. It swung its head, tendril whiskers curling and uncurling as it snuffled and snorted some more.

Then something struck it right between the eyes. Startled, it blinked its sideways eyelids and looked down at . . . absolutely nothing. So it looked with its nostrils instead, and the smell of a hero took shape in its olfactory senses.

"Here, you big crocodile!" shouted a bold voice. "Come and get me!"

Something else struck the Swamp Beast, this time right on the tip of its nose, which is the only part of a Swamp Beast that might almost be called sensitive. The Slavering Swamp Beast let out a high-pitched snort, its curled whiskers momentarily straightening.

Then it roared.

Although it is as bulky as a hippopotamus, with back feet like floppy paddles wriggling uselessly from the sides of its trunk-like tail, the Slavering Swamp Beast moves much faster than anyone might expect, propelling itself along with powerful forelegs, and able to spring forward with its coiled tail.

Eidor fled invisible before it, shouting half in terror, half in heroic bravado. "Hurry up, Crete!" he called over his shoulder as he raced along the edge of the pond, the splashes of his footfalls the only sign of his passage. "Hurry up, hurry-up-hurry-up-hurry-uuuuuuuup!"

The Swamp Beast, fixated on that one smell, failed to notice the tiny shape, little more than the size of a flea, springing across the stones with mighty, heroic bounds until coming to the chest. Crete, though too large to live in a pinhead-sized city, was plenty small enough to leap into the crack between trunk and lid. It was a tight squeeze, but he pushed himself through and dropped into the chest itself.

Something flared. Then another something. Then a third. Silver, orange, and purple somethings lying in the bottom of the trunk.

Crete was much too tiny to wrap his arms around the circumference of even one of the wands. But he touched one and, with a moment of effort, forced it to conform to the size of his hand. He was slightly out of practice, but once a homunculus, always a homunculus! He reached for the second wand and the third, and these reduced more easily than the first. Soon he held all three wands. With a spring, he squeezed himself back through the narrow opening.

The Slavering Swamp Beast, passing at speed, swished its tail and sent the trunk crashing into the water. Crete, knocked right along with it, held onto the wands as tightly as he could. Water closed over his head, water deep as the ocean . . .

The next moment he was full-sized again, standing in a pond up to his knees.

"*Hurry uuuuuuuuuup!*" Eidor's voice flashed across the cavern just ahead of slavering roars.

Crete shook himself, waded across the pond, and climbed out on the side nearest the door. "Come on, Eidor!" he shouted, waving in the general direction of his friend's voice. "I've got them!"

"'*Bout tiiiiiime!*" yelled the dwarf, though his words were drowned by a particularly ferocious roar. The Slavering Swamp Beast gathered itself up on the muscular coils of its tail. Then, with those muscles uncoiling like a spring, it launched itself across the cavern, its immense jaws gaping, ready to swallow both heroes in a single gulp!

But that's when it hit the end of its magical chain.

Eidor and Crete, feeling Beast foam splatter the backs of their heads, dove through the narrow door one after the other into the corridor beyond. In the cavern, the Swamp Beast keened in frustration, tearing furiously at its chain. But the chain had been woven of pure enchantment and would not break.

"Are you there, Eidor?" Crete asked.

To his vast relief, the empty space by his elbow answered, "Sure am." The dwarf shimmered back into view, covered in slaver but unharmed. He shook himself off and grinned. "Now *that* was proper heroics!"

The two heroes got to their feet and trotted down the corridor to rejoin Franz and the ghost. Neither of them saw a secret door open in the wall of the passage just after they left. Neither of them saw a shadowy figure approach the den of the Swamp Beast.

Chapter 10 ◆

ADY MARA stood on the threshold of the Beast's den, peering from behind her veil first at the iron chest half submerged in the stagnant pool—unopened, its magical locks intact—then at the poor monster straining on its chain. She saw no bones or pools of blood and decided it was too much to hope that the Slavering Swamp Beast had managed to injure at least one of the heroes.

She strode into the cavern, right up to the beast, which turned its dripping jowls her way and rumbled forlornly.

"What's wrong, my pet?" she asked the monster even as she picked up the end of its heavy enchanted chain. "Do you want to hunt down those nasty heroes who dared try to steal from you?"

With a flick of her wrist, she broke the chain and freed the Swamp

Beast.

"Go!" she cried. "Find those heroes and that skinny little banker's clerk! Go, my Beast!"

A toad poked his warty head up out of her pocket, dismayed to see the Slavering Swamp Beast crash through the narrow door, sending bits of wall tumbling as it rushed forth in pursuit of its luckless prey.

Mara caught the toad in one hand and hauled it up to meet her gaze. "Failed again, Paisley," she said with a snarl. "Obviously you have no talent for treason. Muteness may not have been a pleasure, but now that you face the prospect of ending your days in this form, perhaps you wish you hadn't dared cross me yet again!"

The toad blinked sad eyes at her—not so very different from his elf eyes—kicked his long back legs out straight, and said, "*Graaaup.*"

Lady Mara laughed. "Hardly a sight to please the eye of a fair princess!" she declared and dropped him into the deepest pocket of her gown.

Roselee flared a brilliant green when the two heroes appeared through the shadows of the tunnel. In Crete's powerful fist the three wands glowed their triune hues like the most beautiful of torches. Roselee recognized them at once.

"They did it!" she whispered, then shot out from the wall and whirled about. "You did it, you did it!"

Unaware of her ghostly exuberance, the heroes merely nodded at Franz, and Crete held the wands high. "Success!" he declared with a grin, slowing to a jog as they approached.

Franz smiled in return, though his heart felt a strange jumble of emotions. He was relieved to see the two heroes well and whole after their encounter with the Beast, and he was overjoyed that they had managed to retrieve the wands. But . . . they'd done it without him.

Thoughts of heroism had never plagued him before, back in his . . . for want of a better word, back in his *real* life. Would he ever be able to go back to those days? Would he ever be able to live without the question at the back of his mind: *Are you man enough? Do you really have what it takes?*

Shoving that thought away, he fell in step with the heroes and asked Roselee, "Can you lead us to the tower now—"

His voice was lost in the roar of the Slavering Swamp Beast.

The two heroes, the ghost, and the clerk spun around and stared down the dark dungeon passage in a frozen moment of terror. Could it be . . . ? Were their ears mistaken . . . ?

Was that roar *coming closer?*

"It's loose!" shouted Crete, his words barely audible above the clamor. "Hurry!"

"This way!" shouted Roselee, beckoning to Franz.

"This way!" Franz echoed, beckoning to the heroes.

The three of them set off running, Crete and Eidor following Franz, Franz following the bobbing green glow of Roselee, and Roselee desperately hoping she remembered the way out! Oh, if only she'd not been such a coward! If only she'd spent more time exploring these dark passageways! But how could she possibly have guessed that at the end of the Magic Cycle she'd find herself leading not one but *three* heroes in a mad escape from the Slavering Swamp Beast? If she could not find the stairway up to the castle courtyard, would the Swamp Beast swallow them whole? Or would it merely maim them to avoid bringing the no-killing curse down upon Mara's head?

Either way, she knew she dared not make a single wrong turn. But she had no time to think, no time to stop at any of the twists and turns to consider. Instinct alone drove her, and she swished here, wafted there, with Franz desperately careening after her in his efforts not to lose sight of her in the dark.

The floors shook and the walls trembled at the raucous pursuit of the Slavering Swamp Beast behind them.

Roselee found a stairwell leading up. Oh, let it be the right one! "Hurry, Franz!" she shouted as she dashed up, leaving little puffs of ectoplasm in her wake. Franz scrambled behind her, almost falling, using his hands to keep himself upright. Behind him, the two heroes pushed and prodded, Crete sticking him in the small of the back with wand-points to goad him on.

Roselee floated right through the closed door out into the courtyard. Yes! This *was* the right way! She whirled about . . . only to realize that the door was shut fast, and her three heroes were on the wrong side.

"Batwings!" she cried, flinging herself at the bolt. But her hands went right through it. "Batwings, buzzards, and bilge rats!" She tried to punch the door, probably hitting Franz in the face on the far side. She heard helpless hands pounding on the door, her poor heroes, trapped!

And the Swamp Beast squeezing itself up the stairs just behind them.

"Move aside, Franz!" a mighty voice cried. Then, "Hold these, Eidor."

A tremendous blow struck the door so that it rattled. A second blow, and the door splintered. After a third, it crumbled into a pile of kindling and Crete tumbled forth, landing face-down in the wreckage.

"Well done, mate!" cried Eidor, scrambling over the bulky hero, the wands now clutched in his fist. Franz burst out behind, and the two of them helped haul Crete back upright.

"Hurry!" Roselee urged. The stairwell echoed with the roar of the Swamp Beast, and she knew it was only a few turns behind them now. "Hurry, Franz! We've got to get you to the tower!"

Once on his feet, Crete shook splinters from his shoulders and declared himself all right. The three heroes set off across the courtyard at top speed, Crete in the lead, his powerful legs driving hard. Eidor followed close behind, for despite his shortness he was a True Hero, and a True Hero knows how to *run* when need arises. Franz puffed along at the back, unused to this much action and adventure after years behind a desk.

Roselee streamed ahead, darting between elf statues, until she reached the tower door. "Up there!" she cried to Crete and Eidor as they neared. "Get the wands to the fairies! I'll make sure Franz is right behind."

Neither hero could hear her, of course, but they reacted as though they could. Crete pushed open the door and paused for Eidor to pass through ahead of him, since the dwarf still held the wands. It was in that moment that a terrible pallor swept across Crete's dark skin, leaving him ashen. One huge hand pressed to his heart—to that empty place on his shirt where a jeweled pin ought to be.

"My kingdom!" he gasped.

Franz, just approaching through the foremost ranks of elf statues, saw the hero's gesture, saw the movement of his mouth and guessed at the words. He saw how Crete's eyes swam as he gazed out desperately into the courtyard, searching, searching . . .

Though he knew he should not pause, Franz skidded to a halt and looked back. Some instinct told him where to search, and his gaze shot directly to the pile of kindling that had once been the dungeon door.

There, gleaming in the light of new dawn, lay a gold pin with a bright jeweled head.

If Franz had stopped to think, he would have left the pin where it lay, rushed headlong to the tower, and done everything humanly possible to put distance between himself and the slavering roar echoing up that dark, winding stair.

But in that moment Franz was not a thoughtful banker's clerk. In that moment he was a hero, through and through.

He dashed back across the courtyard. He sprang to that gaping doorway. Two red eyes glowed at him from the darkness, and slaver sprayed out, dampening his face and shirt. Franz, his mind so numb with heroic zeal that he couldn't even feel his own overwhelming fear, reached out and snatched up the pin.

The Slavering Swamp Beast appeared in the doorway, its jaws gaping.

"*Franz!*" Roselee screamed.

In an instant, a green bolt of lightning shot across the courtyard and zipped directly into the Slavering Swamp Beast's eye. It passed right through and out the other side of its head, but the sensation was just disconcerting enough that the Swamp Beast swallowed its own slaver in surprise and stood blinking, its bandy forelimbs bulging the doorframe on either side of it, its tail smacking the stairs into rubble behind it.

Allowing Franz the time he needed to pick himself up and run for all he was worth across the courtyard.

Then the Swamp Beast, its predatory nature snapping back into play, fixed slitted eyes upon its fleeing prey. With a shake of its whiskers and a roar that could topple the stars, it lumbered out into the yard in hot pursuit.

Franz darted between the statues. He knew he would never reach the tower doorway in time, for though the Swamp Beast was low and bulky, its massive tail propelled it along so quickly that he felt jaws snapping just one step behind him. If he staggered or tripped, he would be lost for sure!

In desperation, he did the only thing that occurred to him in that moment—he leaped for higher ground.

Which in this instance meant bounding into the arms of the nearest statue and clambering up to perch on a pair of stony shoulders. He was vaguely aware that his free hand grasped the pointed ends of what might be a crown, but he hadn't time to consider this just then.

The Slavering Swamp Beast circled the statue but could not raise its head high enough even to snap at Franz's toes. It pushed against the statue's legs, but not even a Beast could budge solid marble. The squat creature slavered and snorted, and its whiskers curled and straightened and curled again in wrath. But it could not reach Franz.

"I've got it, Crete!" Franz cried, adjusting his position on the statue's shoulders to call out to the two heroes standing in the tower doorway. He held up the pin, its jeweled head gleaming bright. "Quick! Get the wands to the fairies!"

Eidor and Crete nodded and disappeared up the tower stair. Roselee, recovered from the weird sensation of passing through a Swamp Beast's brain, whirled about Franz, so delighted she would have kissed him if her lips wouldn't go through his skin. "Oh, Franz!" she cried. "You did it! You did it!"

"Not yet," Franz said, shakily. The Swamp Beast let out another hideous roar and flung itself at the statue's knees. The statue rocked slightly, and Franz wrapped his arms about the stone head. "I don't know how I'm going to get to the tower now!"

Roselee gazed up at the balcony and saw a chicken and a lizard watching from the window. Once they had their wands, maybe . . . maybe . . .

Crete and Eidor, moving at the speed of heroes, sprang up the stairway. They saw the open door at the top, saw the spinning wheel in the center of the chamber where a squirrel pushed frantically at the treadle.

"Here!" Eidor cried, waving the wands. "We've got these!"

A brilliant light of hope swept across the squirrel's whiskered face. "Lolly! Viola!" she squeaked.

With a flutter of feathers and a flick of a spotted tail, chicken and lizard darted from the window and across the chamber. "Throw them through," Lolly squawked, feathers bursting in a cloud of excitement around her.

Eidor looked at Crete. Crete gave a shrug. Eidor drew back his hand and flung the wands through the open door.

The barrier only worked on people, after all.

In a colorful arc of silver, orange, and purple, the wands flew into the room. The chicken flapped her wings, hopped a few feet into the air, and caught the orange wand in her beak. The lizard stood up on the end of her tail, her short arms waving, and just managed to catch the purple wand.

The silver wand landed on the floor. Alicia, at the treadle, dared not move to fetch it. "Hurry!" she cried, her squirrel squeak surprisingly commanding. "Help the Chosen One!"

Lolly and Viola scurried back to the window. Viola, using her tiny hands, worked its latch and pushed it open. They looked down into the yard where Franz perched on the shoulders of King Pintamore, with Roselee whirling around him like a small green tornado and the Swamp Beast soaking the king's knees with slaver.

Lolly turned her head. A pulse of magical potency brimming with orange light built up on the end of her wand. The magic stored up in her fairy being for five hundred years surged inside it, eager for release, eager for direction. "*Bwaaawk, bwok-bwok-bwok!*" Lolly cried and shot enchantment in a stream from the wand's end.

Viola cried, "Be small, furry, and cute!" She blinked her goggly eyes at her friend. "That's what you meant, right?"

Lolly shrugged.

Magic flew in a brilliant arch, lighting up the dawn courtyard with orange glow as bright as midday. Then it fell like a streaking star. The Swamp Beast looked up, its mighty jaws gaping, and the magic plummeted directly down its slavering gullet.

The Beast gulped. Then it hiccupped.

One last burst of orange sparkles, and Franz stared down at a bulldog puppy worrying away at the feet of King Pintamore.

Franz let out a huge sigh of relief. Roselee, floating at his shoulders, gave him an enormous, glowing smile. "Quick now, Chosen One!" she said. "You've only got to climb the stairs, and your princess awaits your kiss!"

Franz, still holding tight to Crete's pin, started to slip his legs from around the statue's shoulders . . . when suddenly the world went dark.

Chapter 11

L ADY MARA stepped through the ruins of the doorway leading up from
the dungeon. Two handsome henchmen followed her, but they were
difficult to see for the raging, roiling storm of darkness that wrapped
the Mistress of Briardale in a maelstrom of malice.

From behind her wafting veils she saw the red-haired bank clerk
perched on the shoulders of the stone king. She saw her cute little Slavering
Swamp Beast snorting and pawing at the statue's knees, its curly tail
wagging. She saw the fairies high in the tower window . . . holding their
wands.

A sneer creased her lips, unseen by all and yet somehow sensed like
the shiver of ice on a spring morning.

"Do you imagine I will allow my curses to be broken after all this time?" she cried, and even her henchmen flinched away at the terrible thunder of her voice. She raised her right arm, her fingers curling and kneading the air as she formed a ball of enchantment between her long black nails. She aimed directly at Franz and cried, "*Il'v*—uggggh!"

Her eyes could not perceive the stream of green vapors that whipped across the courtyard quicker than thought, darted through her veils, and plunged into her mouth, choking the enchantment before it could be fully spoken.

Franz, clinging to the stone crown, stared aghast at the little puffs of ectoplasm vanishing in his ghost friend's wake. "*Roselee!*" he cried, straining his eyes for some sign of her appearing out the other side of Lady Mara's head, even as she had darted through the Swamp Beast's eye.

But there was nothing. Not even the faintest green glimmer.

Crete and Eidor, almost falling over themselves in their haste, burst out the tower doorway into the courtyard. Their mission of delivering the wands accomplished, they did what True Heroes must do—charged back into the thick of the action. "Hurry, Franz!" Crete shouted even as his mighty legs propelled him across the statue-littered yard. "Get up there!"

Lady Mara, still choking and gagging, almost doubled up against the sickness boiling in her stomach, gestured wildly with one arm. Her henchmen, understanding the silent command, drew their swords and ran out into the yard. The raven-haired one would have caught Franz by the back of the collar even as he leapt free of the statue, but something furious and invisible head-butted him in the stomach and sent him sprawling.

"Some hero you are!" Eidor, now visible, snarled at the brawny human who lay groaning at his feet. "Picking on a skinny little banker's clerk . . . *pshaw!* Why don't you pick on someone *half* your size for a change?" He kicked the former hero in the ribs.

The golden-haired hero dodged behind a great stone horse then sprang leapfrog-like over the shoulders of an elegant lady elf who had stood for centuries half bent, adjusting her skirts. Franz, with a desperate glance to one side, saw a mighty arm reach out and knew he lacked the speed to outrun a True Hero, however false that hero may have proven himself.

But with a battle roar, Crete sprang between Franz and his assailant, swinging his huge arms. Without a thought for himself—because true True Heroes never think of themselves when rescuing the helpless—he knocked aside the golden-haired hero's sword with his left fist and planted his right fist in the man's chiseled jaw with a satisfying *crack*.

"Go on, Franz!" he cried.

Franz picked up his pace, finding reserves of speed he never knew he had. He was so desperate to reach the tower doorway that he couldn't even spare passing notice for the bulldog puppy yapping at his heels. He was almost there! He was going to make it!

Suddenly a wicked voice bellowed in a horrible croak: "*Il've!*"

Franz braced himself, fully expecting to turn into something hideous. Instead, he heard a low "*Mooooooo!*" somewhere behind him.

"*Il've!*" Lady Mara shouted again, and this time Franz heard a forlorn donkey's bray.

He had no time to think of this, however. He must get through that door, climb that stair, kiss that princess!

Hardly knowing how he got there, he found himself racing up the tower stairs, one hand pressed to the wall for support—for he was very out of breath—the hand holding Crete's pin pressed against his side where a painful stitch stabbed him with every gasping breath. Yet he did not pause, did not hesitate. He climbed those stairs as fast as any hero ever could, turning the last bend and seeing an open door before him. He raced for it—

And hit the invisible barrier.

"Ow!" Sparks flashing before his eyes, he crumpled on the top step, one hand clapped over his nose, blood trickling between his fingers. The *whir-whir-whir* of a spinning wheel filled his ears. His vision cleared, and he saw the squirrel at the treadle in the middle of the room, pumping for all she was worth.

A chicken and a lizard stood just beyond the doorway, wands gripped in beak and claws. Magic brimmed up in those wands . . . but magic of only two colors.

The lizard twisted her little head around. "Alicia!" she cried. "We need you too! We can't open the barrier without you!"

The squirrel stared desperately at the silver wand lying on the floor between her and the doorway. "Someone's got to turn the wheel!" she squeaked.

Darkness filled the stairwell, rising up like a rushing tide. Franz staggered to his feet, his whole face throbbing. He turned, looked down, and saw the roiling smoke of evil. Flashes of red enchantment tore through the darkness like lightning. Lady Mara had entered the tower.

"*Bwok-bwok-bwok!*" scolded Lolly around her wand. And Viola lashed her spotted tail. "Hurry, Alicia! We've *got* to try!"

The squirrel pushed at the treadle, her tail flicking. Her snapping black eyes fixed on the hero standing just outside—the skinny, stoop-shouldered, utterly unheroic hero. Was he worth all of this?

Did she have a choice but to hope?

She gave the treadle one last vigorous push. Then she sprang for her wand, snatching it up in her tiny claws.

The wheel spun . . . it slowed . . .

Alicia took her place between her sisters. "Barrier BREAK!" the squirrel cried.

Orange, purple, and silver light flashed from the wands. Then orange, purple, and silver cracks appeared in mid-air, like shards of glass. Something shattered.

The darkness billowed up, ready to choke Franz. He staggered forward, bursting through the last remnants of the barrier and into the tower room.

. . . the wheel slowed . . . slowed . . .

Casting about, he saw the stone girl on the floor, her face partially covered with stone curls. With complete disregard for his knees, Franz flung himself to the floor beside her, almost falling atop her.

. . . slowed . . . sloooooowed . . .

No time for thought. No time for doubt. No time to worry over the fact that he wasn't *really* a hero.

Franz kissed the princess right on her stone mouth.

. . . the wheel stopped . . . .

Chapter 12

THE WHEEL stopped . . . and nothing happened.

No crack of doom. No crumbling to dust. No final, tragic death wails of souls lost.

Alicia, Lolly, and Viola exchanged glances. Then Viola exclaimed, "Your . . . your *faces!*"

But Franz did not see or notice this. He still knelt beside the beautiful stone princess, his mouth slightly puckered from the kiss he'd just given, staring hard. "Please . . . please, Roselee . . ." he whispered.

Was that a flush of pink staining those gray cheeks? No question about it! And the flush spread and spread, and then the stone folds of the gown were lavender, and the parted lips were rosy, and long eyelashes fluttered over sparkling green eyes, and a dainty hand reached up to brush away curls of . . . bright blue.

Blue?

The most beautiful young woman in all the world frowned, wrinkled her nose, and groaned. "I seem to have hit my head on something! Bother that." She blinked those amazing eyes again, her gaze focusing on Franz. "Who are you?"

Franz gaped at her. "Your . . . your hair is blue."

The princess sat up, pushing blue locks from her eyes, which she narrowed upon Franz. "Did you just *kiss* me?"

"Uh, yes, I—" Franz gave a yelp and pulled back as her sharp slap stung his cheek.

"Ugh!" The princess shuddered and wiped her lips with the back of her hand. "Filthy, disgusting . . . and you're *human* too, aren't you? Ooooooh!" She shook her head, stuck her tongue out, and gagged. "How did a *human* boy get in here? Auntie Alicia will turn you into a rabbit, you know. She really will!"

"No, she really won't," said a voice of pure silver.

Franz turned then and saw three glorious women—not quite as beautiful as the princess, of course, but otherworldly and amazing in their own right. One wore a purple fur coat, and her eyes were like two enormous violets. One wore a peaked orange cap trailing veils of saffron hue, and her hair was the color of fresh-squeezed citrus juice.

The third had white hair pulled back severely from her startlingly young and lovely face. She carried herself like a queen in her silver gown, though when she spoke, one might glimpse the faintest trace of rather overlarge front teeth.

"Well, boy," said Guardian Alicia, moving to stand over Franz and the princess. "It seems you are a True Hero after all."

"Me?" Franz gazed wide-eyed up at the stern fairy, realizing that she must be right since his kiss *had* worked to break the curses on Briardale. "B-but how?" he stammered, trying to get to his feet and finding his legs too rubbery for the effort. "I've never moved a mountain or slain a dragon or . . ."

Guardian Alicia's wand tapped on Franz's hand, and it turned and opened to reveal the bright jeweled pin lying in his palm.

"You have saved a kingdom," said Alicia, smiling despite herself. "The whole Kingdom of Homunculi owes you its undying gratitude for preventing it from being crushed by the Slavering Swamp Beast. No mean feat for any True Hero!"

Franz blinked at the pin. A kingdom! And he, a bank clerk . . . he'd saved it!

The princess crossed her arms and shrugged her dainty white shoulders up to her ears. "What *are* you going on about, Auntie?" she demanded.

Guardian Alicia addressed herself to her charge. "Princess Maralyn, allow me to introduce you to your hero and rescuer—Franz Happernickle."

"My hero?" repeated the princess, giving Franz a look of mingled disbelief and disapproval. She sniffed. "A *human* hero?"

"As it turns out, True Heroes come in all shapes and sizes," Guardian Alicia replied, nodding sagely. "That silly girl Roselee may have more sense in her head than I gave her credit for."

Franz, hearing this, turned suddenly back to the princess. Though she was overwhelmingly gorgeous and gazing at him with an expression not quite as disgusted as it had been, he found his heart sinking with sudden realization. "You aren't Roselee," he said.

She raised a pretty eyebrow. "Who's Roselee?"

Guardian Alicia gasped in astonishment, her eyes flashing down at Franz. "You thought *Roselee* was the princess? Whatever gave you *that* idea?"

Franz blushed almost as bright as his hair and couldn't meet the fairy's eye. "It's just . . . I thought maybe . . ."

"Gracious, boy, Roselee is the furthest thing from a royal elf princess you'll ever find!" Alicia continued with a toss of her silvery head. "Why, she's nothing but a—"

"Bwok—*ahem!* I mean to say, Alicia!" came Lolly's voice. Everyone turned to the orange-hatted fairy at the tower window. She pushed open the casement, stepped out onto the balcony, then turned and beckoned to the others. "Come and see this!"

Everyone crowded onto the balcony, except for Franz. Even the princess picked herself up, dusted herself off, and hurried to squeeze herself between fairies for a foremost view. "Look!" Franz heard her say. "Father's come to visit. Why are that donkey and that stumpy little cow in the courtyard though? And . . . is that Aunt Mara? Ooooh, Father does *not* look happy with her!"

Alicia drew back into the room, pulling the princess by the hand along with her. "We'd best go down and explain the situation to King Pintamore," she said, speaking to her two sisters. Then she gave a sigh, shaking her head at the princess. "Though how I'm going to explain *this*"—she plucked up a blue curl and rubbed it sadly between finger and thumb—"I really don't know. Why did you have to enspell it such a horrendous color?"

The princess huffed and threw up her hands, turning to Franz. "Do you see what I put up with? They don't let me do *anything* I like! This is why I ran up here to hide from them; they put up such a fuss over nothing!"

Franz had no answer to offer. When the three fairies and the princess started down the stairs, he trailed after, still carrying Crete's kingdom in his hand. His heart sank further with every step he took.

Where was Roselee? Everyone else seemed to be waking and freed from the evil enchantments . . . but what about her? Was she still a ghost?

Was she really dead?

Did she sacrifice herself when she plunged down Lady Mara's throat?

This thought made him sick. Granted, he'd not known the green girl for long, and she'd caused him far more trouble than he'd ever hoped to experience in the whole of his life. Because of her, he'd been straight-jacketed, sent to a lunatic asylum, thrown into a dungeon, almost devoured by a Slavering Swamp Beast or hacked to pieces by henchmen's swords . . . but . . .

But she'd also believed in him. She'd seen a hero in him when no one else did.

What if she was gone for good?

As Franz followed the others through the tower doorway, he heard a high-pitched yelp and felt a worrying at his foot. He looked down to discover the Slavering Swamp Beast savaging the lace of his shoe. He gave it a gentle nudge that did nothing to discourage it, then shrugged and ignored it.

"Father!" exclaimed Princess Maralyn in delight, rushing across the courtyard—a courtyard suddenly crowded with many gloriously clad and radiantly beautiful elf courtiers and steeds. Standing in the center of that throng was the most glorious and radiant of them all, a noble king fully seven feet tall and wearing a crown (which Franz remembered having held onto rather tightly, and blushed again).

Maralyn flew through the gathering and flung herself into her father's arms. "Oh, it's so good to see you!" she said brightly. "Have you come to celebrate my birthday?"

Only then did Franz see the hunched figure kneeling before the king—a figure in ratty black robes, unglamorous without enchantments. Her veils were gone too, revealing a face no longer beautiful. Indeed, all of the elfin glory Lady Mara once possessed had faded away over the last five hundred years, leaving her face scarred by her own bitterness and evil. She was little more than a shriveled hag huddled in a heap at the feet of her mighty brother.

King Pintamore, his expression stern and severe, softened visibly at his daughter's embrace, no doubt relieved to find her healthy and whole. "Are you well, my dear?" he asked her earnestly.

"Perfectly so!" the princess replied.

The king looked unconvinced. "What happened to . . . your hair?" he asked, lifting a lock from her face. "It looks appalling."

Maralyn's smiles vanished into disdainful frowns. She sniffed and pulled away from her father, crossing her arms and rolling her eyes. "You're just as bad as Auntie Alicia," she declared. "Everyone wants me to be *perfect* all the time! But maybe I don't want to *be* perfect. Maybe I want to be *me* now and then!"

King Pintamore, well accustomed to his daughter's dramatics, offered no argument to this, saying only, "We'll discuss it later. For now . . . Guardians Alicia, Lolly, and Viola? Where are you?"

The crowd of elf courtiers parted, and the three beautiful fairies passed through, wands glinting, translucent wings wafting in the morning breeze. They curtsied to the king, who acknowledged them with a gracious nod. "What has happened here?" he asked. "I'm guessing we did *not* avoid my sister's sleeping curse after all."

"No, indeed, Your Majesty," Guardian Alicia replied. "In fact, the situation became much worse than any of us might have guessed!"

She, Lolly, and Viola went on to explain what had transpired over the last five hundred years. It amazed Franz how easily King Pintamore accepted and even disregarded the fact that half a millennium had flown past while he slept in stone. Elves live according to very different streams of time, Franz guessed.

As the story unfolded, Franz looked around, feeling uncomfortable and out of place in this gathering. Off to one side of the crowd he saw a donkey and a stubby-legged bull. Something about them seemed familiar, particularly the bull's incongruous bristling beard. Deciding that since he was a True Hero himself now—officially speaking—he might as well be with the other True Heroes, Franz shuffled over to stand between them, dragging the Slavering Swamp Beast with him (for it had clamped its jaws on his trouser leg and refused to let go). He offered his friends awkward smiles. The bull glared, but the donkey gave him a friendly ear-twitch.

"And so you see," Guardian Alicia finished grandly as the elf king's court listened with rapt attention, "Franz Happernickle proved himself a True Hero at the last and awakened Princess Maralyn from her sleep."

King Pintamore glanced around, his gaze at last resting on Franz standing there between donkey and bull. "Is this true?" he asked, his noble voice full of the music of ancient stars . . . and utterly intimidating. "Did you rescue my daughter?"

"I . . . I kissed her awake, yes," Franz replied, bowing awkwardly and blushing more brilliantly than ever. "But I couldn't have done it without the help of my friends. They're True Heroes too, you see. Crete, Eidor . . . and Paisley."

He frowned, his gaze darting about the crowd. He saw the raven-haired and golden-haired heroes bound and held by two tall elf lords. He saw Lady Mara kneeling before her brother, grinning her ugly grin. But . . . "Where *is* Paisley?" Franz asked.

"*GRAAAAAAUP!*"

Something wriggled in the depths of Lady Mara's pocket. Then out popped the sad face of an enormous toad.

"Oh, you *hideous* thing!" Princess Maralyn shrieked.

But to everyone's utmost surprise, she followed up this shriek by striding over to her aunt and plucking the toad right out of the pocket. Then she held it up for everyone to see, its back legs kicking out straight behind, its buggy eyes blinking. How much more revolting that warty body looked in the delicate white hands of the fairest maiden in all the land!

"Really, I don't think you could *be* any uglier!" the princess declared, then deliberately planted an enormous kiss on those toady lips.

The toad's eyes bulged. Its legs kicked rapidly.

Then, with a little *pop!* it vanished in a puff of smoke. The smoke churned then cleared . . . and standing there hand-in-hand with the princess was Paisley. Though he was hardly any better looking than the toad.

Lady Mara laughed. The laugh began in her gut, rumbled up through her throat, and poured out from her thin, snarling lips like an overflow of venom. "Now, Paisley!" she cried in the creaking voice of a crone. "Now let your pretty lady see your *true* face, unhidden by my beauty spells! Now see how fast your friendship *really* is! *Ah hahahaha!*" She shook her head wildly, her eyes rolling with wickedness. "You should never have betrayed me!"

Paisley ducked his head, looking as though he wanted to melt into the courtyard paving stones. But before he could even cast about for a place to run and hide, Princess Maralyn's hand cracked across his face. Franz winced, knowing how much power the dainty princess could put into a slap.

"*That,*" said Maralyn, "is for being *unpardonably* rude."

Paisley blinked at her in shock. She made a face and tweaked his nose. "Don't you even remember what you said?"

"I . . . I . . ." Paisley hung his head. "I should never have laughed at you for coloring your hair."

"You're absolutely right!" Maralyn replied with a haughty toss of those brilliant blue locks. "Honestly, you're as old fashioned as my father! Laughing at a girl like that. Is it any wonder I told you I'd never see you again?"

"I'm so sorry, Maralyn," Paisley said, his eyes full of remorse and longing. "I never should have laughed. I should have . . . I should have . . ."

"Yes?"

"I should have told you what I truly think . . . that you are the most beautiful woman in the whole wide world!"

Maralyn narrowed her eyes. "And my hair?"

"Is the most beautiful hair in all of existence!"

The princess smiled. And if her face had been beautiful before in its frowns, it became unbearably brilliant with that one smile. Right there in front of everyone, she caught the ugly Swamp Elf by his enormous ears and kissed him full on the mouth with just as little care as she'd kissed the toad.

Paisley looked as if he might faint.

When the princess pulled back, she spoke lightly, "You're forgiven. Come meet my father."

Franz exchanged glances with the donkey and the bull. A tiny part of him felt insulted. Kissing Paisley didn't seem to bother the princess one jot, while kissing him had given her the shudders! Oh, well. So being a True Hero didn't always mean getting much appreciation.

King Pintamore received his daughter's sweetheart with some reserved coolness but expressed gratitude nonetheless for the brave part Paisley had played in rescuing the princess. Then he turned and addressed himself once more to Franz. "And are these all of the heroes?" he asked.

"All but one," Franz replied. "There was also . . . Roselee. We couldn't have done what we did without her. She traveled the whole world over to find all of us and risked herself again and again to help us."

The donkey brayed and the bull lowed in agreement, nodding their heavy heads. The Slavering Swamp Beast, sitting on Franz's foot (which by now stood in a pool of slaver), wagged its curly tail and yipped.

King Pintamore looked thoughtful. "Where is this Roselee?" he asked.

The crowd of beautiful elves murmured. Even Lady Mara and the two handsome henchmen looked around, searching the various corners of the courtyard. Franz felt his heart sink again. Was she gone forever, swallowed by the evil enchantress?

Then a little figure clad in a somewhat threadbare dress appeared in the doorway of the asylum. She looked out at the assembly, gulped, and lowered her gaze. When she managed to look up again, she met Franz's wondering eyes . . . and smiled.

He knew her at once. She might not be green anymore, or even remotely ghoulish. But she was definitely Roselee!

"Ah!" said Guardian Alicia, moving lightly across the stones to take the girl by the hand and lead her forward to meet the king. "Here she is. Your Majesty, meet Roselee, a human housemaid we employed to help with the menial chores while my sisters and I focused our attentions on watching your daughter."

Franz remembered then with a jolt—remembered a passage in Paisley's book he had read and entirely overlooked! *"The princess was lonely in her solitary life, hidden away at Briardale. With only her three fairies— disguised as her aunties—and a housemaid for company . . ."*

The housemaid! Poor Roselee, just a little housemaid, summoned to do the monumental task the fairies had intended for the king himself! And yet she'd done it, laboring over five hundred years.

If ever there was a True Hero in this world . . . Franz shook his head in disbelief and amazement.

Guardian Alicia explained quickly about summoning a ghost to help them when the three fairies found themselves trapped in the tower. She explained how Roselee had gone hunting for heroes. "It wasn't her fault the first several didn't succeed. As a human, it was only natural she'd try human heroes first, little realizing how susceptible they are to greed and ambition." She cast a withering glare at the two handsome henchmen with these words.

"But in the end," said King Pintamore after listening to all, "it was a human who rescued our princess."

"A true-hearted human," Roselee piped up bravely, offering a little bobbing curtsy as she did so. She looked around and grinned at Franz again. "The truest-hearted I ever saw."

Franz felt his heart swelling at her words. He thought he might burst with joy and pride!

Embarrassed, he looked down at his feet and met the gaze of the Slavering Swamp Beast, which wriggled and rolled onto its back, kicking stubby feet in the air. Why, Franz realized, even Slavering Swamp Beasts no longer held any fear for him! Roselee had named him a True Hero, and a True Hero he was . . . thanks to her.

He knelt and rubbed the Swamp Beast's belly, too delighted in that moment even to speak.

Epilogue

FRANZ SAT on the front steps of the castle he had once thought would be his doom. Now, waiting in the early morning light for the carriage that would carry him home, he was surprised to realize how reluctant he was to leave Briardale behind. His experiences there had been weird, otherworldly, even harrowing . . . but they were experiences he would never forget!

After Pintamore magically changed Crete and Eidor back into their appropriate shapes and banished Mara and her henchmen to the same dungeon cell she'd used to imprison the heroes, the king of the elves had set to the real work—restoring the broken minds of all the lunatics Mara had gathered into Briardale's halls. This had taken such a long time that the three fairies eventually shooed Franz, Roselee, Crete, and Eidor away to catch a few hours of sleep. After all, they'd had a full night of heroics and were properly worn out!

That evening, the princess's birthday feast was held in the courtyard of Briardale under myriad brilliant lanterns. The True Heroes had been invited to attend, naturally. In the middle of the feast, Maralyn had announced her betrothal to Paisley the Swamp Elf, much to the scandalized delight of all those present . . . and the stern interest of her father, who told the young couple that they would discuss the matter later. Franz rather thought from the look in Maralyn's eye that she would have her own way in the end. He was glad for Paisley, who was so happy that his ugly face became *almost* handsome.

Following Maralyn's announcement, Pintamore summoned the True Heroes to him one by one . . . starting with Roselee.

"You, Roselee the Housemaid," he declared in a solemn voice before all the court, "shall henceforth be known as Lady Roselee the Valiant, Heroine of the Elves."

Roselee blushed and smiled shyly as a great cheer went up for her among the gathering. King Pintamore placed a jeweled collar around her neck then bade her resume her seat. She almost fell into her chair next to Franz, whispering to him, "Batwings and buzzards! I never expected that!"

Crete and Eidor were summoned next. They both looked bold and properly heroic (now that they were restored to their proper shapes) as they bowed to the king and accepted jeweled collars of their own. Then Pintamore asked them what wish he might grant them in gratitude for their services.

"Well," said Crete, fingering the pin on his vest, "ever since I left home, I haven't been able to shrink *quite* small enough to return. It's the curse of leaving Homunculi. My king warned me about it. Do you think . . . is there anything you can do?"

Pintamore nodded and touched Crete on the top of his head. A little flash of light, and Crete smiled suddenly, relieved. "That's fixed it!" he cried. "I can feel it! I'll be able to return home as soon as I want."

The king nodded and addressed himself to Eidor. "And you, Son of the King Under the Low Ceiling?"

The dwarf shrugged. "My dad's going to be furious at me for being away two hundred years without notice. A few extra jewels and some gold would certainly make my homecoming easier!"

Pintamore solemnly declared that jewels and gold would be granted in abundance. Crete and Eidor returned to their places on either side of Franz and Roselee, both delighted with their rewards.

"Next, Franz Happernickle," King Pintamore said.

Franz, his knees knocking, rose and presented himself to the king. He would never get used to having so many elfin eyes fixed on him at once. He hadn't even believed elves *existed* a few days ago!

Pintamore presented Franz with a jeweled collar which would no doubt purchase all of Mr. Teabody's bank and half of Yoleston besides. Sweat broke out across Franz's brow at the mere weight of it.

"And what wish might I grant the True Hero of Briardale, Waker of the Sleeping Beauty?" King Pintamore asked.

Franz blushed and looked away, uncertain what to request. His gaze happened to alight upon a sad little shape tethered to a post on the far side of the courtyard, lying with its heavy jowls between its paws and feeling very sorry for itself. When it caught Franz's eye, it wagged its curly tail faintly.

"I'd . . . I'd really like to keep the Slavering Swamp Beast," Franz said, shuffling his feet nervously. "If it's all the same with you."

King Pintamore looked bemused. "Your wish is granted," he declared. "Bring the Slavering Swamp Beast to the True Hero of Briardale!"

So the Beast was fetched, yelping delightedly as it was placed in Franz's arms. It sat on his feet through the rest of the feast, slavering mightily every time Franz or Roselee slipped it a tasty tidbit.

That was all yesterday evening. Now Franz sat on the front steps of Briardale with the Slavering Swamp Beast on its leash beside him. He was to return to Yoleston today. Yoleston, which had branded him a lunatic and sent him off in a straightjacket to meet his fate. To be sure, Yoleston was quite likely to welcome back with open arms a young man as wealthy as Franz now found himself—his pockets bulging with gold and the jeweled collar hidden under his shirt. He should be able to make a place for himself and maybe do some good for other unfortunates who suffered under the cruelty of the likes of Mr. Teabody and the judge.

Still . . . Franz sighed and looked around. He'd hoped his friends would show up to say goodbye. Crete and Eidor, perhaps. Had they already set off for their homelands? And what about . . .

"What about Roselee?" he whispered.

The Slavering Swamp Beast whined and tilted its head at him. Franz rubbed it behind one floppy ear. "It's all right, boy," he said. "At least we have each other."

Hearing a rumble, Franz looked up to see the king's own carriage roll out into the middle of the courtyard. He would certainly arrive home in Yoleston in style! With another heavy sigh he stood, scooped up the Slavering Swamp Beast under one arm, and cast a last glance about, just in case he should happen to spy a friendly face. Then, knowing he couldn't put it off any longer, he walked over to the carriage, opened the door, and—

"You get to sit next to Crete," said a cranky voice. "He gets carriage-sick."

Franz blinked into the bearded face of a dwarf and the grinning face of a homunculus. "Eidor! Crete! What are you doing here?"

"We're escorting you home," said Crete, reaching out a hand to help

Franz climb aboard. "We discussed it and decided that, as True Heroes, we can't let you go by yourself to face those idiots who condemned you to an asylum. No, we'll make sure you're properly established before we go. You, and Roselee too, of course."

"Roselee?" Franz took his seat beside Crete, settling the Slavering Swamp Beast in his lap. His vision adjusted to the dimness inside the carriage and he saw . . .

"Isn't this exciting?"

He saw a bright-faced young lady wearing a neat frock with white cuffs and collar, her hair done up in two braids atop her head. She may not be green or glowing, but she was utterly and completely Roselee.

"You're coming to Yoleston too?" Franz gasped even as the coachman shut the door and the coach rattled into motion. "I thought you'd been named Lady Heroine of the Elves. Don't you want to live at King Pintamore's court?"

Roselee laughed and shook her head. "I'm human! I don't want to spend my whole life among shiny, solemn *elves*. Besides, I've been a ghost for five hundred years—a lot has happened in the human world during that time. Electric lights! Indoor plumbing! There's so much I want to see and experience."

So saying, she reached out and grabbed Franz's hand, giving it a squeeze. He realized that it was the first time she had actually touched him since getting her body back.

Eidor snorted and crossed his arms. "Stop grinning at each other, you two saps! Can't bear sentimental tosh, certainly not for the whole ride into town."

But Franz couldn't stop smiling. Whatever life in Yoleston held for him in the future, he knew somehow that it was going to be much more . . . *interesting* than it had ever been before. Meeting Roselee's cheery gaze across that little distance, he suspected there would be many more grins in his future.

ABOUT THE AUTHOR

GRACE MULLINS, who lives in North Carolina, has loved fiction since she was very young. When she's not hiding away in her room and writing stories, she reads/blogs fiction, devours sweets, daydreams of traveling the world . . . and teaches a K-3 class that can be as challenging as anything to be found in adventure fantasy. One of Grace's dreams has  been to be published, and she thanks God for giving her the desire of her heart.

To learn more about Grace, visit
www.ItsSimplyGrace.blogspot.com

To Caroline, Holly, Isaac, and Heidi—
my own little magic makers.

RIAR FEN Castle lay shrouded in thorns and silence. Lona didn't know which was worse, though both were her own doing. The thorns grew in a dense tangle around the castle grounds, creeping over battlements and towers, and squeezing through cracks in the crumbling walls. Over a hundred years ago, Lona had enchanted them and trained their spreading arms into a living fortress to keep people away, but now they encroached where they weren't invited.

They snagged her cloak as she walked past them in the courtyard. "Cheeky thorns," Lona muttered. She tapped them with her wand and they quivered and fell away. "If I weren't vigilant, they would swallow us whole." Then realizing that she was talking to the length of red fur in her hand, a squirrel she'd caught in a snare, she laughed. "Not that you care. You're dead.

And on your way to my soup pot."

Lona proceeded through the crumbling ruin, remembering its glory days. It had never been as magnificent as White Thorn Castle, Timber Vale's royal seat, but it had been grand. Now it held only rotting tapestries, tarnished suits of armor, and rooms long ago abandoned to dust and spiders.

Birds and small animals that took shelter in the ruins flew and scampered about as her presence disturbed them. She huffed at their distrust, forgetting that she dangled one of their fellows in her hand.

In early years she had wondered if the lack of companionship would affect her sanity. Sacrificing a bit of magic, she had enchanted some of the animals, giving them speech. However, even with human words on their tongues, the animals' thoughts seldom strayed from finding food or a mate. Finally, she gave up trying. Indeed, she'd stopped worrying about her sanity altogether, for what did it matter?

She entered the large, dark kitchen and stepped surely to the worktable, though the red coals on the hearth provided little light. With gentle care she laid the squirrel down to rest while she stoked the fire and set a pot of water on to boil. Then, by flickering firelight, she prepared the squirrel and gently lowered it into the steaming water.

"There, isn't that lovely?" She paused, frowned, and then added ingredients to the pot. "Here are some carrots and turnips to keep you company while I check on the princess."

Princess Arabella's chamber was in the west tower, on the same side of the castle but down a dark, narrow passage and up a winding, uneven staircase. Upon reaching the top tower room, she scanned the chamber for any sign of change. Satisfied that all was as it should be, she placed her torch in an iron ring on the wall and said, "Well, Your Highness, and how are you this evening?"

Arabella's golden curls lay over her shoulders, gleaming in the torchlight, and the pink of her lips and cheeks cast shame on the roses that bloomed among the briars climbing around the chamber walls.

"Such beauty, and none to see it but me." Lona *tsked* and shook her head. "But there is dust on your face, and I know you hate that." She blew along the length of her wand, and a ribbon of wind swirled, fluttering Arabella's gown and hair as it whirled away the dust and carried it out the small window.

A distant thud sounded deep within the castle, startling Lona into stillness. "Someone opened the passage. It must be Lady Rhoswen. Surely it is, for who else knows of it? I must go."

Lona took the torch and scurried down the tower steps, along the passageway in the outer wall, across the courtyard, and into the great hall built against the craggy cliff that guarded the rear of the castle. Behind the hall was the royal chamber, where a secret passage opened into a tunnel that led to a natural cave overlooking the Sage River. But Lona didn't make it that far.

Lady Rhoswen walked across the throne room, her face illuminated by a torch in the grasp of a tall, broad man whose face was lost in shadows. Only his ear and a sliver of his face caught the glow of the torch, but Lona knew it was John, Rhoswen's personal guard.

As Lady Rhoswen drew near, Lona dropped into a curtsy. "My lady. I didn't expect to see you again so soon."

"No. I did not know that I'd be coming myself. But we must talk. Do you have a fire lit anywhere?"

"Yes, my lady. In the kitchen."

"Excellent. Take me there. I am chilled from the caves."

Lady Rhoswen was a petite creature whose delicate air of fragility was deceiving, Lona knew. The woman was made of iron. Still, Lona led the way without hesitation.

Lona glanced around the kitchen as she entered, trying to see it as Lady Rhoswen would, and felt uncomfortable about entertaining such a grand lady there. The wall around the hearth was blackened by soot, bundles of drying herbs dangled from the ceiling beams, and there was nothing but a stool to sit on.

But Lady Rhoswen's face revealed no disdain as she looked around the room and crossed to the hearth. The gold roses embroidered around the hem of her forest-green riding habit glinted in the firelight, as did the bright red ringlets falling over her shoulder.

"What is this you have simmering?"

"Squirrel soup."

The lady shuddered. "How can you? I cannot understand why you scavenge for food when you can simply wave your wand and have anything you want to eat."

"But at what cost? You know that I drain my well of life with each bit of magic I use. It is far more practical to eat real food and spare my magic for important things."

Lady Rhoswen rolled her eyes. "My dear, you are overly cautious. A pleasant meal would not cost you much."

"My sisters were less careful with their magic, and they are gone. So much wasted, so much lost."

"They used their magic to protect the princess," Lady Rhoswen said, her voice measured but sharp. "Do you consider that a waste?"

Lona refused to let her eyes drop. "No, never that. But that was not all they were asked to do."

"Without their help, I never could have spared my people from the worst of my father's ravages upon this kingdom."

"But at what cost to my people?"

With shaking fingers pressed to her face, Lady Rhoswen turned away. "Stop speaking of what cannot be undone."

Boots scuffed against the stone floor behind Lona, and she spun around. She had forgotten about the guard.

"Are you well, my lady?" he asked.

Lady Rhoswen turned slowly, visibly struggling to compose herself. "Yes, John. Wait for me in the passage."

The man hesitated, but bowed and strode from the room.

With weary steps Rhoswen moved to the stool and sank down on it. "I must not tarry. I have come because of my father. He is dead."

This was astounding news, but Lona was not surprised to see no sorrow on Lady Rhoswen's face. She had been at war with her father for a century.

"How did he die?"

"He had a fitting end for one who poisoned his own brother. His supply of the Elixir of Abeyance ran out, and in desperation he tried to make more."

"And poisoned himself as a result," Lona finished for her, nodding.

"The youth it gave was hard for him to relinquish, aside from his ambitions to take the throne. I expected this to happen, now that no one but you was left to provide him with the potion."

"And I wouldn't have given it to him." Lona had despised Rhoswen's father, Galloran, nearly as much Rhoswen herself did, for what he'd done to Arabella.

The younger son by ten years, Galloran had grown up with no thought of inheriting the throne from his elder brother, Wesley. But when the king and queen remained childless long after Galloran had grown, married, and fathered Rhoswen, he had begun to set his heart on becoming king someday. Then, long after anyone would have believed it possible, the frail and aging queen conceived. Upon the birth of a healthy baby girl, Galloran had conspired against her innocent life.

And thus had begun a tragic chain of events.

"I am grateful that I have always had a potion of your making to take," Rhoswen said, breaking into Lona's thoughts. "I would trust no one else's hand with something so volatile."

"I have always taken the greatest care with yours," Lona said somberly. Then her eyes brightened. "But you will no longer need it. With your father gone, you may resume your natural life. You can even bear children if you wish. I am sure you will no longer be barren once the potion is out of your system."

"I intend to do exactly that, and many other things. I will marry again and forge ties with another kingdom. I will restore our agriculture and trade so that our people may flourish once more."

"But surely, my lady, that will be work for Arabella to do. You have inherited the regency, but now that your father is gone, we may concentrate on breaking the curse. You should send out a proclamation calling for princes and lords to come. Send away the dragon and move soldiers into the fens to clear out the thieves so the journey is safe."

Lady Rhoswen's face had been bright and expressive, but now it smoothed into impassivity. "No. Such effort would be fruitless, and the monarchy must be made secure or the kingdom will erupt into chaos. All these years, I have hoped to see my dear, sweet cousin take her rightful place, but we no longer have the luxury of time. We must face the truth: This curse will never be broken."

"It's a spell now, not a curse," Lona argued, feeling as if the floor were shifting beneath her feet but not sure why.

"Ah, yes. Well, you did what you could there. Such a shame you were so young and inexperienced. A wiser fairy wouldn't have placed such an impossible impediment to the spell's being broken."

"I didn't mean to say it," Lona said, her voice quiet with shame. "I was going to say she would be awakened by another prick with the spindle, but Isemay spoke in my ear and her words came out of my mouth before I could stop them. *True love's kiss.* Of all the shatter-brained ideas."

"Exactly so. Thus I fear there is but one merciful thing to do."

Lona's eyes grew round. "Merciful? What do you mean?"

"I mean, my dear fairy, it isn't kind to let Arabella remain forever in an enchanted sleep. The kingdom cannot bear it either. I have made my decision: If she has not awakened by the waning of the moon, we shall release her from the curse however we must."

An icy chill ran through Lona's veins. She knew exactly what Lady Rhoswen proposed; she could see the answer clearly in the lady's eye. "I won't let you do it," she said.

Lady Rhoswen stood and wrapped her cloak around her shoulders. "Truly, I mean it as a kindness. You have served her long and loyally. The best thing you can do for her now is to let her go."

"I will never give up."

Gently patting Lona's red cheek, Lady Rhoswen said, "Of course not. That is why I must do this for her. For you. I have told you now so that you might prepare yourself, and for no other reason. Do not let your heartbreak lead you to any rash actions."

"I will tell her what you intend to do."

"I expect you will." Rhoswen gave her a wry, sad smile. "But consider how unkind it is to cause her worry. Let her rest in peace for the time she has left."

On those parting words she left, and John's torch briefly illuminated the stone walls beyond the doorway as he lit the way for her.

Her breast heaving with panic and confusion, Lona raced back to the tower room. Once there, she paced back and forth, assessing Lady Rhoswen's parting words. Thorns caught at Lona's ragged dress, and she tore free with a jerk of frustration. Then her gaze fell on Arabella, who lay as still as a statue though flushed with the color of life.

Two tears, one from each eye, slid down Lona's cheeks. She caught them on the end of her wand and let it absorb the tears. Fairy tears were powerful, and she didn't want to waste them. She would need all the power she could muster in coming days. She knew this as surely as she knew that she must warn Arabella even though it would alarm her.

Lona sat on the stool beside Arabella's bed, took one of the girl's soft hands in her own calloused one, and tugged on a string around her neck, drawing from under her gown a long, pointed spindle—the very spindle that had initiated the enchantment more than a century ago. Lona always carried it on her person; for it was not only the source of doom, it was also the source of the one blessing afforded during long years of isolation.

It was Lona's key to the dream world.

Holding the smooth wood in her fingers, she wondered again why Lady Rhoswen had never once asked to make use of it. Sighing, she closed her eyes and willed herself to fall asleep. Soon she felt the familiar pulling on her mind and allowed unconsciousness to draw her into its stream.

She emerged from dark mist into Arabella's chamber again, but now in the dream world instead of the waking one.

"Arabella, you are in great danger," she said in a rush as soon as she saw the elegant princess standing at her window, which was larger here. Unlike a window in the real world, this one showed a changing landscape, visions of the outside world.

Arabella turned. "What do you mean? In danger from what?"

"From Lady Rhoswen. She means to kill you." Arabella's blue eyes reflected confusion and disbelief, so Lona took a breath and tried to speak calmly. "She says she intends it as a kindness, to spare you from this curse. And perhaps it would be merciful, but I could never allow her to kill you."

With a faraway look in her eye, Arabella asked, "When does she mean to do it?"

"At the waning of the moon."

"A fortnight then, no more. I wonder if anyone can fall in love so quickly."

"Not if they aren't around to do it." Lona paced and planned. "I shall have to hide you somewhere."

"Perhaps, but not yet. There is hope."

"What hope?"

Arabella turned to look out the window again. "Someone is coming."

ACROSS THE border between Stone Haven and Timber Vale lay a vast, desolate plain. There were no trees, no thriving farms or pasturelands. Edmond and his companion had been traveling across it for three days. They had passed no villages and met no other travelers on the road. On the second day, a patrol of a dozen soldiers had detained them briefly.

Edmond had expected mockery or suspicion from the soldiers upon hearing that he was a prince in search of the sleeping princess. But the battle-hardened men had accepted his words without question and wished them good fortune. As if they actually believed in the legends.

Edmond studied the clods of dirt Martin's horse left in a trail before him. The soil was soft, dark, and fertile. Rivers and streams crisscrossed the vast flatlands, some flowing down from the mountains of his own country and some fed by the springs and marshes of Timber Vale. It was no wonder his father so desperately wanted control of this land.

King Osden was a hard and calculating man who asked much but gave nothing, even when saying farewell to his own son.

"Edmond, I hold little expectation of seeing you again. No one has yet survived the trials of Briar Fen to reach the sleeping princess, but I am not completely without hope. Remember your training and think of your homeland. If you should succeed and bring back the princess to be your brother's bride, it would mean the salvation of our kingdom. Go with honor."

Edmond had expected neither affection nor concern. But surely sending a son to face almost certain death should have awakened some sort of reluctance in a father's heart, or at the least inspired some ceremony. Instead, the King had seen him alone, and he and Martin had left unheralded. Edmond's bitterness was complete.

"Martin, I am a fool," Edmond called.

Reining in his horse, Martin turned his craggy face to look back in surprise. As Edmond drew even with him, Martin inquired, "Would Your Highness wish me to agree with you or disagree?"

The corner of Edmond's mouth twitched. Martin was the only person who had ever been able to make him laugh. "Agree with me, certainly, for it is the truth. Why else would I ride to almost certain death so that my brother may gain a rich and beautiful bride?"

"No reason I know of, unless it be love of your father and loyalty to the kingdom."

"Well then, I am proven a fool."

"Yes, Your Highness."

Edmond glanced sideways at Martin. With his high forehead and jutting cheekbones, the man could have been carved from the mountains himself, but he was not a native of Stone Haven. Nearly a decade before, the king had made a bargain with Lord Galloran, regent of Timber Vale. In return for helping him find and capture one of the feared black dragons that sometimes nested in Stone Haven, Lord Galloran had sent King Osden precious timber and one other gift—a soldier of the Royal Guard.

Martin was that soldier.

Stone Haven had its own formidable army of well-trained soldiers, but a man trained in Timber Vales's fighting methods and familiar with its geography, legends, and people was invaluable to King Osden's ambition.

One might have thought a man would harbor resentment at being bartered like livestock between two monarchs. Nevertheless, Martin had always treated Edmond with respect and, at King Osden's orders, had set about training the young prince with stern diligence.

"Now that we are returning to your homeland, where do your loyalties lie?" Edmond asked.

As clouds obscured the setting sun behind them, the sky above them darkened, making Martin's expression difficult to see. He was silent for so long, Edmond wondered if he would answer. When he did, his words surprised the prince.

"In truth, Your Highness, my first loyalty lies with Princess Arabella and her people. Though I have no liking for Lord Galloran or his bargain with your father, I have always thought my task in training you to be in accord with my duty to the princess. Have no doubt: As long as waking the princess is your goal, I am your man."

"Then you cannot like my father's plans. As her bridegroom, my brother will strip her lands of their riches and suck the kingdom dry like a marrow bone—all to fulfill his ambition."

Martin shook his head. "It is an evil plan, but I have little fear of its being carried through."

"And why is that?"

"Have I not drummed the legend into your head since you were a boy? You will be able to waken the princess only if you truly love her. Could you hand over the woman of your heart to the devilfish that is your brother?"

"I wouldn't hand over a dog I liked to that man."

"There you are. And now we must ride hard before we are overtaken by the storm behind us. There is a keep just ahead."

Edmond looked back to see that the lazy grey clouds overhead were being chased by angry black clouds that churned in the skies. "How far ahead?" he asked.

"About two miles," Martin answered, and urged his mount to a gallop.

The horses seemed as anxious as their riders to outrun the storm, but they were still several hundred yards from the keep's walls when the clouds broke over their heads.

The rain was cold and drenching, penetrating the men's heavy cloaks. Fierce gusts of wind blew the rain into their faces. Blinded, Edmond trusted his horse to follow Martin's and hunched his shoulders against the onslaught of the skies. Only when their horses' hooves clumped onto the heavy wooden drawbridge of the keep did Edmond relax. Never had a sight been more welcome than the torchlight in the stone battlements above.

"Who goes there?" called the gatekeeper.

Martin answered, "Prince Edmond of Stone Haven."

There followed a creak and groan as the guardsmen raised the portcullis, and they rode through into the courtyard.

"I'll take your horse, sir," a boy said, shouting above the tumult of rain and thunder. Edmond relinquished the reins to him as he dismounted. His boots sank into mud, and the wet wool of his cloak clung to his shoulders as he followed a guard across the wide courtyard. The guard hauled on an iron ring set into one of the heavy doors; and as it opened, sounds of music and revelry spilled into the miserable night.

Eager for shelter from the rain, Edmond strode inside and paused just beyond the threshold to peel off his dripping cloak. He wished he might remove his boots as well, but the thought of vermin in the rushes on the floor dissuaded him.

A dozen or more men seated on benches around the hall ate steaming pottage from trenchers and drank spiced ale. In one corner, a minstrel played a lively tune on his lute; a few soldiers joined their voices with his.

Soon after Martin entered, carrying their packs, the chamberlain, a portly man with receding hair and beady eyes, appeared and welcomed them. He directed a page to lay their cloaks by the fire to dry, and said, "Your Highness, we are honored by your presence tonight. Do you intend to travel through Timber Vale, or do you pass along our border?"

"We will travel though. I desire to see if the legends about the sleeping princess are true."

The small man's head bobbed as if his neck were a spring. "Oh yes, sir. They are true—though it is unlikely you will see her. Regardless, the Lady Regent wishes us to offer hospitality to all foreign princes, so I'll give you food and lodging for the night with her great goodwill."

"Lady Regent?" said Edmond with some surprise. "What has become of Lord Galloran?"

A shadow seemed to pass over the chamberlain's face. "He died recently," he said, but something in his voice implied there was more to the tale, perhaps something sinister. "His daughter, Lady Rhoswen, is now regent of this land."

Edmond nodded. He had heard of Lady Rhoswen before now: Lord Galloran's beautiful russet-haired daughter. He wondered if she would prove as iron-fisted as her father had been, and how she would view any attempts to break the curse on the sleeping princess, for surely it was not in her best interest.

"On the morrow," the chamberlain continued, "you must journey to White Thorn Castle and present yourselves to her."

Although he disliked the highhanded tone of this statement, Edmond nodded politely. When the chamberlain bowed and left to see to their dinner, Edmond strode over to warm himself at the massive hearth, standing with his back to the fire and keeping a wary eye on the soldiers around them. Martin sat on a bench nearby and leaned back against the stone wall, but Edmond knew that he, too, would stay alert.

Soon, a girl with a tattered dress and downcast eyes brought trenchers of pottage and jugs of ale. She set the food on a table near them and slunk away. As they sat down to their meal, the chamberlain came to inquire after their comfort. Before he left, Edmond asked, "What can you tell me of Lady Rhoswen?"

With a small nod, the chamberlain said, "She is all things lovely and wise, though she is well over a century in age. 'Tis said she drinks a fairy potion to keep young so that she might guard our kingdom until the sleeping princess may take her throne."

Edmond kept his voice light and pleasant. "And Lady Rhoswen will relinquish all her power if the spell is broken?"

"Yes, for such has always been the desire of the good lady's heart. The princess is her very own cousin, and she loves her as a sister. Indeed, it was well known that Lord Galloran wanted nothing more than to take her life and thus become king, for the chains of law fettered his power as regent, but Lady Rhoswen has protected her all these long years."

"She sounds a good and worthy lady," said Edmond, keeping his doubts to himself.

After eating, Edmond and Martin wrapped themselves in thin blankets provided by the chamberlain and lay near the dying embers in the fireplace of the great hall. Because of his nobility, a cot was found for Edmond, with a goose-down mattress and even a linen sheet, but Martin was left to sleep on the rushes.

Long after Martin fell asleep, Edmond stared at the vaulted ceilings above him, thinking. The people here believed in magic, even as Martin did. But could there really be a regent who never aged and a princess that never woke?

III

THE LANDSCAPE before Arabella swirled with images and colors, but one spot of clarity remained fixed before her: a man's face, half illuminated by firelight. His features were carved in noble lines, though his skin was darkened and weathered by sun and wind. He was accompanied by an older man seemingly fashioned of leather and stone, who treated him as his master. From the obsequious bows of the chamberlain, she knew that the younger man was a lord—perhaps even a prince.

And all of her hopes rested on him.

Would he survive the treacherous journey through Briar Fen? Perhaps, for he looked to be made entirely of sinew and steel. Only two other men had ever made it to the castle. One had been carried off by the dragon as he tried to find a way through the thorns. Arabella had watched helplessly from her dream window, unable to call to Lona to help him. The other man had made it as far as her chamber, and Lona suspected he had come through the tunnel, though how he had known of it they never learned. He had certainly not come through the thorns.

She had only known he was coming when she heard the scrabble of loose stones disturbed on the stair and the heavy tread of boots across the floor. Lona came and went with sure steps that fell like a whisper, so Arabella had instantly known that a stranger approached her.

She cringed, remembering the indignity and helplessness she had felt as hard lips rammed against her own, bruising them. Paralyzed yet fully aware of the smell of sour breath and stale sweat, she had wished for the first time that she might actually be as dead to the world around her as she appeared. But it was her curse to experience every dragging, eternal moment of the century as it passed, and every discomfort of a kiss so desperately unwanted.

When his first kiss did not awaken her, the man had tried again, sure that success must only require a different technique; but still the enchantment remained upon her. Apparently he then remembered the requirements of the spell, for he'd said, "O beautiful princess, I do truly love you with my whole heart and soul," then kissed her again. She was as helpless against that as she was against the ringing slap he had dealt her cheek when she didn't wake up.

Lona had burst into the room then in a fury of words and magic. She'd turned him into a fish and released him into the murky water of the fens. There, Arabella knew, he would spend the rest of his life hiding from the herons and snakes that stalked the shallow waters in search of easy prey. In her opinion, it was the perfect fate for such a man.

"Where is he now, Your Highness?" Lona asked from behind her.

Arabella turned to her. Lona had changed little in all this time. She was as dainty and spry as most fairies were (or as they started out, anyway), and though she was half out of her mind from her hermitic existence, her eyes still sparkled with an intelligence and pragmatism that had helped spare Arabella's own sanity.

"In the keep at the edge of the forest," Arabella said.

"Do you think he is a nobleman?"

"He is highborn, though he is no stranger to work or to battle, I believe. As to whether he is noble . . . we shall see."

The next morning dawned bright, though the storm of the evening before had left its mark in the form of damp boots and clothing. After a loaf of rye bread, salted cheese, and a jug of ale to break their fast, Edmond and Martin readied their horses for the day's ride. Though the stable boys had done a fine job of brushing mud from the horses' legs and seeing them fed and warm, the two men preferred to saddle up for themselves.

A short while later they led their horses across the quagmire of mud and straw in the courtyard. The inhabitants of the keep barely looked their way, bustling about on their own business. Only the chamberlain wished them a good journey as they mounted on the open drawbridge and rode away.

They followed the road that led through a village behind the keep and into the thick forest of trees bordering it on three sides. Edmond trailed warily behind Martin. His whole life had been spent on the sparse crags and slopes of his home, exposed to wind and sun but open to the freedom of the sky.

Sparrows and finches flew and twittered around them, disturbed by their presence, while squirrels ran across their path and scolded them from the safety of high branches. Pale morning sun filtered through the branches of soaring trees, sending shafts of light between their columns. Edmond cast his awed gaze at Martin and caught a hint of pleasure upon the older man's face as he took in the beauty around them with eager eyes.

"It's a wondrous place," Edmond said in hushed tones.

"Yes," Martin said. "But like all beautiful things, it is dangerous as well. Stay on your guard."

"How far is it to White Thorn Castle?"

"Only half a day's ride. The keep guards the border. White Thorn Castle guards the fens."

"A grand castle to guard a marsh?"

"The fenlands are rich with mystic power, and their springs are the lifeblood of our fertile lands."

"Tales describe the fens as a charming place, with quicksands and bogs and . . ."

"Blood-sucking devilfish," Martin added.

"I cannot express how delighted I am that the sleeping princess lies in Briar Fen Castle."

"So you should be. Few people have dared go nigh the place, thus the princess remains undisturbed—almost as if she has been waiting for you."

Edmond narrowed his eyes at Martin's teasing. "Perhaps the castle is closely guarded to hide the fact that the princess does not exist."

Martin shrugged and shook his head.

They arrived at White Thorn Castle when the sun was high overhead. The castle itself burst upon their view suddenly because of the closeness of the surrounding forest. Its turrets soared among the trees' uppermost branches, and their thick trunks appeared to support its walls. But while the trees were a rich tapestry of greens and browns, the stones of the castle were a brilliant alabaster white. Vines, ivy, and sprays of ancient roses climbed the walls and framed the shuttered windows.

The road became smoother here as it crossed over a stone bridge spanning a quiet river and ended at the drawbridge of the castle. The great gates were open to those on the road, but entry was delayed as the guards carefully examined each cart and wagon lined up to get inside.

"Let us ride ahead. They will not expect us to wait with the merchants," Martin said.

Edmond nodded and followed Martin in a weaving path around the wagons and carts. At the gate, a guard held up a hand to stop them. "State your name and business here."

Edmond did not wait for Martin to announce him this time. He gave his name and said, "I desire speech with the Lady Regent."

"I will inquire, Your Highness."

The guard waved to another to take his place before he set off through the bustling market of the courtyard and into the great hall of the castle. He was gone long enough that dozens of carts had moved in ahead of them, but at last he returned and motioned to a couple of stable boys. When he had approached near enough to be heard over the surrounding din, he said, "The Lady is pleased to see you. If you will come with me?"

Edmond and Martin dismounted, turned over their horses to the waiting stable boys, and followed the guard into the great hall.

There were few windows, so the hall was dim and cool. Edmond could just make out that the carved woodwork on the pillars and ceiling was designed to look like tree branches sweeping out in all directions and generously laden with wooden leaves, fruits, and flowers. Heavy tapestries depicting dancing fairies with blossoms in their hair hung on every wall. Elegant courtiers stood in clusters around the room, and all turned toward Edmond and Martin as they walked behind the guard, who led them down the hall to the raised dais at the end.

A diaphanous pillar of light fell through a wide, glassed window in the ceiling, highlighting a mosaic depicting the stages of the moon, which was inlaid in the stone floor before the dais. Just beyond the light, Edmond saw the hem of a white gown and the tips of dainty gold slippers, but the rest of the figure was lost in shadow.

Edmond knelt there on the mosaic before the throne with one hand on his sword, knowing full well that the lighting set him at a disadvantage. The Lady Regent was free to study him at her pleasure while he was kept in ignorance of her.

"Prince Edmond of Stone Haven?" a sweet, refined voice said. She spoke with precision, lingering over the syllables of his name and title.

"Yes, my lady. At your service."

"I have long waited for your father to send one of his sons."

"Indeed, my lady?"

"Certainly. Ever since I declined to marry your father thirty years ago, I have expected this. He could not have this throne himself, but he intends to see a son upon it. You seek Princess Arabella, of course."

As Edmond's mind struggled with this startling new information, instinct warned him to be cautious with this woman who may be guarding her throne jealously. "But surely the sleeping princess is no more than an old wives' tale," he said. "Would we not do better to seek stronger ties with the true power of the land?"

"Your kingdom is not known to be content with alliances."

"I hope we have grown wiser, my lady." Silence met his remark, but a lifetime in his father's court had hardened Edmond's fortitude. His face remained impassive.

Lady Rhoswen leaned forward until the light revealed her face. Edmond's breath caught at the youthful vision before him. Her skin was as pale and translucent as the light spilling over her, and every line of her face and form bespoke her noble heritage. Fine auburn brows arched as she caught his scrutiny. Then she whispered, "No. You do not seek an alliance."

Edmond kept his eyes steady on hers, giving nothing away.

She stood abruptly, sending her guards and attendants into low bows. "I desire an audience with you, Prince Edmond." She turned to walk behind a tapestry being held aside for her, and a guard with one hand on his sword motioned for him to follow her.

Edmond hesitated, feeling he was safer while still in public view, but it was impossible to deny her request. A soft shuffle of feet at his back alerted him that Martin stood ready to follow, but Edmond held up a hand to signal him to stay. Edmond knew with sharp certainty that Lady Rhoswen intended this to be a private conversation.

Behind the tapestry lay a cozy chamber where Lady Rhoswen sat in a large, cushioned chair. She was attended by several pretty young ladies with carefully downcast faces. After one of these handed her a silver cup, Lady Rhoswen asked, "Will you take refreshment, Your Highness?"

"I would relish a drink, my lady."

Lady Rhoswen took a sip, eyeing him over the rim of her cup. When she lowered it, the wine had tinted her pale upper lip. He found it difficult to look away from the splash of crimson on her fair countenance as he thought of the youth potion she was said to drink.

Handing her cup to the girl waiting behind her chair, Lady Rhoswen gestured with slender fingers to Edmond. As the girl brought him the cup, Edmond realized she intended him to drink from it.

"Do not worry," she said. "It is only wine. The Elixir of Abeyance is much too valuable to share."

After taking a drink, Edmond asked, "What is this elixir you speak of?"

"It suspends my body in time. So long as I take it, my body does not age or change in any way."

"Making you immortal?"

"No. The ingredients used in it are toxic and slowly poison the body over time—or all at once, if a careless hand prepares it. But having lived more than a century, I cannot think anyone would enjoy immortality for long."

Edmond finished the wine, and the girl who had given it to him relieved him of the empty cup. "Leave us," Lady Rhoswen said to the girls, who curtsied and scurried out.

When they were alone, she rose with languorous grace. "You are quite the noble specimen," she said, inspecting him. With slow, floating steps she walked around him. Her finger brushed his shoulder, tracing across his back and down his arm. "So strong."

Edmond remained silent, but his nerves jumped. "No more so than any man."

"Humble too. Surely good characteristics for a king."

"Perhaps."

Lady Rhoswen took her chair again and drummed her fingers on its carved wooden arm. "If you desire a crown, there are alternate paths before you."

"Are there?"

Her nod was slow and deliberate. "You interest me, young Edmond. It would be such a waste to throw your life away in a vain pursuit."

"And what pursuit is that?"

"You cannot deceive me. I know you have come to find Arabella. But do you know the dangers ahead of you? The mires and thieves and dragons? You do not even come with a force of soldiers at your back."

"I thought you would be opposed to so many armed foreigners traveling across your land. And I have Martin, of course." One of the lady's arched brows lifted in question, so he enlightened her. "The guard your father, Lord Galloran, sent to my father in exchange for . . . other goods."

"Indeed? I did not recognize him. If you truly have one of my own countrymen with you, you will fare better than most. But you will fail in the end."

"Because there is no princess?"

Lady Rhoswen laughed. "No. Because you cannot love her."

Edmond crossed his arms. "I have heard that you love her. How is it impossible that another should do so?"

With a smile still upon her lips, Lady Rhoswen's cheeks lifted, and her eyes narrowed as if at some private joke. "Ah, but I have the benefit of knowing her."

There were depths to this woman he could not yet fathom, but clearly she intended to dissuade him from his quest. Edmond did not like to be manipulated, so he murmured quietly, "Perhaps all that is needed is for our souls to touch."

"You are not such a fool as to believe that. You will discover nothing but a crumbling castle and a poor soul trapped forever in an evil curse. But here, power and riches could be yours for the taking."

"How so?"

"My kingdom needs an heir. I offer you what I have offered only one man before, and that long ago."

"What offer is that?"

"Myself. Marry me and rule this kingdom at my side."

Edmond caught his breath at this new danger. She had the advantage here, with armies at her command. Though he was a prince, he was a younger son, disposable to his father. An insult could prove deadly.

But to accept was unthinkable.

"Who was the other man?" Edmond said, prompting her to speak and buy him time.

"My first husband. I married him long ago, and he has since passed from this life. I did not know then that the elixir would make me barren, but so it has. I will not be drinking it much longer, and my body will once again resume its natural functions. I want strong sons and daughters, and you could give them to me."

"I am honored at the compliment, my lady, but I pray you will allow me time to consider your generous offer."

Lady Rhoswen's lips tightened. "Very well. You may remain as my guest until you decide."

Edmond bowed but said nothing.

Her whole expression hardened and she waved him away. "Leave me, but return in the morning with your answer."

Edmond bowed again, and his footsteps echoed behind him as he left, as did her words. She would be outraged when she found him gone in the morning, but urgency consumed him. Instinct told him her offer was a ploy to keep him from his quest, and why would she make such a bold move unless she feared he might be successful?

IV

THOUGH HE and Martin arose and sought out their horses before dawn, hoping to go unnoticed, they were not alone. Six other horses were being saddled.

Edmond met Martin's eyes and motioned him toward one of the stable boys. Understanding his silent command, Martin asked the boy, "What is all the stir about?"

"A prince is come with his knights. They ride to Briar Fen Castle."

"Is that so? I did not see them yesterday."

"No, for they came late in the night and ride out now on the Lady Regent's business."

"You're a smart one, aren't you? What is the name of this prince?"

"Nicol of Windemore."

Martin produced a small coin and handed it to the boy, who deftly pocketed it before any of his fellows could see.

Edmond heard all this as he saddled his horse nearby. "What is the Prince of Windemore doing here at the beck and call of Lady Rhoswen? Nothing good, I expect," he murmured to Martin.

"True, sir, but this may work to our advantage. I had misgivings about how we would be able to leave, for the guards may have orders to not let us go, but now we may ride out on their heels."

Edmond felt his muscles tense, knowing their backs would be exposed to arrows from the battlements. But unless they escaped on foot, this was their only option. "We must not draw attention to ourselves. Keep to the shadows."

The eastern sky turned pale, but no sunlight breached the castle's high walls. Only a few torches dotted the dark courtyard. Edmond and Martin led their horses to a shadowed area of the wall near the gate. When, with a creak of wood and rattle of chains, the portcullis was slowly raised, they mounted and stood ready.

Six mounted men clinking with mail and armor passed through the gate in single file, their horses moving at a trot. As the last one passed onto the drawbridge, Edmond and Martin dug their heels into their horses' sides. Their mounts leapt forward into a mad gallop through the gate and around the horses in front of them, quickly passing them by. The guards, taken by surprise, could do no more than shout "Halt!" after them.

Glancing back over his shoulder, Edmond saw a mad scramble among the dark figures silhouetted on the battlements and knew that their departure was indeed more of an escape. Behind them, Prince Nicol and his men increased their pace, endeavoring to overtake them, but Martin signaled for Edmond to follow him off the deeply rutted road and into the trees.

It was nearly impossible to ride horses through the dense foliage and scrub, but Martin found a clear path with the surety of a woodsman. For a short while they heard sounds of the other men struggling to follow, but by sunrise they had left all signs of pursuit far behind. Martin did not return to the road but pressed on into the forest.

The leaves of oak and beech laced the canopy above, obscuring the weak morning light. Brambles and thickets pressed upon them from all sides, showering them with dew as they passed, but the animals of the forest had made a sure path among them. Martin followed the winding path up and down the slope of the land and around rocky outcroppings. Before long, Edmond had lost all sense of direction.

"You do know where you are going?" he asked Martin, realizing that he was following his man blindly.

"Yes. I travelled this way many times in my youth. The main road is quicker, but it turns north half a day's ride from the castle. Besides, I doubt that any pass that way in safety unless the Lady permits them to, and I do not think she will be content to let us go."

"Nor do I."

Eventually the trees began to change to elm, and still the land sloped downward until the elms were joined by great drooping willows. The two men forded a small stream, pausing halfway across to let their horses to drink.

"We are nearly to the fens," Martin said, patting his horse's sweaty shoulder. "You must be very careful, my lord, for the marsh is deceitful. What looks like sturdy ground may actually be water grasses growing over deep mires. There are water snakes to watch for and quicksand. I will seek out the ancient path through the fen, but much of it has sunk beneath the stagnant waters, and the way is hard to find. There is a place ahead where we can pass the night in safety and leave the horses. It would be foolish to risk them in the fen when we can travel faster by foot anyway."

Edmond nodded. "Lead on."

Martin pulled his horse's head up from the stream and moved on, soon turning onto a broader path. They journeyed through the rest of the day, slapping at biting insects, moving slowly to watch for dangers. Often they had to cross through deep waters, swimming alongside their horses, and Edmond was thankful for Martin's insistence that he learn to swim as a boy. There were no deep rivers or lakes in his mountainous kingdom, only one pool at the base of a waterfall in a narrow valley. Most of his training had taken place in that valley; there he had honed his skills with weapons and developed skill and confidence in the water.

As they waded through one pool of stagnant water, Martin suddenly sank to his waist and shouted, "Quicksand! Stay back."

Edmond led his horse from the water onto solid ground, tied a rope around the pommel of his saddle, and threw the other end to Martin. By this time, the man had sunk until only his head was above water, but he'd managed to keep his arms free of the sand. He caught the rope and twisted it several times around his wrist, tying a knot, and was thus able to maintain his grip on the rope as Edmond turned the horse and, with great effort, pulled Martin free of the sand's deadly suction.

Lying on the bank, nearly swallowed up in ferns and covered with grey mud, Martin struggled to catch his breath as Edmond crouched over him. At last he sat up and gripped Edmond's arm. "I owe you my life."

"And after being in this forsaken place a day, I owe you mine a dozen times over. You prepared me well, but it is a wonder anyone survives here."

"There are many who do. You will be their guest tonight. We shouldn't tarry. You do not want to spend a night here without shelter."

A snake slithered out of the ferns, and Edmond's sword flashed out. With the flat of his blade, he flung it into the water. "No, I most certainly do not."

As twilight fell upon them, their path ran alongside a rocky ledge. Edmond was amazed to see an orange glow emanating from a large cavity in the rock. The cave was the height of two men, and they might easily have ridden into it . . . but were halted by a threatening voice overhead.

"Stand!"

With muscles tense and heart pounding, Edmond reined in his horse and looked up to where a man stood on an overhang with an arrow nocked, ready to draw his bow. There was a rustle in the branches of a tree to their left, and Edmond searched until he saw another man standing ready to loose an arrow. With amazement, he heard Martin laugh.

"Warren, you dog. Do you not know your own brother?"

The man on the overhang lowered his bow and leaned forward to get a closer look. "Never say it's you, Martin."

"By your life, I swear it is," Martin said. Then he laughed again. "I'm disappointed. We rode into the middle of your camp with nary a man to stop us."

The man drew his bow. "I could stop you now."

"Or you could come join us by your fire," Martin said, his voice unperturbed.

With a grin, his brother said, "Go on inside."

Edmond began to relax as he dismounted and led his horse behind Martin's into the mouth of the cave. The horses' shoes rang against the rock and echoed through the chamber. A large fire burned in a pit on the floor, but the cave's ceiling was too high for its light to reach.

Running footsteps approached from behind. Warren passed them, carrying a torch, and said, "I'll help you find an empty stall for your horses."

The stalls were formed by gates made of cut saplings that closed off the open ends of natural alcoves in the rock. It was impossible to see much, but the place smelled of animals and hay. The shuffling sounds of hooves and various bleats and grunts revealed the kinds of animals kept here.

"We keep them in here at night because that is when the dragon does most of its hunting. It's not always safe in the daytime, but the creatures don't do well kept inside all the time."

"Dragons must have a fierce appetite," Martin said, leading first his horse and then Edmond's into a large alcove with a tall ceiling.

"It's been a sore trial having the dragon around. He's eaten most of the game, and if it weren't for the fishing and the odd caravan that comes up the north road, we'd have all had to move on or starve. As it is, there are no more than a dozen of us left. Of course, the supply wagon for the castle comes by every fortnight, but we take that only when we have to. After all, we're loyal subjects of the princess, bless her."

"Glad to hear it," Martin said in a dry tone.

"Oh, always. I'll see about getting you some food. Come to the fire when your horses are settled." Warren handed Edmond the torch and started off.

"Don't you need a torch?" Edmond asked him.

"I've been walking these caves my whole life. I don't need light to find my way."

Martin chuckled as he unsaddled Edmond's horse. "He hasn't changed, the old rogue."

With ill-hidden humor, Edmond asked, "Why didn't I know you were related to thieves?"

"Well, sir, it isn't something a man should boast of, now is it? But I figured you'd overlook it for the sake of a safe night and helpful information. Warren is sure to have plenty of that."

This proved to be true. As the three men sat around a fire, eating small fish fried in a pan over the flames, Warren talked of all the strange sights he'd seen in the forest during the dozen or so years since he'd last seen his brother. As he told stories, a few children played a game with assorted rocks nearby, and several women sat weaving baskets of reeds, listening to the talk. The other men of the camp were on guard duty.

"And what goes on in the rest of the kingdom?" Martin asked.

Warren scratched his beard and said, "Well, 'tis said that Galloran died."

Sitting up straighter, his attention now sharp, Martin said, "So we heard. And we had audience with the new Lady Regent."

"Lady Rhoswen, yes." Warren nodded. "It is good, we hope, that she is now regent. All this time she has protected Arabella from her father and his stratagems and rebellions. So long as he retained his youth through magic, she has done so as well, and has protected the princess from his attacks. Her soldiers patrol the roads and the fens, and her dragon defeats anyone that slips through. Galloran wasn't able to get close to the princess even though she lies in his own castle."

"Nor can anyone else," Edmond said, staring into the blackness overhead while his brain churned.

"I suppose not," Warren said, his voice thoughtful.

Edmond clenched his hand on his sword. "She offered me marriage, claiming she could make me a king, but I could not understand why she had waited so long to act against the princess. Now I know. She could not act so long as her father lived."

Looking around to see if the others followed his line of thinking, he saw that the men and women around him all wore tense expressions.

When Martin spoke, the dread of a loyal subject rang in his voice, "Surely she could not be capable of such wickedness."

"I fear that if we do not reach Briar Fen Castle soon, we will learn the worst. Martin, we leave at daybreak."

By noon the next day Edmond began to wonder if he would ever be dry again, or if his feet would rot in his boots. For most of the morning they had traveled across solid ground, but streams and bogs rose up constantly before them. They had left their horses behind with Warren, knowing the poor beasts would be useless in the terrain ahead.

"How much further, do you think?" Edmond asked, anxious to find the castle.

"Not far now. With luck, we should be there in another hour. See that ridge ahead of us? You can just make it out beyond those willows."

"Yes. I see it."

"Briar Fen castle lies on the other side. Indeed, it is built against it, the rock forming its fourth wall."

As soon as he finished speaking, they both froze as a sharp shriek rang through the air, sending a chill of fear down Edmond's spine. "The dragon. Curse my father for sending it here!"

"I could not tell its direction, could you?"

"No. Keep a sharp eye out."

They walked on, wary now, their eyes constantly scanning the sky. Edmond groaned when their path disappeared beneath mud and puddles of stagnant water, especially since slogging through it would slow them down and leave them exposed.

The trees, almost all willows, grew sparsely here, and the heavy smell of decay rose up from the marsh. They waded around the shallows of a lake with a small island in its center, upon which stood an abandoned stone tower. Only the bones of civilization remained to indicate that anyone had ever lived here, but vivid life flourished among the decay. Delicate white lilies with bright pink centers floated on the water, and strange birds on long legs waded through the pools. Bird calls filled the air, frogs croaked, and minnows teemed in the shallows. Life and death held hands in this strange green world.

"Here's the path again, Your Highness."

Martin waited until Edmond stood beside him. A cobbled road stretched ahead for ten yards before sinking again beneath still water.

Edmond heaved a sigh. "I will never curse the dry season at home again."

As they proceeded, jumping from tussock to tussock through the maze of water and mounds of earth, or wading through when these grassy stepping stones were too far apart, Edmond realized that he no longer even felt the water seeping into his boots. The clay was deep here, however, making it difficult to advance, as they had to pull their boots out of the muck at each step with a sucking, squelching sound. "It's a good thing we aren't trying for stealth," Edmond said after a particularly difficult step in which he nearly lost his boot entirely.

"The music of the fens," Martin said cheerfully.

As they emerged from another grove of willows, the ridge rose before them. But a river flowed between, with their path to the castle resuming on its far shore. "This is the Sage River," Martin said. "It runs deep and has strong currents."

"How do we cross?" Edmond asked.

"Come on, lad. You can swim."

"Yes, but that river looks treacherous."

A new and rapid ripple drew their attention, caused by a small black head rising up from the water. "Snake," said Martin.

"Better and better," Edmond said. As he glanced around, something caught his eye a short way down the river where it took a bend to the right. "Is that a rope?"

"Aye. No doubt Warren put it there," Martin said, and led the way along the muddy bank toward the bend. They saw that a giant tree had fallen across the river here, and above it a length of thick rope stretched between two trees on opposite sides of the river at the height of a man's reach. The narrow end of the tree rested on the opposite bank, which was lower than the one they stood on. Even with the rope, crossing would be difficult.

Without hesitation Edmond climbed the twisted roots that rose above his head, reached to grasp the rope, and took a step forward. After a few careful steps he got comfortable with the angle of his feet on the slanting tree and kept himself balanced by grasping the rope above his head. "It seems secure," he called to Martin, "though it is a good thing neither of us is short."

Martin scrambled up behind him, and they moved carefully across the river, their confidence rising until the trunk sloped down at an angle that seemed much steeper than it had looked from the bank.

"We may take a dunking after all if we don't manage this well," Edmond said, pausing to collect himself.

"Yes, but we have worse trouble."

Edmond looked back at Martin then followed his gaze downriver. The dragon hung there, silhouetted against the sky, its body arching up to charge forward as it caught sight of them. Its battle-torn wings spanned the whole width of the river, and its sleek body was taller than any warhorse, with a huge tail doubling its length. The ridge of spines crowning its head and the claws on each of its feet chilled Edmond's blood. As it came closer, the sunlight glinted off a heavy gold chain encircling its neck

With the predator tearing toward them, there was no time to wonder about the chain. Edmond let go of the rope and slid down the tree, crouching low to keep his balance. His weight kept him on course nearly to the bottom, where he fell off and plunged into the river.

Keeping his eyes tightly shut, he felt by the rush of water and bubbles next to him that Martin had fallen in beside him. Deciding it was safer to stay underwater, he swam as far as he could and surfaced only when his lungs screamed for air. Through the water streaming over his eyes, he could just see the enormous black dragon mounting the sky, preparing to plunge down in another attack. He dove again as deep as he could go, kicking furiously. Because dragons preferred the rocky desert lands on the borders of his own kingdom, he hoped the dragon couldn't swim, but a splash in the water spurred him to keep kicking downwards.

Death awaited him on the surface, yet he had no choice but to come up for breath. The current dragged at his aching legs, but he kicked hard. His boots and sword were a hindrance, but he was glad not to have lost them.

When he finally broke the surface, his head banged into something and he reached up, groping for a handhold. He managed to grab a limb and pull himself up. Shaking his head to clear the dripping hair from his eyes, he saw that he had surfaced beneath a tangle of limbs and broken trees.

While pulling himself further into their shelter, he looked around for Martin and saw him upstream, clinging to a root on the bank. The dragon was swooping down toward him.

"Martin. Here!" Edmond cried out.

Martin turned sharply and saw him. He dove, but not deep enough. The dragon hit the water, claws extended, and caught him by one leg. It pulled Martin out of the river, streaming water behind as it flapped its wings hard, trying to gain altitude.

As Edmond's heart lurched, Martin took a knife from his arm sheath and pulled his body forward with incredible strength to stab at the dragon's leg, piercing between scales. With a scream of pain the dragon released him, and Martin fell into the water, landing on his back. He drew breath and dove again quickly.

Martin was underwater long enough to worry Edmond, but at last Martin's head quietly broke the surface beside him under the branches. Neither spoke as they searched for the dragon. It shrieked and emerged from over the ridge that towered over the riverbank, then dove and skimmed the water, searching for them. It passed directly overhead and swooped into the sky again.

"It's seen us," Edmond said.

"Some of these branches extend beneath the water," Martin said. "Use them to pull yourself down and stay submerged."

With their lungs full of air, they held themselves under as the branches shook around them, churning the water into a whirl of bubbles and debris. Edmond feared their shelter would soon break apart.

When they were forced to come up to breathe, flames burned above them. Only the dampness of the wood saved them from emerging into an inferno.

Martin coughed in the smoky air, his chest heaving. "Where's the dragon?"

Ducking underwater again, Edmond pulled himself through the tangle and emerged on the other side, ready to dive back under. But though he looked in all directions, he saw no sign of the dragon.

"It's gone. Let's move before it comes back."

Martin joined him, and they maneuvered around the pile of debris until they could climb up the bank. Martin led the way along the base of the ridge, and soon they heard shouts and screams ahead. Running, they burst through a stand of trees and saw, across a narrow open field, the thorn-covered walls of the castle.

On the far side of the field, Prince Nicol and his men engaged in deadly battle against the dragon, their backs to the thorns, which burned with dark orange flames belching columns of smoke.

As Edmond and Martin took in the scene before them, the dragon swooped down and grabbed a man off his horse, crushing him in its terrible teeth. Having claimed its prize, the dragon flew away directly over their heads, so close that they dropped to the ground to avoid the spikes on its whipping tail and, looking up, they could see the sheen of the purple scales on its underbelly.

They stayed down until the dragon disappeared over the tree line, then stood up and faced five swords brandished by men with hard faces and steady hands.

Bleeding, wet, and exhausted, Edmond and Martin weighed this new threat.

"On the bright side, Your Highness," Martin said, "we've found the castle."

NEVER HAD Arabella so keenly felt the chains of her curse. Watching from the dream world, she was powerless to offer aid of any kind to the prince who had faced so many dangers on his way to her castle. His escape in the early dawn from White Thorn castle had taken her by surprise—not that he'd been able to evade the castle guards, but that Rhoswen had tried to hold him there.

As he travelled the forest and crossed the fens, anxiety had been her constant companion. He had fought his way past many dangers, but Arabella had seen several others which he managed to evade by sheer good fortune.

Now another prince had come as well, one she had often seen visiting Rhoswen of late. He had never come to Briar Fen before, and she wondered why he chose to now. But her attention was always drawn back to the first prince.

With all her heart Arabella wished that she could hear in the visions, for she burned with curiosity about the discussion he'd had with Lady Rhoswen. Her cousin's attraction to him had been clear, but he had remained aloof, though he displayed the manners of court with perfection. He was young, but she saw the way the courtiers had eyed him with respect, as if drawn to his confidence. Even the thieves in the wood had shown him deference.

Now he was so very near, standing in the small field beyond the fortress of thorns. A gash on his head bled, the bright red blood diluted by the water streaming from his wet hair. He held himself with courage, but no man could go through what he had endured and not be exhausted. And he faced a foe of five with only one to stand beside him.

Lona, who had joined her in the dream, tried to comfort her with a touch, but her hand passed through Arabella's arm. Nothing was real here. "Princess, have courage. He seems a valiant man. All is not lost."

"Go to him. Save him."

"I will stand ready should he need me." Lona turned, and her figure shimmered until it disappeared.

Arabella watched the scene below. The five men moved steadily to form a circle around the two, four of them on foot, the prince remaining on his horse. Words were exchanged between them, and she longed to hear what they were saying. It could not have been anything peaceful, for in the next instant the battle commenced.

With sword and knife at the ready, Edmond stood with Martin, their backs together as their foes advanced. From their years of training, Edmond and Martin fought well together, but they were outnumbered. Before Edmond swung his sword to counter a heavy blow aimed at him, there was a guttural cry a short distance behind as one of Martin's throwing knives found its mark.

Martin would need room to avoid his next opponent, so Edmond advanced on his own foe, forcing him to fall back under a rapid series of thrusts and cuts. Wary of exposing his back to one of the two other men, Edmond darted to the left and turned so that his back was to the wall of thorns. Then, as his opponent thrust toward him, Edmond swung his own weapon. Their blades met, vibrating with the force of the clash. Edmond's timing and angle gave him the upper hand, and he drove his opponent's sword to the ground. He stepped on the blade and stabbed his knife into the man's shoulder, rendering his arm useless. The man dropped to his knees but staggered up again to run away.

Edmond looked for Martin and saw that he had the third man on the ground beneath him. Martin would finish that one off soon, but they still had two men to defeat. Expecting to face them both in a joint attack, Edmond was surprised when only one advanced on him.

Prince Nicol stayed well back on his horse, awaiting the outcome of the battle.

"Run away and live," Edmond offered his new opponent.

"Heed your own advice. You are nearly spent, and I am fresh."

The man mocked him, but Edmond did not answer. Instead, he swung his sword and, edge striking edge, the steel sparked. Edmond slid his sword forward, keeping pressure on the other weapon until the hilts touched. At this close range, Edmond hooked a foot sharply into the man's ankle, throwing his balance backwards. In that second, knowing his opponent's weight to be on the wrong foot, Edmond lifted his sword and drew back for power. He cut down, slicing into the man's arm and severing the flesh to the bone.

With a rapid step, Edmond withdrew. "I offer again to let you run away."

The man roared and charged at Edmond, who spun away and twisted his blade so that the broad side of it hit the man in the back and sent him crashing to the ground. A simple rotation of his grip on the hilt, and Edmond drove the point of his sword into the back of the man's shoulder, between the neck and shoulder blade.

"Run before I cut off your legs and leave you for the dragon."

Sure that the prince would be upon him or Martin at any moment, Edmond left the wounded man on the ground and turned to face his last adversary. However, he caught only a glimpse of the other prince as his horse disappeared into the trees.

Martin ran up beside him, breathing hard but perfectly well. He waved at the thorns and said, "We need to find a way through here."

They walked along the thorn wall in search of a place where the thorns might be less dense, but there was none. Even where the thorns had been charred black by the dragon's fire, new branches sprouted before the men's eyes.

With Martin standing guard, Edmond took out his sword and hacked at the briars. Though his sharp blade cut through the branches, they were so dense and interwoven that making any opening was difficult. Even with his hard leather gauntlets it was dangerous to push them out of the way.

After cutting at them until his face gleamed with sweat and he could barely swing his arm, he'd managed to push deep into the thorns. Just as he clenched his teeth and raised his sword again, Martin shouted a warning. "Run, Prince Edmond! They are cutting you off."

Edmond turned and saw that the vines were indeed growing quickly, closing together behind him. He would soon be trapped and likely killed by barbs as long as his hand. With room enough still to swing his sword, he cut his way through; but by the time Martin helped to drag him out, there were dozens of thorns embedded in his leather jerkin and a long gash crossed his cheek.

"It's impossible," Martin said.

But Edmond was set on completing his quest. He had fought too hard to walk away now.

A shriek that had become all too familiar pierced the sky high above them. Shading their eyes, they looked up to see the dragon, its massive wings spread, gliding across the blue expanse.

"Is it possible that thing knows to guard the castle?" Edmond asked with imperturbable calm.

"Likely, I'd say, though it must be compelled to do so through magic," Martin replied. "Whatever its aim, we are at its mercy. There's nowhere to hide."

The crackle and rustle of scraping branches sounded behind them, and they turned to see the thorns curling back on themselves, creating a clear path.

"Come on," Edmond said without hesitation. It might be a trap, but it was their only chance. He grabbed Martin's arm and pulled him into the opening. Seeing the way clear before them, they ran.

The thorns closed in behind them and wove more tightly together overhead, shielding them from the sky but keeping well clear of their bodies. Edmond realized they were running over the rotten wood of a drawbridge, and then their path opened into a courtyard. Their feet skidded on loose rubble as they halted abruptly and looked around.

In front of them stood a young woman with masses of curly brown hair as tangled and wild as the thorns around them. She wore a tattered gown and a triumphant expression. Her eyes were slanted and her cheekbones sharp and thin, betraying her fey origins, as did the knobby white wand in her hand.

Still staring at her, Edmond and Martin failed to see that the thorns were closing in behind them until they felt points as sharp as needles dig into their backs. They jerked away and ran forward.

"Stop!" the woman cried.

They could not stop, however, or they would be impaled.

"Oh, you vexatious things," the woman said in a roar of anger. With a wave of her arm she sent an arc of blue light toward the thorns. The light buzzed briefly, and then the thorns drooped.

Martin checked the wounds in his side and back as best he could, but Edmond stared steadily at the fairy before him. "Thank you for saving us," he said. He bowed, unsure what the protocol was for meeting a fairy but not wanting to be disrespectful.

"Thank Arabella. She told me to save you."

"The princess?"

"Of course, you slug-footed luggard. Who else?"

"Pardon my ignorance. I didn't know she was awake."

"Of course she's not, you blithering fool. Do you think I would have brought you in here if she was?"

On these words, the fairy turned and strode forward without an invitation to follow her. Edmond hesitated to go through the dark arch of a doorway nearby, but a shriek overhead reminded him that he was standing in the open.

"Hurry, Martin."

"But she's raving mad."

"Clearly, but I do not think she means us harm."

"Come along," the fairy called back, motioning with her hand. The two men fell into step behind her. "You must see the beauty you seek."

With a heavy thud of his heart, Edmond realized that the moment he'd been waiting for his whole life now lay before him.

VI

THE FAIRY woman led the way up a dark and twisted stairway to the top of a tower. The men followed, and though Edmond's legs felt heavy and his wounds throbbed, his heart pounded with anticipation. He knew it was an odd reaction, considering his years of resentment and cynicism, and yet there was magic here. He could feel it.

Realizing that the woman was mumbling, he tried to catch her words but failed. Then, as they passed through another arched doorway into a dim chamber, he forgot about her entirely.

Thorns grew through the window and through cracks in the walls and holes in the roof, winding around the room. Though the thorns outside had been bare, here they were covered in bright green leaves and blooming roses of every color. A shaft of light from a small window stretched across the floor and up onto a velvet-covered bed, illuminating two dainty, slipper-covered feet and a royal blue gown. Two white hands clasped at the waist of a bodice embroidered with gold, and there, just at the trailing, dimming edge of light, was the most entrancing face Edmond had ever beheld or dreamed of.

Her skin was fair but tinged with a healthy, vibrant flush. Dark, curling lashes rested upon her pink cheeks, and her bosom rose and fell with gentle breaths. She looked as if the slightest noise would disturb her. Her eyes were poised to flutter open, and the curve of her lips promised a waiting smile. Framing her face, long golden curls were carefully arranged over her shoulders, glinting in the light.

"Good heavens," Edmond breathed. Unconsciously he stepped forward to study her more closely.

"If you kiss her, I'll ram you down that dragon's throat myself."

Made aware of his companions again, Edmond straightened and stepped back but did not look away. "I thought kissing her was rather necessary."

"Not until you fall in love."

"Love?" Edmond asked, turning now to face the fairy woman. "What are the chances of true love between any two people? And to make it more unlikely still, she is asleep."

The woman just looked at him.

"What if the legend is wrong?" he asked.

"It isn't wrong. I did the spell myself."

"Really?" Edmond asked, raising an eyebrow. "And you called *me* a blithering fool."

Her face soured. Her lips moved as she ground her teeth, and her wand shook at her side. "Of course it was foolish!" she burst out. "If that silly, romantic blossom-eater with a mouth wider than her ears hadn't been talking behind me, it never would have come out that way."

Wanting more and more to know the whole story, Edmond said, "I think it is time for some introductions. Then perhaps we can figure the rest of this out. I am Prince Edmond of Stone Haven, second son of King Osden. And this is Martin."

The fairy curtsied. "Prince Edmond, may I present Her Royal Highness and future Queen of Timber Vale, Princess Arabella. Princess, may I present Prince Edmond." This was all done with a courtly grace that belied the fact that he was being introduced to an unconscious body. Then, leaning toward him, Lona whispered. "She cannot see you when you are in this room with her, but she can hear you."

Try as he might, Edmond could make no sense of this, but he responded politely though awkwardly, "I am pleased to meet you, Your Highness. This is Martin, a man of your own country. I apologize for our intrusion here."

"You don't need to apologize. She told me you were coming days ago."

Edmond glanced between the fairy's scowling face and the still face below them. "So you talk to her?"

The fairy huffed. "Arabella, I think he might be dimwitted. He's handsome as a devil and seems a good man in a fight, but he's as dim as the night is long." She faced the princess as she spoke then turned back to Edmond. "Of course I do. And you'll have to talk to her as well. Her life depends on you, doesn't it?"

With a solemn nod, Edmond said, "I'm afraid it does."

"Well, so long as you understand that, I'll let you begin courting her."

"But how?"

"Questions later. Right now we need to see to those wounds."

She turned to leave, but Edmond said, "Wait. What is your name?"

"Lona. Now don't say you're pleased to meet me or any of that other nonsense. I've no time for it. Come along."

The two men whispered behind her as she led the way to the kitchen. They must think she couldn't hear them. So they thought she was mad. Well, maybe she was, but they'd soon learn that she knew what she was talking about just the same.

In her sternest voice she said, "Come in, and we'll get you cleaned up. I can't have you bleeding all over my floor."

"I'd prefer not to bleed all over anything," Edmond said. As he spoke, his sharp eyes roved around the room.

"All this is worse than useless these days with only myself to feed," Lona said, motioning to the cavernous kitchen.

With his eyes still studying the various implements and oddments, Edmond said, "But amazing just the same. I have never seen anything like it."

Lona nodded, knowing that Briar Fen castle was one of a kind, built as it was against the stone of a cliff. The kitchen's back wall was the cliff itself. Its vaulted ceilings soared overhead to allow the smoke and heat of many fires to rise above the army of cooks needed to feed a castle full of people. A small spring trickled out of the stone wall into an overflowing stone basin, wetting the floor all around before draining through a hole rimmed by flagstones. Wisps of steam rose from the basin, for it was a hot spring, the key factor determining the location of the kitchen when the castle was built.

One of the four fireplaces was so massive that three men could stand comfortably within it. Dozens of fowl and even whole oxen could be roasted on spits across its coals. The once great kitchen no longer belched heat and smoke or clamored with the work of a dozen cooks, but when Lona sat on her stool in the evenings, eating her solitary meal beside a meager fire, the ghosts of the past crowded around her.

Life emanated from these two men, however. The strength and vibrancy of their presence was a welcome but unsettling change in her world.

Needing action, Lona filled her cauldron from the spring and swung it over the fire. She threw in some herbs—thyme, cloves, yarrow, and calendula. "Hurry up and boil."

"What was that?" Edmond asked, looking up from pulling off his boots.

"I wasn't talking to you. Now strip off your clothing please."

The men eyed each other uneasily.

"What are you afraid of?" she asked, fetching clean linen rags.

"Many things," Edmond said. "I'm not yet sure if you're one of them." Then slowly, as if reluctant to admit his need, he added, "But I do long to be clean and dry again."

Handing them the rags and several lengths of linen, Lona directed them to the basin of hot spring water. "You'll find soap on the rock ledges above the basin. When you've scrubbed off the mud, I will tend to your wounds."

She then turned back to her cauldron, which was already bubbling, since the water had been hot to begin with. Now that it was infused with healing herbs, she ladled some into a clean bowl to cool then glanced over at the men. Gauntlets, jerkins, and tunics had dropped to the floor, and they vigorously scrubbed at their skin and dumped buckets of water over their heads. Though they were mostly hidden by shadow, Lona still blushed at the sight and looked away.

When they returned to the fire, clean and loosely draped in linen sheets, Lona examined their wounds. Edmond had only a few puncture marks on his back from the thorns and cuts on his forehead and cheek, but Martin had a deep cut on his side. It no longer bled, but it could easily get infected. Both men were also covered in bruises that would continue to darken, and one of Martin's ankles was ringed with swollen red lines.

Lona shook her head. "I guess I'm lucky I don't need to reattach any of your limbs."

"Could you?" Martin asked, raising his eyebrows in disbelief.

Lona blushed. "No. Like I said, isn't it lucky I don't need to?"

She carefully cleaned their cuts with the herbed water to prevent infection then told them to stand still. With studied care she pulled her wand from her hair where she'd stashed it for safekeeping. Directing it toward their worst wounds, she sent out a blast of energy to seal them. It was the surest way of healing she knew, so she ignored their gasps and groans.

"That is amazing," Edmond said, running his finger along his cheekbone where his cut was now closed. "Why bother with medicine when you could heal all our wounds with magic?"

Lona carefully applied a salve to the smaller cuts on Martin's arms. "Because it isn't worth the cost. Don't you know anything about magic?"

"Very little," Edmond said.

"It drains her life to use it," Martin said.

Lona narrowed her eyes at him. "You know all about it, do you? Then you should know what a gift I gave you just now. All living things possess within them a portion of spirit, or energy. Fairies are born with an abundance of this energy. We are able to use this well of power to act upon the natural world, but when we do so, it is spent and cannot be regained. We can live for centuries, but each use of magic shortens our life until it is gone and we are left shriveled and wasted. Death comes quickly after."

"Why use it at all?" Edmond asked, his shrewd eyes trained on her, bright with curiosity.

With a smile Lona said, "Some fairies use it to gain power, to manipulate and enslave. Most of us use it to serve—to heal, protect, or cheer. We believe it is our calling in this world."

Martin stared into the fire, pensive. Edmond sat down on the stool, though it looked as if it could crumble beneath him, and stretched his feet toward the flame. "I never knew that dry feet were a luxury."

"In the fens they are. Your boots will take longer to dry than your clothes, and I want you to visit the princess this evening," Lona said. "I will dry them for you."

As Lona fetched her wand from her hair again, Edmond held out a hand to stop her. "Nay, dear lady. I would not ask that of you."

Flapping a hand at him, Lona said, "Tut now. I give only what I feel is wise. Indeed, my sisters often mocked me for my parsimony. But I spare nothing in service of Princess Arabella."

Lona tilted her head to the side and considered how best to dry the leather boots. Then with a nod she twirled her wand slowly around them, concentrating hard, and brought forth each drop of water that had soaked into them. The droplets shimmered and spun in a whirlpool in the air until she flicked her wand and flung them against the hot stones of the hearth. They sizzled and steamed away. She did the same for Martin's boots, pleased with the results. "You will need to brush the dust from them though."

"'Tis better than a show at the fair," Martin said.

"Of course it is, simpleton," Lona snapped. "Do you dare compare me to a common magician?"

"Only favorably," Martin said, tugging at his nose.

Mollified, Lona sniffed. "There are some who know a fair bit about herbs and minerals, though most are frauds. It takes a great deal of study to use such things safely. I mix a great many potions and elixirs myself. By using ingredients that hold the power of life within them too, I am able to use less of my energy."

"And what of your wand?" Edmond asked. "Does it hold its own power as well?"

"No. We create them ourselves. They are enchanted to direct and store our magic. The spell costs us dearly, but we can strengthen the wand's power with our tears and blood when they spill out so that none of our energy is lost."

Edmond nodded and sighed deeply. "It is a wonderful gift your kingdom has to be blessed with fairies. Stone Haven has no such gift."

"Few places do, and Timber Vale is not as blessed as it once was. I am the last in the kingdom."

Martin looked up sharply at this. "But there were still half a dozen or so of your kind left when I was sent away."

Feeling her bottom lip tremble, Lona pursed her mouth tightly. Once her emotions were under control she said, "Even they are gone now, sacrificed for the sake of the kingdom, so Lady Rhoswen says. They aided the armies and saved failing crops, for the people had as much as they could bear with heavy taxes and little trade. But much of their magic was also used to aid Rhoswen as she hid from her father. Over the years, the fires and food and a dozen other things that might have been done by hand, leached their life away. It was the effort to train that infernal dragon that finished them off."

Drawing a shuddering breath, she caught the two teardrops spilling from the corners of her eyes with her wand then shoved it back into her hair. The two men's faces were solemn in the flickering firelight.

Edmond leaned forward, clasping his hands over his knees. "Dragons are not uncommon in my land, but I have never heard of one being trained. How did they do it?"

"It's a spell, of course. Dragons are intelligent creatures but fiercely independent. When Lord Galloran bargained with your father for a dragon, he commanded my sisters to create a spell binding the dragon's mind to his.

But when they realized that he meant to use the dragon to put an end to Princess Arabella, they stole the dragon and harnessed it to Lady Rhoswen instead, for after all, she was Arabella's fiercest defender."

Lona sniffed but blinked back any threatening tears. "Rhoswen can see through its eyes and command it at will with no more than a thought. The spell is bound with a golden chain around its neck. But she has found that her control is not complete, for it fights against its captivity."

"I saw the chain you speak of. If it were removed, the spell would be broken?"

"Yes," Lona said. "There is always a way to break a spell, but never an easy one."

"No, getting a chain off a dragon's neck would certainly not be easy."

Tired of standing, Lona sat on the floor between Martin and Edmond, and only then realized how far she had to crane her neck to look at them. "Now tell me about yourself," she said to Edmond.

Edmond straightened, and Lona remembered that he was not likely accustomed to being commanded like a servant. But he merely nodded his head and said, "I have had but one purpose in life, one given to me by my father. From the time I could hold a knife, I've been trained for this quest. My father wishes to unite this kingdom with ours through marriage."

"Such is the way of kings," Lona said, nodding.

"But I wanted nothing more than to try and to fail. My goal was to survive and find my freedom. I no more believed in a sleeping princess than I believed in true love. Clearly I was wrong about the first. I am left to wonder if I was wrong about the second."

"I pray you are, good prince, else my princess will never awaken."

"Martin has told me the story of the curse, but certain aspects of it intrigue me. I don't know what is legend and what is real. Will you tell me the story from the beginning?"

"That I can do. I've known Arabella since she first drew breath, for I and six other fairies attended the birth to make sure it went well. The queen had waited long to have a child, and she was fearful because of her age. The king asked us to ensure the safety of the queen and the baby. It was a long night, but the baby girl was born healthy and strong.

"The king held a banquet to celebrate the birth and to thank us for our service. We were invited to eat at the royal table and were made her godmothers. After the dinner we each wished to give the princess a gift. I nearly walloped some of my sisters for the useless gifts they gave her." Lona snorted. "She was already a pretty baby and a princess. She would be spoiled and petted enough, I thought, but they were determined to give her every perfection. It would have made her insufferable, so I intended to give her the gift of snoring."

Edmond burst out laughing, and Lona glared. "What? I tell you, it never did anybody any good to have no faults!"

"I take it you changed your gift then, for she isn't snoring now."

Lona briefly reflected on her disappointment and then said, "I was not given the opportunity. I was hiding behind a curtain, afraid of the reaction my sisters would have if they suspected my plan—for I was the youngest of them—when the ceremony was interrupted. Unbeknownst to us all, the king's brother, Galloran, conspired against the new heir. He bargained with Sybil, a fairy who was old and feeble, withered of heart from her years of performing dark magic, to come to the feast and curse the princess. She entered the great hall, and before we knew her intent, she cursed the innocent baby to prick her finger on a spindle on her sixteenth birthday and die."

"Why did this fairy not kill her that day?"

"No fairy can kill with magic, for magic gives life. They may, however, set into motion events that will lead to death."

"Why did the other fairies not force her to undo the curse? With so many there, you must have been able to compel her to do so."

Lona shook her head sadly. "When she spoke the curse, the hall erupted into confusion and the king commanded the guards to clap Sybil into irons. But the spell had cost her dearly. She dropped to the stone floor and withered before us until her last breath rattled from her throat. It seemed hopeless, but I could not bear the tears in the queen's eyes and offered to do what I could to save the baby.

"I conferred with my sisters, and we all agreed that the curse could be altered to put her to sleep instead of killing her. But Sybil's curse was powerful. It had seeped deep into Arabella's soul and carved itself in the lines of her fate. The best I could do was alter the chains of death into chains of a profound one-hundred-year sleep. Isemay, one of my fairy sisters, kept mumbling about true love's kiss. I would have nothing to do with that, I tell you. Was there ever anything more foolish? But as I was pronouncing the spell, Isemay said those words behind me, and in my nervous state I repeated them before I knew what I was saying."

"A pity that happened."

"Yes. And such an uproar as there was! The king and queen were devastated that she would sleep for a hundred years, for they would not live to see her awakened. They had every spindle in the kingdom destroyed so that the kingdom had to trade for every scrap of new cloth and everyone quickly became ragged. Secure in their efforts, they thought all would be well, but on the days leading up to her sixteenth birthday, everyone grew nervous. Arabella was kept in the dark about everything because we did not wish her to live in fear, but we should have told her. If we had, disaster might have been averted."

Edmond leaned forward and asked, "How so?"

"Rhoswen invited the royal family to stay at her father's holding here in

Briar Fen for the impending birthday. The King and Queen were desperate to do something and thought it the perfect place to guard her closely because it was the most fortified castle in the kingdom, being built into the stone ridge as it is. How could any of us have known that here, in a dusty, unused tower, was the one spindle left in the whole kingdom?"

Edmond stood up and paced around the shadows of the room. "So Lady Rhoswen invited her here, and by chance Arabella came across a spindle. Has no one wondered at that coincidence?"

Lona stood as well and felt the fabric of their tunics to see if they were dry. But as Edmond's question sifted through her brain, she spun around to face him. "No. Lady Rhoswen has always protected Arabella. She learned of her father's role in the curse when she heard him speak of it in a drunken rage. She was still a child and afraid to speak out against her father, and she told no one. Then, when Arabella fell into this cursed sleep, Rhoswen found the king and queen dying and discovered her father's greatest betrayal: He convinced them to take a youth potion so that they might live to see their daughter wake, but he gave them poison instead.

"Galloran took the regency upon their deaths, but he had lost his daughter's loyalty. For over a hundred years Rhoswen and I have kept her safe from Galloran's many attempts on her life."

"And yet Lady Rhoswen herself now conspires to murder her."

Lona's heart sank and cold fear ran down her spine. "Yes. But how do you know this?"

"I will tell you of my audience with Lady Rhoswen and my meeting with thieves in the fens, but right now I need to see the princess. There is a deep game afoot, and we must keep her safe."

VII

LONA WALKED before him carrying a torch, and Edmond carried a pail of hot water from the spring. The fairy wished to bathe the princess's face, which seemed an odd thing to do at that moment, but he was content that they would be near her. Foreboding ran through his veins.

Once they entered her chamber, Lona directed him to light a fire on the shallow hearth. As he did so, she plucked a few roses from the vines on the walls and pulled the petals from them. After dropping these into the water, she bathed the princess's face and neck. "It gets very dusty in here," Lona said as she worked. "She feels everything that touches her and cannot stand the dust since she is unable to brush it away."

"How do you speak to her?" Edmond asked, beginning now to believe that she might really be able to do it. "With magic?"

"Yes, but not my own."

With the fire now caught, Edmond walked over to the bed. "Will I be able to speak to her?"

"I see no reason why not, though I do not know for certain. Lady Rhoswen would never try."

"Does Lady Rhoswen visit often?"

"No. A few times a year perhaps. Though she was here only days ago, the same day you crossed the border into this land." Lona waved a hand to stop him from speaking. "Do not ask me how I know. Ask her. It will give you something to speak of."

"I do not think there will be a shortage of things to discuss." Edmond smiled and reached for Arabella's hand but pulled away when he realized what he was doing.

"Go ahead. You will need to hold her hand."

"I will?"

"Yes. And hold this as well." Lona pulled a string from around her neck. It was tied to a long wooden spindle which she held out to him.

Edmond took it warily. "Is this the spindle that brought the curse on her?"

"Yes. I think that is why it is able to do what it does. It has a connection to her. I discovered it by chance." Lona pulled a stool up beside the bed and beckoned for him to sit down. He did so then gently took the hand nearest him on the bed.

Her skin was soft and warm but slack. The pulse throbbing in her wrist reassured him.

"You must go to sleep, for she can only talk to you in the dream world. I have learned to fall into a light sleep from which I can easily rouse myself, but I do not know if that will work for you."

Edmond relaxed and awaited further instructions.

"Go to sleep. The spindle will do the rest. And do not worry. Martin and I will stand guard."

Lona left the chamber, and Edmond thought for a moment how strange this all was. But he was tired, and the feather mattress seemed to call to him. He wished he could stretch out on it, for he hadn't slept in a bed for over a week; but he settled for leaning his head on it, with the hand holding the spindle beneath his forehead as a pillow.

Sleep found him quickly, and he was pulled into a vortex of colors from which he emerged into Arabella's chamber again. It looked precisely as it had before except that there was no bed here and no sleeping princess—only a very awake one.

He saw that she was taller standing than he had expected and more regal with her perfect posture and tipped-up chin. Even more striking were her blue eyes, as clear and blue as a deep lake.

After a moment he realized he was staring and tore his gaze away. He bowed low and said, "Princess Arabella, I am honored."

She gave him a regal nod. "As am I, Prince Edmond." Then she laughed, a short, breathless sound that betrayed her nervousness. "Perhaps now you will feel more as if we have been introduced. I don't think you quite believed the last one."

"Do you blame me?"

"No." Arabella gestured to the space around them. "How do you like it here? This has been the sum of my existence for over a century now."

Edmond looked around, finding the room empty of furnishings and ornaments of any kind. The window, however, swirled with colors. Walking over to it, he looked out and found that he could see for miles around. If he focused on any one thing, he could make out every detail of it.

"This is how you were able to see me cross the border as Lona said."

"Yes. I can see anything within my kingdom."

Amazed, Edmond said, "My father would give his whole fortune to do that. Everything you see is real?"

"So far as I can tell. Certainly they have always been proven true from what we learn of the outside world, though that isn't much. But I cannot hear anything in these visions of the real world, and I do not see everything, so most things remain a mystery."

"And yet, I wonder if you don't see more than most."

"It is true that I have learned much about human nature and the masks people wear."

"People like Lady Rhoswen?"

With a slight, hesitant nod, Arabella said, "Yes, her most of all. Though I still don't know what to believe. She has always been my older, wiser cousin. I do not think she has ever loved me, but she has loved my people. They are her people too, after all. But just as she has sacrificed the lives of so many of the fairies, she is now prepared to take my life for the good of the kingdom."

"I am sorry, but I cannot credit her with such pure motives."

"And what can you, a stranger here who has only met her once, know of her motives?"

"Perhaps more than most because of the very fact that I am a stranger. I may observe her with new eyes." Edmond folded his arms across his chest and wondered how Arabella would react to his next words. "She proposed that I should marry her."

Arabella's eyes widened and she tilted her head. "That is certainly interesting."

"She was careful to point out the advantages of marrying her if I wished to be king rather than risking my life to find you."

With a delicate shrug, Arabella sighed. "Her logic is solid. And she had already determined to end my curse the only way she could."

With one sharp shake of his fist, Edmond said, "Exactly. The only way *she* could. She knew, however, that there was a chance I might break it another way: by waking you. And she has tried to stop me using every means available to her. I barely escaped her castle, her dragon attacked me by the river, and I feel in my bones that she has another scheme in play with Prince Nicol."

"But all these years she has protected me."

"All these years her father was alive and heir before her. Now there is nothing between her and supreme power in this kingdom but one defenseless sleeping princess who is in her keeping."

Her eyes troubled, Arabella paced between Edmond and the window. "I cannot believe that she has planned this all along. Has power corrupted her?"

"Power has that effect on most people, so it is possible. I do not claim to know all the answers here."

Arabella stopped pacing and looked at him. "And yet you have discerned so many of them already."

"I am well versed in scheming and manipulative royals." Edmond heard the derision in his voice and wondered if Arabella would question it. But though she studied him briefly, she said nothing of it.

Her voice was soft when she spoke again. "Yet you are willing to love me, a royal, and break my curse."

Edmond's muscles tensed. "I will be honest with you, Princess Arabella: I did not come here expecting to love you or even believing that I could."

Arabella's head drooped, hiding her expression. "Then why come at all?"

"I came because my father sent me. Indeed, he sired me, his second son, only for this purpose—a gamble that might pay off, and one for which he was willing to gamble my life."

"This still does not explain why you came."

"No, I suppose not. I came because I have not been allowed in the whole of my existence to choose for myself. But if I survive this quest, I might escape any more of my father's interference in my life."

Arabella smiled a polite, courtly smile. "So your reward does not depend on breaking this curse."

There was a long pause. "No. It doesn't. And I have no desire to be anyone's king."

Arabella turned and leaned against the window sill, looking out into the swirling images.

With a surge of frustration rising in him, Edmond spoke more sharply than he intended. "Where is your spirit? Do you not want to be free of this?"

She only turned her head, but her words jabbed at his soul. "You cannot know how I want to be free. The chains of this curse are such as I wouldn't wish on my worst enemy. But I am at your mercy, sir."

"Then find your courage. Enthrall me until I am at your mercy as well. You have beauty, grace, and wit to aid you. I have nothing to offer you but a soldier's skills and a heart that has never known gentle emotions. But they are yours to command. I never said that I was unwilling to stay at your side and try."

With a choked laugh, Arabella turned fully to face him. "No man has ever dared speak to me as plainly as you do."

"I brave it only because at present you are in no position to throw me into a dungeon and torture me."

"You forget my loyal protector. Lona wields her magic with discretion at all times—unless she is angry."

Edmond grinned. "Then I hope you will account my words as I meant them. I want to see justice done here, and I can do it only if you fight by my side."

She laughed again, this time with a bubble of true mirth. "Now I know why others watch you and respond to your presence as if you were a king among them, whether you want to be one or not. You are sharp and hard like an arrow in flight—a force for good, and one to be reckoned with."

"Perhaps not a poor choice to give your heart to then?"

"Perhaps. Though I believe love is no slave to wisdom. I wonder what does rule it? If we could command our hearts, this would be easier."

"I am entirely uneducated in the science of love. I must have words with Martin about neglecting so important a matter when he trained me for this quest."

"Martin seems very loyal."

"Yes, and his loyalty lies first with you. I—"

Before he could finish, Arabella focused her attention elsewhere. "No!" she screamed. "Someone is touching me."

"What? Do you mean in the waking world? I am holding your hand."

"No." She gave a disgusted, frightened gasp. "Someone is kissing me!"

Alarmed, Edmond asked, "How do I get back?"

"You must wake up."

"How?"

"I don't know."

He shouted inside his head, "Wake up, you fool!"

With a heavy, foggy feeling, he pulled himself back into consciousness and opened his eyes to see Prince Nicol on the other side of Arabella's bed with his head bent over hers. In a flash, Edmond pulled a knife and shoved its point against the man's white neck.

"You will stop at once," Edmond said with venom in his voice.

Prince Nicol froze, lifting his head only a fraction. His hands quivered slightly as he raised them off the bed, but his voice was calm. "May I stand back?"

A little awkwardly, Edmond drew his sword while keeping his knife against the other man's skin. "Yes, though if you are wise, you will do so with great caution."

In slow, careful degrees, Prince Nicol straightened. Edmond held him at sword point as the distance grew between them.

"It is a pity she didn't wake up," Prince Nicol said. His voice was refined and bored.

"Did you expect her to?"

"No, but it was worth a try. Now I shall have to kill her, which is a shame, don't you think?"

"Sorry to disappoint you, but the lady is under my protection."

Prince Nicol leapt backward and drew his sword. With the bed between them, Edmond was forced to vault over it after him.

"I am a fool, I suppose," Prince Nicol said. "Lady Rhoswen was most insistent that I not kill you, only the princess. I gather you are to be her new plaything. But now I shall have to kill you anyway, and it would have been so much easier while you were snoring."

Edmond kept his face a careful blank though his temper burned. "Yes, you should have taken the opportunity. You won't get another."

Moving cautiously like a cat afraid of startling a bird, Prince Nicol adjusted his stance. "You are grown confident after besting my men, I see. However, you face a different class of foe now."

"Not so different. One class is poorly trained and the other is cowardly."

Edmond's mockery broke Nicol's caution. The man sprang forward, swinging his sword. Edmond met it with a crashing blow of his own. The collision jarred his wrist and shoulder, but his muscles held firm. He was able to disengage and draw back several paces. He dared not glance toward

Arabella where she lay still and defenseless, so close to danger. His need to protect her hampered his ability to attack.

With a cry, Edmond rushed on Nicol, cutting and jabbing with violent strokes, driving him back against the thorn-covered wall. Before he could corner him, Nicol spun away. Edmond fell heavily against the wall and pushed off again, thorns digging into his unprotected hands, then turned in time to see Nicol raise his sword over Arabella.

With a running leap, Edmond tackled him from behind. The sword went flying, but Nicol crashed on top of Arabella. The adversaries slid off the high, narrow bed, bringing Arabella down with them. Edmond heard her head hit the ground, but he could not help her. Nicol was pinned beneath him, struggling to break free; so he punched his fist into the side of the prince's face once, twice, and a third time before the man went limp.

Just as Edmond stood and rolled the other man across the floor in a heap, Lona burst into the chamber, her wild eyes searching in the dim light. "Is the princess safe?"

"Safe, but likely hurt." As Martin ran in, Edmond pointed at the unconscious prince. "Guard him. If he wakes up, don't be gentle about knocking him out again."

He leaned down and examined Arabella. She was as peaceful as ever on the surface, though she breathed more quickly and shallowly than before. "Forgive me, Arabella," he whispered, both for letting her be hurt and for what he needed to do next.

He slid his arms beneath her and lifted her back onto the bed, carefully laying her head on the pillow. Then he ran gentle but firm hands down her arms and legs, searching for breaks. "Nothing seems broken, but I do not know where she hurts. How can I ask her? I couldn't possibly go to sleep now."

"Let me," Lona said, holding out a shaking hand for the spindle.

After a quick search Edmond snatched the spindle off the floor, handed it to the fairy, and watched, amazed, as she slipped effortlessly into sleep. A moment later she shook her head to wakefulness and said, "Her head aches terribly, and she feels bruised all over but believes she is well. She wishes me to thank you for saving her."

Edmond said nothing. But he gripped Arabella's warm hand in his and mentally thrashed himself for not protecting her better.

Lona scowled down at the limp prince as Martin stood over him. "Curses! Who is this? How did he get in here?" She pointed her wand and directed the thorns to slither across the floor and wrap themselves around Nicol's ankles and chest, binding his arms to his side. The thorns cut his flesh wherever it was not protected by leather or steel armor, but he didn't stir.

Edmond was thinking hard. "He is Prince Nicol of Windemore. I suspect Lady Rhoswen told him about your secret tunnel. Where were you two all this time? How did he get past you?"

"That blasted dragon was trying to burn down the castle, so Martin and I were out in the courtyard doing what we could. Then it flew away and we heard the commotion up here."

"A diversion then," Edmond said, nodding. "He was here at Lady Rhoswen's bidding, sent to kill Arabella."

"Then she is not holding to the time frame she gave me," Lona said.

Edmond met Lona's eyes. "She's desperate now that I'm here. I threaten all her ambitions."

FEW THINGS remind a person they're alive quite so vibrantly as pain. Arabella felt oddly comforted by it. But she could tell by the grip of his firm, calloused hand that Edmond was distressed. And it was just as clear that Lona was furious.

Arabella's mind could move freely between the realm of dreams and the darkness behind her eyelids. She preferred the dreams because she hated feeling blind, but she wanted to be present in the real world to fully grasp what went on around her. To her left, Lona spoke.

"I'm going to turn him into a slug and put him out on a stone in the sun."

"Will you at least wait until we question him?" Martin said.

"You wish to question him, do you? Then I know what to do. I'll be back."

Martin spoke again in his low, rough voice. "What do you suppose she's doing?"

"I wouldn't dare hazard a guess," Edmond said. In contrast to Martin, he spoke with refinement, but his voice was firm and decisive. And it was directed toward her so that she knew he was looking at her.

"She's a rare beauty, isn't she?" Martin asked. "The princess, I mean."

"Rare indeed."

"Did you really talk to her in the dream world like Lona said?"

"As strange as it seems, I did. She can hear us, you know. It feels strange to speak of her as if she isn't here when I know she's listening." Then Edmond laughed, a deep rumble that took her by surprise, and said, "Martin, you're blushing."

"No, I'm not. It's hot in here, what with that fire outside and running up all those steps."

Lona's voice erupted into the room, vibrating with purpose. "I found it."

"A birdcage?" Edmond asked.

"Just wait." There was a soft whooshing sound and then shouts of "Catch it! Catch the mangy thing!"

After much jostling and exclaiming, metal clanged, and a squeaky voice said, "Turn me back! Turn me back! How dare you do this to me?"

"Because you are a rat, a filthy vermin, creeping in here to kill my princess. Now you look like what you are."

"I am a prince, woman."

"You are muck. Answer our questions or you will find that a worse fate awaits you."

"Prince Edmond, I appeal to your mercy," Nicol said. "Torture me, slay me . . . anything but this!"

"We shall see how forthcoming you are with information," Edmond said, his voice as hard as granite. "Take him to the kitchen, Martin. Lona, see what you can discover from him. I'll join you in a moment."

Their footsteps faded away, as did Prince Nicol's indignant squeaking. Then Arabella felt a tickling sensation on her cheek and realized Edmond had brushed back a strand of her hair. "I cannot possibly express how sorry I am that I failed you, Princess. I will not do so again, I assure you."

Then he too was gone.

Time seemed to crawl at half its normal speed before Edmond returned to visit her in the dream world, though it was only the next morning.

"Martin and I blocked off the tunnel," he said as soon as he appeared. "There was plenty of broken furniture, crumbling statuary, and loose stones from the courtyard wall to do the job. If anyone tries to use the tunnel, they won't get through easily or with any degree of stealth."

"I'm glad. But Rhoswen won't give up," Arabella said.

"No, she won't, and I'm very aware that she has a dragon to do her bidding. I think we should move you to a safe location."

Arabella turned at that. "You mustn't. Lona believes the magic to be tied to this chamber. If you move me, I might well be trapped in my sleeping body and no longer able to speak to anyone."

"We will keep you here for now, though it makes me nervous."

"Have you learned anything from Prince Nicol?"

"Not much, but enough. Lady Rhoswen was blackmailing him with something he refused to speak of but which he says would destroy him. He was so anxious to be rid of her threats and demands that when she offered to keep her silence in exchange for one little favor, he agreed. The favor, of course, was dripping poison into your mouth."

Arabella watched as anger burned in his eyes and his jaw clenched. Clearly he was having difficulty speaking of it, but she wanted to know more. "But how did he get here so quickly?"

"Rhoswen received word of my coming from the patrol Martin and I encountered at your border. Prince Nicol was in Timber Vale, though in the south. Word of a prince who had come searching for you unnerved her, so she sent for him before I even arrived at her castle."

"Well, you may rest easy concerning Prince Nicol. I doubt Lona will let him out of his cage anytime soon."

Edmond shook his head, and an ironic smile curled his mouth as he spoke. "I believe she is beginning to like having the rat to talk to. At first she fumed and threatened him. Then she began to merely lecture, and when I left her just now, he was regaling her with all the gossip he could recall."

"She has been very lonely," Arabella said. Her heart ached for her friend who had endured so much loneliness on her behalf.

"One would have to be desperately lonely to waste time talking to that creature!" Edmond shook his head ruefully. "I must go now. I do not want to stay too long and risk endangering you again."

With that he was gone, and he did not return for several days. Life became shapeless and void, and Arabella could hardly bring herself even to look out of her window. Not even Lona had time for her now, save for very brief visits during which she communicated little.

Arabella began to despair of Edmond's returning, until one evening she heard him climbing the stairs. Already she recognized the sound of his step.

He approached the bed and stood over her, silent for a long time. Then the legs of the stool scraped against the floor and he grasped her hand, running his thumb over her fingers as soft as a whisper.

Edmond sighed. "I wish to talk to you, Arabella, but it may be some time before I can relax enough to sleep."

To Arabella it did indeed feel like a long time. But she waited in her dream world, and at last he appeared before her. The expression on his face gave no hint of his thoughts, so she remained still, trying to calm herself, until he spoke at last.

"Are your eyes this beautiful in real life? Every time I see them, I am surprised."

She'd hoped for something . . . different. But she answered him, if a little coolly, "Most likely. They are one of my fairy gifts. Eyes like sapphires, I think it was."

"Why do you frown? Do you dislike compliments?"

She paused, trying to put into words the doubt that had plagued her since she was very young. "How would you like to be complimented and valued your whole life for beauties and virtues that are not naturally yours?"

"I did not intend to insult you."

"I know. You could not know how your words would affect me. When I was a girl, I was vain and silly. I know that now, though I didn't then. Everyone lavished praise on me, and I always wanted more. But I have had time to realize that I want people to see who I am without the gifts."

"What gifts *did* they give you?"

Arabella lifted her shoulders and sighed before giving him a full account of all that was false about her. "Besides my eyes, a voice like music, perfect beauty, curls of gold, grace of movement, and . . . " Arabella paused, embarrassed, then continued, ". . . sweet breath."

Edmond chuckled. "That last one is a treasure beyond price."

Seeing the humor in it, Arabella laughed a little. "Yes, indeed. Isemay gave it to me. She was always kissing the soldiers about the palace, so I suppose she thought it very important. She could not have known when she gave it to me, of course, that I would someday need to be awakened from a hundred-year sleep by a kiss."

"Was your mother beautiful?" Edmond asked, his voice thoughtful.

Surprised, but pleased to speak of her mother, Arabella said, "I thought so, and I know my father did as well. But her beauty was different from mine. It radiated from within. She was kind and gentle. Though she was often frail, she always showed affection to those she loved."

Edmond nodded. "The fairies did you a great disservice. You would have been much admired without their gifts, just as your mother was. But now you will never believe it."

"Don't feel sorry for me, please." She turned away, unable to bear his gaze which seemed to see everything. "If you find my eyes beautiful, so much the better considering what I need from you."

"Arabella, please don't hide from me."

Hesitantly she turned back. "Yes?"

"I would not fall in love with golden curls or sapphire eyes, no matter how enchanting they might be. It is your courage I most admire."

"But you told me I needed to find my courage."

"Yes, *find* it . . . because I know you have it. You have borne the weight of this curse, endured every moment of this captivity, without becoming bitter or vengeful. You have a good heart and a strong mind. I am in awe, for these are qualities no fairy magic could bestow."

Arabella felt light and warmth fill her heart at his admiration, but she saw that his expression was now grim. "You haven't come to see me for two days," she said softly. "What troubles you?"

He bowed his head briefly then met her eyes. "I have been struggling with whether or not to tell you something. I do not want to distress you, and above all I don't want you to think ill of me, but you need to know about my father. He is determined to tie our kingdom to yours through marriage to gain the wealth of your natural resources, especially your timber. Our own land is nearly barren of everything but what we can mine from the mountains."

Arabella nodded. "I would not object to opening trade with your nation. Such an arrangement would benefit both kingdoms."

"Yes, if trade were his intention, it would. But he means to possess Timber Vale."

"I would never let that happen."

Edmond's hands curled into fists at his sides and his jaw clenched. "If you knew him as I do, you would prepare to defend your throne. He has wanted this land far longer than even I realized. Lady Rhoswen claims he proposed marriage to her, and she refused. At that time there was still a quarter of a century to wait before your curse could be broken or I am quite sure he would have made you his aim. As it was, he had time enough to raise sons. He trained my brother, his heir, to be subservient to him in all things. I was trained to fight and survive. I was always meant to find you and to bring you back to wed my brother."

A cold knot formed in Arabella's chest. "And you were a willing party to this, even knowing that if you were successful, it would be because you loved me?"

Edmond threw his hands up in a gesture of frustration. "I never agreed with the idea, but I didn't believe any of this was possible. I have lived in bitterness toward my father, who cared more for a legend than for me. I thought only of escape and freedom . . . but I found a crumbling castle surrounded by enchanted thorns and sheltering a princess who has been asleep for over a hundred years. It is too incredible to be real, but here it is. And now true love no longer seems impossible either."

Warmth rose within Arabella's bosom like the morning sun. "My kingdom has a long history of intrigue and political strife. It is a daunting prospect. But I hope I would not face it alone. Would you defy your father for my sake?"

"Without question. The thought of how near you came to death just days ago, and under my watch, has tormented me. Not a minute goes by that I do not think of you, your safety, and your future. But I will bring chaos into your life even as I restore you to it."

"My life has been nothing but chaos and intrigue since I was born, though I did not know it. Regardless of what your father may do, the rest of my life will not be a peaceful one. My people do not know me. Those who did know me have long since died. I am afraid that if Rhoswen does not step down, civil war will ravage my kingdom."

Edmond paced before the window, his steps slow and methodical. "We could go away and leave Timber Vale to Lady Rhoswen and my father to his machinations. Your people would be at peace."

Arabella allowed herself a brief moment to consider this. It was so very tempting! But the weight of duty would drag her down into regret if she did not obey it. "You are free to do as you wish, of course. But I must stay. Though Rhoswen has done much good here, all of her efforts have revolved around magic, and that resource is nearly exhausted. Her intentions were good, I do believe, but her actions were unwise. Already I see the veneer of prosperity wearing thin."

"And you believe that you could do better?"

Arabella very nearly felt insulted by this question, but there was no mockery in his voice. He sincerely wanted to know if she believed in herself. "I *will* do better. The people have become as dependent on magic as Rhoswen has, and they have lost their pride and spirit. Under Rhoswen's continued rule, they would flounder and suffer when hard times come. I mean to see them thrive under the merit of their own labors."

Edmond nodded. "Such wisdom is unnatural in one with such a

youthful face."

"Perhaps so. I scarcely know if I am young or old. I was born one hundred twenty-three years ago, but I have lived only sixteen of those years. I have lost so much through this curse, yet I have gained one very important thing: perspective. And that changes everything."

"I see that you are resolved on this course, and I cannot find it within me to keep such a noble queen from her people. I will do everything in my power to set you on your throne."

Arabella laughed. "Even fall in love?"

With an answering smile, Edmond said, "Even that."

IX

L ONA WAS pleased that Edmond now spent so much time visiting
Arabella, since for days he hadn't at all. But it also frustrated her. He
guarded the spindle like a selfish boy with a new treasure, and Lona
missed visiting her princess. He needed to move things along, and if he
didn't do what he needed to do soon, she was going to have to take matters
in hand.

"Why doesn't he get it over with?" Lona asked, chopping a carrot.

Martin didn't look up from sharpening his knives. "Get what over
with?"

"I wasn't talking to you."

With a glance at the rat prince leaning glumly against the rusted bars
of his cage, Martin raised an eyebrow. "Of course you weren't. How foolish of

me."

"Well?" Lona asked, prompting Nicol to answer. "Why hasn't he kissed her yet?"

"Don't ask me!" Nicol squeaked. "I didn't hesitate to kiss her. I never hesitated to kiss any passably pretty girl."

"You'll find it a harder task now," Martin said, laughing.

"Oh, stop it," Lona said. "You're always mean to him."

"Me?" Martin pointed at his chest. "I didn't turn him into a rat."

After another savage chop, Lona pointed her knife in the direction of Arabella's tower. "It isn't that hard. He just needs to pucker up and squish his lips on hers." Lona saw Martin's wince of disgust and grinned at him. "Want me to show you?"

"That's quite all right. I'm well versed in the mechanics, as is Edmond. The issue is the repercussions of a kiss—what it means if she wakes up and what it means if she doesn't. He's afraid to find out."

"Pig bristles. He'd better find some gumption soon. We're out of time." Lona slammed her knife down on the table. "He needs a kick in the seat. You two get along till I get back."

In Arabella's chamber she found Edmond, very much awake, sitting on Arabella's bed. He held her hand loosely in his, but his face was lined with strain and the longing in his eyes was plain to see.

"You fool of a man, kiss her already."

Edmond opened his mouth to answer . . . But before he had a chance, an unearthly screech ripped through the air, sending shivers of dread down Lona's spine and deafening her ears.

"The dragon!" Edmond cried, dropping Arabella's hand and rushing to the small window. Lona ran after him but couldn't see past his broad shoulders until he lunged backward. The dragon flew past, its wing nearly brushing the tower walls.

"Nicol said it would return," Edmond growled, leaning through the window to see where it had gone. "Do you think Rhoswen sent it?"

Lona gripped her hands together. "I don't know. Her control over the dragon is not complete, as Nicol found out when it attacked his men though he was here at her bidding. Rhoswen commands it, but it can act on its own as well."

"Maybe it is just scouting and will go away again." Edmond sounded mildly hopeful.

There was a howl like rushing wind and the roof overhead erupted into flame. Ash and burning debris rained down on them.

"No such luck," Edmond growled as he rushed to Arabella's side.

"Get her out of here!" Lona screamed, but Edmond was already hauling her up and over his shoulders.

With a panicked look at the flames around them, Lona followed Edmond in a mad dash for the stairs. They'd made it halfway down when a jolt shook the whole tower. Lona lost her footing and slid down several steps. Edmond only managed to stay upright by pressing his shoulder against the wall until the swaying stopped. He hoped he hadn't accidentally struck Arabella's head against the stones.

Edmond shouted to Lona as she scrambled up. "The dragon's ramming the tower! Hurry before he does it again or we'll be crushed in the rubble."

They ran, but even without another jolt from the dragon, the walls crumbled around them and the stone steps became treacherous. Lona lit the way with her wand; without that light they would never have made it out before the second blow brought the tower crashing down behind them.

"Martin!" Edmond yelled. Then he coughed as dust filled his lungs.

"Here, sir!" Martin called from the passage ahead. When they met up with him, Lona saw that he was carrying the birdcage. Prince Nicol was curled up in a ball, trembling, on its floor.

"You brought Nicol," Lona gasped, amazed since she well knew how Martin disliked him.

Martin shook his head, his expression a strange mixture of alarm and wry humor. "The whole place is burning and the dragon is knocking it to pieces. I couldn't very well leave him to die—though if we don't get out of here, none of us stands a chance."

"To the tunnel!" Lona declared, running ahead of them.

As they ran through the great hall, one wall had already collapsed and the crumbling tapestries burned around them. In the royal chambers beyond, they halted at the pile of rubble they'd so carefully heaped over the passage door. Martin shouted in frustration, "We'll never clear it in time!"

Lona didn't bother to answer. He would soon know what she could do. With a flick of her wand, she lifted the pieces of the barrier into the air as if they were as light as milkweed and flung them to the far end of the room. She jerked the door open and lit the way with her wand, ignoring Martin's grumbling behind her that she should have used magic to build it in the first place.

But once they were safely inside the tunnel, Lona dropped back beside him to say, "You know I do not waste magic when a task can be accomplished with a little effort. But now I must save our lives, and that is another matter entirely."

The tunnel dipped down and grew colder and narrower. The rock became slick with water and the air grew heavy. "Where does this come out?" Edmond asked.

"Over the Sage River," Lona said, then added tersely, "I am certain Rhoswen will be waiting at the other end."

"We'll be coming out blind," Edmond said, his brow darkening with an uneasy frown.

"Can't Arabella see what is going on out there?" Martin asked.

Lona shook her head. "She may not be able to now that we have taken her out of the tower."

"We can still try to ask her," Edmond said. "Will you take her, Martin?"

Martin set the cage down and sat beside it; then Edmond transferred Arabella to his arms. Grasping the spindle, which hung from the string around his neck, he sat down next to Martin with his back against the rock wall, closed his eyes, and tried to go to sleep. After several minutes his shoulders slumped in defeat. "I couldn't possibly sleep now."

"Let me." Lona knelt before them, impatiently grabbed hold of the spindle, and took Arabella's hand from Edmond. She closed her eyes and searched for that misty, sleepy state which allowed her to be pulled into the dream world. Yet as hard as she tried, somehow she could only see the darkness behind her own eyelids. "It isn't working."

"We'll have to think of something else," Martin said.

Lona agreed, but her attention was on Edmond's frozen face as he looked down at Arabella, clearly realizing that he would never speak to her again unless he could wake her up.

Edmond stared at Arabella. Her face lay against Martin's shoulder, illuminated only by blue fairy-light. Dark shadows carved out the hollows and curves of her face, but the pink flush of life was still there. The thought of never speaking to her again made him feel cold and desperate.

Surely only love could inspire such a ferocity of dread as he now experienced!

Lona spoke, almost in his ear. "Let us hope Rhoswen has not brought an army. I will go out first and buy you some time. Martin will guard the entrance to the cave. You must awaken her now, Edmond. She cannot be left defenseless."

Edmond said nothing but motioned to Martin to give Arabella back into his keeping. As they made their way through the end of the tunnel, it sloped up and widened into a cavern. A circle of light ahead showed the way out; Lona extinguished her light as they approached it.

"Stay in the shadows," she said.

Vines and dripping moss lined the stone opening, and rushing water sounded below. The birdcage clanked against the rock as Martin set it down and joined Edmond at the entrance. Edmond recognized the place. To their right was the large tree that spanned the river with Warren's rope strung above it. The dragon had attacked them here, so they'd been in no position to notice the cave entrance. "I hate this river," Edmond said.

Lona pointed across the river. "There she is. She has only one guard with her, that big fellow, John. But we cannot forget that she has the dragon."

Then, without warning, Lona cupped her hand around her mouth and shouted, "Rhoswen, Arabella is awake! Isn't it wonderful?"

Edmond heard Lady Rhoswen shriek with fury across the river. The sound echoed off the rock of the cliff and chilled his blood.

"You fools!" Lady Rhoswen shouted. "All these years I have kept this kingdom safe from her, and now you would give it into her keeping? Never! Not so long as I draw breath."

"I accept the challenge!" Lona shouted back, abandoning her fake pleasantry.

Edmond watched Lona jump out of the cave and disappear from sight. Turning away with Arabella still draped over his shoulders, he said, "Martin, guard the entrance."

With a curt nod, Martin pulled a knife in each hand and jumped out of the cave onto the narrow ledge below.

Edmond knelt on the rock floor and let Arabella slip down to rest upon the ground, supporting her head and shoulders with his arms. "I wish I could awaken you to the peace you deserve instead of the danger you will face. But Lona is right: It is time."

Then, tipping her chin up, he leaned down and pressed his lips firmly to hers. Though they remained still beneath his, they were warm and sweet like the sun-kissed petals of a rose. Emotion surged through him until he thought his heart would burst. Surely only love could feel that way! But was it enough?

Slowly he raised his head but kept his eyes shut, afraid to look and find her still sleeping.

"Don't you want to see if my eyes look the same in real life?" a dear and familiar voice asked.

Joy and relief raced through him, and he didn't know which was stronger. He pulled her tightly against his chest, and this time she returned his kiss in full measure. She was not lost to him any longer, and he was determined to see her safely through this.

The cave went dark as a shadow passed over its entrance, and the two broke apart. The full force of his love for her left him speechless, but there was no time for words anyway. Only true love could have broken the curse, and their steady gaze into each other's eyes affirmed the miracle of that reality. Later they would speak of little else, but not yet.

He had a dragon to face.

As Arabella gazed into his eyes, he saw much more than sapphire blueness. He saw the strength and courage of a queen.

"Come, my love," she said. "Our friends are in danger."

Edmond pulled Arabella to her feet and made sure she was steady, then ran to look out. The dragon flew in a circle around Lona and Lady Rhoswen, who faced each other on the far bank. Then the great beast landed next to Lady Rhoswen, settling down like a tame dog beside her.

UNSTEADY ON feet that hadn't held her weight in far too long, Arabella struggled to compose herself as Edmond drew the string with the spindle over his head and held it out to her. "Take this and hide in the tunnel," he said.

She put it over her head and pulled her hair out of the way then clutched at his arm as he turned away. "Let me go with you."

"If we are to have any chance of surviving this day, I must get the chain off that dragon's neck and break the spell. Worrying about your safety is a distraction I can't afford. Here." He pressed something else into her hand; she recognized by touch the hilt of his knife. "Just in case," he whispered.

Then, after one last look, a world of emotion in the gleam of his eyes, Edmond turned and jumped down onto the ledge.

Stumbling forward, Arabella sank down on the rock and leaned out to watch. A steep path snaked down the sheer side of the ridge. Martin was halfway down, struggling to defend himself against John, a much larger man. Edmond sprinted down to aid his friend, sliding more often than running.

Across the river, Lona waved her wand toward Rhoswen several times, but Rhoswen simply regarded her with an air of mild contempt, apparently impervious to any spell Lona might cast. But then Rhoswen noticed the struggle across the river and, with a pointing finger, directed the dragon's attention toward the men fighting near the riverbank.

Horrified, Arabella watched as the beast took off and flew straight toward its targets. She shouted, hoping desperately to be heard, "The dragon!"

Though Edmond looked up first, he had no time to do more than jump into the river. Martin stumbled and rolled forward, but somehow managed to land in the river as well. When their heads broke the surface moments later, relief surged through Arabella.

Until she saw that John was climbing up the path toward her.

Looking around, she saw dozens of large rocks scattered over the cave floor. Lifting one, she threw it as hard as she could toward the guard's head. It struck the ground in front of him and rolled under his feet. He stumbled but kept going. With shaking hands Arabella picked up another one and hurled it at him, not worrying about aiming or waiting to see if it hit him. She threw rocks, one after another, as fast as she could until she heard a dull thud and a grunt of pain. She'd hit him on the brow above his right eye. Blood streamed down his face, but he was still standing.

She looked around for another stone, but she'd already thrown all that were near the entrance. She ran deeper into the cave to look for more, found one, and turned around holding it just in time to see the dragon land on the lip of limestone jutting from the cave's entrance.

The huge beast's body blocked nearly all of the light, but she knew that its glowing yellow eyes had spotted her. Arabella had witnessed what this beast could do, and her only defense was a knife.

Summoning what courage she still possessed, she fumbled with the blade until she gripped it in both hands and pointed it toward the dragon.

With sinuous steps the dragon approached, drawing back its head like a serpent preparing to strike. Certain that it was about to breathe fire, she seized her only chance. Grasping the knife in both hands, she ran forward, aiming for its heart. Her knife bounced off the dragon's scales, the impact knocking her to the ground. As she lay there, dazed and hopeless, a blue light filled the cavern. She cringed, waiting for the inferno.

But the fire never came.

Instead, Arabella was enveloped in a cloud of steam and white debris. The dragon roared as if in pain and fled from the cave, the breeze from its hasty retreat whipping Arabella's hair and dress. Unable to breathe, she sat up, coughing and waving her hands frantically to clear the air around her face. Hearing Lona call her from the mouth of the cave, Arabella staggered to her feet then stumbled toward the fairy.

"Where's Nicol?" Lona asked, her face wild with panic.

"I don't know," Arabella said, gasping.

Lona disappeared through the white fog, and Arabella soon heard the cage's metal door squeak open. "Go on, get out of here," came Lona's voice from the shadows. "But if you ever want to be human again, you'd better come back to me!"

Prince Nicol scuttled past Arabella without a glance but turned at the cave's entrance and sat up, whiskers twitching. "Then you had better live through this, fairy!" he called back in his high squeak, then slipped outside.

An instant later Lona's hand grasped Arabella's wrist and pulled her to the mouth of the cave. "Jump!"

She'd trusted Lona for over a century and was not about to stop now. She jumped.

They landed in a heap on the path below the cave and struggled to stand up. Arabella grabbed at the white things caught in her hair and pulled at one to see what it was. "Feathers?"

"It was the first thing that came to my mind," Lona grumbled. "Fire to feathers. Saved you, didn't it?"

Arabella nodded, looked up to see feathers flying out of the cave and fluttering down, and gave a choke of strained laughter. But an instant later all humor vanished. "Where's Edmond?"

"I don't know." Lona scrambled down the path.

Still desperately scanning the landscape for a glimpse of her prince, Arabella followed as best she could. At the bottom of the ridge, near the riverbank, they had to step around the guard's body. Arabella cringed at the gash her rock had inflicted on his head, but from the angle of his neck she thought he must have died from a fall. "Later," she whispered, not wanting to worry over his death when they were still in danger.

"What was that?" Lona asked from where she stood on the bank of the river.

"Nothing."

"Well, don't talk to yourself. People will think you're mad."

Arabella didn't bother to answer. On the far side of the river, Edmond and Martin climbed the muddy bank while Rhoswen looked down on them in disdain, a mocking smile twisting her face. The dragon once again circled above its mistress.

Lona grabbed Arabella's shoulders. "Rhoswen is wearing a charm that protects her from my magic, and the Elixir of Abeyance prevents wounds. I need help." So saying, she ran toward the tree that stretched across the river.

With amazing grace and balance, the fairy ran across, easily navigating the awkward angle as the tree sloped up. Arabella did not know if she could manage to cross, but she was determined to try.

She removed her torn silk slippers, hoping she could climb better in her bare feet, and stepped up on the log. With her arms out for balance, she managed to make it halfway across, but the shouts and screams of the others terrified her. Though she dared not look away from her task, she looked down at the river and froze with fear.

She couldn't swim, and in her heavy gown she would be powerless against the strong current. Terrified, she closed her eyes and lost her balance. Feeling herself tip backward, she flung herself forward and gripped the tree trunk with all her strength. She scraped her hands against the rough bark but managed to cling tight.

She turned her head, scraping her chin on the bark, and saw Lona and Rhoswen struggling together as Lona tried to tear off something strung around Rhoswen's neck. Edmond and Martin stood between the dragon and the fighting women, keeping the great beast's attention focused on them. The dragon still belched feathers instead of fire, but it slashed at them with its wicked claws, and they could not get close to the chain around its neck.

With painful urgency Arabella clawed her way up the rest of the tree trunk. Her gown caught and pulled against the bark and branches, but she managed to make it across. Rolling down on to the grass, she landed in a heap and stood quickly.

As she ran to help Lona, she could think only one thought: The men needed Lona's help with the dragon. So with no sign of grace or elegance, Arabella rammed into Rhoswen from behind and sent her down in a sprawl. As Rhoswen fell, she grabbed Lona's wand, but Lona held it tight. Lurching to her feet, Rhoswen twisted the wand around and pulled with all her strength. Lona lost her grip, and Rhoswen sent the wand spinning into the river.

With an anguished cry, Lona ran to the riverbank. "Get that charm from around her neck!" she called over her shoulder as she chased her wand downstream.

Rhoswen turned to Arabella and smiled. Her smile was strangely similar to Arabella's, for they were alike in many ways, these two cousins. But that smile was a warped and twisted thing on Rhoswen's face. "You can try to take my charm," she said, her lip curling back in a snarl. "But you're a delicate little flower, aren't you?"

Arabella clenched her hands into fists. "I am a different person from the girl you once knew."

"Perhaps, but now I have all the power."

As Rhoswen spoke, the men shouted, and Arabella turned to see the dragon crawling straight for her, one heavy step after another.

"Do you like my pet, Arabella?"

But Arabella was frozen in fear like a bird before a serpent, and couldn't answer. Then, as though in a dream, she saw a most unexpected sight.

With the dragon forced by compulsion to focus on Arabella, it could take no notice of any distractions. So it did not pause to shake off or scratch at the human climbing up its back, gripping the spikes along its bony spine. Soon Edmond straddled its shoulders. Martin tried to follow, but the dragon whipped its massive tail and sent him flying.

Arabella took a step back and tripped over the torn ribbons of her skirt. She hit the ground hard and lay there gazing up into the dragon's cavernous mouth with its deadly teeth. Just as it began to lower its head, she saw Edmond swing his sword in a mighty arc, hacking into the gold chain.

The soft gold was no match for Edmond's steel, but it was thick. The dragon, feeling the jolt of that weapon behind its head, swung itself from side to side, trying to dislodge him. But Edmond hung onto the chain with one hand as he hacked at it with the other, and the dragon could not shake him off.

Arabella clawed her way up from the ground, trying desperately to get away before she was trampled. Hearing a cry, she turned back in time to see Edmond flung to one side and land hard on the ground, nearly rolling into the river. He curled up in pain, but he held the broken chain in his hand. The weight of his body being thrown had severed the weakened links.

The dragon roared, and feathers erupted into the air. Through the swirling cloud of white, Arabella saw the great black beast rise into the air on its massive wings and race away through the blue sky to freedom.

"My dragon! What have you done?"

Startled at the raw fury in Rhoswen's voice, Arabella turned and saw her cousin clutching her own temples, her face white with wrath.

"It is free now," Arabella said, "even as I am. You hold us captive no more."

Rhoswen turned to her, eyes huge, teeth bared. "The grave will be your prison now!" she cried in a voice scarcely human. She reached to her side and pulled a gleaming knife from a leather sheath. With trembling hands she clutched its carved handle and strode toward Arabella.

Stepping backward, Arabella lifted both hands. "Haven't you taken enough from me?" Though she saw only madness in her cousin's face, she tried to keep her voice calm and reasonable.

"Not yet, I haven't! I've always hated you, my perfect cousin, and I could not allow you to hurt this kingdom. Consumed by your pleasures and vanities, you were no more fit to rule than my father was in his greed!"

"And are you fit to rule, Rhoswen? You, who have driven the fairies nearly to extinction? Are you, with murder in your heart, as benevolent as you believe?"

"I do what I must!" Rhoswen screamed. Then she charged forward, the knife raised high, its deadly blade flashing.

Arabella flung her hands up then saw the charm at Rhoswen's throat. With no more than a whisper of a movement, Arabella grabbed it and pulled down with all her strength.

The charm broke free, and Rhoswen froze as still as a statue, her face contorted in a snarl of rage but her eyes rolling in confusion. A faint blue halo of magic hovered over her.

Arabella had only an instant to marvel that she had not been stabbed. Then, in an instant more amazing still, she saw the spindle that hung around her neck spring into the air, almost as though of its own volition. It pricked Rhoswen on the breast above her heart.

Time seemed to stop as Arabella and Rhoswen both stared at that sharp point, stared at that tiny bead of crimson bubbling up from Rhoswen's skin.

Then Rhoswen's eyes closed. She sagged forward and fell to the ground.

With her red hair fanning out over her face like a veil, Rhoswen lay still on the grass. Feathers swirled above her and fluttered down like falling leaves. Arabella turned her over with trembling hands and saw that her cousin was lost in an enchanted sleep.

The spindle's curse had entwined her in its grasp.

RUNNING FOOTSTEPS approached, and Edmond caught Arabella to him. "Are you hurt?"

"No." Her limbs shook, but they were whole. She pulled back a step so that she could look at him. Blood from a cut trickled through the sheen of sweat on his brow. "Though you are."

"I was never better," Edmond declared. He framed her face with his hands and kissed her with the same firm precision he did everything. Arabella put her hands on his arms and kissed him back, rejoicing that they were together and safe.

But a moment later she pulled back and demanded, "Where's Lona?"

They both turned to search and saw the fairy nearby, sprawled on the grass and gasping for breath. Breaking away from Edmond, Arabella ran to her friend's side. "You saved me, didn't you? You made the spindle prick her."

"Yes. Though why you took so long to get the charm off her I don't know!"

"Well," Arabella said, smiling, "there was this dragon, you see. How did you think to use the spindle? Did you know that it would curse her too?"

"I only hoped. But I've always known there was great power in it."

"How did you find your wand?"

Lona sat up and waved her hand as if brushing away one of the feathers that floated by. "You'll never believe me. Nicol saved my wand! It was caught up in a tangle of fallen trees and branches downstream. He ran across and plucked it out of the river for me. Doesn't that prove that he is sorry for his misdeeds?"

"It proves he wants be a human again," Edmond said, raising a brow and folding his arms.

"Yes, well, I took care of that already," Lona said.

"What?" Edmond's voice rumbled like thunder. "Where is he?"

"How should I know, you blithering fool? I was busy saving the princess while you lay unconscious like the greatest glump!"

Then Martin called to them from where he stood over Rhoswen. "She doesn't look dead, but she is as still as death."

"She's fallen into an enchanted sleep," Arabella said.

"Probably for one hundred years," Lona added. "But who knows?"

"Ah!" Martin nodded then shrugged. "Seems fitting. What are we going to do with her?"

"I'm definitely not taking her," Lona said. "I've done my share."

Edmond turned to Arabella and asked, "What do you wish us to do with her, Your Majesty?"

Arabella felt a little thrill in the pit of her stomach. *Your Majesty.* It was true. Though not yet crowned, she was queen of this land. She drew herself together, calling to mind the strength of her father, the courage of her mother, and all of the virtues with which she had been born, not magically blessed.

"We will take her back to White Thorn Castle," she said. "She will be safe there until we understand her curse better and can make an informed decision."

His face took on the solemn expression he wore when deep in thought, but he took her hand in a gesture of affection and respect. Such a small token, but powerful. Peace and courage flowed into her heart, and, if possible, she loved him even more.

"We must go to White Thorn anyway to arrange the coronation." He smiled at her then, tenderly and with just a hint of teasing in his eyes.

"There's something else we must do first," Lona said, brushing feathers from Edmond's shoulders as if they were pesky flies.

"Yes," Arabella agreed. "We must get cleaned up. I cannot go anywhere looking like this."

"No, no, no!" Lona shook her head so that her wild hair danced like a briar in a storm. "We have to get you two married."

Arabella stared at her in amazement. "Just like that?"

Edmond put his arm around her waist. "Consider this, darling: My father can hardly force you to marry my brother if you are already married to me."

At this Arabella laughed, but she still asked, "Will he be satisfied to let us live in peace?"

Edmond shook his head and shrugged; but before he could answer, Lona interrupted with a snort. "Of course you won't live in peace! Who ever heard of a married couple being peaceful? What with that great lummox Martin clunking about the castle, Lady Rhoswen lying around collecting dust, and the collection of spoiled children you'll no doubt produce in no time at all, it is well for you that I shall be there to help."

Smiling, Arabella reached out one arm to catch Lona in an embrace. "Yes, indeed. I will need you more than ever, my dear friend!"

ABOUT THE AUTHOR

MICHELLE PENNINGTON spends her days quoting movies with her husband, making messes faster than her four kids, and generally tolerating General Lee, their autocratic cat. She only puts up with him because apparently it's a *thing* for authors to have a cat. She loves to make magic by stringing words together, but she also creates designer sugar cookies, sings loud in church, and reads fiction like it's her last day on earth.

To learn more about Michelle, visit
www.Michelle-Pennington.com

ASHLEY STANGL

OUT
OF THE
TOMB

To Alex, Graci, and Morgan,

whose help and encouragement made this story possible.

T HE HOVERCAR soared over purple-leaved trees, but Tanza didn't care about the planet's autumn splendor. She pulled on thick black plasti-skin gloves, slid her feet into human-made boots, and secured the pack over her shoulder. She straightened seams, charged tech, and ran over the plan one more time, so that when the dome appeared through the foliage, all she had left to do was smile.

"Oh, aren't you a beauty?" she whispered.

The morning sun brought out the veins of color—pink and purple, blue and green—in the dome's smooth white stone. Thorns choked the building beneath as if even nature wanted to protect the splendor inside.

Nature could deal with disappointment.

Tanza gripped the steering column, resumed manual control, and landed the compact metal hovercar on the forest floor in a whirl of fallen leaves.

Keffer's voice crackled through the hovercar's comm system. "You've landed?"

Tanza pressed the reply button on the console. "Light as a drift bug."

"She look like a winner?"

Tanza smiled. "She's made of aurolith."

Keffer whistled low and long. "Someone had a lot of money to burn."

"And a burning need to take it with them, I hope."

"You ready to go in?"

Tanza tried not to be offended. She failed. "Of course I am."

"Your hair tied back? Remember the Tekka job."

Tanza ran a four-fingered hand over the brown curls safely gathered within her hair binder. "I will never forget the Tekka job. Especially since you'll never let me."

She could hear the smirk in Keffer's voice. "Someone's got to keep you humble, *charit*."

Tanza cringed as Keffer's human tongue mangled the tephan term of endearment. Keffer had worked on Arateph so long that he spoke Common Tephan in daily life, but no human could manage the tephan naming tongue. With their less complex vocal cords and less sensitive hearing, humans could neither hear nor speak the lower layers of sound in the complex language tephans used to construct their names. Humans looked so similar to tephans that Tanza sometimes forgot how alien they were.

She said, "I'm shutting down comms."

"Just this once, take comms inside."

"Impossible. Comm units cause havoc with security nets."

This wasn't true, but as long as Keffer believed it, Tanza could do these jobs in privacy. She couldn't skim off trinkets for herself if her employer watched her every move.

Since Keffer had never visited a tephan tomb, he still fell for the excuse. "Wouldn't want my best supplier fried even for the sake of hearing my dulcet tones."

"Me neither," Tanza said and slammed the comm system's kill switch. She didn't have time for chit-chat. She had a tomb to rob.

She left the hovercar and approached the tomb with swift, emotionless efficiency. Long experience had given her laser focus. On a tomb job, she had no emotions, no outside concerns. Nothing existed except the contest between Tanza and the tomb's defenses.

She cast an appraising eye at the tomb. Judging by the dome's design, the tomb was about one hundred fifty years old and built by those who hired the most expensive designers. Although it stood far from any of the old Houses, Tanza knew she'd found the family tomb of one of the last lords of Arateph. The security would be formidable—the greed of Arateph's nobility lingered long after death.

A wall of annet branches with thorns as thick and long as Tanza's hand surrounded the edifice. Tanza circled the tomb twice before glimpsing a door. She reached into her pack for a compact metal cylinder and unfolded it into a blade as long as her forearm. When she pressed a button, a shimmering coat of blue energy surrounded the blade and cut through the thigh-thick branches like paper, revealing a set of double doors wide enough for five people, blocked by heavy metal bars. Tanza touched the bars and brilliant light flashed, but the energy pooled around her gloves and fizzled into nothing. Without the gloves she'd have been paralyzed for an hour at least.

She activated the security field again and this time tracked the strands of energy to the left of the door. Constantly testing the energy field, she cut another path through the branches and located the field's source box behind an aurolith panel at the base of the wall.

Lying flat on her stomach, Tanza tore away the panel and examined the control box. It seemed a standard neuroblock model, though the number of switches, screens, and blinking lights made her adjust her estimate of the tomb's age: barely a century old. She could deactivate this neuroblock model with her eyes closed. She reached for the leftmost switch on the top row.

A white light blazed and the world spun. Tanza's stomach heaved and spread her breakfast on the forest floor beyond her left arm. Afterward she rested her head on her folded arms, every nerve quivering as she gulped in five desperate breaths. Then she rose unsteadily to her hands and knees, wiped her face, and gave the panel a look of grudging respect. She hadn't seen a stunner on a control box since the Tekka job.

"Nasty little thing, aren't you?"

Fighting dizziness and her heaving stomach, she reached into her pack to pull out a syringe of hospital-strength nausea medication, then brushed the red micro-sensor covering one end of it over her left elbow. When the sensor beeped wildly, she knew she'd found a vein. Tanza injected the dose of medication then tucked the syringe back into her pack. In minutes, her head cleared and she remembered how to outwit the stunner.

She used an annet thorn to pop off a piece of the plastic in the top right corner of the control box, revealing a screen and several small buttons, then scanned it with her Coalition-issue program scanner—a formidable computer shoved into a brown plastic box that fit in her hands. The modern decryption technology broke through the ancient security measures in minutes and provided the stunner's shut-down code.

After neutralizing the stunner, Tanza blazed through a complex pattern of switches and buttons on the field's main control panel; the next time she touched the tomb wall, she felt nothing except bare stone. The neuroblock field was down.

She returned to the entrance and pulled at the bar across the right-hand door. As expected, it didn't budge. She beat a staccato pattern across the bar until a laser-light grid—sixteen little boxes, each with a different symbol—appeared on the metal. These were the oldest and most common electronic locks on tephan tombs, and Tanza had long ago learned to defeat them using a glitch in the hardware.

She held a square mirror—precisely the size and shape of the pad of laser-light buttons—just above the bar and passed a hand between bar and mirror from all four sides. Then she held the mirror against the buttons for a count of three. The laser-light symbols faded, a series of heavy clanks sounded from within the tomb, and Tanza pulled open both doors . . .

. . . to reveal another set of doors as white, flat, and solid as those she'd just opened. These were secured with fifteen mechanical locks. Tanza had never before seen a tomb with so many on the inner door. She couldn't rely on her knowledge of historical security technology to get past these locks; there were no standard configurations to research or glitches to exploit. Nothing could help her now except old-fashioned trial and error.

Tanza tore off her gloves and grinned. She loved this part. This was pure thievery, with only her fingers and instincts to guide her as she listened to tumblers, picked locks, and felt her way around knobs and switches. Since the tomb sat miles from any living soul, she could luxuriate in the challenge.

Tanza didn't enjoy much about her chosen profession—she scraped to pay the bills, kept company with untrustworthy people, and only by constant vigilance evaded the authorities—but she loved the challenge of tomb robbing. Usually, tephans from the charity houses were hired only for mindless menial labor, but Keffer's jobs made use of Tanza's intellect and love of history. Keffer had taught her the art and science of thievery, and she had taught herself the history behind the tombs and their contents. Though she liked research more than robbery, this was her favorite moment of a job, when the mechanical locks challenged her with one last puzzle of pure skill. If she solved it, she could claim the tomb's riches. Little in life was so straightforward.

After two hours' work, the last lock fell away and Tanza pulled open the doors. She reached into the darkness and found a panel to the left of the door; if the security systems were operational then the lights would be too. The heat from her hand activated the switch, and the hall blazed with light.

The glory nearly struck her blind. Even the inside walls were made of aurolith. Its colors glittered at her from every direction, a silent promise that the riches inside were even rarer than the walls that hid them.

Tanza shut the doors behind her. She might be miles from another living person, but she felt certain that such blazing beauty could be seen from space. Ten locked doors lined this hallway alone, and a staircase held the promise of further wealth on a second floor. *Dozens* of nobles could have filled the chambers with expensive honor gifts. After seven years of tomb robbing, it took a lot to impress Tanza, but this tomb set her heart fluttering like a drift bug.

She rushed toward the closest door, her imagination reeling with visions of the life this tomb could buy her. No more dusty tombs, no more Keffer. A mansion somewhere in the mountains, a whole fleet of her own hovercars, enough money that the humans *had* to let her take a history degree.

But inside the chamber she found only two canvas chairs and some plastic wrappers. The chamber looked like a campsite, not the final resting place of one of Arateph's nobles. There wasn't even a coffin shelf.

The next two rooms were no better, offering only a metal washtub, some buckets, old food wrappers, and a portable cold-storage box. She could make no sense of it. Had a homeless person taken up residence? But surely no squatter could have outwitted all the security measures.

She found the first corpse in the fourth room. Atop padded sheets on a waist-high coffin slab was a young man's body clothed in a white burial robe. The man was no older than thirty, without a sign of decay on him. This wasn't unusual in newer tombs. Sentimental or queasy families sometimes opted for preservation fields to keep the body fresh.

Yet Tanza had never seen a body look so little like a *body* before. His cream-colored skin was smooth and supple. His long, muscular limbs seemed relaxed. His bright gold hair hung slightly over his eyes. His jaw was square, his nose blunt, his lips full. He seemed familiar, but she couldn't trace the resemblance. She'd probably robbed one of his relatives.

Tanza turned her attention away from the corpse and toward his coffin slab's preservation field. She pried away the front panel of fake woodgrain, knelt to examine the parts, and was baffled yet again. She felt like a complete amateur as she stared, uncomprehending, at this preservation field's unfamiliar tangle of plastic, metal, and wires.

Finally, near the center she recognized a power cell. She pried out the pink metal cylinder with a lock pick and cradled it in her palm. This power-cell brand had gone out of business after Arateph joined the Interplanetary Coalition, but enthusiasts found the old brand more reliable, more efficient, and more valuable than modern versions.

Tanza shuffled the still-hot power cell between her hands. Once it cooled, she clutched it in one hand and kissed it. "No offense," she told the corpse. "You've been pretty long enough. This beauty's going to buy me my own hovercar."

She hid the power cell in a side pocket on her supply pack. Keffer wouldn't get his hands on a treasure like this.

She pried a few more parts out of the preservation field then snapped the front panel back in place. The room contained nothing else of value, so

Tanza shot the corpse a final salute and moved to the room across the hall.

This room contained piles of long, shallow wooden boxes, almost like jewelry boxes. The first box held a selection of thin metal rods—scalpels, picks, needles. The next box contained several syringes, the ancient medications long ago decayed and evaporated.

Tanza gaped. Medical tools? What kind of tomb *was* this?

She grabbed a strange tool from the floor. The ornately carved wooden handle was thick, round, and curved in the middle. A thin metal skewer protruded from the handle's flat end, and the light danced on its oily sheen. Tanza brushed her thumb across a bump on the base of the handle, and the skewer gave an electric buzz.

Tanza dropped it and jumped back, heart racing. That was no medical tool. That was a spindle. A real, working spindle, the gory feature of every revolution-era drama. One stab of that skewer and one press of that button would activate an energy pulse that could shred a person's organs in thirty seconds.

Spindles had been outlawed on the planet since Arateph joined the Coalition, but groups like Cornerstone still used them, believing tephans should fight for independence with a true tephan weapon, no matter how brutal. That spindle was more valuable than the power cell, more valuable than anything Tanza had ever taken from a tomb.

She would never touch it again. Any person who would buy a working spindle wasn't someone she wanted to sell to. Keffer could never hear about this.

She turned her back on the spindle and rifled through the boxes of antique medical tools, falling into a quiet rhythm as she searched for anything of value. Most people found tombs eerie, but Tanza luxuriated in the peace.

A man's voice, deep and smooth, flowed through the silence. "I beg your pardon, but are you robbing me?"

Tanza's heart seized. The tools clattered on the floor. She whirled around to see the corpse standing in the doorway.

THE YOUNG man, burial robe hanging to his knees, looked as hale and healthy as if he hadn't been dead a few minutes ago. His golden hair and white robes glowed in the tomb's light. He looked at Tanza with wary amusement, as if uncertain of proper etiquette toward one's tomb robber.

Tanza couldn't breathe, couldn't move. Couldn't process the reality before her.

"You . . ." she rasped. "You were dead."

"I'm afraid not," he said, spreading out his hands.

She gave a harsh, cynical laugh, the kind she saved for Keffer's tougher cronies, because laughing was a better plan than going mad. "I never believed in ghosts, but this tomb *would* be the first to have one."

His lips twitched in amusement, but his eyes showed concern—a mischievous but not cruel spirit. "I swear to you, I'm not a ghost." He held out his hand. "Here, touch me. I'm flesh and bone."

Tanza wrapped a shaking hand around his fingers. They were solid, warm, and living. If this man was dead, then she was too.

She cast away his hand and felt a fool for believing in ghosts. This man had never been a corpse. He was a rival thief who'd reached this tomb before her and decided to mess with her head. That must be why the chambers were empty.

She stood up, crossed her arms, and demanded, "Where'd you put the body?"

He tilted his head. "Excuse me?"

"That preservation slab must have held a real body. Where'd you put it?"

"There never was a body. Just me."

"I'm not an idiot. This is a tomb. I might be a thief, but at least I don't steal bodies."

"I didn't steal—"

"Or did you just hide it away for a sick joke?"

"Why would I steal a body?"

Tanza remembered that the tomb had been surrounded by annet thorns. A wall like that would have taken at least fifty years to grow and had been unbroken before she'd sliced away the thorns. Tombs couldn't be breached from below or above. How could he be a rival thief?

"But . . ." she stammered. "You can't be a ghost."

He rolled his eyes. "I thought we'd established that."

A swath of golden hair fell over his right eye. He ducked his head, lifted his hand, and swept the hair aside with two fingers. Tanza recognized the motion. She'd seen those exact movements in a hundred history presentations and chronovids. The nervous quirk had been imitated by dozens of actors and satirists, but no one could do it perfectly. Except for this man, with that hair, that hand, and that face.

She stumbled back. "You're Prince Auren."

He tensed. "Is that a problem?"

"No," Tanza said. "Except you've been dead for a hundred years."

Prince Auren looked as if he'd taken a blast from his tomb's stunner. "What do you mean, 'dead'?"

Prince Auren's capture and assassination at rebel hands had been the first step in toppling Arateph's monarchy. Soon afterward every member of the nobility had been killed, and the People's House had ruled the planet until first contact was made with the alien Coalition. The prince was a relic of a lost regime, and his name should have faded into the dust of history.

But Prince Auren was greater than history. He was legend. The rebels had never produced his body, and that sliver of doubt had sparked the planet's imagination. Some said the prince had escaped and would mount an army of supporters to reclaim his throne. Some said he'd gone into hiding with no memory of his royal past. Tanza had liked the legends, but she always knew that Prince Auren had died by rebel attack or old age, and that no one would find anything except his remains.

Which she had just found.

Walking around and looking just like the man from the chronovids.

That preservation field was actually a *stasis bed,* technology meant to keep him asleep, unaging . . . and alive.

While Auren stood in stunned silence, Tanza stumbled through a summary of the history he'd missed. By the time she finished, Auren looked ill and as pale as the robes he wore. "I've been missing," he choked. "Presumed dead. For a *century.*"

"If it helps, I'm as surprised as you are."

He stood tall and imposing in his desperation even as his hands shook. "You're lying," he said at last. "They wouldn't abandon me."

"I can prove it," Tanza said. She reached into her pack, pulled out her program scanner—his eyes went wide at the unfamiliar technology—and activated the main screen with its time and date stamp.

Auren read the display, and his face twisted in confusion. "I've gone *backward* in time?"

Tanza looked at the numbers and realized her mistake. "It's the new calendar." She adjusted the settings. "That's the tephan date."

His face went slack. "A hundred years," he gasped.

"The centennial was two weeks ago."

His eyes flashed. "You adjusted the display. You could have put any number on there."

She put her hands on her hips. "Why would I do that? What possible gain could come from it? You saw me—I was stealing your things. I thought you were dead because this tomb is more than a hundred years old."

He wouldn't believe her until she showed him the annet thorns outside; then he wandered back to the chamber, looking more like a corpse than ever. He leaned his elbows against a stack of crates and looked ready to collapse. "My entire world is dead, and only a tomb robber knows I'm alive."

"In my defense," Tanza said from the chamber's doorway, "you should be a corpse. How does a long-lost prince wind up in stasis in a tomb?"

He met her eyes. "I'm not sure I should tell you."

Tanza glanced around. "Who else are you going to tell?"

He considered, brushed the hair from his eyes, and sighed. "Oh, what's the worst that could happen?"

As he looked around the room, his gaze caught on the spindle Tanza had tossed into the far corner. His face flashed shock, then horror, then sorrow, as he moved uneasily toward it. He touched it with one finger as though it were a frightened animal, and when it didn't bite, he grabbed it in one hand and ran a finger along the curves of the handle.

When he faced Tanza, his gaze was turned so far inward that she had no fear he might use the spindle against her. He spoke in a distant manner: "The rebels attacked one of the summer palaces. I was the only royal in residence. They agreed to spare the servants if they could have the crown prince."

"You let them capture you?"

He nodded, eyes on the spindle.

"That was stupid."

His gaze met hers, strong and sharp as sunlight. "It was right," he said, and then his gaze turned inward again. "They held me for three days before deciding to kill me." He held up the spindle. "With this." He rubbed beneath the right side of his rib cage. "My organs were shredded. I . . . don't recommend it."

"How did you survive?"

He let out a deep breath and sank onto a pile of boxes. "They didn't think I deserved a quick death. They sustained the pulse for only about fifteen seconds."

Long enough to give him injuries beyond mortal endurance but too brief to bring immediate death. He would have lingered in unimaginable agony as his life drained away. Tanza felt grateful that the tomb's stunner had already emptied her stomach. History had made it clear that such a spindle strike brought the most painful death possible.

She pushed away her feelings of disgust and horror and focused on the facts. "The pulse was barely too brief to kill you," she said. "You should have died within the hour."

Auren explained, "Lord Rimath—the head of the local House—had secretly planned a rescue. His men reached me just in time and took me from the palace."

"That doesn't explain the tomb."

"Lord Rimath had suspected I'd be injured. He couldn't take me to a House or a hospital—the rebels would look for me there. But House Rimath had just built a brand-new tomb nearby. No one would look for me in a tomb, and no building could have better security, so his men brought in a healing bed and medical supplies from a local hospital. Everything was ready before my rescue started. They had me here within minutes." Auren gave Tanza a faint, sad smile. "I only learned this in flashes, you understand. I was rather busy . . . dying . . . at the time. Lord Rimath made certain I understood before the healing bed activated, and after that . . . I woke up here."

Tanza considered the story, but one piece wouldn't fall into place. "A healing bed shouldn't have kept you in stasis," Tanza said. "Not if it healed your wounds."

Auren replied, "Most healing beds have a stasis setting."

"Why was it activated? And why did no one come back for you?"

"I wish I knew."

Tanza's mind seized the challenge. She paced, thinking. "This is a tomb with state-of-the-art security. You must have lumiscopes."

"The lumiscopic feed would be transmitted to a guardhouse."

Tanza shook her head. "The guardhouse is long gone, but all security recorders have internal memory as extra back-up."

She raced across the hallway and climbed atop Auren's empty healing bed. She found a small lens in the ceiling just left of the bed and used a stolen scalpel to pry away a large, paper-thin panel of aurolith. Behind it she found a large, black box.

Tanza pulled the recorder from the hidden brackets, set it on the floor, and smiled at the maker's mark. "A Berimac. Your Lord Rimath spared no expense." She pulled a panel off the side of the recorder. "That's good news for us."

She aimed the lumiscope's lens at the blank aurolith wall, and a black-and-white chronovid appeared, showing Tanza taking the instrument from its hiding place. "Not only do we have a chronovid," she explained to Auren, who stood in the doorway in a state of vague bafflement. "We have a chronovid projector."

Auren stepped into the room, eyes riveted to the image but focused on the date stamp, not the chronovid itself. "A whole century," he said. "The recorder couldn't store so much data."

Tanza said, "The interior security recorders are motion-activated. They only log when moving people are in the tomb."

She fiddled with some buttons, and the date stamp changed to a few days after Auren's disappearance. The chronovid showed an unconscious Auren on the healing bed, blood-stained clothes piled nearby. Now that Tanza knew Auren wasn't dead, it was easy to see that his robe was a hospital gown, not burial clothes.

She sped through the imagery, watching people come and go with medical equipment and sober expressions. When the record ended, Tanza reversed the chronovid to the last time a waking person had been in the room.

In the image, a bald man scanned Auren with unfamiliar instruments and adjusted the healing bed's settings. "Stasis functional," he called out the door, his refined accent similar to Auren's.

A short woman with dark curls peered through the doorway. "You're certain he can't come with us?"

"Too fragile. Stasis is safer until he has someone to supervise the healing."

"Someone should stay."

"The new orders override this duty," the man said. "Hundreds will die if they don't get help. Auren would want us to go."

The real-life Auren spoke to the screen. "I might, Hanet, if I knew where you were going."

"If the worst happens," the man said, oblivious to his future viewers, "Kenni's coming to restock in two days. She'll know what to do."

Tanza asked, "Who's Kenni?"

Auren said, "Lord Rimath's daughter. Lady Ikennir."

The name sparked a faint memory from historical research, and Tanza looked at the date stamp. Her hand flew to her mouth. Her veins turned to ice. "No," she gasped. "They're going to Alogath."

Oblivious to the meaning, the woman in the chronovid planned a route to Alogath. Auren's head snapped toward Tanza's face. "What happens in Alogath?"

Tanza couldn't look at him. To Auren, Alogath was merely a suburb of the capital, not a symbol of the bloodiest day in tephan history. Not every schoolchild's first lesson in the brutalities of warfare.

"I shouldn't tell you," Tanza said. "You don't need to know. Not right away."

"Tell me, thief," Auren demanded, every ounce of his royal authority in the words. Tanza met his eyes and his face softened. "Please," he begged. "It can't be worse than what I'm imagining."

"It is," Tanza said.

She turned off the projector and locked her gaze on the colored veins in the aurolith wall. "Lord Dassin betrayed the king. He helped the rebels lure dozens of the king's supporters to Alogath under false pretenses. It looks as if he drew in your doctors with a story about some kind of disaster. No one knew that the rebels were anywhere near the capital, and no one knew that Lord Dassin had joined them. Alogath became a slaughterhouse."

Images from historical chronovids flashed through her mind—people shot down in waves, nailed to the sides of houses, sliced to pieces bit by bit. Tanza had little sympathy for the decadent, corrupt nobility, but no one deserved Alogath.

To spare herself and Auren the details, she rushed to the end. "Alogath was the beginning of the end for the monarchy. After that day it became the rebels' preferred execution center. Nearly everyone of noble blood died there."

Lady Ikennir's death had been infamously gruesome, and now Tanza knew why: Her father had taken Prince Auren from the rebels. Of course they would torture her.

Auren *definitely* didn't need to know that.

She finished: "By the end of the month, the king and queen were dead and the People's House came into power."

Auren said, "With Lord Dassin in a comfortable position, no doubt."

Tanza shook her head. "When Lord Dassin saw the brutality at Alogath, he threw himself from his House's highest parapet."

"I see." Auren stared at the wall. "Everyone dead?"

"Very nearly," Tanza said. "Anyone who survived went so deep into hiding that they were never found again."

"Everyone," he breathed. "Everyone I ever knew." He glanced at the healing bed. "Everyone who knew about me."

"Mystery solved," Tanza said with a note of mournful irony.

Auren didn't speak for a long time.

TANZA'S MED scanner showed Auren to be in complete health and thus capable of leaving the tomb . . . once he found something other than hospital clothes to wear. Tanza rummaged in the hovercar and found a set of Keffer's clothing crumpled in a storage nook. For once, Tanza was grateful for Keffer's haphazard organizational skills. The wide blue shirt and boxy gray pants were a far cry from palace finery, but they were clean, so she brought them inside the tomb.

While Auren dressed, Tanza wandered in the woods behind the tomb. A light breeze rattled the leaves, and drift bugs floated by on their ribbons of colored silk, but the peace did nothing to calm Tanza's mind.

She'd wanted a *tomb*, with some precious metals and valuable antiques and salvageable tech parts. What was she supposed to do with a long-lost prince of legend? As a child, Tanza had loved those legends—it was hard for a child of the charity houses not to be enthralled by the glittering luxury of Prince Auren's world or the romanticism of the lumiscope dramas that imagined his escape from the rebels—but now she was an adult, and the reality was far from picturesque. Prince Auren was no hero; he was a royal from a decadent ruling house that had drained its people dry and driven them to revolution. Now Tanza—even less of a hero—was obligated to introduce him to a new century.

This discovery would rock Arateph, and Tanza wanted no part in the media mayhem that would follow. People would want to know about the woman who found Prince Auren. Though Tanza called herself an amateur historian, the title wouldn't fool the Coalition media or the police.

She didn't want a prison cell.

She wanted to fly far away from this mess. Instead, she hopped into the hovercar and brought it near the tomb's entrance, then stepped out and leaned against the vehicle with her head in her hands.

"What am I going to do with him?" she moaned.

Auren emerged from among the annet thorns. Keffer's clothing hung strangely on his slightly shorter, leaner, and differently angled tephan frame. "What are my options?" he asked.

Tanza lifted her head. "Not much," she replied, deftly hiding her own distress behind a cool mask. "You have no surviving family, no assets. I should take you to the nearest government office."

His face paled. "No," he insisted. "Not that."

"The Coalition replaced the rebel government," she assured him. "The Coalition is human-run; they don't know anything about the old monarchy or the revolution."

"They might consider a tephan prince a threat to their rule."

Tanza shook her head. "The Coalition has twenty-seven planets. A resurrected prince might appeal to a few crazy independence groups like Cornerstone, but it won't threaten the Coalition government."

Auren's face took on that stunned, faraway expression again. "Ruled by aliens in a different star system. Our rockets had barely reached our third moon."

Tanza smiled sympathetically. "The humans brought a lot of changes."

"I can't put myself at the mercy of unknown aliens." He met Tanza's eyes. "Please don't tell them of me."

His desperation stole Tanza's breath. Tears of sympathy threatened to flow; instead, she laughed and said, "Honestly, I don't want to go anywhere near the government. But what else can we do?"

Auren said, "You could take me to Alogath."

Tanza's limbs stiffened. "What?"

Auren said, "I want to go to Alogath. Everyone I ever knew died there. I need to honor them, even if I'm a hundred years too late."

"And you trust a tomb robber to take you there?"

Auren gave her an appraising glance. "I spent my life surrounded by security. I understand threat assessment. You won't harm me."

His confidence unnerved Tanza, but he was right. She shrugged and said, "I'm a thief with standards. I won't hurt you."

His expression eased. "I can't say as much for the rest of Arateph. Will you help me?"

Tanza cradled her chin and considered. "I could. I keep a place in Alogath—I grew up there, and rent's cheap in a place with so many ghosts." She glanced at the hovercar. "But my . . . employer . . . wants to meet me in Lorantz. I'll have to check in—drop you off somewhere first, of course—and take you to Alogath after that."

Auren's eyebrows rose, but he said, "I understand."

The words had a note of finality, like a judge's decision or a king's decree. Tanza stood stunned. She hadn't expected assent. She'd expected hesitation, a distrust of the criminal and her associates. At the very least she'd expected questions. She'd given Prince Auren less than half a plan.

"What happens after Alogath?" she asked. "I can't stay with you forever."

"I can stay in Roshen," he said, referring to the old capital city, which bordered Alogath. "It's the city I know best, and they must have resources to help displaced persons."

Tanza stared. "That's your plan? Live like a beggar?"

"Better a free beggar than a prisoner of your Coalition."

Tanza wavered. She sympathized with the philosophy, but Auren's plan put him in remarkable danger. A prince couldn't possibly realize the threats of street life! Yet it was the best way to save Tanza's livelihood; after only a few days he would disappear, and life would return to normal. He'd be left alone and destitute, but what other choice did they have? It was either this or the police, and Tanza didn't want to approach them any more than Auren did.

Finally she shrugged and replied, "Whatever you say." She gestured to the hovercar door. "Your ride awaits."

Auren nodded. "You have my gratitude." He approached the hovercar with caution, peering around, into, and beneath it. "This is your vehicle?"

"A hovercar," Tanza said. "It flies."

"With no wings?"

The question unbalanced Tanza because she'd never thought of it and felt as if she should have. The rounded metal capsule had no external features that showed it capable of flight. "Anti-gravity," she said. She put up a hand to forestall further questions. "Human technology. I just drive it. Trust me, it flies."

Auren nodded slowly. "I trust you, thief." He ended the sentence abruptly then said, embarrassed, "I shouldn't keep calling you that. What is your name?"

"Tanza."

"Tanza," he repeated as he climbed into the passenger seat. He pronounced every layer of the name's sound with the perfect tones and timbre of the tephan naming tongue. "A strong name to live up to."

"I know," Tanza snapped as she climbed into the other side of the hovercar. "'Thorn.' 'Wound.' The name for a child nobody wants."

Auren said, "That's only its basic meaning. Listen to the undertones. The name suggests strength, determination, protection."

Tanza's soul stilled. She'd never dreamed anyone would have bothered to give her name's undertones meaning. She tried the tones on her tongue and found Auren's translation accurate. She could have cried at the notion. Instead, she sniffed disdainfully. "A nice idea, but nothing like yours."

He smiled sadly. "My mother had a long time to consider it."

After losing nine children before birth, the aging Queen Marastel had named her son Auren. The basic meaning was "first star," but the undertones gave it deeper meaning—the star that brings light to blackest darkness, the arrival of hope in the midst of despair.

Once they'd settled in their seats, Tanza secured the safety harnesses and put the hovercar into flight. Its whisper-quiet engines brought it up through the tree branches and sent Tanza and Auren soaring across the open sky.

As Auren watched the countryside pass beneath them, he asked, "What is your virtue name?"

Tanza's hand twitched on the control column, and the hovercar swerved. "You want to know the virtue name of the woman who robbed your tomb?"

"A name is important whether you live up to it or not."

Tanza shrugged. "I wasn't given one. My mother abandoned me three hours after birth."

"Oh. I'm sorry," he said earnestly. "But you must have taken one at your coming-of-age."

"No one takes virtue names anymore."

Auren's face fell. "No one?"

"No one except for lunatics who think Arateph needs 'cleansing' from moral decay. The whole practice was ridiculous to begin with."

His jaw dropped. "How can you say that? A virtue name guides every part of a person's life."

Tanza snorted. She knew her history. She doubted a virtue name had ever done anyone any good. "Really."

"I tried to live up to mine."

Tanza glanced at him sideways. "All twelve of them?"

"Fourteen. You're forgetting my coming-of-age name, and I received thirteen virtue names at my naming day."

"No one counts the thirteenth one," Tanza said.

Auren murmured, "I did."

Prince Auren's naming day had been legendary even while he lived. Tradition held that the king and queen should choose their child's ordinary name and select the heads of two or three Great Houses to bestow virtue names. The idea was that each House could bestow a name on a royal child, but Prince Auren had been born too late for anyone to hope for royal siblings. Thus his parents had invited the heads of all twelve Great Houses give the prince a virtue name.

A virtue name told the world each House's hopes for their future monarch. House Jorith named him *Luchrit*, meaning beauty, but beauty of soul above that of body, a striving of spirit to cherish all things fair and worthy. House Thommat named him *Corigrat*, calling for humble grace and wisdom in his speech and actions. Tanza could never remember all of them, but each name dripped with meaning and set high expectations.

House Kepha bestowed the twelfth virtue name, *Petrior*— determination and strength that triumphs over every obstacle. This should have ended the ceremony, but as Lord Kepha left the stage, a thirteenth man appeared, one who'd not been on the guest list.

This moment of the recording had been recreated in paintings and lumiscopic dramas a thousand times in the century since—a man in a simple black shirt and trousers, surrounded by the elaborate headdresses and vividly colored clothing of Arateph's nobility. Carabos had been the fourth son of the fifth Great House, but he'd broken away and founded a Thirteenth House that had recently proclaimed itself "the People's House." No one had recognized Carabos's House or deemed him a threat. Until now.

Because Carabos said, "I name the child *Moritain*, for his greatest act of virtue will be to die before his twenty-fifth year and so spare us from the rule of kings."

No one knew how Carabos had entered; he was dragged from the hall two moments later. But the damage had been done.

Auren told Tanza, "That name shaped my life more than any other. People took it as a prophecy; I dodged twenty-six assassination attempts before I turned seven. In the end, the curse of Carabos fell. The spindle struck me four weeks before I turned twenty-five."

"Yet here you are, alive."

"There is that," he said. "For how long, who knows?"

He pulled something out of his pocket and rolled it on his fingers. Tanza glanced over and saw he held the spindle.

Tanza's nails dug into the hovercar's yoke. "Please," she growled through gritted teeth. "Put that away."

Auren held up the spindle. "This?"

Tanza threw her torso against the opposite window, barely keeping her grip on the control column. "Yes," she said, fighting back a quiver in her voice. "There's no need for it. I won't hurt you."

Auren pointed from Tanza to the spindle and back, eyes wide. "Do you think I'm threatening you? I don't mean to. Look, it's sheathed and the safety's on."

"I don't *care*," Tanza said, urgency lacing her words. "Put it away."

Auren slipped the spindle back into his pocket, and Tanza sat straight again.

Once she had full control of the hovercar and her breathing, she whirled upon Auren. "Why do you even *have* that?"

Auren said, far too casually, "I couldn't leave it behind. If I'm going to risk your world, I might want a weapon."

"Not that one. Just *owning* one will get you several years in prison."

Auren brought out the spindle again and considered it. "The new government's done *some* good, it seems." He shook his head. "I probably couldn't use it anyhow. Not after . . ."

He wedged the spindle end into a joint in his seat, snapped off its handle, and slipped both pieces into his pocket. Tanza hid her astonishment. The prince who could snap a spindle in two would have little need of weapons.

She said, "Get rid of that thing after we land. Throw it in a trash heap. I don't want it near me."

"As you command," he said with a crisp royal salute.

Moments later a light blinked on the console and the comm screen displayed Keffer's name. Tanza bit back a curse. The last time she'd ignored Keffer after a job, he'd remotely grounded the hovercar until she answered. So she took a deep breath, told Auren to keep quiet, and prepared a few lies.

For the first time, she wished Keffer did his business in a human language; the virtue prince would understand every word of their Common Tephan, and Tanza couldn't switch languages without arousing Keffer's suspicions. Auren seemed to like Tanza; he might not after he heard her discussing business with Keffer.

She opened the audio link. "What do you want?"

Keffer asked, "How rich are we?"

"The tomb was a bust, Keffer."

"What do you mean, a bust? You promised me treasures."

"I promised nothing."

"Aurolith walls!"

"It was too new. No one had been buried in it."

"I trusted you, Tanza."

"You know every tomb's a gamble."

Keffer sighed. "I only like gambling when I win. Look, we can figure out how to regroup. I'll see you in three hours."

Tanza's jaw went tight. Keffer was never *this* picky after a job. She'd thought she would have plenty of time to settle Auren someplace safe from Keffer's eyes. "Don't be a tyrant, Keffer. I just spent four hours breaking into a tomb. I don't even want to think about business until I've eaten, showered, and napped."

"Or until you've unloaded the last bit of loot. I'm not an idiot, Tanza."

"I'm not lying to you. Since when have you set me a curfew?"

"Since you tried to tell me an aurolith tomb was empty. Have you forgotten who provided that hovercar? Who found you a program scanner? Who gives you a nice little salary between tomb jobs? If you think you can double-cross me now . . ."

Tanza rolled her eyes and filled her voice with disdain. "Don't get your tubing in a twist. Just let me have a lunch break."

"If you so much as slow down, I will ground you so fast you'll be spitting dirt for a week. Come here and prove you're not holding out on me."

Tanza sighed. "Yes sir."

She turned off the audio link and settled back into her seat with a sigh. "That could have gone better."

Auren looked as if he'd just tried to sprint through a neuroblock net. When he regained the power of speech, he said, "Your employer's a demanding fellow."

"That's one word for it," Tanza replied as her mind produced a flurry of more colorful adjectives. She had *not* planned on introducing Prince Auren to Keffer.

After a few frenzied moments of thought, she reassured Auren—and herself—by saying, "Don't worry. Keffer's a decent guy, for a career criminal. You'll be fine."

THREE HOURS later, Tanza landed on the flat black expanse of Keffer's roof. Keffer emerged from a doorway on the far end of the roof and swaggered toward the hovercar.

Auren stared at him through the windscreen and murmured, "What's wrong with him?"

Tanza couldn't understand what Auren found so troubling. George Keffer was a tall, broad man in his early forties with a square, sun-tanned face and thick brown hair. Unlike most in his profession, he had no scars or prison tattoos and kept himself well groomed. Most people considered him handsome.

Then it hit her. "Keffer's human," she explained. "You've just seen your first alien."

A human's eyes were slightly lower on their foreheads, their eyebrows thinner, their ears a little further back. Their nostrils flared wider, and each hand and foot had five digits, not four. No one of these features, except the extra digits, would have been remarkable in a tephan, but together they gave the impression of something very alien. Five-year-old Tanza had been frightened by her first sight, and she'd known about humans her whole life. Auren had to be terrified.

Auren murmured, "It looks almost tephan, but it's *not*. I'd have preferred aliens with tentacles or five heads."

Tanza helped him out of his seat. "You get used to it."

She escorted Auren onto the landing pad. Keffer and Auren goggled at each other in mutual astonishment until Keffer glared at Tanza. "You brought a *passenger*?"

Tanza shrugged. "You wouldn't let me take a lunch break."

"Then he was in the car *before* I called. I monitored your path. You never stopped."

"I found him at the job. He needed a ride."

Keffer scanned his gaze over Auren. "Is he wearing my clothes?"

"Long story."

Keffer's arms flailed in silent distress. Auren watched every movement of Keffer's ten fingers, so nervous that he brushed the hair from his eyes several times.

To end the standoff, Tanza made Keffer take them to a kitchen on the building's second floor. She prepared Auren a fish sandwich and a salad—his first meal in a century—while Keffer stared daggers at her. The moment she finished, Keffer dragged her down the hall to his office.

Tanza never liked Keffer's office, but she found it especially oppressive after the beauty of an aurolith tomb. Sickly yellow afternoon light trickled through a small window and splashed over the brown wooden floor, its brown floor weaving, Keffer's enormous wooden desk, and the unadorned brown and gray cabinets lining the walls. Everything in this room had been chosen solely for function, as if Keffer had surgically removed every scrap of beauty that crossed the threshold of his office.

He kept his supplies scattered in a haphazard layer throughout the room, using a mental map of the mess to locate anything he needed. It drove Tanza to distraction. As they entered the office, Tanza barged past Keffer, swept aside a pile of junk on the corner of his desk, and sat in the clearing, staring at him boldly while he closed the door. She'd long ago given up verbal arguments about Keffer's organizational skills but couldn't resist these silent jabs.

Keffer didn't notice. When the door clicked shut, he leaned against it and asked, "Is that Prince Auren?"

Tanza's hand crashed onto a pile of digi-records. "How did . . . how could you possibly know?"

Keffer smiled smugly and sauntered around to the other side of the desk. "He did the hair thing," he said, and demonstrated with his hand across his forehead.

"How do *you* know about the hair thing?" Tanza asked, twisting her body to keep her eyes on Keffer.

Keffer dropped into a cracked brown office chair. "The centennial was two weeks ago. I couldn't link up to a showstream without seeing a history program or lumiscopic drama."

He made Tanza explain her discovery. It took a long time; security fields and healing beds were technologies humans hadn't invented, and they baffled human science so completely that those industries were the only two that remained in tephan control.

Once Keffer understood, he grasped Tanza's hand, his eyes gleaming like coins. "Do you have any idea how rich we are?"

Tanza pulled her hand back. "You won't see a cent."

Keffer went stiff. "What do you mean? I financed . . ."

She jumped off the desk and stabbed a finger into the space she'd cleared. "No one can know I found him. If we tell the world we found Prince Auren, the media's going to dig up all they can on the 'daring heroes' who rescued him. They *will* find out the true nature of your business."

Keffer mused, "We don't have to tell the media. Other people would pay for Prince Auren."

Tanza's lip curled ferociously. "Don't go there, Keffer. You don't sell people—and if you do, it'll put you in much grimier company. They'd destroy you in days."

Keffer was silent a moment then scowled. "Then what did you bring him here for?"

"He's been asleep for a century. The least I could do is give him a ride."

"Then what? You let him go, he runs to the nearest police point and tells everyone about the tomb robber who found him."

"He won't go to the government," Tanza said. "He doesn't want attention. He just wants me to take him to Alogath, so he can disappear into an ordinary life."

Keffer frowned. "Why Alogath? He can 'disappear' in Lorantz, too."

Tanza said, "He wants to be near Roshen. It used to be the capital. I can take him to my place in Alogath and get him on his feet."

"I need you here."

Tanza huffed, sitting back on the desk and crossing her arms. "You can spare me for a couple of days."

"Not to babysit a moldy old prince."

An argument blazed. Keffer wouldn't let Tanza waste time helping a stranger when he needed her for paying jobs, but Tanza couldn't back down. Keffer's human mind didn't understand the power of Prince Auren's legend.

Besides, she couldn't abandon the prince right after she'd dragged him into a new century.

Finally Keffer seemed to realize he wouldn't win. He grabbed a thin square datapad from a desk drawer, plucked a crumpled piece of circuit-plastic from under Tanza's hand, spread the latter atop the former, and pressed a button to make a flat green map hover at Tanza's eye level.

"Tell you what," Keffer said as he manipulated the datapad screen to make a few lines of text hover next to the map, "I need a package brought to Verith. It would be on your way. Take it there for me, and I don't care if 'Prince Auren' rides along."

Tanza noted the text entry was incomplete, nothing but a price and a delivery site. "It's illegal goods, isn't it?"

"If it weren't," Keffer said, "I'd ship it via Coalition delivery services. It's almost like we're *criminals* or something."

Tanza threw her arms up in exasperation. "I don't want to commit a crime with the *virtue prince* next to me." Virtue names might be meaningless, but Prince Auren's legend hadn't lost all its power over her.

"I can give you a cut."

Tanza's arms fell to her sides. "How much?"

"Fifteen percent," Keffer said

Tanza examined the hovering datapad display and did some mental math. She needed the money, especially after such a bust of a tomb. Auren wouldn't approve, but he'd be out of her life in a few days, and her work would keep her fed for a lot longer.

"Twenty percent," she countered. "Verith's had higher Cornerstone activity this month."

Keffer waved a dismissive hand. "You'll be fine. You're not human."

"That doesn't matter if we're in a group Cornerstone considers 'morally tainted.'"

"All right, twenty percent. Just because I like you."

"Deal. Put it in the hovercar for me."

Keffer snorted. "I am not wasting a *hovercar* on a delivery run. Do you know how much fuel costs?"

Tanza threw a hand toward the map. "How am I supposed to get there?

"You have a car, don't you?"

"A *ground* car! I pulled it out of a tomb! I'm lucky if it gets me to the market!"

Keffer shut down the datapad display, leaned back in his chair, and crossed his arms. "Then hope you're *really* lucky."

Keffer had already compromised on Tanza's payment. If she pushed him any further, she would lose her chance to go to Alogath. "Fine," she said, storming out of the office. "I'll see you in a few weeks."

"Have a nice trip," Keffer called after her just before she slammed the door.

TWO DAYS later, Tanza sat on the blue and orange elastifoam floor-covering of her house's gathering room, shoving supplies into two giant backpacks. Auren emerged from one of the bedrooms wearing boxy gray clothes that made him look like any modern laborer. Though Prince Auren had owned palaces larger than her entire neighborhood, he had adapted to Tanza's cramped home surprisingly well. He hadn't even cringed at the eye-searing flooring or the feathered window coverings that Tanza's human landlord insisted upon. Perhaps the house wasn't worth comment in a world full of much stranger changes.

Tanza shoved a fishing set into one pack, forced the zipper shut, then turned to the other pack.

Auren hefted the first pack and groaned. "Are we going to Alogath or crossing the Nightmare Wastes?"

"I like to be well prepared," Tanza said, her voice tight. She had long ago learned that it was better to be over prepared than stranded without supplies, and she had no patience for teasing while she tried to make ready for such a long journey.

The pack was half Auren's height, and he bowed beneath the weight. "Will it fit in the car?"

Tanza added a small radiant heater into her pack, next to a bundle of clothing. "Why don't you find out?" she snapped.

Auren swiped a hand across his forehead, but since Tanza had cut his hair almost to the scalp, he found nothing to brush aside. He turned it into a royal salute and staggered out the front door with his burden.

As the front door sealed shut, the back door opened and Keffer strode into the house. "Good, you're still here!" he boomed. "I've got a package for you."

Tanza sprang to her feet and whisked Keffer into a back bedroom. "Not so loud," she hissed as she shut the door. The room was in disarray due to Tanza's packing efforts, and she hated that Keffer had entered her house the *one time* it looked as disorganized as his own office.

Keffer smiled, and Tanza couldn't tell whether he was amused by the mess or by her demeanor. "Oh, that's right. You're ashamed to show me to your high-and-mighty friend."

Tanza sighed. "I don't want to announce my crimes to *the virtue prince*. What do you want? I already have your package."

He whipped a small green paper box from behind his back. "Got another one. This package goes to Alogath."

"You said one package!"

"It's worth ten times the other one. A simple dropbox. I sent you the address. Just set the box inside, the sensors will chart it, and we'll get filthy wads of cash. Two minutes of your time."

"Give me the hovercar," Tanza said.

He eased the box back. "I can always find someone less demanding and keep you here in Lorantz."

Tanza snatched the package. "Fine."

He smiled. "Oh, and change of plans on the Verith box."

"Again?" Tanza moaned. The client had already changed the delivery site three times.

"He wants it delivered straight to his house," Keffer said. "I sent the address to your datapad. He wants you to come alone, and he wants it in two days."

"Two *days?*" Tanza screeched. "I'm driving a ground car that was built before the revolution! Tell him I'll get there when I get there."

Keffer crossed his arms. "One doesn't say no to Denfor Berimac."

Tanza almost dropped the box. "He's still alive? And willing to deal with a human?"

Denfor Berimac was the last living heir of the family that had manufactured the lumiscopes and security nets for most of Arateph, including the tombs that Tanza robbed. When Arateph joined the Interplanetary Coalition, Berimac had holed up in one of his many houses and rarely emerged since. He viewed humans as a security breach on a planetary scale.

"He doesn't know I'm human," Keffer said, "and he's desperate for what I'm selling."

"I won't even ask."

"Good girl." He pointed to the package in her hands. "Alogath." He pointed to the main room, where the original package waited in her luggage. "Verith, two days. Remember that."

Tanza rolled her eyes. "I'm not an idiot."

The front door slammed, and Auren called from the main room. "Tanza? Where are you? We do *not* need anything more. I've sent off platoons with fewer provisions."

Keffer smirked at Tanza. "No, you're not, but you're traveling with one."

Tanza stuck a finger between his eyes. "Do *not* let him see you," she growled, and slipped into the hallway, slamming the door behind her.

"Coming," she called. She bustled into the main room, forced the green box into the pack, and threw the pack over her shoulder before Auren could ask any questions. "Let's go," she said, and led Auren out the front door.

Tanza's pack still held the power cell from Auren's healing bed. If she sold it, she could buy her own hovercar, but Keffer would suspect something if she made such a huge purchase after giving him nothing from a tomb job. Thus Tanza was forced to drive an ancient ground vehicle. It was a classic High-Runner, with large, narrow wheels, high, rounded fenders, raised headlamps, and no roof—a car for rich people driving on sunny days through flat country, not for cross-continent trips. The car was prone to breakdowns, and replacement parts hadn't been manufactured in a century; but with careful driving and constant maintenance, Tanza *might* be able to make it to Verith in two days.

She threw the pack into the front storage compartment, checked the engine in the rear, then climbed into the driver's seat while Auren settled into the passenger's place. "Ready to go?" she asked.

The front door to Tanza's house burst open. Keffer raced outside and skidded to a stop in front of the car, nearly tumbling over the windshield.

Tanza's glare could have melted aurolith, but it didn't make a dent in Keffer's smile. He presented Tanza with a brown wallet. "You forgot something."

Tanza glanced at the wallet and her insides blazed. She needed this, but she wouldn't have forgotten it if she hadn't been so concerned about hiding Keffer from the prince.

She handed the wallet to Auren, not trusting herself to look at Keffer without exploding. "This is yours," she said. "It's that ID we talked about. Just in case."

Auren looked inside the wallet and his face twisted. "Arthur Lateph," he said, choking on the sounds of his new name. Tanza had given him a human alias, since a tephan of his apparent age would have been born in the height of the human-naming craze. He'd yet to forgive her for it.

Keffer quickly surveyed Auren's features. "You look like an Arthur," he said.

Auren glared. "It's the name of a *beast*," he said in a voice that could have killed plants. "How savage is Earth, that you name your children after beasts?"

"What is he *talking* about?"

Tanza rolled her eyes. "He insisted on looking up the meaning. The name Arthur means 'bear.'"

"A brushbeast with legs!" Auren moaned, as if this proved his entire point.

Keffer gave him an amused, condescending, and slightly offended look. "People naming their kids 'Arthur' aren't thinking about a bear. More likely thinking about a king."

Auren relaxed, though only slightly. "Is that so?"

"Honest," Keffer said, putting up a hand the way humans did when taking oaths. "King Arthur. Legendary king of England. Code of honor and all that stuff."

Tanza fought her history-loving urge to investigate this claim. "Well, isn't that a nice, civilized namesake?" she said, waving Keffer back while starting the car. "Thanks for the history lesson."

The car roared forward, leaving Keffer standing alone in the street.

Auren's face, bright with relief over his assumed name, became darker as they drove through the city. So far, Auren's every impression of this modern, space-faring Arateph had included disappointment. He found the architecture dull and utilitarian (modern society loved its clean, practical lines), found the clothing drab and shapeless (modern fashion considered the clothing of Auren's time unspeakably gaudy), and was dismayed to find tephan traditions obscured by human customs and technologies. The city's spaceport, with its vast landing strips, forests of control towers, and several hundred varieties of spaceships, left him nearly ill from the effort to comprehend it.

Eventually they left the city for the countryside. Farms were larger now and tended by giant automated machines, but a century hadn't changed the crisp snap of a fall morning, the rush of the wind, or the rustle of seedpods ready for harvest—or so Tanza guessed as she watched the strain melt from Auren's face.

Auren savored a lungful of fresh air and smiled. "Now *this* is worth waking up for," he said. "There's nothing like a drive through the country in a High-Runner." He ran a hand along the curve of the door. "This is the first thing that seems familiar since the tomb. If there were a couple of guards in the backseat, I could almost pretend . . ."

He stroked the dashboard instruments, and his hand paused near the center of the car. His smile disappeared. "Did this car come from a House Eckler tomb?"

Tanza's throat went tight. "What makes you think that?"

He pointed at one of the power gauges. "It's stuck on zero," he said, "and the glass is cracked. I did that to the elder Lord Eckler's High-Runner when I was eight years old."

Tanza tried to brush aside the implications. "Those instrument panels are so easy to break."

Auren traced his finger along the web of cracks. "No, it's exactly the same shatter pattern. I remember—I thought Lord Eckler would kill me for scarring his beloved High-Runner. Instead, he had it buried it with him a few years later. He didn't even replace the original glass—he was a purist."

Tanza sighed. "It did come from a tomb." She made her next words sharp to mask her embarrassment. "I don't think he'd mind. I needed a car. I never thought you'd recognize it."

Auren's lips made a thin, tight line. "I knew you were a thief. I just didn't know it so . . . clearly before." He watched the fields fade in favor of forests. "Have you robbed many tombs?"

"Enough to get good at my job."

"Your job." His smile was halfway between humor and horror. "That's all it is to you. You're happy to make your living off the bodies of the dead."

"I don't steal bodies," Tanza snapped. "Just the stuff they're greedy enough to hoard after death."

"And that you're greedy enough to take."

Tanza slammed the brakes. Auren's head nearly hit the windshield.

She set the handbrake and leaned close to Auren, venom on her breath. "Listen, *Lirishan*." She pronounced the term of royal respect without its naming tongue undertones, turning it into an insult. "Your fourteen virtue names don't give you the right to lecture me. I wasn't born in a palace. I didn't get buried in a tomb more expensive than most houses. I do what I need to do to survive. You know what sort of work I do, and if it bothers you so much, you can get to Alogath without my help."

Tanza rejoiced when she saw the terror in his eyes. "Are you throwing me out?" he asked, his voice little more than a whisper.

Her smile was hard. "I am very close." She let him wait through two frantic breaths before adding, "You can stay if you don't mind the taint of the criminal classes."

Auren nodded. "Understood."

Tanza stomped her foot on the accelerator, but instead of roaring ahead, the car spluttered, rumbled, and fell silent. Tanza swallowed a mountain of curses, slammed her hands against the steering column, and then climbed out and stormed to the back of the car. She looked over the engine, fetched the tool kit, and fiddled with the engine's usual trouble spots, but the car stayed silent each time she tried the remote start.

"Have you tried the overload inhibitor?" Auren asked.

Tanza snapped, "There's no such part."

Auren sprang from his seat and came to her side. "Yes, there is." He pointed to a loose square metal piece buried behind a fluid pump.

Tanza tapped the piece into position and clicked the remote start. Nothing. She smiled. As if a prince knew anything about engines. "Didn't work," she said.

"Of course not," Auren said. "You need to reset all the energy points."`

The words held no malice, but all Tanza heard was a proud royal condescending to the hired help. This day had been stressful enough, and she didn't need Prince Auren standing over her shoulder being *helpful.*

She slapped a wrench against his chest. "If you're such a genius, you fix it."

She stormed off before she did any more damage. The virtue prince might not have a throne, but killing him would probably still count as assassination.

Twenty paces from the road she disappeared into a clump of trees, dropped on a pile of leaves at the base of a whisper tree, and buried her scream in the foliage. Why had she agreed to this? Keffer was right: She should have left him to shift for himself in Lorantz. Prince Auren was much more impressive in chronovids or lumiscopic dramas. In real life he was nothing but a spoiled, self-righteous scion of a royal house that had rested upon virtue names while sneering at starving widows.

Who cared where the car came from? It wasn't as if she'd stolen it from a family of fifteen with infants to feed! She'd taken it from a man decades dead, rich enough to bury whole *cars* with him. She noticed that Prince Auren, who'd been so ready to condemn the vehicle's acquisition, was more than willing to help repair it when *he* had somewhere to go.

She fumed in this way until she heard the High-Runner's engine roar. She wouldn't have cared if Auren drove away without her except that the packs were in the car and it would be a long walk back to Lorantz. She shifted her tingling limbs and rose from the leaf pile.

And heard a scream above her head.

A red-furred quadruped hung from a tree branch, the poisonous spikes of its tail a hand-span from Tanza's nose. The deathtail was not happy to wake up and find an intruder in its territory.

Tanza inched away from the long, thin whip of a tail, but the rattle of the leaf litter pushed the deathtail into a crazed frenzy. It plummeted to the ground and charged, tail flying.

Tanza took off running and plunged through the trees with the deathtail on her heels. She emerged into the clearing at the edge of the road just as Auren closed the car's engine cover and lifted his head.

Tanza had no breath for a warning, but an angry deathtail wasn't easy to overlook. Auren raced to the front of the vehicle, where the raised cover to the storage area still blocked the windshield.

Five strides from safety, Tanza slipped on a patch of wet leaves and fell. Almost instantly the deathtail's claws tore into her right ankle.

She swallowed a scream. The claws hurt, but only the tail was poisonous.

The tail swung back, gathering momentum for a strike.

Tanza would die in convulsions.

At least Auren would be safe. He knew how to drive and he had the supplies. He could survive without her, but he'd never survive a deathtail.

The tail arced, a fiery red streak. Tanza turned her head, unwilling to watch her own death.

A shadow loomed over her, and she heard an awful crunch. When she dared to look, she saw Auren several paces away, standing over the motionless deathtail with a tire-lift in his hand.

"I don't think it's dead," Auren said. "We'd better get out of here."

He lifted her into the backseat then sprang into the driver's seat and drove away. When the deathtail was out of sight, Auren stopped the car and turned to Tanza. "What just happened?"

Tanza said, "A deathtail and I wanted the same tree."

He glanced at the rivulets of blood flowing from her ankle onto the beige upholstery. "You should have let him have it."

She laughed wearily. "I tried."

Auren jumped out of the car and retrieved the medical kit from the storage area. Then he helped Tanza hobble from the car to a grassy patch at the side of the road, well away from any trees. He propped her foot on a thick fallen branch and peeled back the shredded, blood-soaked bottom of her pant leg, sending a flash of hot, stinging pain through Tanza's wounds. Three cuts spanned the outer half of her right ankle, barely visible through the pooling blood.

Auren winced. "I think we should find you a clinic."

"Not unless you want Arateph to know you're alive," Tanza said. "Arateph Med survived the revolution. The archives will have your voice print."

Auren paled. The undertones of a tephan voice were unique to each person. If Auren spoke to medical personnel or called a clinic, the voice-recognition technology could match him to his records in seconds.

But he persisted, "You need medical attention."

Tanza gestured to the medical kit. "I have everything we need."

Auren opened the red box to reveal an expansive display of bandages, ointments and medications. "I see. You brought the clinic with you."

Tanza smiled faintly. "I have a good supplier."

He unrolled a strip of cloth. "Bandages haven't changed much. I'll do my best."

As Auren cleaned away the blood and applied sterilizing ointment, Tanza gave a more detailed account of her adventure with the deathtail. At the end she asked, "Did you actually *hit* the deathtail?"

He nodded but kept his eyes fixed on her bleeding leg.

She asked, "Why didn't you run?"

He placed healing mesh over the scratches. "It would have killed you."

He said it as if she didn't know, as if that realization wasn't spreading a shadow of terror through her soul. "Yes, but . . ."

Did he really not know what he'd done? What horrors he'd risked for a common thief? How deeply Tanza was indebted to him? If he didn't realize, how could she explain it?

Finally she stammered, "No one runs *toward* a deathtail. Not even for family. One scratch could . . ."

Auren wrapped a thick white bandage around the ankle. "That's why I had to help. I'm named Nivalith."

Nivalith—courage that risks death to save life. Maybe virtue names were good for something after all.

"About that . . ." Tanza wasn't sure whether she should start with thanks or with an apology, or what words to use for either one.

While she considered this, Auren wrapped several layers of bandage around the foot and ankle, then, with Tanza's consent, cut away the bloodied tatters of her pant leg. He frowned at the sloppy results. "Are you sure you don't want a clinic?"

"It's fine," Tanza gasped. The adrenaline had faded, and the wounds throbbed and burned beneath the bandages.

Auren's brow furrowed. "You're in pain."

She thrust a hand into the medical kit, pulled out a syringe of pain medication, and injected it expertly into her arm. Then she swallowed a dose of an antibiotic and told him, "I'm fine. These meds are really good." The pain faded in seconds. "Let's get moving."

Tanza clutched the empty syringe in one hand while Auren grasped her other hand and hauled her to her feet. She walked two steps unassisted before the world wobbled and she tilted to one side. Auren caught her just before she fell.

Tanza mentally cursed her supplier. "Human pain meds," she slurred.

Auren lowered her into a sitting position on the grass. "What do you mean? Did you take human medications?" he asked, looking more frightened than he'd been by the deathtail. "Are they poisonous?"

Irritation and amusement swarmed sluggishly through the thick glaze of Tanza's thoughts. "Supplier gave me . . . wrong kind. Bad label . . ." She sniffed the empty syringe. "Yes. Human. Had it before. Just . . ." Her eyelids drooped and her head fell.

"Tanza!" Auren shouted, tapping her cheek. "Stay with me!"

His terror jolted her into alertness. "I'm fine!" she yelped. "Not dying! Just sleepy!"

"You're certain?" he asked.

"Yes," she said with as much force as she could manage. "Don't worry. I'll sleep it off." She shifted her arms and legs, trying to remember how to stand. "Help me walk."

Auren helped her to her feet and supported her the last few steps to the car, where he eased her into the backseat.

"I'll drive," he said as he fastened her safety restraints.

"Not safe," Tanza slurred.

"I probably have more experience driving a High-Runner than you have. We're on country roads. I know the route you planned. We'll be fine."

Auren disappeared into the driver's seat, and the car rumbled forward. The hum of the wheels and wind lulled Tanza to sleep before she could thank him.

WHEN TANZA woke, red light and shadow filled the air, and tall buildings crowded the street. They'd reached Debben, a city larger than Lorantz. Tanza ordered Auren to stop. The medication had faded, and she didn't want Auren learning about new traffic laws in the middle of a crash.

Auren eased the car to the curb and stopped the engine. The sleek new metal-and-glass buildings along the road sported signs in three human languages, the tephan translation a tiny afterthought at the bottom. Near a storefront not five paces away stood four muscular young human males. At the car's approach, their heads turned and their expressions darkened.

Tanza leaned over the driver's seat and murmured in Auren's ear, "Turn the car around. Now."

"But you just said . . ."

"I don't care. Get us out of here."

Before he could move, the men blocked the paths of all four wheels. The tallest of them, a square-jawed man with sunburned skin, loomed over the driver's door. "What are you doing here?" he asked in clumsy Common Tephan, pronouncing the words as though the language itself disgusted him.

Tanza said, "Just switching drivers. We only stopped for a moment."

The tall man raised an eyebrow. "Two tephans stopping in a human neighborhood at sunset? I think you're Cornerstone, come to blow up some humans."

"We're not, I swear," Tanza said.

The man tapped Auren's jaw with the back of his hand. "How many virtue names you have, small-brain?"

Auren nearly answered the question, but Tanza rushed to speak up first. "I wouldn't take a virtue name to save my life. Neither would he. Just let us leave."

"I asked *him,* lady."

Tanza knew that one of Auren's virtue names was related to honesty. These humans would think fourteen virtue names proof of Cornerstone involvement. Could she trust the virtue prince to lie?

Auren rolled his eyes and said, "If you must know, I think I took *one* a hundred years ago." He flipped the ignition switch, and the engine roared to life. "We're late, so if you'll excuse us . . ."

The man smiled cruelly. He leaned over the door and reached toward the ignition switch. "You're not leaving."

Auren didn't even glance at him. He released the brakes and pressed the accelerator, and the four men dove out of the car's path nanoseconds before the wheels crushed their legs. Auren sped away, and despite his outdated knowledge of traffic laws, Tanza wouldn't let him stop the car while they remained in the human neighborhood.

As they drove, Tanza shouted above the wind, "Are you out of your mind? You could have run them over!"

Auren adjusted a mirror as casually as if nothing had happened. "I knew they'd run. All bluster, no bravery. Not a virtue name among them."

She stabbed his shoulder with a finger. "What if they hadn't moved? You'd have injured four *humans.* The police would skin us alive."

Auren's eyes widened. "Literally?"

"Very nearly," Tanza said. "You know who the police are? Humans. They'd see two tephans attacking humans, call us Cornerstone, and lock us away for life."

"What *is* Cornerstone?"

Tanza had never heard anyone ask that question before. Cornerstone filled the infostreams, factored into political and personal debates, cast clouds of worry over most minds on Arateph. She hated to destroy Auren's blissful ignorance. "They call themselves a tephan independence group, but mostly they kill humans and blow up their technology."

"Why did those humans expect Cornerstone to have virtue names?"

"Most Cornerstone members take at least three virtue names. They're almost the only tephans who do anymore."

Auren struggled to keep his eyes on the road. "How can they have virtue names and practice such violence?"

"Cornerstone thinks humans have destroyed tephan life and morals. They take virtue names to prove they're 'true tephans' and show 'purity in a fallen world.'"

"But that . . ." Auren would have driven into a lamp post if Tanza hadn't shouted warning. "That's a perversion of virtue names. They're not meant to be trophies. They're meant to inspire people to greater virtue."

"Cornerstone's not known for nuanced philosophy. You're good or you're bad, and if you're bad, you're dead."

This so troubled Auren that Tanza refused to let him ask any more questions until they'd parked the car outside a tephan flower shop. Immediately he turned around in his seat.

His first question surprised her. "Did you mean what you said to those humans? That you wouldn't take a virtue name to save your life?"

Tanza laughed. "Remember who you're asking. A virtue name wouldn't do me much good."

"Would *anyone* outside of Cornerstone want one, or are virtue names tainted beyond repair?"

Tanza felt a stab of pity for Auren. Virtue names were vital to him, but modern Arateph considered them irrelevant and old fashioned. No one wanted a virtue name because no one cared. But when Tanza saw the sorrow and desperate hope in the prince's face, she couldn't tell the blunt truth.

"Well," she said, "people associate virtue names with Prince Auren as much as they do with Cornerstone."

He let out a sigh of relief. "Then . . . would you mind if I chose one for you? I'd like to, before we reach Alogath."

Tanza's jaw dropped. "Why?"

"I don't want to be the only person outside Cornerstone with a virtue name. I think you'd bear one well."

"Me? You're crazy if you think I have any use for virtue."

"You wouldn't be helping me if you had no sense of virtue."

That wasn't virtue. That was guilt. Tanza couldn't have come with him at all if not for those two illegal packages hidden in the car. Auren thought Cornerstone perverted virtue names, but giving one to a tomb robber wouldn't be much better. If he knew her whole history, he wouldn't talk about virtue. He wouldn't want to talk to her at all.

Tanza sighed and asked, "Does this really matter that much to you?"

"It does."

Well, he *had* just saved her from a deathtail. She could humor him.

Shoving aside thoughts of tomorrow's delivery, Tanza said, "All right. Name away. Just keep your expectations low."

He slid over into the front passenger seat. "I will give you a fitting name," he said, "once I take a few days to consider. I have more practice receiving virtue names than giving them."

She climbed over the seatback into the driver's seat and started the car. "No rush." If it took long enough, maybe he'd abandon the idea entirely.

Having slept away the day, Tanza drove through the night. Even though the car broke down five times the next day, they arrived in Verith at sunset. The only available tephan hotel had only one un-booked room.

As Tanza fretted in the hotel lobby, Auren suggested, "We could keep driving."

"Can't," she said quickly. "I can't drive any farther, and *you* can't drive through cities."

A good excuse, since she couldn't tell Auren about tomorrow morning's package delivery. This hotel was less than ten minutes' walk from the delivery point Keffer had provided.

As Tanza and Auren settled into separate beds, Tanza planned her mission. She couldn't let him catch her on her errand. His century of slumber had made him reluctant to sleep, but he usually slept most deeply in the hours surrounding dawn. She sent a datapad message to the client, confirming a delivery time just after sunrise, then turned off the light and tried to snatch a few hours of sleep.

When she woke, gray light filled the sky and Auren slept as heavily as a molting brushbeast. She retrieved Keffer's brown box from her pack, threw a black jacket over her sleep-rumpled clothes, and moved toward the door as quickly as she dared.

Auren remained sleeping as Tanza slipped into the hallway. Her trip would take less than half an hour. In the unlikely event that Auren woke, he would assume she'd slipped out for breakfast, and she planned to return with food before he suspected otherwise.

She left the hotel and hastened along the winding streets until she reached the city's edge and found a giant, brown brick house dripping in angular, animal-inspired Evris statuary. Two hundred years ago, Evris statuary, which mocked that king's infamous wildlife gardens, had been faintly subversive, but its modern admirers romanticized the old monarchy.

Tanza tore her mind from the history and focused on the more important matter of security. The house boasted two towers and was surrounded by enormous, lush gardens. The fence of energy-net filament—strong enough to stop a car—could sustain four different security nets at once.

Tanza walked behind the house and waited outside a giant gate. A jungle—trees, shrubs, flowers, vines, and grasses in every color Tanza knew—flourished on the other side of the fence with far too much vigor for this autumn weather. Tanza couldn't even see the house. Such a garden needed a micro-climate generator, which meant Berimac was a serious gardener with a serious amount of money.

A man hobbled out of the lush greenery on a walking stick and two unsteady legs, clad in a scarlet dressing gown as brilliant and expensive as any of the flowers. Even in his frailty he looked like a man who commanded empires and captured souls with fresh-carved coins, and Tanza recognized Denfor Berimac.

As Berimac approached the gate, he pressed some buttons on a black box in his palm and the energy walls outside the fence fell. His deep voice could have come from a man half his age and twice his size. "Do you have my package?"

Tanza held the box through the fence, and Berimac tore it open. Two orange and yellow falls of silken petals flipped over the edge, while smaller brown capsules rattled on the box's moist bottom.

Mizzen swampblossoms! This whole trip was for a flower? An illegal flower, yes—highly endangered after invasions of Earth species and not allowed outside the marsh reserves—but not the crime that Tanza had feared. Nothing dangerous.

Suddenly, electronic screeching filled the gardens, startling several birds and making Tanza shrink inside her skin. Berimac's face became stone. The energy walls whipped across the gate again, and Tanza took several steps back. What had she done? How had she angered the old man?

Two heavily muscled tephan men, attired in gold and brown suits that resembled those of the historical King's Guard, walked toward Tanza along the outside of the fence, dragging a man who resembled the historical king.

One guard hit some buttons on a black box on his belt, and the alarms went silent, but Tanza's ears still rang. "A-Arthur?" she exclaimed, calling Auren by his assumed name at the last second. "You followed me?"

Berimac turned on her, his face harsh. "You know this man?"

"Unfortunately, yes," Tanza called back. She gave Auren a glare sharper than any spindle. "You should be back at the hotel."

"So should you," Auren replied.

"*I* had an appointment. *You* weren't invited."

"An apt phrasing," Berimac said. "My instructions were clear. The courier was to come alone. I rarely approach the gate in person, and I don't want the whole city to see when I do."

Tanza leaned as close to Berimac as the energy walls allowed. "I didn't know he would come."

"Clumsy of you." Berimac's face twisted in a sneer. "People in your line of work should be capable of detecting a tail."

"I swear he's the least dangerous person on Arateph. He doesn't approve of my line of work. He's harmless."

Berimac stared at her for a long moment. "I believe you," he said at last. He nodded to the guards. "Make sure he doesn't come back."

The heavier guard nodded. The other guard twisted Auren's arms behind his back while the heavy guard threw a punch at Auren's torso.

"You said you believed me!" Tanza shouted at Berimac, fury almost drowning her fear.

"I do," Berimac said. "But mercy doesn't keep a man safe. A beaten man has a better memory."

Tanza had a horrible suspicion that *beaten* man and *dead* man were not vastly different concepts to Berimac.

Panic obliterated all thought. Before she realized what she was doing, Tanza found herself standing between the gasping Auren and one very large fist. It collided with her abdomen and expelled her breath in a pained grunt, but she had endured harder punches from harder men. She immediately lashed at the guard's vulnerable areas, fighting with all the desperate savagery she'd learned as a child in Alogath. After a few jabs she landed a blow on her guard's chin, which dazed him long enough for her to dart out of his reach.

As she turned to help Auren, she found the prince doing his own fighting. He threw his head into his guard's chin and smashed his captor's foot. Then, in motions almost too fast for Tanza to follow, he twisted his arms out of the guard's grip, threw his elbows into his opponent's stomach, and swept his foot behind the guard's legs. The guard fell like a stone.

Tanza's guard had recovered, but before he could strike, she grasped Auren's hand and pulled him away from the fight. They dashed past the gate and along the rear fence, and old Berimac watched with a disgusting expression of amusement.

Tanza fumed at Berimac's cruelty. All this trouble for a few endangered plants? The old tyrant must have thought them sufficiently chastised—or sufficiently amusing—because as Tanza and Auren disappeared around the corner, she heard Berimac order the guards to come back into the garden. Even without pursuit, neither Tanza nor Auren slowed until they reached their hotel.

After slamming the door to their tiny hotel room, Tanza found enough breath for a tirade. She locked the door and pushed Auren toward the center of the room. "What is *wrong* with you? Why did you follow me?"

The hint of anger in Auren's expression took Tanza by surprise. "I saw you leave the hotel."

"You couldn't wait for half an hour?"

He paced between the beds. "When I woke and found you'd left, for a moment . . ." He ran a hand over his face then pierced Tanza with his gaze. "What was I supposed to think? How could I know you planned to return? Why didn't you *say* something?"

All of Tanza's anger at Auren turned to hatred for herself. She hadn't thought . . . hadn't even considered what it would look like to him if he woke up alone. All she'd cared about was secrecy. She hadn't even left a note.

These thoughts deflated her pride, and she sank heavily onto her bed. "I didn't want you to know," she said.

Auren sat across from her on his own bed, and some of his anger faded. "You were on Keffer's errand, weren't you? That package . . ."

"He wouldn't let me take you to Alogath unless I made some deliveries for him."

"Deliveries? Are there more?"

She couldn't bear to tell him about the green box hidden in her pack. One delivery was crime enough in Auren's eyes. She couldn't reveal that their entire trip was a delivery route.

Since she didn't need to deliver the package until after she and Auren parted ways, it wasn't technically a lie when she said, "No. That was the last one."

"Then our trip to Alogath will have no more surprise sunrise excursions?"

Tanza stared at him. His words were casual, even friendly, with none of the anger or judgment she'd expected. "You still want to travel with me?"

"What's done is done," he said. "I don't approve, but you threw yourself into a fight to save me, and I'm not likely to find that kind of help elsewhere."

Tanza didn't point out that he wouldn't have needed the help if he'd traveled with anyone else. Instead, she asked, "Where did the virtue prince learn to fight? You *flattened* that guard."

Auren gathered stray supplies near the bed and brought them to his pack. "I had a call for my assassination broadcast globally when I was a week old. I know how to defend myself."

"Glad to hear it," Tanza said, pulling her pack from the closet. "I don't think Berimac plans to hunt us, but I won't relax until we're out of the city."

"Berimac?" Auren asked. "As in the lumiscopes? He must have been a child the last time I saw him."

"I don't think he's *that* old," Tanza said.

"He could be," Auren said. "I remember a young Berimac child at a palace function." He grimaced at the memory. "Beastly creature. Bruised my knees. This Berimac seems much the same."

"He just likes his privacy," Tanza said. "And his flowers. That's all that was in the package, you know. Flowers. Not weapons or drugs or anything. Just a swampblossom. You're not supposed to plant them outside the reserves, but it doesn't do any harm. Probably has a better chance of survival in that garden of his . . ."

Auren chuckled. "Tanza, you don't need to justify yourself to me."

Yet she always felt that she had to. She'd robbed dozens of tombs without a sting of conscience. Now one prince with a list of virtue names made her feel guilty for delivering a flower to an old man. If she were smart, she'd leave Prince Auren here.

Instead, she brought him and the luggage to the car, and within the hour they continued on their journey to Alogath. She'd grown good at making bad decisions.

MID THE picturesque beauty of the hill country—soaring rises covered in autumn purple, majestic cliffs of rock—Tanza scowled down at the High Runner's engine. The steep inclines had overwhelmed the car; this was the seventeenth breakdown since leaving Verith two days ago.

"That's it," Tanza said, throwing aside a wrench. "Needs four parts that haven't been made since the revolution. Can't be fixed."

Auren agreed, so they eased the car off the road and into the ditch.

As Tanza shoved all the supplies into their packs, two hovercars zipped overhead, and Tanza barely held back a frustrated scream. If Keffer had just let her use the hovercar, this trip would have ended two days ago. Hovercars were still too expensive for everyday transport, but Keffer could have spared the cost of fuel to spare Tanza's sanity. But no, that would have required *generosity,* and now Tanza was stuck in the middle of nowhere with an injured ankle, an ancient prince, and no transportation.

Not even Auren's power cell would get her a hovercar now, Tanza reflected as she yanked the packs from the car. Even if she dared to cross Keffer, she wouldn't find a power-cell buyer or a hovercar dealer until Alogath.

She slammed the cover over the storage area and held out a pack to Auren. "Time to start walking."

Auren pointed to a small smudge near a forest on the horizon. "I think I see a town."

Tanza hefted her pack over her shoulder with a sigh. "At least it's downhill."

Against stiff autumn winds they plodded toward the smudge, which resolved, after an hour of walking, into a collection of buildings on the edge of a forest. The gathering of houses and shops could barely be called a town, but it sat on a silver ribbon of magna-track and boasted a small stone building that proved to be a flash-transit station.

"Flash-transit; that's something," Tanza said as she and Auren crossed a grassy town square. She tucked a few wind-battered curls back behind her head. "The fare will cost me three months' rent, but we'll reach Alogath by nightfall."

"Flash-transit?" Auren asked.

After four days of ground-car travel, Tanza had forgotten how little Auren knew of modern transportation. "Think of rail-caravans," she explained, "but four times as fast and carrying three times the passengers."

Auren's face twisted as he stared at the track, evidently attempting to visualize this mode of transport. "Sounds uncomfortable."

"It's . . . not bad," Tanza replied. "It's fast, anyway."

Long-distance railways in Auren's time had been designed for comfort, not efficiency. Even basic fares received plush seats, elaborately decorated surroundings, and wide views of the countryside. Tanza thought she'd have preferred such inefficient transport to the cramped, windowless metal casing of flash-transit.

The tiny gray-brick transit station had silver roof panels and wide windows of colored glass—an outdated building of entirely tephan design. The Coalition hadn't bothered to build a new station for such a rural area; Tanza was surprised they'd built a flash-transit line through here at all. The only update was an ancient security column—probably taken second-hand from a larger station—installed in place of a boarding-pass desk in a deep nook in the outside wall of the station's waiting area.

Tanza led Auren up cracked stone steps and into the sheltered nook that held the security column. A circular metal desk formed the bottom portion of the column, and two-foot-thick plastiglass formed its upper half and ceiling, which stood at roof height. The column's entrance door was warped and rusted, and the interior was just large enough for a computer, a scattering of office supplies, and an ancient tephan woman.

"Branch line's being repaired," the woman drawled through the communication grate. "Cornerstone strike."

Tanza wasn't surprised. For the last few months the infostreams had been filled with reports of Cornerstone strikes between Verith and Roshen. Cornerstone hated technology introduced by humans, and the flash-transit lines were among the easiest public targets.

The old woman said, "First shuttle runs tomorrow."

Tanza pressed for more details about travel times, prices, and security. The station employee researched each question on an ancient computer so slow that Tanza considered giving up and walking to Alogath. Eventually Tanza paid a fee to reserve two seats, but when she turned around, Auren was gone.

She clambered down the stairs in a panic and found a town square transformed. A colorful, bustling city had sprouted in the space between the transit station and a row of businesses at the far end of the wide, grassy square. Tephans had made mountains of wood in the center of the square and rings of rocks on the sides. Male tephans assembled a stage on the far end while old women strung instruments, and another group had just started assembling a row of booths near the train station entrance.

Tanza peered at the sky and saw the shadowy shapes of three moons overlapping each other. Of course! Moon-cross! Tanza knew little about the traditional celebration, for the harvest festival had died out in most parts of Arateph, but smaller towns held onto the customs. Tanza could easily imagine Auren rushing toward the familiar sights on the same wild impulse that made him charge deathtails and trust thieves.

She located him in the branches of a tree at the square's far end and reached him just as he dropped to the ground. "What's wrong with you?" she demanded. "Climbing trees! I thought something had happened to you."

"Sorry," Auren said, his smile unharmed by the scolding. "I couldn't resist. I had to catch it." With a lopsided, child-like grin that Tanza had last seen on chronovids of a five-year-old crown prince, Auren presented a huge hat made of thin, textured fabrics of red and blue-green shot through with gold and silver. The outer edges of its brim brushed his shoulders.

Tanza shielded her eyes before the colors blinded her. "What do you call that monstrosity?"

"It's a hat!" Auren said, and set it on his head. "Isn't it wonderful?"

Tanza wanted to curl up and die. The fashions of the last century included everything but taste. "No," she moaned. "Why would you *want* it?"

His hands left the brim of the hat and spread wide. "To win the game, of course!"

Tanza's opinion of the prince's fashion sense improved slightly. "It's a game?" she asked.

Auren froze. "You've never joined the hat hunt? What sort of moon-cross do you celebrate?"

"None. I grew up in the city."

"As did I . . ." he said, his confused tone inviting further explanation.

Tanza hated to destroy another part of his world. "It's not an important festival. The Coalition doesn't recognize it, and tephans don't mark it. I mean . . . I know *when* it happens, but I haven't seen a celebration since I was four, and I don't remember much of that."

His face fell. "No moon-cross."

"Except in primitive country towns."

He stood motionless and blank as he considered this. Then, as if a switch flipped, he burst into a blinding grin as he grasped her hands between his. "Tanza," he said, "you are going to love tonight." He removed the hat and placed it on her head. "We start, as all the best things do, with a hat." With that, he led her toward the heart of the festival.

Apparently the hat hunt was a moon-cross tradition. The hat's comically wide brim was made to catch the autumn winds. Once it was knocked from a head, anyone could chase the hat and claim it until the wind took it again. Whoever held the hat at sundown claimed victory. At first only children played, but as adults escaped the workday they joined the chase, and the hat and the hunt wove wildly around the festival grounds.

Tanza didn't play long. Her ankle wounds ached, so she kept watch over the packs. She preferred to watch Auren play. He dove, tumbled, ran, and climbed with all the energy one would hope a man to have after a century of sleep. He trained children in the finer points of hunting, learned local ground-rules from town elders, and was more at ease than Tanza had ever seen him even in chronovids. History showed Prince Auren as the golden child, the last hope of Arateph, the man of virtue in a house of decadence. It had never shown him *laughing*.

At sundown a twelve-year-old girl claimed victory, but Auren showed no disappointment as he stood with Tanza to watch the bonfire lighting. The pile of wood and dry stalks blazed into a mountain of flame, and then the real festival started. Torches from the main fire lit smaller fires around the festival grounds. Jugglers tossed flaming knives, dancers spun fire in sun-bright arcs, and shadow puppets gave life to heroes and monsters of legend.

Meat pies, root vegetables, and sticky sweets flowed from sellers' stalls and generous hands. As Tanza and Auren stood among the stands near the transit station, wearing their packs and sipping at syrupy drinks, a withered old lady gave Tanza a fireblossom from her garden. Caught up in the spirit of the festival, Tanza blew off the petals, which exploded in ribbons of light. Bits of the glow caught in her hair. Auren's joy gave his face its own glow.

Tanza glanced at the station and at its ancient employee still at her desk inside the security column. "I'm glad we had to wait," she told Auren.

As the words left her mouth, music blared from an open second-story window in the station. The recording was poor, but Tanza recognized the bracing chords and soaring melody.

Auren smiled. "The kingdom anthem."

But Tanza's limbs went cold. That song stood for only one thing these days . . .

She seized Auren's hand and ran. He gave a cry of protest and tried to tug free, but she gripped him harder and gasped, "Cornerstone! The building's being bombed!"

Frantic crowds raced away from the station. Everyone had heard of attacks like this. The building would explode at the song's end, and only a scant few bars remained.

Hatred of Cornerstone flared through Tanza. Hundreds of innocents filled the square tonight; most nights, she doubted the whole town contained more than a hundred people. Cornerstone would endanger lives and destroy a tephan festival just to prevent a flash-transit line from running. If Tanza weren't so terrified, she'd have been sick.

The crowd surged around Tanza, dozens of people terrified past all sense. Auren scooped up a little girl who'd been lost in the chaos and scanned the crowd for her parents.

A dissonant, multi-layered tephan shriek sounded from the transit station. Tanza whirled around to see the desk attendant battering the door of the security column with weak and withered fists. The latch of the column's warped door had jammed, trapping the woman.

In that moment a veil dropped over Tanza. Her emotions disappeared; sound muted. A glassy stillness focused her thoughts on the facts. She had the skills to break open the door and the necessary tools in her pocket. The woman would die if she didn't act.

Tanza dropped her pack at Auren's feet and sprinted toward the station.

Auren started to follow before he remembered the child in his arms. Then he scooped up the extra pack with one hand, settled the screaming child on his hip, and ran the other direction.

By the way the door rattled, Tanza knew the woman had disabled the electronic security. Tanza only needed to break the physical barriers. She barely heard the chaos as she pulled out a metal file and jammed it beneath the door latch. She pressed against the file with one hand and pulled up and out on the door handle with the other hand. With a shrieking scrape of metal, the door flew open.

The old woman cried out in wordless relief and panic. Tanza dug her nails into the woman's shoulder and pulled her out. Half-carrying the old woman, she raced away from the station as the last notes of the kingdom anthem sounded.

The train station erupted in fire and smoke. The explosion drowned out the screams of the crowd. Falling chunks of stone left craters only inches behind Tanza and the woman. Had they been a second slower, they both would have died.

Shaking—and coming to a slow realization of the danger she'd just escaped—Tanza fell to her knees, and the woman fell beside her.

Auren ducked and wove toward them against the current of panicked festival-goers, his face white and his eyes wild. "Tanza!" he shouted as he struggled to bring the heavy packs through the crowd. He jumped over someone's leg and twisted out of someone else's path, then crouched at her side. "Are you hurt?"

Tanza rose unsteadily to her feet. "I'm fine."

Auren knelt beside the old woman. "Are you hurt, *morikah*?"

Tanza hadn't heard that honorific—which indicated great respect and friendliness toward an unfamiliar older woman—since she was a child. At the moment she could barely remember how to speak Common Tephan, and Auren was constructing obscure terms in the naming tongue.

"No," the woman rasped, her expression that of a frightened child. Tanza reeled under the sudden realization that Auren was decades older than this ancient woman.

She also realized Auren's arms were empty and asked, "The little girl?"

"Found her parents," Auren replied. He helped the old woman to her feet and asked her, "Is your family at the festival, *morikah*?"

As if in response, two young tephan women burst through the crowd and embraced the old woman. "Grandmother!" the taller one cried, apparently too modern to make it a proper naming-tongue title.

As the family members shared their relief and fear, a thousand facts flooded into Tanza's mind, and she snapped back into action. The explosion was over, but the danger hadn't passed.

She took one of the packs from Auren, grabbed his hand, and dragged him away. "We have to leave."

"What?" Auren asked, looking back at the woman and her granddaughters. "What about them? Is Cornerstone coming to slaughter?"

"They'll be fine," Tanza said. "Cornerstone gave warning. This was a statement, not a cleansing." Certain that the chaos covered their voices, she told Auren, "The med and fire teams are coming. Their scanners might have access to your voice print. Worse, they might suspect something about 'Arthur's' identity card, and you don't want to be caught with fake papers after a Cornerstone attack. We'll go through the woods and catch a train in the next town."

Auren nodded, face stoic, as he shouldered his pack. "Very well."

In the confusion, no one noticed two strangers slipping out of the town square, and they traveled through the forest by the light of crossed moons.

OURS LATER they made camp among the trees by the Lessin River, Auren now grateful for Tanza's overzealous preparations. The heavy packs contained two insta-tents to keep out the rain, radiant heaters to keep out the chill, and blankets to hide them from thoughts of the disaster.

Early the next morning, when Tanza crawled crusty-eyed from her tent, she found Auren sitting under a tree next to a sack spilling over with fish. Too weary for conscious thought, Tanza croaked, "What? How?"

"Couldn't sleep," Auren said. No surprise there. He'd slept fewer than four hours a night since leaving the tomb. "Thought I'd take advantage of the river—and that astonishingly good fishing set you tucked into my pack."

Auren swept up a shining glitterbelly in one hand, flipped open a knife with the other, and sawed off a fillet in one clean cut.

"You're good at that," Tanza said as he stripped the sparkling blue scales from the flesh.

He flipped the fish and cut off the other fillet. "A lot of practice."

"How?" Tanza asked, astonished.

Auren tossed the fillets onto a clean towel and the remains into a pile at the edge of the campsite. "Whenever the death threats became too serious, my parents would send me upriver—up this river, actually—to camp at the headwaters. I'd spend a few weeks away from any living soul, except a few guards and servants, and go back to the palace when the danger passed. I did a lot of fishing."

"Didn't the servants clean them?"

Auren grinned. "The fish were disgusting. Why would I let the servants have all the fun?"

For a few moments Tanza watched the dance of his hands and the flash of the scales, but then realized all those fillets needed cooking. She piled firewood, pulled a sparkstick from her pack, snapped the little cylinder's red paper coating, and threw it on the pile. Soon bright flames crackled.

Auren didn't notice. He'd finished with the fish and now stared upriver.

"Looking for something?" Tanza asked as she unfolded two palm-sized packets into low fabric seats.

"A fishing boat," he replied. "They'd usually haul to Roshen this time of day. Captains were known to give rides."

Tanza snorted. "In your time, maybe. Now you'd need three forms of ID and a letter of reference before they'd let you within shouting distance."

"*Some* kindness must remain."

Tanza shrugged and sat on one of the chairs. "People are smarter now."

Auren brought the fish over and sat in the chair on the opposite side of the fire. "I prefer being the fool, especially if it gets us a ride."

Tanza let him hold onto the hope but made plans for several days of walking.

Using Tanza's cooking pan, oil, and a few basic seasonings from his kit, Auren turned the fillets into a golden-brown breakfast of flaky flavor and soaring aromas. As Tanza savored the first bite, she said, "You're not what I expected in a prince."

"I'm not a prince anymore," Auren replied between bites. "The crown didn't wait for me."

"I think you'd have made a good king," Tanza said and meant it. The decadence and corruption of the nobility was historical fact, but Prince Auren had proven himself to be everything good in the royal regime: caring, humble, brave, noble. *King* Auren could have reformed Arateph's ruling class without civil war.

"I'm glad you think so," Auren said. "Though it does me little good now." He set aside his fish half eaten and watched the river race toward Roshen. "When I woke, I thought there might be a place for me in government; I still care about Arateph, and you claimed the Coalition wasn't hostile to the Houses. Now I realize . . ." He shook his head. "The changes are too great. I know nothing about this world, certainly not enough to be of any use."

Tanza claimed another slice of fish. "You could always be a fisherman."

He laughed and took another bite.

When the fish was nearly gone, Tanza thanked Auren for the meal.

"You supplied everything," he said. "Your fishing gear. Your cooking gear. Your knives. Without you, I'd have been helpless." He finished his fish and pointed toward her. "Which reminds me: I've found a virtue name for you."

Tanza went stiff. The easy emotion of the morning vanished. Once again he was the virtue prince and she the tomb robber. Not even his gratitude for her help could hide her flaws or erase what she was.

She fought down her shame. Virtue names were a meaningless tradition. Nothing he said could affect her life.

With a cynical laugh, she said, "Really? What would that be?"

Auren's gaze held centuries of tradition, his face royal solemnity. "I name you *Irimitha*."

Tanza's breath caught and her heart raced. *Irimitha* stood among the strongest of the virtue names. *Pure of heart* was the basic translation, but the undertones gave it more profound meaning. This was purity that blazed like fire and stood strong as stone, purity that required action and bravery to fight against evil and promote all possible virtues.

This name had come from Prince Auren, the virtue prince of legend. Great dignitaries had dreamed of such honor. Tanza—liar, thief, and tomb robber—deserved none of it.

She could have cried. Instead, she laughed, the same laugh she'd used when she first found his body come to life in a tomb. "You're crazy. Give me something a *little* believable. Did you forget how we met? Who I work for? I'm not pure of heart and haven't been since Keffer first found me a tomb to rob."

"Not yet, perhaps," Auren said, his voice gentle, "but virtue names aren't about the virtues you already have. They're about what you *can be*. The name isn't too heavy for you. You've helped me in so many ways since leaving the tomb. Last night you nearly died for an old woman you barely knew. The woman who did all that can give honor to the name Irimitha if she chooses to."

Tanza snapped, "I don't choose, Auren. When we part ways in Roshen, I'm going right back to Lorantz to get new orders from Keffer. I'll make my living the way I always have, the only way I know how. Irimitha will make me starve."

Auren leaned toward her. "How do you know unless you try? There are other options, Tanza."

She inched her chair back. "I believed that once, a long time ago. I even tested for university, too dumb to realize that no human would give a penniless tephan a scholarship."

Auren's head tilted. "Why would humans have any say?"

"They run the universities!" Tanza's voice rose as long-suppressed anger overwhelmed her. "They run everything. They're supposed to guide us to the standards of life in the rest of the Coalition, but everyone knows they'll never give up control. We're inferior: two-percent smaller brain capacity, our technology decades behind. Tephans don't get into university unless they have money or connections, and I don't. Now, any other possible future is closed off because of the path I chose. I'm already a criminal. Virtue's not going to change that."

Auren studied her face. "I think," he finally said, his voice heavy, "that virtue's the only thing that *can* change it. Virtue is not a burden; it's a tool. Maybe it would help show the humans that tephans are worth something."

He rose and looked out over the river. A fishing boat floated into sight, and Auren smiled. "There's our ride, if it has a foolish captain."

He raced toward the shoreline and hailed the boat. To Tanza's surprise it stopped, and after a few shouted negotiations, Auren hurried back from the river, grinning. "They'll take us to Roshen," Auren said. "The captain had a good haul, and he's in a generous mood."

As they packed up the camp and made their way to the boat, Tanza was glad Auren had proven her wrong about the ride. Could he be right about the virtue name too? She wanted to believe it; Irimitha had such a nice sound. But she was no fisherman—too modern and too smart.

Virtue was far too dangerous to consider.

AUREN LINGERED near a plaque outside a gray brick house, reading about the first deaths of the Ambush of Alogath. Tephans called this place the Killing Square, and Tanza had known its history since childhood, but she'd never realized the scope of the tragedy until she watched Auren mourn. To him these were not plaques with names and photos of strangers decades dead—he'd known most of those who died here, had talked and laughed with them and called them by nicknames. It wasn't right to gawk at his grief, to make him a living history exhibit in this museum of the dead.

Tanza approached him from behind and whispered in his ear, "I'll meet you at sunset."

He nodded vaguely. She doubted he'd even remembered she was there.

She was shocked to see the sun shining as she left the square. That place always had its own cloud of sorrow, and Auren's grief had made it seem as dim as downpours. But the rest of Alogath was as lively as ever, filled with people rushing about their business, gazing at datapads or fiddling with the earpieces and handheld screens of their portable comms systems. No one noticed Tanza as she slipped into a fourth-story apartment in a nearly empty, rundown building and came out with a green paper box.

The dropbox wasn't far from the apartment, so Tanza walked. She pointedly didn't think about the prince she'd left behind or about what he'd think of the errand she was on. He might call her Irimitha, but Tanza had bills to pay. Besides, the last package had held plants. Tanza doubted this one contained anything more dangerous.

As she walked, the streets became narrower, the houses battered and broken. Dark crevices gaped in the sidewalk, and broken bits of concrete stuck up like giant claws. She peered down an alley and saw the dropbox: a panel of rusted metal on the wall of an abandoned restaurant. Tanza only needed to stick the box behind it.

A chunk of broken concrete dug into her wounded ankle, and she collapsed. The green box skittered from her arms and split as it smashed into a wall.

The box buzzed, and Tanza's insides went sour.

She tore through the box and layers of padding and uncovered a broken spindle. The carved wooden handle lay in one corner, its trigger button pressed against the side of the box. The glimmering tip of the metal skewer, severed from the handle, pointed at Tanza's heart.

Auren's spindle.

Impossible! He'd buried it in a garbage heap. But Tanza had forgotten that animals like Keffer forage in the trash.

Stumbling on her injured leg, she raced back to the apartment, eyes and hair wild. Once inside, she slammed her door, secured all ten locks, and closed the blinds. Then she turned on the wall comms and entered Keffer's code. She even turned on the visual link. She wanted Keffer to look her in the eye.

Keffer filled the screen, perched on his cracked office chair like a throne. His smile made him look the fool. "Tanza!" he cheered. "You made it to Alogath! Did you make the delivery?"

Tanza could barely speak through her tightened jaw. "I started to. Then I saw what was inside." She held half of the spindle in each hand. "A spindle, Keffer. You know what I think about spindles."

"It's broken," he said.

"But fixable, or else you couldn't have sold it."

"The buyer was enthusiastic. I downplayed the damage."

"The buyer is Cornerstone, isn't it? You hate Cornerstone."

He shrugged. "They're friendlier to humans who have spindles. Money's money."

"There isn't enough money in the universe to make me sell this."

Keffer tilted his head. "Let me get this straight: You want to throw away a money magnet because you're scared of Cornerstone?"

"No, it's because I know what a spindle does, and I know what Cornerstone does, and I refuse to have anything to do with either."

Keffer leaned back in his office chair, arms crossed. "She's all high-and-mighty, is she, now that she's traveled with the virtue prince? Remember how you make your living. You've sold things to people twice as bad as Cornerstone without batting an eye."

"Doesn't matter. We're done, Keffer. Finished. I'll destroy this spindle, and you'll never see me again."

He leaned forward until his nose brushed the comm screen. "Tanza, calm down. Think about this."

Tanza's nails dug into the spindle handle. "I can't stand to look at you. I'm done."

"That's it?" Keffer's laugh burrowed under Tanza's skin. "You think you can just leave? You're a thief, Tanza. You rob tombs, and you need me to help you do it."

"Not anymore," Tanza snarled, and cut power to the comms. She paced the room and screamed out her frustrations, then destroyed her kitchen knives by hacking the spindle handle to splinters. When she finished, the ruined kitchen matched the ruin of her life.

What had she done? She disagreed with Keffer's tactics, but she'd done that before. She could have refused the job and stayed in Keffer's good graces. Instead, she'd blazed and burned away her world. She had nothing left.

But she knew a man in the Killing Square whose world had ended too. Maybe . . . maybe they could navigate this new world together.

She cleaned the kitchen then walked the streets of Alogath by the light of the setting sun. She found Auren atop the steps of the museum, looking like the ghosts with whom he'd spent the afternoon.

"All right?" Tanza asked.

His gaze was far away. "Alive," he said, "and making my peace."

Tanza gripped the stone post at the base of the stairs. "I should have stayed with you."

"No," Auren said. "I needed to face this alone." He descended the stairs and took Tanza's arm as they walked to the apartment. The memories had unlocked more of the prince in his personality.

Tanza asked, "Do you want to talk about it?"

"Someday," he said.

They entered the apartment, and Auren didn't notice the new dents in the countertop. Tanza warmed up some fish they'd brought from the boat, and they ate it at her tiny kitchen table.

Tanza pushed her fish around her plate. "I was thinking," she said. "I won't go back to Lorantz."

Auren put down his utensils. "You won't?"

"I'd rather stay with you. You'll need someone to guide you for a while."

"Keffer approves?"

"I don't care what Keffer thinks." She would have left it at that, but if she wanted to escape Keffer's world, she couldn't keep secrets. She sighed and said, "Keffer tried to make me sell the spindle."

She told every detail: Keffer bringing her the package the first day of the trip, her lies after the disaster with Berimac, her trip this afternoon and the ensuing argument. Auren stayed silent throughout the tale—whether still numb from the Killing Square or stunned by her sins, Tanza didn't know. She knew only that the guilt was too heavy to hold inside.

Her story told, she could have cried, but instead she set her jaw and said, "I know Keffer's sitting in that chair, waiting for me to come crawling back. But I won't. I'm tired of tombs. I want to live."

Auren reached across the table and grasped her hands. "You will," he said. "I know it."

Tanza found strength for a smile. "I'll try."

As they cleaned the kitchen, Auren asked, "Will Keffer punish you for the betrayal?"

Tanza shook her head. "It's not his style. He'll rage about it, make sure everyone knows what an idiot I am for destroying a spindle, but he's taken larger losses. After the next client, he'll forget I ever existed."

When the kitchen was clean, Tanza and Auren collapsed into separate bedrooms, both too exhausted from the emotions of the day to even change clothes. Tanza's mind went black the moment her head hit the pillow.

A sound woke her in the middle of the night. A thunder of heavy steps sounded in the hall, and her front door rattled beneath a blow. Tanza bounded out of bed and hastened toward Auren's room. He stood in his doorway, wide awake. A moment later the front door splintered, and eight black-clad tephans rushed into the apartment. Before Tanza and Auren could run, the intruders reached the hall and pulled them into the main room.

The men around Auren muttered reassuring words in Common Tephan—friends, help, rescue—and called him by his title. The three intruders who held Tanza were less gentle. They twisted her arms and dragged her with far more force than her useless attempts at resistance required.

The intruders brought them to the kitchen and stopped before a tall tephan woman with a sharp face and sharper eyes. Her red, gold, and white armbands told Tanza that the intruders were Cornerstone.

The woman brought her face a hand's-breadth from Tanza's and snarled, "Not enough to desecrate the tombs of the dead. You must steal the living too." She spat on Tanza's cheek. "Virtue punishes those who stray. Especially the enemies of the virtue prince."

The woman stepped away and nodded to one of the men holding Tanza. "Give her what she deserves."

The man at Tanza's right unsheathed a spindle and placed its point against her ribs.

"No!" Auren screamed, trying to tear himself out of his captors' grasp.

The sharp-faced woman stared in surprise. "You want to spare this monster?"

Auren stilled and took two deep breaths. "She woke me," he said with the voice of the chronovid prince. "That's worth something. Let her live."

After a silence, the knife-faced woman turned to Tanza's captors. "Make sure she doesn't follow us." One of Tanza's captors cracked something heavy against her skull, and the world went black.

10

WHEN TANZA woke, faint light streamed through the window and her head had a lump as wide as her palm. She crawled to her bedroom and found the under-bed drawer that held this apartment's stock of pain medication. She swallowed a nausea pill and then, after double-checking that the syringe held tephan pain medication, injected a dose of it into her arm.

The med scanner showed only minor concussion, so when she could walk without dizziness, she returned to the main room and turned on the comms. She needed to rescue Auren, and she'd never do it alone. But who to call? The police would lock her up as a tomb robber, and she couldn't go crawling back to Keffer.

The comm screen beeped and flashed. Keffer was calling. Tanza answered and kept her face neutral.

"Morning, *charit*," Keffer chirped. "Had a change of heart?"

"Auren's gone," Tanza said, her voice dull but underscored with menace. "Taken by Cornerstone."

"Then you're available. Excellent. Got my eye on a nice tomb in the southern hemisphere."

The truth trickled into Tanza's recently concussed mind. "You told them," she growled. "You sold Auren to Cornerstone like he was a piece of machinery, you nameless child of . . ."

Keffer shrugged, untouched by her slanders against his heritage. "Since I couldn't give them the spindle, thought I'd give them their beloved prince instead."

"People will find out you sold him, Keffer. And you're going to wish for death."

"So what if people know? Cornerstone won't hurt him. They're into that virtue stuff and that frilly old aristocracy; he'll feel right at home."

"No, he won't. He hates what Cornerstone does, and they'll kill him for it."

"If his philosophy gets him killed, that's his problem. You should be glad I got him out of your hair."

"Glad?" she choked. "Glad he's dead?" She moved her hand to cut the call, but a thought stopped her. "Who'd you sell him to?" she demanded. "Who's your contact in Cornerstone?"

"Someone with enough money to make it worthwhile."

Cornerstone had a patron. That was why the attacks had increased in recent months. This patron had a lot of money to burn and a distrust of humans . . . and security recorders that offered a closer look at Auren's face.

Tanza said, "Berimac. You sold him to Berimac."

Keffer smirked. "He's a paranoid freak, but he has money to spare, and he loves your prince. He'll take good care of him."

Tanza remembered Berimac ordering his guards to beat Auren just for standing too near his gate. "I doubt that," she said.

She cut off the call and paced the room as anger, guilt, and despair smothered her attempts to plan. She had failed Auren. He'd trusted and defended her despite her crimes, and she had delivered him to death. If she hadn't raged about the spindle . . . if she had hidden Auren from Keffer . . . if she were anything better than a depraved criminal . . . Auren wouldn't be the prisoner of a faction of crazed zealots.

Yet he *was* a prisoner, and Tanza had to change that. But how? She had no time, no money, no help, no resources, and no idea where Auren was. She ransacked the apartment, gathering items at random—her program scanner, the comms, her syringes of tephan pain medication—but couldn't formulate a coherent plan.

Then inspiration struck. She rushed to the bedroom, dove for her pack, and scratched at a hidden pocket to uncover a small pink cylinder. The power cell was all that remained from Auren's tomb, and she had no reason to hide it now that she'd cut ties with Keffer.

Tanza told the power cell, "Little beauty, I believe you're supposed to buy me a hovercar."

She knew where to find Auren. Berimac would want to see his merchandise in person. Cornerstone would take Auren to a dark old building surrounded by plants that hid an ancient man who should have rotted long ago.

Tanza had one last tomb to rob.

11

ANZA PEERED through the fence at Berimac's unnatural greenery. Just enough daylight remained for her to see the house—and for the security recorders to see her. Her black clothing and Cornerstone armbands would mask her once she was inside the house, but she didn't want to hide just yet.

She pressed a gloved hand to the fence, and brilliant strands of energy streamed away. A neuroblock field—just what she'd expected. Seconds later the alarms sounded, and two guards approached her, one from each side. Right on schedule.

Tanza unfolded a small metal cylinder into a blade surrounded by blue energy. The guards—second-rate muscle accustomed to guarding one reclusive old man whom no one cared about—hesitated. Safety measures kept the blade from cutting flesh, but it made an intimidating weapon, since few people recognized the tool.

Tanza lunged toward the first guard, and he stumbled headfirst into the neuroblock field. His limbs seized and he fell, eyes open and body paralyzed.

The second guard saw this and used the black box on his belt to drop the neuroblock field. So Tanza struck his skull with the side of the blade. He fell down senseless, but the blow shattered the blade.

Tanza knelt by the fragments, mind racing. She'd planned to bring that intimidating blade inside the house. She'd have to improvise.

After pocketing the handle, Tanza stole the larger guard's control box, used it to lower the other three energy barriers around the fence, then climbed the net of energy filament and dropped into the gardens.

After the chilly atmosphere of the autumn twilight, the heat and humidity from Berimac's micro-climate generator felt like an oven. Sweat droplets sprouted on Tanza's forehead and dampened her long-sleeved black garments. Fortunately her research had shown her how to manipulate the climate to her advantage.

She pulled a sparkstick from her pocket and attached a newly purchased smoke-patch to its side. She snapped the stick and tossed it into the driest plant in sight—a squat Jem bush just beginning to go to seed. Then she crouched behind a tree, sheltered her head with her arms, and waited.

The sparkstick kindled the smoke-patch, and thick gray smoke spilled through the entire back garden. The micro-climate generator responded to the simulated fire, and dark rainclouds blotted out the remaining sunlight before bursting into thick sheets of rain. Tanza ran in a haphazard pattern toward the house, knowing that not even a Berimac recorder could see her through the smoke and simulated storm. After a minute the sparkstick was drenched and the rainclouds disappeared, but Tanza had already reached a back entrance.

With the guard's control box she undid the electronic locks and alarms, and her lock-picker's tools made quick work of the three mechanical locks. She slipped inside an abandoned pantry then plunged into the hallway and moved inward. Cornerstone wouldn't keep Auren anywhere near windows or external doors.

As Tanza neared a large door in the center of the first floor, she heard a voice that sent shivers through her core.

"Find her," Berimac demanded in the same tones he'd used to make his guards beat Auren. "The thief's on the property. Find her before she finds the prince."

Five armed Cornerstone fighters streamed toward the open door, and Tanza scrambled up a staircase to avoid them. She emerged in a hall and saw three Cornerstone fighters at the other end. They'd discover her the moment they turned their heads.

Tanza dove into an open doorway and shut it noiselessly. Down the hall, unfamiliar voices argued about the proper search pattern, showing no signs of leaving. She was trapped.

Her hiding place was a large balcony overlooking an elegant room with a glass ceiling and a wide, sparkling floor. Once this room would have been the center of a glittering party; now it held only three people: Denfor Berimac, grotesque with anger and wearing a gaudy old-fashioned suit; a familiar sharp-faced woman in Cornerstone black . . . and a still figure in white who looked more like a prince than ever.

Tanza hid in a corner of the balcony behind a sprawling sofa, peering through the railing at Auren as she assessed her options of escape.

Berimac gestured imperiously at the Cornerstone woman. "Convince him, Novi."

Novi stepped toward Auren, her voice as sharp as her face. "*Lirishan*, you must retreat to a more secure location."

Auren stepped back, now directly under the balcony. "You mean a tighter prison."

Novi put a hand on his shoulder. "We did not kidnap you. We rescued you."

Auren shrugged away her touch. "With armed men in the middle of the night? From the woman who saved me from a hundred years of sleep and did all in her power to help me?"

Berimac looked as though he wished he'd held back a few more men to handle the prince. "From a known criminal whose crimes endangered you as you traveled with her. Cornerstone only wants to help you reclaim your kingdom."

"Cornerstone wants to kill innocent people," Auren said flatly.

Novi growled, "You haven't seen Arateph, the way the humans control our world and take everything for themselves. They destroy our culture and demolish virtue."

"I've seen enough, and I hate it too. But this is not the way to change it."

Novi stared. "What other way is there? For virtue to thrive, evil must be punished. You of all people should know that. *Petrior*—good that conquers evil. *Kaibreth*—the firm hand that brings justice."

Auren said, "You love my virtue names, but you forget the one I chose for myself: *Marenith*—mercy."

The name meant far more than that. This was mercy as gentle as a whisper and as devastating as lightning, mercy that forgave the unforgivable. After a childhood plagued by an enemy's curse, Auren should have wanted revenge. Yet he'd chosen unconditional forgiveness as the virtue to define his adult life.

Tanza marveled at the name. Novi sneered at it. "That's not virtue, that's weakness. Allowing evil to thrive in others."

Auren said, "So you slaughter those you find lacking. Destroy them so you don't have to teach them a better way. *That* is evil, and no matter how long you keep me here, I will not condone it."

In the dark, heavy silence that followed, Tanza heard the fighters outside her balcony disperse, but before she could escape, Berimac's answer froze her in place.

His voice sounded like the walls of a tomb. "Novi," he said, "we've made a mistake. If this is Prince Auren, we have no use for him. He'd be more of a danger than a help to our cause."

Novi nodded. A spindle point flashed in the light of the newly risen moons.

Tanza had waited too long. Unlike the rebels of a century ago, Cornerstone would kill the virtue prince quickly with a single, sustained pulse of energy. She couldn't fight her way out the door and down the stairs in time to stop them.

So Tanza leapt. She vaulted over the balcony and fell upon Novi. Bones crunched—some of them Tanza's. Novi screamed, and the spindle point stuck in Tanza's right side. Novi twitched a finger and the spindle buzzed, only for a moment.

To Tanza it was an eternity of agony. Pain ripped through her core as the energy ripped through her organs. But Tanza's pain-shredded mind had the animal instinct of *away*, and she rolled off the spindle point.

Auren snatched the spindle from Novi's hand and knocked her unconscious before she could move again. The spindle's energy had burned Tanza's bloodstains off its skewer.

Tanza's lungs spasmed ineffectually as waves of pain scraped through her core. When she finally inhaled, the pain exploded like a bomb and she struggled to remain conscious. Each breath was agony, but she forced her lungs to take in air.

To keep her mind from her suffering, Tanza calculated her chances of survival, drawing from her knowledge of spindles. A spindle strike lasting twenty to thirty seconds was immediately fatal. This strike had lasted three seconds at most. Her organs were damaged, but she would survive if she stayed still and reached a healing bed within a few hours.

Auren was trapped in a Cornerstone stronghold. Staying still was not an option.

The pain receded as adrenaline kicked in. Tanza could breathe without feeling as if her chest contained a million shards of glass. She even raised herself on her hands and knees and looked around the room.

Auren knelt over Tanza, white as death. "Tanza!" he cried. "Did she stab you?"

Tanza shook her head, and Auren's expression wavered between relief and disbelief.

Behind Auren's back, Berimac put in a comms earpiece.

Tanza pointed a shaking finger at Berimac and rasped to Auren, "Stop him."

Auren looked back and jumped to his feet, pointing the spindle at Berimac. "Don't call them back," he said. "I'm armed."

Berimac's lip curled as he positioned the earpiece. "The virtue prince would gut an unarmed old man?"

Tanza knew Auren wouldn't, but he did a good job of pretending. "I think virtue's on my side," he said.

With that, he lunged, and Berimac's shaky legs collapsed. Auren hit him with the spindle handle, and he dropped senseless.

Auren returned to Tanza's side. "Can you move?"

Tanza wanted to never move again, but Auren would never escape without her. She patted the pockets of her outfit until she found an unbroken syringe of tephan pain medication. The medication wouldn't last long against these injuries, but it might last long enough for them to escape the house.

She brushed the vein sensor over her left elbow. When she found a vein, she administered the dose before her hand could shake. In a few moments the pain disappeared under warm, hazy numbness, and Tanza staggered to her feet. "Now I can," she gasped.

Auren glanced from the balcony to Tanza's landing place, obviously calculating what sort of injuries the fall could have produced. Perhaps he believed this the only source of her injuries. Her black outfit hid the bloodstain from the spindle wound.

"Are you sure?" he asked.

"Yes," she rasped.

"I could carry you," he said.

Auren couldn't fight Cornerstone and carry her at the same time. Tanza scowled and walked past him with firm steps, leaving him no choice but to follow.

Moving as quickly as she could while the medication remained effective, Tanza led Auren through the halls. Not wanting to risk a fight unless absolutely necessary, she and Auren changed routes or ducked out of sight every time they neared a Cornerstone fighter, but eventually they escaped their labyrinthine path and reached the front door.

They peered out a window. Three Cornerstone fighters followed a search pattern in the front gardens.

"Any plans?" Auren asked.

Pain smoldered beneath the fading effects of the pain medication, but Tanza ignored it as she pulled out the control box she'd stolen from the guard. She activated the alarm furthest from the front door. The

Cornerstone fighters raced toward the sound, leaving the front garden open. Tanza and Auren reached the gate; but as Tanza opened it, a fighter standing near the right side of the house spotted them, alerted his comrades, and gave chase.

Tanza and Auren slipped into the street, dodging traffic to hide their path. Outside Berimac's phony paradise the night air was cold, and a scattering of snowflakes floated down. Tanza led Auren blindly down alleys, not knowing whether she led him toward or away from the waiting hovercar. They reached a business district and lost their pursuers amid the crowds seeking restaurants and entertainment for the evening, but Tanza didn't dare stop running despite the pain that grew sharper by the step.

The medication's last effects faded, and the pain returned, stronger than it had been in Berimac's ballroom. This pain was like nothing Tanza had ever before experienced, so harsh that it had color and taste and temperature, with the spindle wound burning like the sun in the center. And this was a minor blow compared to Auren's spindle strike! How had Auren endured? How had he lived through that much pain?

Tanza stumbled a few more steps and collapsed upon a trash heap at the end of an alley.

Auren knelt beside her, his breathing harsh and fast. "Tanza!" he gasped, then saw the small dark stain on her right side. "The spindle stabbed you!"

Tanza coughed, and blood bubbled in her throat. "I know."

Auren's expression filled with guilt. He sounded on the verge of tears as he rambled, "I feared as much, but I let myself believe . . ." He tore off one of Tanza's armbands and held it over the spindle wound. His other hand felt for her racing pulse. "I didn't think it possible. How did you *walk* after a spindle strike?"

Tanza couldn't answer. Her quick, shallow breaths sent shards of glass scraping through her chest.

Auren's face, looming large in Tanza's foggy vision, hardened into a mix of sorrow and anger. "You should have told me!" A drop of moisture landed on Tanza's cheekbone, a snowflake that burned. "You've killed yourself for a man who should have died a century ago! What were you thinking?"

Tanza mouthed her one word of defense: "Irimitha."

Auren went white.

Then, fighting panic, he leapt to his feet and dashed to the end of the alley. There he almost collided with a young tephan woman in a pink coat and caught her by the arm. "You!" he demanded. "Do you have a communicator?"

The scene seemed distant and faded, like a decayed chronovid of Prince Auren.

Wide-eyed, the woman nodded, touching an earpiece.

"Call a hospital!" Auren ordered. "This woman's dying!"

The woman obeyed, hands shaking. Her earpiece blinked red, a face appeared on her hand-held screen, and she stammered, "Verith Med? I . . . someone needs help . . . on the eighth thoroughfare, in the restaurant district . . . I don't know who, he just stopped me! She looks pretty bad." The woman broke into sobs. "I don't know!"

Frustrated, Auren seized the screen and put in the earpiece. "This is Prince Auren Lucrit Corigrat Verinen Kaibreth Petrior Moritain Marenith, and Tanza's dying of a spindle wound!"

Tanza heard the woman gasp, and Auren continued to shout through the comms, but the world grew too dark to see. The pain melted away, and her hands went cold. She fell into a deep sleep.

12

TANZA WOKE in white and gold. Gold sunlight streamed onto white hospital walls. Gold energy glowed around the white sheets of a healing bed. A nurse in a golden hospital uniform looked up from her adjustment of the healing bed's settings.

"Don't move," the nurse said. "You're safe at Verith Med. You're recovering from some severe internal injuries. Any hasty movements could undo weeks of healing."

Something squeaked to Tanza's left, and she turned her head. Auren sat in a spindly metal chair beside Tanza's bed. He caught her hand between his and asked, "How are you?"

"Alive," Tanza breathed.

He squeezed her hand. "Good. I was so afraid you wouldn't be."

Auren looked different. His spine was straighter, his face more relaxed. He wore a well-tailored, modern-style gray suit more valuable than some cars, and his hair had grown long enough to brush his eyebrows.

Tanza asked, "How long have I slept?"

"Thirty-three days," Auren answered.

The thought made Tanza dizzy. The world was weeks ahead of her. "I missed a lot."

He laughed. "Imagine being me."

She could imagine it better now. The world seemed strange after only a few weeks' sleep—no wonder Auren had wanted to lay low.

Shaking her head then immediately regretting it, Tanza closed her eyes briefly. When she opened them, Auren's face showed concern, and Tanza smiled to reassure him. "Fill me in," she said. "Last I remember, you were telling a dispatcher all your virtue names."

"Only half," Auren said. "You'd have died before I listed all fourteen."

Since Arateph Med still had Prince Auren's voice print on record, his list of names—with all their undertones—had allowed the system to confirm his identity and brought the authorities to them in nanoseconds. They'd rushed Tanza to a healing bed and Auren into a maelstrom of doctors, politicians, and counselors intent on unveiling him to a stunned public and introducing him to the modern world.

As Tanza listened, her heart grew heavy. "I made you face all that. Everything you wanted to avoid. I'm so sorry."

"I chose this," Auren said, "to save you and to gain protection from Cornerstone."

"But Cornerstone's my fault. Keffer sold you out because I destroyed the spindle."

"I thought so. But it's not your fault. It's mine."

Tanza would have bolted upright if the nurse hadn't scolded her. "*Your* fault?"

He said, "I ran from the authorities. If I'd gone to them right away instead of hiding in Alogath, you wouldn't have faced Cornerstone, the spindle . . ." He squinted back tears, and his next words wobbled. "My running almost killed you."

"Hey." Auren's hands still held one of Tanza's, and she placed her free hand atop his. "We're both alive. Let's call it even."

Auren's tears convinced the nurse to give them privacy; she left the room. In her absence, Auren told Tanza the news she'd missed. The police hadn't found the Cornerstone fighters but had captured Berimac. The loss of their patron weakened Cornerstone, and when Auren's story became public, Cornerstone sympathy disappeared.

"I doubt they'll ever eradicate the true believers," Auren said, "but Arateph finds the virtue prince a much more appealing symbol of our heritage."

That symbol burned bright. Auren had spent nearly every moment of Tanza's sleep speaking to crowds and news reporters and being shuffled about by various government officials. He complained to Tanza about the chaos, the interviews, and the patronizing behavior of Coalition representatives.

Yet the more Auren spoke, the more Tanza realized that he'd arrived where he belonged. He'd received kindness and earned esteem. Just by existing, he'd sparked greater respect for the "primitive" tephan customs and achievements. He was quickly learning the nuances of the Coalition government and longed to prove to the Coalition-appointed human "guardians" that Arateph could represent herself in political matters and take control of industry and infrastructure.

"Sounds as if you have a kingdom again," Tanza said.

"Not mine," he replied. "I'll never have political power. But I hope to do some good."

"Can you start with me?" she asked. "Along with saving Arateph, can you visit me in prison?"

Auren's chair clattered as he reeled back. "Prison? Why would you think . . . ?"

Tanza sighed. "Auren, I'm a known criminal. The authorities found me. I have seven years of crime to pay for once I'm healed."

He laughed in disbelief. "Tanza, don't you realize? Tanza Irimitha is Arateph's hero."

The word struck Tanza's chest like a brick. "Hero?" she croaked.

"You found Prince Auren and single-handedly rescued him from a Cornerstone stronghold. You've become legend!"

She stared at him, but his face was entirely earnest. Then she realized that Auren had spoken two names of Arateph's hero, and she looked away. "Does that legend include my virtue name?"

"Of course," he said. "I included it in every telling of the tale. You're stuck with the name now."

Tanza wasn't sure she wanted that private name public. It seemed more daunting. Yet . . . She met his eyes. "I'm glad to have it."

"It fits you well," Auren said with a solemn sort of smile. "Tanza Irimitha won't be punished for Tanza's crimes. You've received full pardon. The Coalition representatives granted my request."

Tanza gazed at the window, and sunlight flooded her soul. Full pardon. True freedom: what she'd wanted from the time she was a friendless orphan. She'd stopped believing she could have it, as her crimes grew and she chained herself more closely to Keffer. But here it was, delivered to her as in some impossible dream.

Tanza wanted to cry. So she did. She let the tears fall in waves and the sobs rack her body as she cried for the years she'd lost and the people she'd harmed and for the new hope that illuminated the coming years. Despite the nurse's warning, Auren put his arms around Tanza as she wept, offering his strength.

When Tanza finished, she was sleepy but very much alive.

"Are you all right?" Auren asked as he adjusted her pillow.

Her smile was so wide, it hurt. "I am wonderful. I'll be that way until reality sets in."

An awful lot of reality waited outside this room. Tanza would face media scrutiny and needed to find a new line of work. But for the first time in her life, reality wasn't an enemy that crushed every source of hope or consolation. Reality held exciting possibilities, and she found herself eager to race toward it.

She drowsed and nestled into the pillow, but a moment later her eyes snapped open. "Do you think Prince Auren's rescuer would be admitted to study for a history degree?" she asked.

Auren's smile was like a star. "I don't think anything in the universe could keep you from it." He gestured to himself. "You already discovered a historical artifact."

Tanza silenced him and closed her eyes. She didn't have time for chit chat. She had a future to plan.

ABOUT THE AUTHOR

ASHLEY STANGL is a
registered nurse who
spends her free time
dreaming up stories and
retelling fairy tales. She
enjoys reading, writing,
singing, and walking and
biking through nature.

She lives in Minnesota surrounded by a large family and lots of
inspiration for further stories.

To learn more about Ashley, visit www.AshleyStangl.blogspot.com

Did you enjoy "Spindle Cursed" By Michelle Pennington?

Don't miss her other romantic titles, including:

A timid stepsister.
A mistaken identity.
A disinherited princess.
A seething planet.
An enchanted circus.

Here are five
beautiful retellings
to bring new life to the
classic Cinderella tale!

Stories by: Elisabeth Brown, Emma Clifton, Rachel Heffington,
Stephanie Ricker, and Clara Diane Thompson

A ship of lost souls.
A haunted abbey.
A curse of stone.
A jungle king.
A monster of legend.

Here are five
magical retellings
to bring new life to the
classic tale of
Beauty and the Beast!

Stories by: Kaycee Browning, Savannah Jezowski,
Jenelle Schmidt, Dorian Tsukioka, and Hayden Wand

Manufactured by Amazon.ca
Bolton, ON

10250768R00284